PURSUIT OF SHADOWS
THE KEEPER CHRONICLES BOOK 2

JA ANDREWS

Pursuit of Shadows, The Keeper Chronicles Book 2

Copyright © 2018 by JA Andrews

Website: www.jaandrews.com

All rights reserved. This book is protected under the copyright laws of the United States of America. No part of this publication may be reproduced, stored in a retrieval system, or transmitted in any form or by any means – electronic, mechanical, photocopying, recording, or otherwise- without prior written permission of the publisher.

This book is a work of fiction. Characters, names, locations, events and incidents (in either a contemporary and/or historical setting) are products of the author's imagination and are being used in an imaginative manner as a part of this work of fiction. Any resemblance to actual events, locations, settings, or persons, living or dead is entirely coincidental.

Ebook ISBN: 978-0-9976144-8-0

Paperback ISBN: 978-0-9976144-9-7

Cover art © 2018 by Ebooklaunch.com

Illustrations © 2018 by Wojtek Depczynski

❦ Created with Vellum

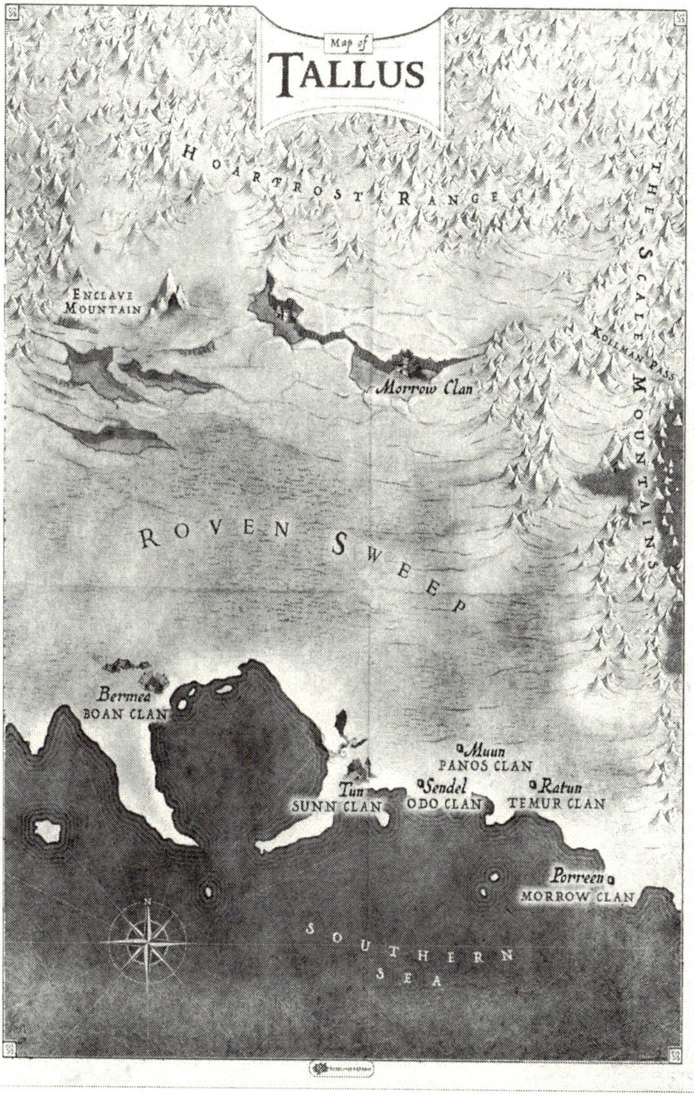

Map of
TALLUS
HOARFROST RANGE
THE SCALE MOUNTAINS
KOLLMAN PASS
ENCLAVE MOUNTAIN
Morrow Clan
ROVEN SWEEP
Bermea
BOAN CLAN
Muun
PANOS CLAN
Tun
SUNN CLAN
Sendel
ODO CLAN
Ratun
TEMUR CLAN
Porreen
MORROW CLAN
N
SOUTHERN SEA

THE FLAMES

THE AIR in the normally drab village square shivered with magic.

Will felt as though he'd stepped into a different world. More people than he'd ever seen were gathered together, the high-spirited crowd causing the weathered buildings around them to fade into the background. The nutty smell of roasted sorren seeds wafted out from the wayfarer's wagon, and Will's mother had bought him not one, but two sweet rolls.

Vahe of the Flames stood far back on the stage, surrounded by dark walls and an arched roof, his voice low as he told of three children trapped deep in the lair of a mountain troll. His fingers toyed slowly with a handful of fire, flickering just above his palm, seemingly burning nothing but air. Will couldn't pull his eyes away.

The wayfarer's black hair and pointed beard mixed with the shadows on the stage. His voice rolled out with dark menace as the trolls crept closer to the children. Will's fist clamped into the sticky dough of his sweet roll, and he leaned closer to his mother. When his arm brushed hers, a jab of disapproval flashed into his chest, off-center and too muted to be his own. His mother watched Vahe with the same sternness she turned on Will whenever he played too roughly with baby Ilsa.

Pulling his arm away from her, the feeling faded. He rubbed his skin as though he could erase the memory of it. It happened more and more often lately, these echoes of what other people were feeling when he touched them.

Vahe continued, his voice still low and foreboding but the spell had been broken. Will remembered that the stage was a wagon. Not a normal wagon—a wayfarer's wagon. Like a house with wheels. Except houses didn't come in dazzling colors, or have fronts that could lay open like a ramp, leading down to the village dirt. Vibrant ribbons fluttered from the edges of the roof, quivering brightly in the evening breeze, but inside, Vahe's dark orange flame lent a brooding feel to the shadows. It caught on unknown things, flashing back glints of burnished copper.

The tale ended with a quick escape by the children and Will's mother put her arm around his shoulder.

"Let's get home." Her disapproval rushed into him again, filling the left side of his chest and leaving a mildly sour taste in his mouth.

"But wayfarers never come here. And he might tell more stories."

"I've heard enough." Her tone made it clear the decision had been made. "Tussy needs milking. And that man takes entirely too much pleasure in frightening children."

Milking a goat was a terrible reason to leave. If only Tussy would run away one of the times she broke out of her pen. With a sigh he felt down to his toes, Will followed her, weaving through the crowd of villagers in the dusty square, hoping Vahe would start a story his mother would be interested in hearing.

Instead Vahe began to do tricks with the strange orange flame in his hand, making it appear and disappear, tossing it through the air, even dropping it onto a pile of dry grass without setting it aflame. He tossed it toward the crowd. It disappeared for a moment when it reached the sunlight, then Will caught a glimmer of it hovering over someone's head. It slid over another, and another, people's hands reaching up and passing through it unharmed. It came close and Will held his breath. When it shifted above Will, the top of his head tingled for a heartbeat. A jolt like lightning shot through him. Every bit of his skin stung like the prickles of a hundred tiny thorns, and the air around him shimmered with yellow light. The flame winked out and the sparkles disappeared.

"The fire likes you, boy!" Vahe cried.

Will rubbed his hands across his arms, trying to brush away the last of the prickly feeling. The crowd oohed appreciatively, and Vahe started another trick. But Will's mother waited at the edge of the crowd, her mouth pressed into that thin line and her brow creased with worry.

The sun beat down on the dirt road leading out of the dingy village, and the whole way home through the low, winding hills, Will couldn't shake the tingly feeling that crawled across his skin.

At the edge of their yard the creak of the goat pen caught his attention. Tussy was shoving her little horns under the bar, pushing open the gate—again. The brand new shoots in the garden almost within her reach.

Will ran forward, stretching his hand out as though he could reach across the entire yard. Too far away to reach her, he could do nothing but hurl fury at the stupid goat for interrupting the storytelling, and for endlessly escaping her pen.

Except the fury *did* hurl out of his hand with a ripping pain and the gate slammed shut.

Agony stabbed up his arms and he dropped to his knees, his own cry of pain drowning out Tussy's insulted bleat. A new circle of winter-brown grass around him marred the summer yard, brittle and dry, like the old, worn out grass of fall.

Shiny blisters swelled on his palms and he curled forward, gasping and choking on the pain. Worry and pity washed over him like cool water even before his mother's arms wrapped around him.

"A Keeper," she whispered, looking from his hands to the withered grass. A fierce pride blazed up in Will and he sank against her, letting her emotions drown out his own fear and pain.

Hours later, he lay in the cool quiet of the cottage and the roiling turmoil in his chest was thankfully all his own. His parents and Ilsa slept in their curtained alcove, the barrage of emotions from them finally quiet. Since he'd closed the gate that had changed. He could feel everything they felt. No one had to touch him now, they only needed to be close.

He rubbed his thumb over the frayed edge of the cloth his mother had wrapped around his blistered hands, his mind spinning.

Magic. He'd done magic. He'd somehow sucked life out of the grass and used it to shut the gate.

The idea hung in the silent cottage both alien and obvious. Part of him was still shocked, but if he was honest, he knew something magical had been happening for months and months. Not with searing, hand-burning pain, but with mumbled, nudging hints. That empty, endless hollowness he'd felt when he shook hands with the butcher at his wife's funeral. Or the day they cheered as Ilsa took her first, wobbling steps—when Will's mother had grasped his shoulder, he thought his heart might burst into a million pieces.

But he couldn't really be a Keeper, could he?

He'd closed a gate from across the yard, and everyone knew the sign of new Keeper magic was burned hands. He stretched his fingers until shots of pain lanced across his palms. If he'd done magic, would the Keepers have to take him? His heart quickened. He'd get to go to the hidden Stronghold. He'd see the queen in her palace. He'd never have to weed the garden or milk Tussy. He'd be rich. He could buy his father a mule, and Ilsa a real doll instead of that ugly rag she carried everywhere.

Will pulled the thin blanket up to his chin, trying not to get too excited. He wasn't the sort of boy who became a Keeper. He was the sort of boy who could never get the goat pen to stay closed.

A foreign terror crashed into him, stronger and darker than anything he'd ever felt and he shrank down into his bed. He strained to hear any sound, but his father's snoring continued, low and steady, and nothing else stirred in the cottage.

He squeezed his eyes shut. *Please don't let me feel their dreams.*

The sensation swelled until he couldn't stay still any longer. He rolled out of bed and tiptoed toward the curtain. The sensation grew stronger. His breath grew shallow and his heart thrummed in his ears as though he stood atop a cliff—or was being chased by something monstrous.

Will pulled the curtain back, desperate to wake them from such a nightmare.

Bright moonlight poured in the window, landing on the bed where his parents lay sleeping. Ilsa and her rag doll curled between them and the wall in a tangle of dark curls. All three were still.

But in the window above them perched a man with a black pointed beard.

Vahe.

Will froze, his hand clutching the curtain. Vahe's gaze snapped up, and Will's gut clenched, whether from his own fear or the wayfarer's, it was impossible to tell. A silver knife appeared in the man's hand, glinting in the moonlight. Slowly, the man raised a finger to his lips.

Will's breath caught in his throat. He needed to yell, scream, something. But his body refused to move.

Vahe shifted his grip on the knife until it pointed down at Will's father's chest.

"Come with me, boy," he whispered, the words barely more than a rustle of wind.

The muscles of Vahe's arm rippled as he shifted the knife over the thin form of Will's parents. Even if Will woke them, they were no match for this man.

A fierce anger stirred in his gut, an anger all his own at this man for threatening them, for daring to come into their house. For being stronger than his parents.

Will stepped forward and let the curtain fall behind him. He flexed his hands slightly. It had worked on the gate. He just needed to push Vahe out the window. Then he could lock the shutters and yell until the neighbors woke.

The desire to push the wayfarer grew stronger and stronger until it filled him, shoving out Vahe's storm of emotions. Every bit of Will wanted that wicked face, that silver knife, and that dreadful excitement out of his home. And out of himself. Will lifted one hand and pointed it toward the wayfarer. Pain shot across his palm as he focused all his fury at the man.

Vahe's eyes widened and he grabbed at the window, bracing himself. "Come," he ordered between clenched teeth. "No one needs to get hurt."

Will pushed harder until his palm burned and the wayfarer threw all his weight against the force of it. Vahe's black hair and beard blended into the night. Will could see only pale cheeks and glittering eyes.

A stray thought wandered across Will's mind, a memory of the withered grass this afternoon. Was the garden outside withering now, fueling whatever he was doing?

He didn't care.

Slowly, a finger's breadth at a time, Vahe slipped backwards.

A small gasp yanked Will's attention down. His mother lay on the bed in front of him, white as moonlight, gasping for breath, her fingers scrabbling against Will's other hand where he clutched her arm. Will snatched his hand back, and the fire racing through him stopped. His fury turned to horror.

It wasn't from the garden. He'd been pulling all that power out of her body.

Everything moved at once.

His mother took a deep, shuddering breath.

His father stirred.

Released from Will's fury, the wayfarer toppled forward, falling into the room, the knife slamming into Will's father's chest. His mother screamed and Ilsa woke, adding her small cries to the chaos. Terror and fury filled Will and he didn't know if it was his or theirs. Pain and panic and desire rushed in, threatening to tear him apart.

Vahe looked up from the knife, his face shocked. He reached toward Will again. "Come here, boy!" he hissed.

Will backed away from Vahe's anger, his mother's terror, and his father's too-still form.

A shout and pounding on the cottage door behind Will made the wayfarer's anger flare hotter. Vahe's eyes bored into Will, his fury thrumming in Will's chest.

Will's mother screamed for help. Vahe hurled a last glare at Will, then snatched up Ilsa. She cried, reaching out toward her mother, her dark curls pressed against Vahe's neck.

"Stop," Will pleaded, taking a step closer.

The door to the cottage splintered and flew open. Neighbors rushed into the small cottage, bringing in a frenzy of emotion.

The wayfarer yanked his bloody knife from Will's father's chest with a snarl. Still clutching Ilsa, Vahe plunged out the window, his anger tearing out of Will, leaving him hollow of everything but his mother's screams.

CHAPTER ONE

Will rode up the interminable slope at a trudging pace, running his fingers through his beard and wondering for the thousandth time why everything on the Sweep was so deceptive. The ceaseless grassland made it impossible to tell distances, and every rise turned out to be twice as long as it looked. On top of that, the seaside road had become mostly sand, and with each step his horse's hooves sank in and backwards, making the climb feel like a continual progression of small defeats.

Endless, faded, tiresome grass rolled down from the far reaches of the northern Sweep to dwindle here, choked out by the sandy beach. In Queensland, or any other wholesome place, the world would be bursting with the greenness and flowers and warmth of spring. But here the grass left over from last year was brown and brittle, the sea was grey, even the sky was barely blue. The emptiness of the Sweep slithered inside him, deepening its roots, tinging everything with hopelessness.

Over the top of the hill, the tip of a jagged peak appeared, and an ache of homesickness squeezed his chest. It was long past time to go home. He'd accomplished nothing here. For his foreignness, he'd been ignored or scorned everywhere he'd gone. All he had to show for the past year were a lingering loneliness and two books crammed full of overheard Roven stories. Granted the books he'd written held more information about the Roven Sweep than the entire Keeper's library, but even that might not cancel out his failure to find the things he'd actually been looking for.

When he finally crested the hill, the Scale Mountains spread out along the horizon like the barren, rocky spine of some ancient monster, guarding the eastern edge of the Sweep. From here the road would take him past the southern tip of the mountains in a day and he'd be in Gulfind. A respectable land with something besides grass. He'd see bushes and trees. He'd be within two easy days of Queensland where he'd have no reason to hide. If people found out he was a Keeper, they'd treat him like an honored guest, instead of calling for his execution.

Something moved in the distance on the road ahead and a mild curiosity stirred his listlessness. He hadn't seen another traveler all day. The Roven clans had already headed north to graze their herds on the well-watered plains near the Hoarfrost Mountains, and there was nothing but grass left here on the southern edge of the Sweep.

A flicker of color caught his eye, and his hand tightened on the reins.

A gaudy wagon with tall sides and a rounded roof stuttered its way over the next long hill. Its garish paint and gleefully clashing ribbons fluttered against the backdrop of the mountains before cresting the hill and disappearing.

A wayfarer's wagon.

A surge of fury and hope blazed up in him. He spurred Shadow forward.

It had been months since he'd found one. The wayfarers were impossible to track. They wandered aimlessly in isolated wagons, spread out across the known world, peddling magical trinkets and cheap performances. Even the Keepers didn't know whether the solitary groups were connected with each other, or whether they hailed from any particular country. The only thing Will had learned in the twenty years since his sister had been taken was that anything he learned from one set of wayfarers was always contradicted by the next.

Will blew out a long breath and relaxed his hands on the reins. It wouldn't be *the* wagon. It was never *the* wagon. In twenty years he'd found almost two dozen of them, but none of them carried Vahe. None of them even admitted to knowing the man.

Still, Will urged Shadow a little faster down the far side of the hill.

Far to the north, a speck winged through the sky before diving down to disappear into the grass. In the space of a few heartbeats it climbed into the air again and flew closer, growing into the shape of an undersized hawk, thin leather jesses dangling from its legs. Talen flapped down, settling on the blue bedroll tucked against Will's saddle horn. The hawk dropped a dead mouse onto the blanket and fixed Will with unblinking eyes.

"That is just as disgusting as the others." Will leaned back from the gift. "You are the worst payment I've ever received. It would almost be worth backtracking a day and losing sight of the wayfarers just to give you back."

Will couldn't flick the thing into the grass until Talen flew away or the bird would think they were playing some grotesque game of fetch and bring it back.

He'd fully expected the sad excuse for payment to have flown off at the first opportunity. But it had been a full day since a herdsman had offered the miniature hawk as payment for scribe work, and he was still here. He'd wing away to hunt, out of sight across the grass, and just when Will thought he'd left forever, the hawk would come back, dangling a dead mouse in his beak.

"Would you like to come with me to Queensland?" Will considered the hawk who merely stared back. "I can see you don't plan on talking back to me. Shadow never does either, and he's been with me for several weeks now." Will patted the mottled neck of the pinto. "But until we reach a place where *people* will talk to me, you two are all I have.

"Can you do anything useful?" He reached out a finger slowly toward the bird. Talen twitched his gaze to Will's hand, but didn't move. Will ran the back of his finger lightly down the bird's chest, brushing over white feathers speckled with veins of brown. "If I drew you a picture of the man I'm looking for, could you fly up to that wagon and give me some sort of signal if you see him? Because he's someone I've been hunting for much longer than a year. And as soon as I've confirmed he's not there, I'm going home." Talen's back and head were darker with ripples of black and auburn. The feathers were so soft they felt almost liquid.

Talon fixed Will with a round, golden eye.

"I'll take your lack of response as a no.

"While you were off hunting mice, I realized I know four different stories where an animal allowed itself to be linked to its master, giving them unique powers. Two of those stories were about Keepers."

Will cast out toward the bird. He found the bright bundle of *vitalle* wound up in its body, strands of energy humming with the potential to burst into flight or dive after yet another mouse. The bird's *vitalle* sat compacted above the broader, slower energy of the horse. Beyond them both, the grass spread out in countless pinpoints of energy, until it ended at the sea.

"Of course, they were a different sort of Keeper than me. Both of them were adept at magic. If you and I are going to communicate, we'll need to keep it more…simple."

Will focused on Talen. "There is one thing I can do, though." *Dispend*, Keeper Gerone would say, *Reach out*. But Gerone had never quite understood Will's unusual talent. It wasn't really the casting out that all Keepers could do to locate energy, this was more of an unlocking or an opening.

Something in his chest loosened, and a nebulous feeling of expectation, or waiting, poured in from the little bird. Not a fully formed emotion, just a…prodding sort of sensation. That was always the way with animals, broad sensations and hungers. They were recognizable. Loyalty, hunger, satisfaction. But only a single emotion at a time. None of the chaotic tangles of emotions that humans had.

"There are no records of Keepers feeling others' emotions." He stroked Talen's head. A warm, contented feeling surfaced on the left side of Will's chest from the bird, in contrast to his own worn-in frustration with himself, which sat more centered and more comfortably inside him. "But it's not a terribly useful substitute for being proficient at magic. Knowing someone wants something isn't the same as knowing what they want."

Thundering hoofbeats sounded ahead of him and two red-haired Roven rangers crested the hill, bearing down on him at a gallop. He had time to wrap one arm protectively around Talen and grab hold of his jesses to keep the small hawk from flying into one of the Roven before they raced past on either side him. Two distinct sensations of scorn blossomed in his chest.

"Off the road, fetter bait," one barked in the harsh Roven accent.

The other ranger kicked out his foot, catching Will's saddle bag, sending it bouncing and clanging, causing Shadow to prance to the side. "Move, fett!"

The Roven tore away down the road, their emotions fading from his chest, leaving only Talen's fear, Shadow's startled wariness, and Will's own irritation.

"I hate this country." Will spoke softly and ran his finger down the back of Talen's head. "You know one of the main problems with the Roven? They think people are fetter bait." When the hawk quieted, Will loosened his grip on Talen's jesses. "Setting aside the fact that you're sort of fettered, I think we can both agree that humans shouldn't be."

Will glanced over his shoulder. The two Roven were heading the wrong way. All the clans that way had gone north for the summer already. With the bird calm, Will closed himself off and the bird's emotions faded from his chest.

They were almost to the top of the rise when Talon let out a piercing screech. Like a needle to the ear. The bird tilted its head and pinned Will with a hard stare.

"A signal like that is exactly what I'm talking about. Although maybe we could pick a more pleasant sound. You could use it to warn me before I'm charged by rangers—"

A jangle of far-off music caught his attention just as the smell of roasting fish tumbled through the air. Will reached the top of the hill and stopped. A wide, low plain stretched ahead of him all the way to the feet of the Scales. Nestled against the ocean sat the small city of Porreen, the winter home of the Morrow Clan.

And around the wall, tents and people crowded together, proclaiming that here, at the very eastern edge of the Sweep, the spring festival was still going on.

"—or ambushed by festivals."

Talen gave another screech.

"Don't try to take credit for warning me." Will nudged Shadow down the hill. "A screech is not a warning."

Like all Roven cities, Porreen consisted of a roundish jumble of lumpy buildings that looked like cattle corralled by a thick earthen wall. With no trees on the Sweep for wood, everything was made exclusively of cob, a mixture of earth and dried grass, shaped by hand without any attempt to make straight walls or sharp angles. The city sat close enough to the sea that the lumpy cob buildings looked like a city built by children on the beach.

The wayfarer's wagon moved along the edge of the festival, heading out of sight around the city wall. Crowds of red-headed, red-bearded, blue-eyed Roven mingled around the tents. Any head that wasn't red was either a foreign merchant braving the unfriendliness of the Sweep, or a foreign slave in a grey tunic.

With a screech that sounded disapproving, Talen launched off the bedroll and soared away over the empty grassland. Will couldn't blame him. The Roven would probably capture the hawk and cage him. It's what they did to foreign things.

Will scratched at his black beard. It hadn't helped, really, to grow the beard. Every man on the Sweep had one and so he'd let his grow to blend in. But theirs were all hues of red, from bright orangey-flame to dark coppery russet. Will's was black. Not a tint of red to be seen. Between that, the rest of his black hair, and his dark brown eyes, his head felt like a signal fire made of shadows, heralding his foreignness. The Morrow Clan's spring festival was bound to be like the others, a mad scramble to buy supplies before the clan moved north for the summer. The hostile stares he was about to encounter dragged at him. He could almost hear muttered "fett" and "fetter bait" already.

The Scale Mountains were so close, and the idea of leaving the Sweep rushed over him like a fresh breeze. He'd glance at the wayfarers, then go. He could be half-way to the mountains by dark. Will flicked the dead mouse off his blanket.

Dismounting, he led his pinto horse off the road, cutting through the grass toward the nearest tents. The tufts at the top of the winter-dried stalks tugged at his pants like greedy little fairies. After a year trying to move unobtrusively through the Roven Sweep, he'd mastered one bit of vaguely sophisticated magic. He cast out, reaching past the dead grass and finding the bits of new growth, just starting to peek out of the ground.

Slowly he extended his fingers toward the ground and began pulling the *vitalle* out of them, drawing it through his hand and into himself as he altered the tiny snips of life-energy into something more elusive. He let the *vitalle* slide out from his other hand, stinging his fingertips as he spread a cloak of disinterest around himself. A suggestion that there was nothing about him worth noticing.

It was done before his fingertips were even singed, accompanied by the usual twinge of guilt at the fact that the other Keepers wouldn't approve.

The influence spell had become unsettlingly easy. Like every other bit of magic Will had ever tried, it had been challenging to cast at first, and even more challenging to sustain.

When he'd first come to the Sweep, he'd only used the influence spell occasionally. But the farther he traveled among the

Roven, the more he realized that the Sweep was always unsafe. They distrusted all foreigners, but had a special hatred for Queensland. Parents frightened their children with stories of evil Keepers who didn't use stones to hold their magic, but pulled it out of living things. It became easier not to be noticed, and now putting on the influence spell was like part of getting dressed. He'd renewed it so often it felt as though it never completely wore off.

The other Keepers definitely would not approve of that. Gerone's eyebrows would dive down into a hairy scowl and he'd say there was something dishonest in it, something slightly dangerous. Which was true, but there was something definitely dangerous about having the people of the Roven Sweep find out Will came from Queensland. Or worse, was a Keeper. So Gerone and his eyebrows could say what they pleased.

Will drew close to the crowd, his hand tight on the reins. But the first person's gaze slipped past him without notice, and he let himself relax. He skirted the edge of the festival. Runes of protection and good luck decorated each tent. The leather vests of the Roven were marked around the armholes and the neck with runes. More were painted onto their bowls and tables, and woven into their rugs. Small gems glittered everywhere. They flashed in rings, hung around necks and wrists, many of them glowing with trace amounts of *vitalle*. The Roven called them burning stones if they held any energy, and Will sighed at how much money he could have made on the Sweep if he'd had any idea how to put the energy of living things into a lifeless rock. The Roven filled the festival covered in runes and gems in an effort to be safe, or lucky, or shrewd.

The wayfarers, with their trinkets that looked magical, whether they were or not, were going to make a fortune in this city. They were probably the only foreign people who walked freely through the Sweep.

Will caught a glimpse of long, brown hair coming toward him, and his fist clenched on Shadow's lead. Opening up without meaning to, the emotions of the crowd rushed into his chest with a cacophony of feelings, shoving aside his own blaze of hope.

The crowd slithered past and the slave woman shuffled into view carrying a pile of fabric. An ordinary clutter of emotions from her blossomed in him. Worry, exhaustion, mild curiosity.

Will searched her face, looking so hard for the resemblance to Ilsa that it took a moment to actually see her and recognize it was all wrong. More than that, she was too old, much older than twenty. She paid no more attention to him than anyone else, and didn't raise her eyes from the ground as she passed. When her emotions faded, Will shoved the chaos of the rest of the crowd out of his chest.

Butter-yellow fruit caught his eye. When he offered the Roven vendor his copper half-talen for three avak, the woman looked surprised to see him for just a breath. Her eyes took in his not-red hair and the fact that he didn't wear a grey slave's tunic, and her lips curled in disgust. She snatched the copper out of his hand with a "fett" and went back to her Roven customers.

Will turned away, blending back into the crowd. To chase away the bitter taste of the slur, he took a bite of the fruit, and the tangy juice burst into his mouth like a splash of brightness in the dusty Sweep. Avak was one of those glorious things that was always better than expected. Like the smell of the air after rain. Or the vividness of a lightning strike. One of those things that breaks into life with the truth that there is far more...*something* in the world than people usually notice.

Will took another bite.

Avak didn't fit here on the Sweep.

The sharp tanginess perked up his mind, as it always did. The afternoon sunlight danced over the orange fabric of the tent next to him. It glinted off a set of metal spoons and shimmered down the red-gold braid of the Roven woman considering them. To the south, the ocean rose in small swells glittering like scales on a sea monster.

A bit ahead of him the flutter of the wayfarer's wagon caught his eye.

The last bite of avak flesh pulled cleanly off the smooth pit and Will tucked it in his pocket. The Keepers' Stronghold needed an avak bush. Gerone would be thrilled. He could plant an orchard of them.

The freshness clarified the reality of Will's situation too. This was just another random, solitary wayfarer wagon. The search for his sister was nothing more than a far-fetched dream, and being on the Sweep was a waste of time.

Will led Shadow around a large red tent filled with blankets and stopped.

At the edge of the festival, flashing with gaudy colors and snapping ribbons, sat over a dozen wayfarer wagons lined up one after the other, in an arc.

Rooted to the ground, Will stared at the chaos of color ahead of him.

He'd had never seen so many wayfarers in one place. Never even heard of a gathering like this.

Wagons with rounded, stout roofs parked next to ones with tall, pointed roofs. One blood-red wagon even had a flat roof, crenelated like a castle. Wildly colored shutters were thrown open and a few of the crooked chimneys dribbled out smoke. A raised stage nestled up against one painted the spiky yellow of a bumblebee, creating the impression that Will stood in a theater.

The stage sat empty, but handfuls of people sat along a row of benches stretching across the back of the makeshift theater, and he sank down on the end, dazed. He let Shadow graze, and watched wayfarers dressed in garish colors unload even more garish costumes and props for the evening's show. A young girl holding a pot passed, trailing the earthy smell of sorren seeds. Tiny shells edging her amber shawl jostled each other with a quiet clatter.

The wagon Will had been following settled at the other end of the arc, calling greetings to the other wayfarers. Will cast out toward the people around him and the energy teeming in their bodies and the bright pinpoints of *vitalle* humming from the burning stones they wore echoed back to him. Countless colored gems, set in rings or pendants, swirled with light and tiny snippets of power.

Will took a bite of the second avak, his surprise fading. He'd found a band of wayfarers doing what wayfarers always did, entertaining crowds and selling marginally magical trifles. The familiar frustration gnawed at him.

A woman stepped up onto the stage wrapped in flowing layers of ocean blues and greens. "Come! Listen to old Estinn!" she called out to the milling crowd with a lilt that made her accent impossible to trace. Bits of grey hair snuck out from under her emerald scarf and her voice rang out loudly from her thin, hunched body. The crowd paused. "When the sun drops over the edge of the world, come witness a battle! Storytellers from near and far will gather, pitting their skills against the skills of Borto Mildiani, in a contest of..." She stopped, then smiled a toothy smile. "*Skills*!

"Are your stories duller than last year's grass? Then keep them to yourself. But if your tales ensnare the ear, come test your mettle against the legendary Borto!" Estinn flung her hand toward the yellow wagon behind the stage.

A black-bearded man in a loose rust-red shirt stepped out, bowing to the crowd with a flourish.

Will's heart froze for a beat.

Vahe.

CHAPTER TWO

Will surged to his feet before he caught himself. Rage and disbelief crashed into each other like wild, frothing waves in a storm.

Will stared at that face, opening up toward the man, as though he could reach past the crowd and feel only Vahe's emotions. There were so many people between them a torrent of indecipherable feelings rushed into him.

Old Estinn stepped off the stage and several other wayfarers joined Vahe. The man greeted them warmly, leading them behind the wagons and out of sight. Will's emotions were so taut he felt almost numb.

A bright dart of curiosity burst into his chest and Will's attention snapped back to the bench. A little slave girl peered at him through strands of long, pale hair from the corner of the nearest wagon. Her emotions were a blazing fire of interest, full of wonder and enthusiasm so strong they shoved everything else inside him to the periphery. She stared at him with large green eyes, as light as spring grass. Her face was so gaunt it was angular.

At her attention he sank back down onto the bench, pushing the deluge of her emotions out of his chest. What he was left with felt almost as foreign. Seeing Vahe's face, after wondering and searching for twenty years, loosed something inside him. Anger and relief strained against each other, but above it all rose a hope, so wild and fierce that it felt almost like terror.

It prodded him to jump up and follow the man. But throttling Vahe and demanding to know where Ilsa was, while he stood among a crowd of his own wayfarers, probably wasn't going to get positive results.

"Are you alright?" The little girl asked, still watching him.

"I..." Why *was* she watching him? He glanced around to see if his influence spell had worn off, but no one else paid him any attention. "I don't know."

She was maybe eight years old, her blond hair as out of place on the Sweep as his black. He took a calming breath, trying to get control of his emotions. Influence spells were always less effective on children. They spent too much time fascinated by new things to be convinced to overlook a stranger.

The little girl inched around the edge of the wagon. Everything about her was dusty in a permanent way, as though she had never been clean. The bones of her shoulder pressed up against her shift like jagged stones and skeletal fingers pushed her hair back. Sitting here among the lurid colors of the wayfarers, her slave's tunic was almost too drab to be called grey.

The Roven bought their slaves from Coastal Baylon and Napon in the east. Criminals in those countries could find themselves as easily on the slave block as in a prison. Debtors were treated the same. A debt large enough would enslave their entire family. But the Roven felt that young slaves were more trouble than they were worth. Until an age where they could be useful, they were kept in a shabby little commune, only fed when they could prove they'd found work. The smallest slaves scurried through the cities with menial jobs, gaunt faces, and tattered clothes.

Will grabbed his last avak.

"Would you like some fruit?" He held it out.

She looked at it suspiciously.

He set the avak as close to the end of the bench as he could. Slowly, she reached forward, then snatched the fruit off the bench. It looked heavy in her hand, like the weight of it might snap her thin wrist.

"It's avak," Will said. "They're my favorite." He glanced around the theater, but Vahe was still out of sight.

She took a nibble of the fruit and cocked her head to the side. "If it's your favorite, why'd you give it to me?"

Will paused. "Would you believe it's my way of countering great evil?"

One of her little eyebrows rose skeptically.

"And," he added, "because you look like me. And I haven't talked to many people lately that do."

She glanced at his black beard and scrunched her nose.

"Well, not exactly like me." He motioned to the Scales. "But where I come from, across those mountains, there are a lot of people who look like you and me. Not everyone has red hair."

She studied the Scales with narrowed eyes. "I don't like those mountains. They don't have any grass at all."

The stony range rose up in a dull brown, jagged and unwelcoming. "True. The mountains are barren, but on the other side the world turns green again and there's grass. Not like here. Over there it's greener and shorter and out of it grows bushes and trees taller than a house." Motion of several people between two of the wagons caught his eye.

She took another bite of the fruit. "There's nothing more wonderful than grass."

Despite everything, the declaration was so unexpected that Will let out a laugh.

She fixed him with a severe look. "Don't you like it?"

"I'm not sure." Will studied the faces between the gaps of the wagons, trying to catch a glimpse of Vahe. "It's a little...empty."

She let out a huff of indignation. "Empty? You could walk for days and not find a bare spot. And all the roots tangle together so the whole world is an endless living thing."

Will dragged his attention back to the strange little girl. He had to press his mouth shut to keep from smiling at the intensity of her enthusiasm. "I've never thought of the grass as being a thing in itself."

"It's the biggest, most powerful thing in the world! It's where everything comes from, and where everything goes when it's too old to move. And"—she glared at him, setting her tiny fists on her hips—"it's beautiful!"

Will sat back. "I stand corrected. I've obviously not been giving the Sweep the respect it deserves." He set his fist on his chest and bowed his head. "I promise not to make the same mistake again."

She pursed her lips in consideration. "And you'll see how beautiful it is?"

Beautiful? Grass too tall to feel like grass, but too grassy to feel like anything else, spread out over the land like the worn, sparse pelt of some massive creature? She waited expectantly.

"I'll try."

"It'll be easy." She leaned forward, her face fairly bursting with excitement. "Summer is coming."

He found himself smiling at her with a smile that felt rusty from disuse. She took another bite of the avak. Vahe still hadn't returned. Will was just about to follow him when the man stepped into view and stood on the stage, calling instructions to a handful of wayfarers, and the surge of hatred that Will felt toward the man almost overwhelmed him.

But Vahe clearly wasn't going anywhere soon. Will settled back and took a deep breath. He couldn't ruin this by rushing into it.

He settled back on the bench. The slave girl still watched him curiously.

"I'm Will."

She considered him seriously for a moment. "I'm..." She let her eyes wander over to the Sweep. "Rass."

Will raised an eyebrow. "Rass sounds a lot like grass."

She grinned at him. "That's why I picked it."

"You're the most interesting girl I've met in a long time." Will paused. He glanced at Vahe. Did Rass know anything about him? He searched for a way to word his next question. *Who owns you?* felt insensitive. He glanced to where she'd been hiding. "Do you live with the wayfarers?"

She let out a giggle. "No."

"You live in Porreen?"

"In the stinky city?" She shuddered. "I live on the grass."

The grass?

"I just came because the colored wagons tell good stories. I love stories."

"So do I," Will said. "I like stories more than maybe anything else in the world."

She cocked her head to the side. "You look like someone out of a story. Sitting here and hiding in plain sight." Her face turned wistful. "I wish I could do that."

Will felt a squeeze of fear in his chest. She could sense his influence spell? Children were unsettling, sometimes. Like they weren't exactly human yet. They were something wilder, brighter. Of course, now that he thought about it that way, maybe it was the adults who'd stopped being human.

Will grasped for a different topic. "I've never seen so many wayfarers together."

Rass sat down on the far edge of the bench. "They come every spring."

"Did..." Will hesitated, but couldn't come up with a better way to ask it. "Did the wayfarers bring you here?"

Rass looked up at him in surprise, then let out a long, rippling laugh. "No one brought me." She licked the last of the avak juice off the pit and held it out to Will. "Thank you."

Will hesitated before holding out his hand and letting her drop the wet pit in his palm. He tucked it quickly into his pocket with the other pit, and wiped his hand on his pants.

"I just come to hear the stories." She pointed at Vahe. "My favorite is Borto."

"Borto?" The name was wrong. Will studied the wayfarer's face. That wasn't exactly right either. The man had too much chin. Or not enough forehead.

"He's the best storyteller on the Sweep."

"The best?" Vahe had told stories, but even as a child Will wouldn't have ranked him any better than the men who told stories in his own village. "Does he do tricks with fire?"

Rass shook her head. "You're looking for Borto's brother, Vahe of the Flames."

Will flinched at the name.

"He comes sometimes, but not as often as Borto."

"Is he here now?" The words came out strained.

"I haven't seen him."

Will's fingers went mindlessly to the gold ring on his finger. The ring had a wide central band that spun with a satisfying smoothness between two thin edges. Will watched Borto closely, a hundred thoughts warring with each other in his head.

"How does your ring spin like that?" Rass asked.

Will held out his hand, showing her. "A friend gave this to me a long time ago."

The Shield, the leader of the Keepers, had gifted it to him over ten years ago, the first time he'd left the Stronghold on his own. *Most rings are a single entity,* he'd told Will. *I've always thought it was interesting that part of this is free to move and spin, affected by the world, while the core of it remains true to the wearer.* The Shield had considered Will for a long moment before nodding approvingly and grinning. *It fits you. And it's extremely satisfying to spin while you think.*

Borto let out a loud laugh and shouted at some approaching wayfarers.

"It's nice to meet you, Rass." Will stood. "I think I'll join the story contest tonight."

Rass's eyebrows shot up. "You tell stories?"

Will leaned toward her and whispered. "Maybe better than Borto."

She clapped her hands and grinned.

Will gave her a slight bow and walked around the edge of the closest wagon.

The influence spell shouldn't have worn off yet, regardless of Rass's attention. And it was awkward trying to have a conversation with someone while the spell tried to distract them. He drew a little energy from the grass at his feet and sent the *vitalle* out through his other hand cutting through the influence spell, letting it dissolve around him. He almost never ended the spell before it wore off, and unlike the ease of putting it on, the unfamiliar act of banishing it burned the ends of his fingers.

Now that it was done, he itched to put it back on. Even back here, away from the crowds of the festival, he felt exposed. The haggling and hawking from the festival seemed louder than before and the smell of smoked fish and roasting sorren seeds was distractingly strong. This might not have been a good idea.

Will started along the wagons toward the place Borto had gone, forcing himself to walk calmly. He caught sight of the man's red sleeve as he sat on a low stool, leaning on his elbows and tinkering with a small box. Will's heart pounded so loudly it was astonishing the wayfarer couldn't hear it.

Borto caught sight of him and rose. His fingers were loaded down with rings that glinted with gems, and at least three larger stones hung around his neck on leather thongs. "Looking for something?"

"You," Will answered, trying to keep his voice pleasant. The resemblance to Vahe made his heart shove up into his throat. He pressed his fist to his chest and bowed, giving himself a moment to calm down. "Do you have room in your contest this evening for one more storyteller?"

Borto took in Will's dirty, drab clothes and worn boots, looking unimpressed.

"I may not best a wayfarer in storytelling," Will said, "but in my own small corner of the world, I once spun a tale so sad it brought a troll to tears."

Borto fixed Will with a probing look. "And what small corner of the world is that? Your accent says southwestern Queensland. Near Marshwell, perhaps?"

Will hid his discomfort at the extremely accurate guess with a smile. "Marshwell is not far at all from where I was raised." Which was true. "But I'm from just over the border in Gulfind." Which was not true. Much smaller than Queensland, Gulfind was surrounded by mountains full of gold mines, making the small population excessively wealthy. It was on excellent terms with Queensland however, and the people along the border from both countries were almost impossible to tell apart. Also, merchants from Gulfind traveled widely and were known for being a bit eccentric. A traveling storyteller from there was unusual, but not unheard of. The lie had served him for the last year on the Sweep.

"I think we can fit in one more storyman." Borto ushered Will back into the stage area. "But I'll warn you, this isn't your homeland. There's no gold for the winner."

"I'm just thrilled to be a part of it." Will wished his pulse would slow. The more he looked at the man, the more differences he saw from his memory of Vahe. "I'm fascinated by wayfarers, and I've never seen so many in one place. There's no better way to learn about people than to hear them tell stories."

"But we won't be telling wayfarer stories. Here on the Sweep, the stories we'll tell are mostly Roven tales."

"It doesn't matter," Will answered, trying to keep the man talking. Borto's voice was different from Vahe's too.

"It doesn't?" Borto looked at Will appraisingly. "If a man tells you of his home and his family, you'll learn something about him. But if he tells you foreign tales, you only learn about foreign places."

"You learn that too," Will agreed. The voice was definitely not Vahe's. "But if everyone knew the same story, we'd still tell it differently from each other." He shrugged. "I think the way a man tells a story reveals more about the man than it does about the story."

Borto studied him. Then a grin spread across the wayfarer's face. "A storyman and a philosopher!" Borto clapped Will on the shoulder and gestured at the old woman standing by the stage. "Welcome to the contest. Give Estinn your name. I want to hear a tale that'd make a troll cry."

Will gave the man another bow and turned toward Estinn. His heart raced like he'd just sprinted across the Sweep, and he took a couple deep breaths trying to calm it. Now he needed to find a place to spend the night and choose a tale. Apparently a sad one. And something that would impress the greatest storyteller on the Sweep.

He could tell The Black Horn. Technically it was from Queensland, and included a Keeper, and it didn't positively end as a tragedy. But it was obscure enough that no one would know if he switched the country. The Keeper would be easy to change to a wise woman and the emotional parts amplified until it would feel like a tragedy. And the only magic in the story was firmly anchored in the horn, leaving it the sort of magic that the stonesteeps on the Sweep used. It never mentioned Keeper magic, drawn from living things.

Will nodded pleasantly at the wayfarers who greeted him as he walked through their area. Leaving off the influence spell felt surprisingly free. It felt like a chain had fallen off, or a window had opened.

Borto knew Vahe. All Will needed to do was befriend him. Here, finally, after twenty years, he had a lead to finding the man who'd taken Ilsa. And following it only depended on telling a good story. There weren't many things Will did well, but storytelling—that was easy.

Will introduced himself to old Estinn and she noted his name.

After getting directions to an inn that served foreigners where he could stable Shadow and stow his bag for the evening, he turned, looking for Rass with a half-formed idea of getting the little girl a real dinner. Instead of Rass, a Roven woman dressed in hunting leathers leaned against the wagon next to his horse. Her hair draped over one shoulder in a long, thick copper braid.

She stood with her arms crossed, watching Will.

Her eyes were narrow, gauging, and her mouth pressed into a thin, flinty line. A hint of unease rolled across the back of Will's neck, but he forced himself to smile at her.

She did not smile back.

CHAPTER THREE

WHEN HE REACHED THE WOMAN, he paused and bowed his head slightly in her direction.

"Lovely evening, m'lady." His smile felt wooden.

She said nothing.

The "m'lady" had been too much. Judging from her leather vest, plain boots, and brown cotton pants, all of which were more functional than fashionable, she was a ranger who spent her life hunting on the Sweep. This wasn't a woman who wanted m'ladying.

Above them a seabird squawked indignantly and Will could still hear the noises from the festival, but an awkward silence filled the small void of space around them.

"I guess it's not a lovely evening if you don't like festivals."

Her foot rested on the bench, pinning down the reins of his horse.

"In which case we could hope for something that will end the festivities, like..." He paused. "A pestilence. Or a plague."

She stayed straight-faced, studying him coldly.

He opened up out toward her to read her emotions and felt...nothing.

Her emptiness seeped into him. She had no anger, no suspicion, no dislike. Just nothing. He'd met people with all different intensities of emotions, but never one with none.

A chill wormed its way through his newfound freedom and he backed up a step before stopping himself.

This woman was dreadful.

"One hour until the epic battle of storytellers commences!" Estinn called out to the crowd.

"That's me." Will took a step closer to Lady Dreadful. He put his hand on the reins, and slowly she moved her boot. He gave her a stiff nod, and led Shadow toward the nearest tents.

It took an age to get to them, feeling awkward the entire time, like his legs had forgotten the rhythm of a smooth gait. Her eyes were probably staring into his back, watching empty and cold. When he'd passed two tents, he glanced back, but saw no sign of her. Climbing into the saddle, he shook off her strangeness and turned Shadow toward the city gate.

Away from the woman, the thrum of excitement at finding Borto resurfaced. What was the best way to befriend the man? Telling a story better than anyone else in the competition tonight was obviously the first step.

He ran over the story of the Black Horn in his mind, as he passed through the gate and into the city. He barely noticed the sharp eyes of the city guards or the way Roven purposefully did not move when he approached, but let him move around them. His gaze ran past the lumpy cob buildings, barely seeing them.

His inn slouched against the shop next to it. Around the door, a stonesteep recarved fading protective runes into the cob, muttering to himself while a faint orange glow hovered around his tools. Will cast out toward the man and felt barely a wisp of *vitalle*. Just enough to make his tools glow. No actual magic was being pressed into the runes. It wasn't surprising. Most of the Roven stonesteeps he'd seen put only enough magic into their work to make it look real. In fact *steep* was such an exaggeration Will had often thought they should be called stonedribbles. But Roven were so used to relying on protective runes and burning stones, they paid the stonesteeps without question. These particular runes were so rough and blocky as to be almost illegible. Protection against weather most likely, a simple spell meant to keep the house safe over the summer while the Roven were in the grasses to the north grazing their herds.

The topmost one could be rain. Or sea, maybe. Definitely something watery.

For the thousandth time, Will wished he'd brought Alaric with him to the Sweep. Alaric was the sort of Keeper who would know immediately what the runes said, what they were intended to do, and why they looked different from the ones the Keepers used. He'd also know how to press magic into them, strong enough to last the summer. Any Keeper besides Will would, for that matter.

He left the stonesteep to his ineffective work and settled his horse in a dingy stable, leaving him with a pile of the cleanest hay he could find. The inn's common room smelled stale, a mixture of old food and neglect, and it took more money than it should have to rent a room. But the innkeeper took his coin without any disparaging comment or look, which was worth something.

The room was as filthy and irregular as the outside of the inn promised. It bent in an elongated triangle shape, one side following the curving outer wall. A low bed smelling of moldy, dried grass filled one side, and the other curved around into a point of empty gloom. A thin rug, still clinging to the memory of bright colors, covered the floor. When Will got back to civilized lands, he was going to stay in the nicest inn he could find. He'd pay ridiculously high prices just to be somewhere clean and bright and friendly.

He spread his bedroll over the windowsill to air. Dropping his bag down on the bed and ignoring the puff of dust that ballooned out of the mattress, he pulled out a bundle and unwrapped two small books. He sat and thumbed through the pages, the soft corners familiar under his fingers, checking for dampness or paper mites. His own handwriting covered the pages from edge to edge, with small drawings and diagrams crammed wherever they fit.

There was a flutter at the window and Talen landed on the bedroll, the usual mouse dangling from his beak.

Will grinned at the little hawk and dug into his bag, pulling out an old bit of dried meat. He set it next to the candle on the little table. Talen dropped the mouse and hopped down, snatching up the meat and giving Will an emotionless stare.

"You're welcome." Will went back to checking his book. Talen moved to the bed with a little hop and fixed his eyes on the flipping pages.

"Shall I teach you to read?" Will flipped back to the beginning. "That would make you a more interesting bird. These are my notes from the past year." He tilted the book toward the hawk, and Talen backed up slightly. "Originally I went to see the elves. Which was the most exciting thing I've ever been asked to do. I only ever found one, though."

A sketch of Ayda filled the next page. "This doesn't do her justice. She's…" She was vibrant and fanciful and her golden hair had almost sparkled. "Mesmerizing. I don't know why she spent so much time with me, but it was weeks. And she never introduced me to any other elves.

"She did show me Mallon the Rivor's body, though. Here on the Sweep you'd know him as Mallon the Undying. Which is a bit dramatic, even if it might be true. He attacked Queensland eight years ago, and was on the verge of conquering us. Until the elves stopped him. We thought they'd killed him, but it turns out they'd just trapped him inside his own mind." He glanced at Talen. "I'd imagine it's like he's a man stuck in a small, drab, little room only talking to himself. And a bird.

"I was headed back to tell Alaric, one of the other Keepers, that Mallon wasn't actually dead, when I heard of an old man named Wizendor who was supposedly coming to the Sweep to raise an army for Mallon. That was troubling enough that a Keeper needed to come to this wretched land." He smoothed the page flat. "At least I assume the other Keepers would have agreed that someone needed to come here. I didn't ask. I wasn't doing anything useful in Queensland. I'd been traveling the country looking for children with the ability to be Keepers for years and hadn't found any. At least Wizendor was someone I might actually find."

With the pages lying still, Talen twitched and looked around the room.

"Maybe I should have stayed, but if there's any Keeper *not* cut out for fighting an enemy with inexplicably strong powers, it's me.

Talen cocked his head at Will, looking at him out of one eye.

"Don't look at me like that. I left a note. Alaric is the Keeper who needed to know, anyway, and he was off in the south running errands for the Queen. I left that note at the palace for him nearly a year ago. By now he's probably been back there for ages, doing important Court Keeper sorts of things like straightening out the world and killing Mallon." He paused. "I wish I could have talked to him before coming here, though. I have no idea what was taking him so long to get back."

"Anyway, all this"—he flipped again and Talen snapped his focus back to the pages—"records me *not* finding Wizendor. Which is dull." He stopped at a page where the writing oozed disappointment. "When I did finally hear him speak to a crowd of Roven, it was still dull. Because the man was not worth the chase I'd just been on. If that old fool succeeded in raising a Roven army, then I'm the best Keeper that ever lived."

Past that, the entries in the book grew shorter and less related.

"By then I was deep in the Sweep, so I decided to learn what I could of the Roven on my way back out. Because, honestly, it feels a little embarrassing to have come all the way here and learned essentially nothing." He flipped past maps of the Sweep, notes on Roven culture, and overheard Roven stories. Records of searches that had begun as fascinating questions, but ended fruitlessly.

Like his attempt to find Kachig the Bloodless, a stonesteep so powerful that he was only mentioned in hushed voices. People were so frightened of the man, it had taken a whole month to discover he'd been dead for ten years.

It was unreasonably irritating that he couldn't even find out the reason for the "Bloodless." A title like that had a story behind it, but whatever it was, no one on the Sweep would talk about it.

The final entries all documented rumors of wayfarers on the Sweep, and any hints at where Ilsa might be.

Talen hopped forward to shove his beak into Will's bag.

"There's no more food in there." Will flipped through the last few pages of failure after failure, but closed the book without his usual sense of crushing despair. Because tonight, none of that mattered. Even though his hope of finding Ilsa hung by the slightest thread—he finally had a thread.

The scent of paper and ink wafted past. It smelled like comfort and home and rooms full of books. He held it close to his face for another breath.

What he wouldn't give to be in a library. Besides these two books, in the entire last year on the Sweep he had only seen five others. Two had been genealogies of the Sunn Clan kept in the wealthy district of Tun, and the other three had been carried by a severe looking stonesteep in a parade at Bermea. Almost no one on the Sweep read or cared to learn how. Limited documents were held in each clan recording births and deaths of the wealthy, businessmen kept minimal ledgers, and very occasionally a contract was drawn up. Will had earned a small amount, including one miniature hawk, by offering to record genealogies for families on the Sweep. The spelling of names was more of an art than a set of rules, but seeing as none of his customers could read, it didn't really matter.

Will shook out the scarf and Talen hopped back away from it. With a tweeting sort of whistle that sounded annoyed, he took off out the window.

Will wrapped his books back up. There was nothing alive in

his room to draw energy from, so Will set his hand on the books and pulled a tiny bit of energy out of himself.

It took so little effort. His palm barely tingled against the books as the energy went into them, wrapping an influence spell around the bundle. It said something that the only magic he was good at involved hiding things. Or himself. He tucked the books in the darkest corner under the bed. Between the shadows and the spell, even if someone came into his room, they wouldn't notice them.

He pulled a red wool shirt from his bag. It wasn't exactly like the traditional scarlet tunics storymen from Gulfind wore, but it was close enough that it would fool anyone but an actual storyman from Gulfind. Hopefully Borto would be convinced. He changed into it and straightened his shoulders. The role of storyteller settled over him like a cloud, and he let himself settle into the safety of it. It would be nicer to get to put on the full role of a Keeper. To keep the storytelling but add in the freedom to do magic and keep records and sit in the library and read books for days at a time. To have the camaraderie of the Keepers, to visit court.

He sighed and tucked a small coin purse inside his shirt and left his bag on the bed. The things left in it weren't worth anything.

The story contest wouldn't begin for a while, but this room was depressing and at the festival he could work on a way to talk to Borto again. He had nothing to draw energy from for an influence spell. Bracing himself against the hostility he was about to encounter from the Roven, he left the inn and hurried back toward the festival.

When the wayfarers came into view he paused to look for Lady Dreadful. Seeing no sign of her or Rass, he sat down on a bench, watching for Borto. As the sky darkened, the area swelled with people. Parents spread out brightly colored rugs on the ground while their children scampered and squealed around them. A sweetbread vendor walked by with a sugary smell of cinnamon. The benches along the back were filling and Will sat along the very edge, avoiding contact with them as much as he could.

A quarter of an hour passed before Will caught a glimpse of Borto passing behind the arc of wagons. With a surge of emotions too tangled to name, Will slipped around behind the nearest wagon to follow him.

There was little commotion back here and Will opened himself up. When he caught sight of Borto, a writhing mass of the man's eagerness and anxiety rushed into Will's chest. He drew back against a red wagon wall and glanced around. There was nothing here to cause so much anxiety.

Borto leaned back against his wagon, his arms crossed, one finger tapping quickly against his arm. A young man with a heavy limp came from the other side, and Borto's emotions flared. Will pressed himself against the red wall until he could just see the two of them.

"Lukas!" The wayfarer greeted him with a wide smile that belied his anxiety.

Lukas answered with a curt nod. He wasn't Roven. Even though his hair and beard were styled like one, they were light brown instead of red. His clothes were the undyed grey of a slave, but they were fitted and clean. He wore half a dozen rings and three necklaces. Even in the sunlight several of the burning stones held enough energy to be visibly bright. Over his slave's tunic he wore a grey leather vest stamped with lines and swirls of runes. One of his legs twisted at an odd angle, and he shifted his weight away from it.

He stood farther from Will, so his emotions were faint, but Will caught a hint of greed, and the twists of fear that always wrapped around it. And behind it all sat a deep, ugly hatred.

The emotions of the two men jumbled together and Will closed himself off to them.

If Lukas was a slave, he was better dressed and he wore more burning stones than any Will had seen. He stood next to Borto like a young lord addressing a servant.

Borto held out a bundle wrapped in a worn, brown cloth. Lukas kept his face impassive as he took it, but his movements were too quick to hide his eagerness. He unwrapped the cloth and Will's breath caught.

A book.

Will took a half step forward before he caught himself.

Not just any book. This was thick, covered with a blue leather binding dark as the night sky with a silver medallion on the front. Even from here, Will could see it promised stories and knowledge. And secrets.

A hungry smile twisted across Lukas's face, and he tossed the wayfarer a bulging bag of coins.

"No trouble getting it?" The words were more of a threatening statement than a question.

"Nothing this doesn't make up for." Borto dropped the bag inside his wagon. It let out a substantial thunk.

What book was worth that much money?

Lukas rubbed his hand across the cover.

"Always glad to help out our favorite clan." Borto leaned back. "And visit our favorite festival. Is the Torch coming to the contest tonight?"

The Torch? If Lukas served the clan chief of the Morrow, that would explain the way he was dressed.

"When he has this to read?" Lukas gave a derisive snort and flipped open the book and thumbed through a few pages. "And he says you're to leave at dawn."

Will stifled a laugh. The Roven Torch was trying to control a band of wayfarers?

"Before the festival is over?" Borto asked sharply. "You'll cost my people thousands of talens."

"Not all of you." Lukas's face turned malicious. "Just you. Says the information he sent you is…" His voice cut through the air as sharp as a shard of glass. "Promising, and you shouldn't dally on the Sweep." Carefully wrapping the book back up in the cloth and without looking at Borto for a response, Lukas turned and limped away.

Borto glared in Lukas's direction for a long moment before turning and ducking back between the wagons, slamming his fist into the side of one.

CHAPTER FOUR

WILL TOOK a few steps toward the empty space they'd left.

That had been intriguing on so many levels.

The Torch of a Roven clan just ordered a wayfarer to go do… something. And it certainly looked like Borto planned to obey, despite his obvious frustration.

Will stepped along the wagons until he could see Lukas's grey form limping quickly toward the city gate. His leg twisting painfully with each step.

Will took a step after him, his longing to see the book outweighing the obvious fact that he wasn't going to be able to get near it. There was no way a Roven Clan chief would let a foreigner into his house, never mind let him read the expensive book he'd just bought in a secret deal from the wayfarers.

Still…

How could he not follow a book like that?

He took another step forward.

"Take your seats!" Estinn's voice called as a jangle of music started. "Come hear stories that will boil your blood, mesmerize your mind, and seize your soul!"

Will lingered for another moment until Lukas disappeared

into the crowd near the gate, before retracing his steps back to the wayfarers' theater.

As fascinating as the book was, if Borto planned to leave the Sweep in the morning, Will had only tonight to impress him. Maybe a good enough tale would convince Borto to let Will travel with them for a few days. If not, he'd follow him anyway.

The sun hung low behind the city, casting the festival into shadows. Smells of roasted barley crackers and smoked fish trickled behind the stage to where Will stood with the other performers, a mix of colorfully dressed wayfarers and leather clad Roven. The wayfarers greeted him cheerfully, questioning him about himself and his story. The Roven stood to the side, coldly.

Estinn settled down the crowd and Will shifted until he could see most of the stage and a slice of the audience between the hanging fabric.

"Our first tale of the night is Yervant, come to share the story of when he followed Mallon to Queensland," Estinn called out, "and killed the Keeper!"

The crowd erupted into cheers and Will's gaze snapped over to the people beside him.

Mallon? No Keepers had been killed when Mallon had invaded. He'd passed through Queensland like some kind of plague, gaining control over people's minds in town after town, holding sway over them even after he'd left. And when he'd controlled enough, he'd brought his armies of Roven to destroy the rest.

One of the Roven, a thick, disheveled man carrying a mug of ale and smelling unwashed, pushed past Will and stepped up onto the stage. Voices called out to him from the crowd, taunting but friendly, and he held up his hand for silence. With a few final jeers, the audience stilled.

"When Mallon the Undying"—Yervant raised his mug reverently at the name—"led our great people 'cross the Scales to crush the farmers o' Queensland, I traveled with him. Our company had men o' the Morrow Clan—" Cheers rang from the crowd. "—and from the Panos Clan." He looked around slowly and the audience quieted.

Will glanced at the faces in the crowd that he could see. Mallon had attacked Queensland only eight years ago. How many of these men were there?

"And we had a giant, with feet so large he crushed three houses with each step!"

The people were nodding along, muttering approvingly and Will held in a snort. Maybe none of these people had fought. Giants' feet were barely large enough to crush a bush, never mind three houses.

Yervant told how the troops had slunk through the woods, approaching a small town right on the northern edge of the Scales. How the giant had gone out first, destroying building after building, then the Roven warriors had swept in. Until Queensland's soldiers had appeared.

"And behind 'em, black like a shadow, a Keeper snuck through the mornin'." Yervant's voice was low and angry. "He had no amulets, no stones, no books. All his magic he sucked from the world around him." The crowd rumbled. "And he didn't help Queensland's soldiers. Not a single soldier had an amulet or a charmed sword. The enemy fell before our blades like grass, and the Keeper didn't even look at the bodies."

Will clenched his jaw in an effort to keep his face impassive. The only Keeper who'd been along the northern Scales was Mikal. And he had done everything he could to protect those men. He'd knocked aside arrows, softened the enemy's steel, thrown illusions onto the field to confuse the Roven.

"Just when we thought we had 'em beat," Yervant said, bitterness creeping into his voice, "the black Keeper stepped up to a burning house and took the fire *in his hands*." A ripple of revulsion swept across the crowd.

Mikal had never spoken of how the battle ended, and Will had never pressed him. He'd been tempted to look into the Wellstone where Mikal had recorded his memories of it, but it had felt invasive. And so he'd only known there'd been a fire. Mikal had always been good at moving flames. He used to light his candles by walking near the hearth. He'd just pull out a bit of flame, dancing on nothing but air, and bring it to his wick.

"The Keeper took the fire in his hands," Yervant continued, "and threw it at us, sending streams o' fire across our men. Burnin' Roven where they stood, poor Andro and Adaom among 'em."

A swell of anger grumbled through the crowd.

Mikal had wept for those men as well. Even all these years later, the Keeper carried those deaths with him like a shadow.

"The black demon burned our men alive!" Yervant shouted. "He drove off the giant with his dark arts. But at the last moment, I drew my bow, and with Andro and Adaom's bodies at my feet, I shot arrow after arrow at the monster."

"And you killed him!" Someone cried out from the crowd.

Yervant nodded. "My last arrow struck home, sinking into his black heart. I saw him fall t' the ground. Dead."

A wildly inappropriate smile threatened to spread across Will's face. Mikal hadn't been shot in the chest. He'd been shot in the shoulder. The arrow had knocked him down, and when he'd gotten to his feet, the Roven were fleeing. Will had changed the bandages on that wound, and it had healed cleanly. The arrow had been nothing. It was the rest of the battle that had left scars.

Yervant finished his tale and bowed to cheers, sloshing his ale across the front of the stage before climbing down and disappearing into the audience.

Estinn stepped back up on the stage. "Thank you, Yervant. Even though you only have one tale to tell"—she paused for some jeers from the crowd—"it's one we don't mind hearing. Year after year after year."

She raised her hand for silence. "Our next storyman is sure to tell something we haven't heard before. A foreigner has offered to entertain us with tales from distant lands." She turned and held a hand out toward Will. "Good people of the Morrow Clan, I present storyman Will of Gulfind!"

A spattering of applause came from the crowd, mixed with murmurs. Will stepped onto the torchlit stage and found himself alone. The sun had set while Yervant talked. The light from the stage torches made the faces of the crowd indistinct, and he imagined they were an audience from back home. Maybe a gathering from a large village. It felt better than a crowd of Roven, but neither really mattered. Tonight the only audience that mattered was Borto.

Will brought a stool from near the back of the stage forward, and settled on to it. He glanced around to make sure the wayfarer was watching, and catching a quick glimpse of the man standing off to the side, he began.

"Good evening. Tonight I bring you the tale of the Black Horn. A tale of old magic worn thin and new magic just born. Of love and sacrifice. Of a vast army and a single soul."

Will opened himself up to the crowd finding skepticism mixed with curiosity. He breathed in the earthy smell of the torch oil spiced with sorren seeds, and looked down at the stage for a long moment, waiting until the crowd settled into silence, their emotions swinging toward curiosity.

"The bag with the Black Horn bounced against Eliese's back like the prodding of a little sprite, cheering her on to adventure and victory..."

As he told of Eliese's early adventures, it began to happen. The two children directly in front of him were drawn in, and their amusement seeped out, mixing with that of their family, with the Roven warrior behind them.

By the time he reached the heart of the story, the emotions of the crowd had risen, each individual's anticipation merging with their neighbors' until it filled the small theater. Instead of feeling it in his chest, it became something more—almost a visible cloud, almost a living thing.

"...on the mantle," Will continued, "the ram's horn sat like a curl of blackness, darker than the shadows. Eliese reached up, her hand hesitating only a moment before picking it up."

Will gauged the audience. Only at the very edges did the mist begin to tatter with distracted people out on the fringes. A dead spot farther along the side circled around someone keeping themselves isolated from the story. But around Borto, the crowd hung together, utterly focused.

The Black Horn moved along simple and well-made, needing little help on his part. An obscure story he'd found tucked away in the queen's library, he'd stitched it together with a similar account at the Stronghold. They'd been easy to merge and the story had become one of his favorites.

Even exchanging the Keeper for a wise woman and leaving out any mentions of Queensland took minimal thought. He just needed to pick up the spool of the story and follow the thread. The words lined up, one after the other. They stretched ahead of him as easy to follow as a wide path through the grass.

Keeping tabs on the emotions of the audience, he slowed down or sped up the tale. And like all audiences, they let themselves be pulled into it, delighting in the feel of the story.

A bright spot of fascination off to his left in the mist of emotions caught his attention. He glanced over to see Rass perched on a wagon wheel in her little grey slave's shift, beaming at him.

At the darkest moment he paused, letting the tragedy seep through the air. The audience sat silent, somber while the darkness of the tragedy felt complete. Speaking just loud enough to carry over the quiet crowd, he drew them back toward the light, with the slightest hope of finding what was lost.

When the final words had been spoken and allowed to fade away, the crowd erupted into cheers and Borto applauded enthusiastically. The emotions of the crowd splintered into individual people feeling individual things, and Will pressed his fist to his chest and bowed his head to the crowd.

He moved to a seat just off the stage to watch the next storyteller. A Roven woman sang next, a long ballad that warbled on the high notes. She finished and the audience talked and laughed and argued with each other while waiting for the next performer. Will sat half-listening to the conversations around him, half-watching Borto. Two men were arguing about whether or not the ubiquitous rumors of frost goblins on the Sweep were true.

The Sweep was obsessed with the idea of frost goblins this spring.

A story about frost goblins would be fascinating to hear. Until recently, he'd always heard the little creatures mentioned as only a nuisance. But this year, the stories sounded more threatening.

"Another report came today," the first man said. "Eight rangers dead."

The second man shook his head. "Just more rumors."

"Magar says they're not," the first insisted.

"Your cousin will say anything to scare you…"

Will opened up toward them, feeling an acidic fear blossom in his chest, even from the protestor.

Will stretched out farther through the crowd, catching more uncertainty than usual. Every town he'd passed through for the last several weeks had an undercurrent of uneasiness. Will had attributed it to the clans readying themselves for the long migration north to their summer valleys, but maybe it was more.

Past everyone, Will felt that dead spot again. A place where emotions were being held tight. He shifted to see past the torches.

Lady Dreadful leaned against a wagon, partially shadowed from the torchlight studying him. His own uneasiness filled his chest.

At least a dozen Roven sat between him and her, but he closed himself off to all but the frost goblin men, then stretched out past people one by one. A young woman with loose, fiery hair spoke to the man beside her, her emotions swirling bright, just under the surface, edged with jealousy. A man whose beard had streaks of grey chatted with the woman beside him, comfort and contentedness running deep. An older man sat alone, humming with a worn, hollow fear. When he reached Lady Dreadful, he found nothing but emptiness.

Night had truly fallen and a boy scurried across the stage adding more torches. Excitement and pride broke Will's concentration on the woman and her blank hollowness faded from his chest. The extra torches drenched the stage with light, obscuring anything past it. Will shifted on the blanket, trying to shrink back into the shadows, wishing he could see Lady Dreadful. But he might as well be on stage, perfectly lit up and unable to see anything.

He turned his attention to the next wayfarer woman who'd taken the stage, trying to push Lady Dreadful out of his mind. Tomorrow morning he'd leave with Borto, or following right behind him. The cold woman could stay here in Porreen and rot.

Borto Mildiani took the stage and Will turned all his attention to the man. It wasn't difficult. From his first words, the man had the audience enthralled.

Even more than his face or his name, this set him apart from Vahe.

Will had forgotten little about the wayfarer's visit to his childhood home. Vahe had told three tales that morning, tales of danger and suspense. As a child, Will hadn't been able to pinpoint what he hadn't liked about them, but he'd told enough stories by now to know. The way Vahe lingered on frightening ideas, the turns of phrase—he enjoyed his audience's fear.

Borto, on the other hand, made the festival laugh. The crowd threw themselves into his hands and he rewarded them with excitement and intrigue. He told the tale of a young Roven girl lost on the Sweep who'd called out to the Serpent Queen for help and Will listened closely, absorbing the story to write down tonight. Most stories were easy to remember, this one was so well crafted and told, it would be effortless. The thread of the story ran perfectly true from the lost girl calling for help, to the sinuous, black shape of the Serpent Queen descending from the night sky, and instead of leading the girl back home, changing her into a shadow and bringing her up to live among the stars.

Will found the Roven myth of the Serpent Queen fascinating. In Queensland, the black cloud-like darkness that wound through the sky was a shadow trail left by the ogre whose constellation sat at one end. Just a lack of stars, a nothing.

But the Roven viewed the darkness as a serpent, slowly devouring every other star. She was the part of the night sky they claimed as their own, different from the rest and bent on destroying it.

Borto finished to thunderous applause and Will rose with the rest of the crowd.

Estinn took the stage long enough to declare Borto the winner of the contest. Will stepped forward to talk to him, but everyone else in the crowd had the same idea and the stage swarmed with people.

Several wayfarers and even a handful of Roven congratulated Will on his excellent story, but the crowd inexorably pushed him back and shut him out. Borto thundered something enthusiastically to the crowd around him. It would be hours before they left the man alone, but Will didn't need to talk to him tonight. He'd be back at dawn, just happening to be leaving at the same time as Borto. Only one route led off the Sweep this far south, and they'd have days on the lonely Sea Road to talk before they'd have a chance to go separate ways.

The obscurity of Will's room called to him. He looked around for Lady Dreadful, but saw no sign of her. Instead of relief, a wave of vulnerability swept over him, like he'd been tossed into murky water where anything might be slithering past.

He slipped into the throng moving toward the city gate and with the darkness and the mood of the crowd, reached the unsavory alley leading to the inn with a minimal number of distrustful glances and no sign of a thick copper braid. The moon wouldn't rise for hours, and the alley sat in heavy shadows. Will paused at the beginning of it. That woman had him rattled.

Still he hesitated. He let out a huff of annoyance at his own fear, even as he cast out down the dark alley, checking for the *vitalle* of anyone hiding in the shadows. He found nothing.

Walking quickly to his room, he slid the insubstantial latch into place, and leaned against the door. Across the dark room on the windowsill he could just make out a lump. It only took a couple steps closer to make it out. A dead mouse. With a small laugh, Will leaned out the window, half expecting an undersized hawk to wing through the sky, but it was empty of everything but distant, cold stars. With a flick, he shot the mouse out the window to land in the alley.

A candle sat on a tiny table beneath the window. Will set his finger against the wick. "*Incende*," he breathed. His fingertip tingled as energy passed through it and a small flame burst into life.

He sank down onto the bed, dropping his head into his hands and staring at the floor, letting the silence and emptiness wrap around him like a breath of fresh air.

"Who are you?"

The woman's voice cut through the room and Will's head snapped up.

Leaning against the wall, tucked back in the narrowest corner of his room, the candlelight showing barely more than her face, stood Lady Dreadful.

CHAPTER FIVE

WILL SHOVED himself up off the bed. "Who are you?" he shot back

She ignored the question. "You shouldn't be here." Her Roven accent bit the words off harshly.

Will stared at her for a moment. "This is my room."

Trying to gauge her emotions, he opened up toward her. The same emptiness blossomed in his chest. He focused more, searching until he felt an undercurrent of anger, deep and...old. Foundational. The sort of emotion that had been there her entire life. Anger surrounded by coldness and emptiness.

He could see her face, but her dark ranger leathers blurred into the shadows. Making her somehow part of the darkness except a glint of silver from a knife hilt at her belt.

She stepped forward and he forced himself to hold his ground.

"I'm usually better at reading people." The shock of her presence quickly wore off and was replaced with anger at her audacity. "I had the impression you didn't like me. Not that you were headed to my room for a midnight visit."

He still felt nothing. This woman exuded less emotion than anyone he'd ever met. His own body, on the other hand, thrummed with wariness and alarm. The door stood between them and Will had the urge to run, but outside this room he would still be just as trapped. A foreigner running down the streets chased by a Roven? That story did not end well.

"Who are you?" she repeated.

Will gestured to his bright red shirt. "I thought the shirt made it obvious. And the story I told tonight."

She said nothing.

"I'm a storyteller." ...*from Gulfind,* he almost added. But the lie felt too blatant.

Her eyes glittered out of the dimness, giving Will the wild impression that she could see through shadows and somehow into him.

"You sound like you're from Queensland."

Will's chest tightened but he kept his voice light. "The people from Queensland and Gulfind sound remarkably alike." Which was one of the main reasons he'd picked Gulfind as his pretend home. "The countries are on such good terms that the family trees along the border are muddled with folk from both countries."

He waited for her to do or say anything. "There's a whole history behind that, but since I make my living as a storyteller, you'll have to pay me if you want to hear it."

"Leave the Sweep."

Her imperious tone was irritating. He sat on the bed and kicked his feet out with a hundred times more nonchalance than he felt.

"I was just considering staying." That lie was blatant, but it was worth it to see the scowl deepen on her face. Will shifted farther onto the bed so he could lean against the wall.

She took a step forward and Will tensed.

He cast out through the room again, looking for a source of energy. The candle flame held too little *vitalle* to do anything. If she attacked, he'd have to pull energy out of her. Which was distasteful. And then he'd—do what? The only spells he worked well were subtle and slow.

His mind offered up outlandish suggestions from old stories: he could split open the ground like Keeper Chesavia had done.

Except even when he told that tale he had no idea how she'd done that. He could call fire from the candle and build it into a wall, pressing her back like Keeper Terrane had done against the trolls.

Of course when Will had tried to manipulate flames, even with a bonfire to draw from, all he'd managed was a little tumbleweed of fire that had scuttled erratically across the ground before fizzling out.

He smiled at her, not bothering to make it look sincere. "Now, I think it's time you tell me who you are, and why you're lurking in my room. It's obviously not to hear me tell a story."

She shrugged. "Maybe I am. There's no better way to learn about people than to hear them tell stories, isn't that right?"

Will's stomach clenched at the echo of his words to Borto. "Have you been following me all day?"

She ignored his question again. "When you tell stories, all I hear are lies," she said, her voice cold. "Go back to…wherever you are from, Will." Her lip curled as she said his name, as though she doubted even that. "You are not what you seem."

Will flinched, and tried to cover it up by running his hand through his beard. "What exactly do you think I am?"

She narrowed her eyes and Will opened up toward her one more time. But her emotions were still clamped down out of his reach. She took two more steps, moving within arm's reach, glaring down at him. The clay wall pressed unyieldingly against his back.

"Go home. Things will not go well for you if you stay."

Irritation flickered at the threat and he took some grim pleasure in letting it show on his face. A bit of breeze slipped into the room swirling the scent of grass with the woman's worn leather and causing the candle to stutter. She glanced toward it and Will's heart stuttered with the flame.

She leaned closer and the uneven clay wall pressed harder into Will's back. "I see you." Her accent dragged the smallest bit along the s, almost like a hiss.

The words cut through him. It took everything he had to not shove away from her.

"Leave." She held his gaze for a long moment before turning and striding the few steps to the door. She glanced back at him with her hand on the latch. "There is much to fear on the Roven Sweep..." Her eyes flickered toward the candle. "For a man like you."

The door closed, leaving Will in the darkness of the empty room. He strained to hear her in the hall. The flickering candle and the wobbling shadows it cast were the only movement.

How long had she been here waiting for him? His gaze searched the room as though it would give him a clue.

His books—

With a rush of fear that splintered like shards of glass, he dropped to his knees and his fingers scrambled back under the bed. For a heart-stopping breath he felt nothing. Then he brushed against the bundle and dragged it out. He clutched the books for a moment, the scarf around them undisturbed, before shoving them into his bag.

He could leave tonight. He could head down the sea road, find a place far from Porreen to wait out the night and wait for Borto to catch up.

He glanced into his mostly empty bag. He needed supplies. Dawn would have to be good enough.

There was no way the woman could prove he had used magic to light the candle, but justice on the Sweep rarely worried about things as trivial as proof. The Roven weren't against magic, but if they found out he could do it, they'd know he wasn't just a story-man. And if they knew anything about Gulfind, they'd know that almost no one there used magic. The questioning from there could only go downhill.

He blew out the candle, dropping the room into darkness.

A raised voice echoed down the alley. Will crawled quietly to the window, and lifted his head just high enough to look out.

Two men stumbled drunkenly down the street. No clan

warriors coming to arrest him, no empty woman with narrow eyes.

Will looked for something to push in front of the door, but the only furniture in the room was the light table and the bed. And if Roven warriors came for him tonight, it wouldn't be furniture or weapons he'd have to use against them. If they came, he'd just have to hope he woke up quickly enough to work some magic.

He let his head fall back against the wall. Except he didn't exactly have an arsenal of magic at the ready.

Blackness bloomed around him, managing to be both smothering and empty. Normally manageable fears grew and shifted, looming like living things. Tentacles of anxiety pried him open.

Even assuming he could befriend Borto, would he find out where Vahe had taken Ilsa? Would Borto even know? It had been twenty years, even if he found Vahe, would the man remember?

Dawn couldn't come soon enough. The hope he'd been feeling faded, strangled out by questions. The fear of failing surrounded him like a wall. No, a wall was too thin. It surrounded him like the grassland outside, vast and empty. He rolled back onto his bed. Fears that felt too real swirled around him. He pushed them back over and over, waiting for sleep that didn't come.

Life felt like one long search after another. He'd spent a year on the Sweep searching for an army that didn't exist, and for Kachig the Bloodless who was dead.

And it hadn't started here. How many years had he spent looking for children born with the skills to be Keepers?

For the past two centuries, Keepers had appeared about every seven to ten years with barely a gap.

Until Will.

After Will had joined the Keepers twenty years ago, not a single new Keeper had surfaced. There should have been at least two more, maybe three. Instead, the existing Keepers grew older and weaker until only Alaric and Will ever left the Stronghold. When fifteen years had passed, Will had begun searching in earnest, traveling Queensland as often as possible, visiting even the smallest towns while the Keepers worried that no more would ever come.

And he'd searched for twenty years for Ilsa. Twenty years of rumors and dead ends. Would this time be any different?

Sometime in the interminable hours of darkness, sleep must have crept into his room, because early morning sounds from the street and a gust of chilly air woke him. The sky had lightened to pale slate, anticipating the dawn.

With as little movement as he could, Will glanced around the room, finding it empty.

Of course it was empty. He rolled his eyes at himself. It was time to get out of the Sweep. He was going to turn into a paranoid mess if he stayed any longer.

The sky was clear. He searched it for a moment, looking for Talen, before rolling up his bedroll and grabbing his bag. Half uneasy, half annoyed with himself for the uneasiness, he cracked the door open just enough to peer into the empty hallway.

It was obviously too late to stop himself from turning into a paranoid mess.

The smell of warm bread floated upstairs from the common room. He let the homey, daytime scent fill up the hollowness that lingered from last night's fear and followed the smell down to where the squinty-eyed innkeeper puttered in the kitchen. Will bought several small loaves and some smoked fish.

Near the door, something rustled. A shadow shifted and the morning light caught on a coppery-red braid.

CHAPTER SIX

WILL's hand clenched his bag. The woman gestured out the door.

"Didn't guess Sora was here for you." The innkeeper leaned his elbows on the counter. "Careful, storyman. That's not a woman t' be taken lightly."

"I'd noticed," Will said. She stood between him and the door. Not that running was an option. Everyone who saw him would vividly remember the black-haired foreigner who'd run through the street. Like a coward.

Even as Will opened up, he knew it would be useless. The innkeeper's curiosity darted into him with an eager brightness, but Sora was nothing but emptiness. In the grey-blue morning light, she looked less like a vicious sliver of darkness and more like a woman. A hostile, unreadable woman, but still a woman.

Behind her the alley lightened. Borto's wagon could be trundling down the road already, the distance between them stretching like a cord. Frustration surged up, battling against his fear. He loosened his hand on his bag.

"Good morning…Sora." He tried to cram as much of his irritation into her name as possible. "Coming to my room wasn't enough last night? You needed to come back this morning?"

A spike of shock and amusement came from the innkeeper.

"Come with me," she ordered.

Will looked around for any other option, but she stood at the only exit. He leaned against the bar, focusing only on her, blocking out the emotions coming from the innkeeper. "No."

She raised an eyebrow, but he felt nothing from her. "Your services are required."

"That's flattering, I suppose. But I'm going to have to decline." He felt the slightest irritation from her.

"Last night," he pressed, looking for more, "you snuck into my room like a gutless thief"—her lips pressed into a thin line—"and ordered me to leave the Sweep. Setting aside the fact that I don't take orders from you, I've decided it's time for me to go home."

He pushed himself off the bar and walked toward the door, but she didn't move out of his way.

"So," he continued, "if your plans for me have changed, and I'd like to point out that it's strange that you have plans for me, I'm afraid you're going to be disappointed."

She crossed her arms. "It's not my plans that have changed. This morning the Torch requires your services."

A cold fear stabbed into his gut. The clan chief?

"You'd be wise to come with me. I'm your polite invitation."

"Yes, you're like a beam of sunshine."

The edge of her mouth quirked up the slightest bit. "If you refuse to come with me, the next people Killien sends won't be as pleasant. And if you try to leave the city...it won't go well."

The walls of the dingy inn pushed in a bit closer. He'd never heard of any foreigner taken to a Torch for a pleasant reason.

"It's not wise to keep a Torch waiting," she said.

"That's true," agreed the innkeeper.

Sora stepped out into the alley and he followed her, his mind racing. He saddled Shadow while she stood in the stable door, blocking his exit. When they reached the end of the alley, the city gate would be within view. He led Shadow out of the stable, his mind scrambling to find a way away from this woman.

But when they reached the street, four guards stood in front of the barred gate.

"You don't want to try that." Sora walked the other way.

Because she'd stop him? Or because the gate was closed for him? Will tightened his hold on Shadow's reins. It was barely dawn, the gate was probably just not open yet. The knot in his stomach didn't go away with the thought, and he followed Sora numbly.

A spattering of Roven moved in the streets, casting unfriendly looks at Will's black hair and beard. Sora turned down one street, then another. Each curved and doubled back intersecting others at odd angles. He felt like he'd shrunk and been trapped in the winding tunnels bookgrubs bored through books. He felt a sudden envy for the grubs. It'd be easier to get out of Porreen if he could burrow himself a new path.

I'm a storyteller from Gulfind, he told himself, attempting to reignite some small hope. *It's worked for months. Everyone has believed me. It'll work a little longer.*

Sora turned onto yet another road.

Everyone had believed him but Sora. The little flick of hope disappeared.

"What's wrong?" A hint of amusement crept into her voice. "Afraid?"

"Yes." He shot her a glare he hoped she could feel. "The Boan Torch is rumored to occasionally arrest any non-Roven he finds in Bermea and sell them on the slave block. I personally saw the Sunn Torch marching a chain of blond-haired slaves to be fed to their *dragon*. No one but Roven live on the Sweep, the only outsiders I've met were passing through. Quickly." He didn't bother to add that the Roven were so uneducated and barbaric that no one wanted to come to the Sweep. "Every foreigner with any sense is afraid to meet a Roven Torch."

Which was why no Keeper had ever met one. The thought caught his attention. Was he about to be the first?

"Ours has nothing against storymen from Gulfind. He's thrilled to meet you."

She didn't sound sarcastic. Maybe this wasn't as dire as it felt. He wasn't under arrest. The Torch had sent a single woman to bring him. And being the first Keeper to meet a Torch did feel significant. Granted the Morrow Clan was the smallest clan on the Sweep, so this was the least significant Torch. But if he had to meet a vicious warlord, it seemed best to meet the smallest one. And offered the opportunity to meet a clan chief, he could hardly run away scared.

Will breathed in a deep breath of the cool morning air. He would meet the Torch and get a sense of the man.

Then he'd run away.

If he could find his way out of this mess of a city.

Borto was getting farther east by the moment, but he pushed the thought away. An hour's head start shouldn't be a problem. Shadow could catch up to the slow wagon.

"You didn't answer my question before," he said. "Why are we going to the Torch?"

She ignored him and he opened up to her again, trying to eek any information out of her that he could. Why couldn't he feel any emotions in her? It was irritating and fascinating. But mostly irritating. He'd never met anyone who could control their feelings this well. Maybe she needed some prodding.

"You do realize I'm a storyteller? If you don't answer me, I'll make something up."

That earned him a response that could almost be called an eye roll, but no emotion.

"The obvious reason," he said loudly enough for the few other people in the street to hear, "is that you've fallen in love with me and we're headed to the Torch to be wed."

She shot him a glare so venomous that he shifted away. But at the same time a jab of indignation shot into the side of his chest from her.

It was thoroughly satisfying.

"Not love then." Maybe more prodding would draw out more emotions. "You must be after money. Has the Torch offered a reward for finding the greatest storyteller in the world?"

She tamped down her emotions again. "If there was a reward, this would be less irritating."

Will stopped. "You're dragging me through town with you at the break of dawn because your Torch wants to hear a story? What are you? His Master of Entertainment?"

She glanced over her shoulder. "Hurry."

He started moving again. The sun crept above the mountains, and in the morning light something about Sora's leathers nagged at him. It took a moment to realize they were plain. Not a single rune marked the dark leather around the armholes or the neck or anywhere. None were sewn into her grey-blue sleeves. The only thing she wore that could be called decorative was a brown cloth wrapped around her upper arm. Leather strips wound around it, fastening on a vicious white claw.

When he didn't look away, she shot him a glare from eyes that were bright green. Green. Roven eyes were always blue. Weren't they? This woman was an enigma. She should be in a story.

The streets widened and the buildings ordered themselves into less primitive shapes. Soon the ends of actual beams of wood, a rich brown against the dull mud, protruded out of the walls holding second floors above them.

Sora made one final turn onto a broad street. It ran past two sprawling houses on each side before ending at one that could only be described as massive.

The entire first level was stone. He hadn't seen a building with this much stone in months. The rock rose out of the ground, unyielding and severe next to all the clay buildings. Wide stone steps spilled into the street like a stack of petrified puddles. Sora motioned to a blond-haired slave who took Shadow. Will spun his ring as he followed Sora past a line of empty wagons and up the steps. He was fiercely envious of her calmness.

An intricate carving of a snake surrounded by stars flowed

across the thick wood door. The tiny scales of the Serpent Queen were coated in something faintly green that caught the morning light and shimmered, one lidless eye flashed red from an inset gem. Light rippled along the snake, making it appear to slither across the door. Knife-thin fangs tipped in a shimmer of red stretched wide around the star-shaped doorknob.

Sora reached for the knob, putting her hand in between the fangs, and Will straightened his shoulders. He needed to keep this quick. Get in, meet the warlord, get out. Easy.

For such an easy thing, it took an inordinate amount of effort to step through the door and follow Sora into the large room. A slave worked along shelves, packing things into reed baskets. The warmth of the room smothered him after the chill outside. A fire burned along the side and torches flickered with the opening of the door, sending a flurry of shadows darting over walls and Roven faces.

The room quieted a little as Sora strode in, and more as Will stepped in behind her. He heard murmurs of "fetter bait" and "storyman" trickle through the room. Sora crossed to a small table where two men sat. One of them was enormous, with a bright red beard and hair so wild and wiry it lay like a lion's mane around his face. Two braids as thick as Will's thumb hung from the bottom of the beard, the ends cinched with thick silver bands. His leather vest was decorated with plenty of runes, tooled in and dyed a deep red. Will paused in the center of the room, feeling awkward.

"Killien, Torch of the Morrow Clan," Sora introduced flatly, "meet Will, storyman from Gulfind."

Will pressed his fist to his chest and bowed low, knowing that when he straightened the enormous man would be towering over him.

But it was the other man who rose with a wide smile.

"Thank the black queen!" He extended his hand. "Someone who can spin me a tale!"

Will reached out grasped the Torch's wrist, the man's hand

locking around his own like a shackle. Killien wore three wide silver rings encircled with runes and inset with small gems on that hand, two more on his other.

The Torch was an average-sized man, dressed in warrior leathers that were not purely functional like Sora's. Intricate protective markings ringed the shoulders and neck, some inset with a coppery dye that caught the firelight. His auburn hair was cut short. His beard was trimmed to a shape only slightly too wild to be called neat, and decorated with thin, subtle braids, bound off with silver beads. He couldn't be much older than Will. At least a handful of years from forty.

"A storyman…from Gulfind." The Torch looked pointedly at Will's fingers spinning his ring. "And with gold to prove it. I've always thought it takes a certain kind of bravery for your people to wear gold out into the world."

"Or stupidity," Sora said.

"Probably a bit of both." Will held up his hand so Killien could see the ring. "I wear this more because it was a gift and because it spins than because it's gold." He turned the band so Killien could see it spin. "That and because I can't get it off anymore. But I don't carry any other gold with me. I'd rather pay for my lodging and meals with stories. Not many brigands want to steal them, and if they do, they have to keep me alive to do it."

The Torch grinned. "Stories work as payment here, too. It's been ages since a storyman came to the Morrow." His accent cut cleanly against the words, refining the Roven harshness a bit.

Will let out some of the tension that had been building in him. Sora had been serious about the Torch. He really did want a story. Maybe this wouldn't be as terrifying of a meeting as he'd expected. A half-dozen short but entertaining stories popped into Will's mind. "I heard a wayfarer, Borto, tell an excellent story last night."

"Yes, Borto's entertaining," Killien agreed, "but I've heard him a hundred times. No one new ever comes to the Morrow. The good ones never manage to get this far away from Bermea and Tun."

"I didn't say he was good," Sora objected.

"Ignore Sora," Killien said. "She told me you had the festival enthralled. That she hadn't seen a storyteller beguile a crowd like that since her childhood."

"Really?" Will turned toward Sora. "I hadn't realized you'd enjoyed it that much."

Sora's gaze turned flinty. "I said, 'manipulate' not 'beguile'."

"I'm sure she didn't enjoy it at all." Killien waved away her words. "But if we based our decisions on what Sora liked, we'd never do anything fun. We'd just hunt. Alone." Unperturbed by Sora's expression, the Torch turned back to Will.

"Tell me about yourself, Will." His voice stayed light, but his eyes turned stony. "What brings you all the way to the Morrow?"

"I've been to Bermea and Tun already, and they were…" Will paused, thinking of how to describe the two largest Roven cities without being insulting.

"Festering slums whose resources are squandered by Torches too stupid to know how to lead?" Killien offered.

Grunts of agreement echoed in the room.

"Well"—Will spun his ring slowly—"I was going to say crowded…but 'festering slums' works too. Everything in Bermea was gray with smoke from that army camp outside the city. And Tun smelled like fish." The smell had lingered on his clothing for days. "They need to move that fish market. I got tired of trying to tell stories while gagging through every breath."

Killien grinned. "I hate those cities." He considered Will for a moment. "But I like you."

Sora made an exasperated sound.

"The Morrow Clan heads north to the summer rifts tomorrow," Killien continued. "You can entertain us tonight in the square and stay here as my personal guest. There's a room upstairs that's been vacant since a piggish stonesteep from Tun was here, charging me too much to renew the wards on our herds."

Will's hand stilled on his ring. Stay here? For the whole day?

"He's leaving the Sweep today," Sora informed the Torch. "I caught him on his way out."

Will could have hugged her. "I am."

But Killien's expression tightened. "A day's delay is nothing."

A day's delay would put him far behind Borto. He might catch up to the wayfarer again, but there was too big of a risk of losing him. Will opened his mouth, desperately searching for a way out.

The enormous man with the wild beard stood up from the table and stepped up next to Killien amused. "Surely an invitation from a Roven Torch is enough of a reason to stay."

No. The only reason he'd had to stay in barbaric, uneducated Porreen was at this moment riding away in a wayfarer's wagon. Will searched for the words to tell a Roven Torch that he wasn't interested in being his guest. He glanced around the room. He was completely surrounded by Roven. His gaze caught on the wall by the door and he stopped, stunned.

Shelves filled the entire end of the room. They were mostly empty, but one shelf held at least fifty—

"Books." His words came out barely above a whisper. "You have books."

CHAPTER SEVEN

He took a step toward them, trying to make out titles. Along the floor in front of the shelves, packed neatly into large baskets, were more books.

Hundreds of them.

"I have a lot of books." Killien led the way over to the shelves. "Most have been packed for the trip north, but you're welcome to read the ones that are left."

Will walked along the shelf reading the titles.

The Clans and the Clashes of the Sweep, History of War in Coastal Baylon, The Gods of Gulfind.

His opinion of the Torch was quickly reforming. Not only were there books, there were a decent number of books about people other than the Roven.

"Do all storymen get this excited about books?" Sora asked. "Or just ones from Gulfind?"

Will's finger froze on the shelf and he glanced up. Sora eyed him with a raised eyebrow, but Killien looked thoroughly pleased to see his books getting so much attention.

Will turned back to the books and tried to keep his voice light. "I don't think you have to be from anywhere in particular to love books."

He slid out a thin book covered in yellow leather and tilted it toward the fire to read the silvery title. *Neighbors Should Be Friends*, by Flibbet the Peddler. Will's eyes tripped over the words and he read it again to be sure. He looked up at Killien. "You have a book by Flibbet?"

"I have three." Killien grinned. "The other two are packed."

A book by Flibbet the Peddler.

Here on the Sweep.

Had anyone found books from the crazy old peddler this far from Queensland? He flipped it open. Flibbet's quirky, multicolored scrawl spread across the page. This book was mentioned twice in other works by Flibbet. The Shield had wanted a copy in the Keeper's library for…for longer than Will had been alive.

"I've never met anyone who knew who he was." Killien crossed his arms and considered Will. "My father met Flibbet just before I was born. The peddler sold him the books and a sword."

Will stared at the Torch speechless for a moment. *"Met Flibbet?"*

Killien nodded. "Said he was the oddest old man he'd ever met. Which, after reading his books, I believe."

"That's impossible."

Killien raised an eyebrow and Sora let out a snort.

"I assure you it happened," the Torch said mildly.

Will bit back his protest. "I just meant that I can't believe the man was still alive. No one's seen him in ages."

"Who hasn't seen him?" Killien looked at him narrowly.

The Keepers. None of the Keepers had seen Flibbet for at least eighty years.

"He's famous in Queensland and in parts of Coastal Baylon. But everyone thinks he's dead. At least everyone I've ever met. The earliest stories of him are a hundred and fifty years old."

"My father said he was old, but one hundred and fifty seems a bit much. Maybe he was an imposter."

Will nodded, then a thought snagged in his mind. "He sold your father a sword?"

"Gave it to him actually." Killien motioned to a short sword hanging on pegs on the wall. It had a wooden grip, a roughly smithed guard, and weathered leather sheath. "Or gave it to me, I suppose. It's a seax, a short sword. Flibbet told my father its name was Svard Naj and it was a gift for his new son 'to help mend the torn'. Seeing as I wasn't even born yet so no one knew if I was a boy, my father assumed the old man was a bit cracked."

Will had never heard of Flibbet giving anyone a weapon. So much of his writing centered around ideas of peace, it felt out of character. But it was more than that.

"He just *gave* it to your father? I've never heard of Flibbet giving away anything. I've heard him make stupid trades, like offering a silver goblet in trade for a handful of chicken feathers, but never just a gift. Is it a good sword?"

"It seems to be. I only use it for ceremonial sorts of things. It's shorter than the one I learned to fight with. And it has a feel to it. Like it's somehow…too serious for a mere fight." Killien laughed and ran one of his hands through his hair. "That sounds a bit ridiculous now that I've said it out loud."

"Not if Flibbet the Peddler really gave it to you."

"Especially if he was already dead," Sora added.

Killien grinned at her.

"I'm glad Sora found you, Will." Killien pointed to the book in Will's hand. "It goes without saying that guests in my house are free to read my books."

Will wanted to read this book. Very much. Whether or not it had really been given to the Morrow by Flibbet, it looked genuine. If he could just read it through once, maybe twice, he'd be able to remember it. Memorizing books was almost as easy as storytelling. He could rewrite it for the Shield later.

But Borto was getting farther away by the moment.

Sora tilted her head and studied Will. "I don't believe he ever agreed to stay."

Killien looked at Will appraisingly. "He doesn't look stupid enough to decline an offer of hospitality."

Sora leaned against the bookshelf and sized Will up. "I don't know..."

Will thought for just a moment about the wayfarer's wagon, trundling east toward the Scales, slipping farther away, the cord between them growing thread-thin.

But he was still surrounded by a room of Roven in the middle of a city of more Roven.

He'd just have to hope that Borto was slow and his yellow wagon was memorable enough that it would be easy to track.

With a nod, he let the idea of Borto go. "What sort of story would you like to hear tonight?"

"Something we haven't heard before. I'm sick of Roven tales with clans massacring each other. Tell me something from a foreign land. Something brave and dangerous and clever."

"The tales from Gulfind are generally clever, if you like tales that revolve around gold. I also have some from Coastal Baylon. Those people are a bit strange and their gods are so...mystifying they end up with curious stories."

"Do you know anything from Queensland?"

The room stilled and Will felt eyes on him. He turned back to the Torch, trying to keep his face nonchalant.

"A few."

"What are they like?" Killien's face stayed friendly, but his eyes were sharp.

"Queensland stories have a certain feel to them. A sort of brightness."

The Torch's eyes narrowed so slightly Will thought he might have imagined it. He did not imagine how much Sora's narrowed.

"Or maybe naivety," Will added. "They really love their heroes."

The Torch looked at Will calculatingly. "I'd like to hear some tales from our enemies. I'd imagine in Queensland the Roven always play the villain."

Out of the hundreds of tales Will knew, he couldn't think of a single story that didn't portray the Roven as the enemy. "The stories I know well"—Or the stories he'd decided he officially knew while he was on the Sweep—"don't mention the Roven at all. But others there are no more flattering to you than your stories are to them."

Killien grinned. "Everyone from Queensland is a villain."

Will forced a smile at that. "As for stories I know best, one is about a young man who is captured by a dragon, and the other is about one of their Keepers."

"Which one?" Killien's voice was sharp and something tightened in Will's gut.

"Chesavia," Will answered. He should have picked something less Queenslandish. Some general adventure story instead of something about magic and Keepers.

"Didn't she die fighting some sort of demon?"

"A water demon." Will's estimation of the Torch rose again. "I'm impressed. I haven't met anyone on the Sweep who knows tales from Queensland."

"I don't know many, but I do know who the Keepers are." Killien's smile held nothing pleasant. He nodded toward the baskets. "I have several books that mention them."

He studied Will. "Tonight, tell us a story from Queensland. It will be fascinating to learn what my enemy thinks is entertaining."

Will nodded. It would be.

CHAPTER EIGHT

"Sora," Killien said, "show Will to his room."

Sora's gaze never faltered from Will's face. "The storyman has managed to travel all the way from—where was it? Gulfind? I think he can find his way upstairs." Without a glance at the Torch, she strode out the door.

Will watched it close before letting his gaze flick back to Killien, expecting anger at Sora's defiance. Instead, Killien looked at the door with a rueful expression.

"I think Sora likes you, storyman." The huge man who'd been sitting with Killien rose.

Laughter rippled through the room and Will glanced around. These people weren't like any Roven he'd ever met. His fear had almost completely dissolved, replaced by a reluctant curiosity. "I'd hate to see how she treats someone she didn't like."

"Don't mind Sora," Killien said. "She doesn't like anyone. But the woman can stalk a white fox in a snowstorm, so we tolerate her attitude."

"I'm Hal." The huge man stepped closer, rising to a full head taller than Will. Everything from his vest to his linen pants to the thick beads in his beard spoke of wealth, but his expression was good-humored. "Do you know any stories about dwarves?"

A spattering of groans greeted his question.

Hal extended his hand and Will grasped it, his fingers barely reaching around the huge man's wrist. "Because you're part dwarf?"

Hal grinned widely. He was dressed much like Killien, runes lining the edges of a wide leather vest, several silver rings spread out across his fingers.

"I know a few dwarf tales," Will said.

"Hal is obsessed with dwarves," Killien said. "No one understands why."

"I do," Will said. "They're strong, they're vicious warriors, they're funny, and did you know they can"—he paused trying to think of the word— "sense rocks? When I was in Duncave, a dwarf gave me a tour of an unused tunnel system and he followed a thin vein of quartz along three different tunnels without ever shining his light on the wall. They say that when there's a different sort of rock, they can taste the difference in the air."

Hal's mouth hung open. "You've been to Duncave?"

"Had an audience with the High Dwarf." Which sounded more formal than whatever had happened. "But it turns out King Horgoth isn't fond of foreigners. He offered me an armed escort on my way out."

"Thank the black queen," Hal breathed, "a real storyman!"

"But he doesn't have to tell the entire story right now," Killien broke in, looking around the room. "Because you all have work to do. It's light enough to get these baskets packed."

Unlike Sora, all of the other Roven obeyed Killien without hesitation.

"I want to hear about Duncave," Hal said.

"After the herds are sorted," Killien said, irritated.

Hal paused on his way to the door. "I'm glad you're here, storyman."

"As am I," Killien said. "I didn't expect someone as...well-traveled as you."

Will shrugged. "You don't learn new stories by sitting at home."

"You do if a storyman comes to visit. Come, I'll show you your room." Killien led Will out of the back of the room.

"You're not exactly what I was expecting in a Torch, either." Will followed Killien to the dark wood stairs. The amount of wood in the house was astonishing. Will slid his hand up the smooth banister as they walked. It was refreshingly solid and unclaylike.

"What did you expect?" Killien asked without turning.

A bloodthirsty villain didn't seem like the best answer.

"I've visited three other clans," Will said. "Admittedly I never met their Torches in person, but the Odo Torch had a decidedly unwelcoming way about him, the Sunn Torch only came out to lead slaves to the dragon's cave, rarely gracing anyone with his attention. And the Boan Torch..." Will paused.

"Was a pompous lump of dead weight?" Killien offered over his shoulder.

Will laughed. "I only saw him from a distance during a parade, but...that is a good description. The Boan with their huge army, and the Sunn Clan with their dragon and their stonesteeps—don't they see the benefit of working together?"

"They see nothing but their own grab for power." Killien turned into a short hallway with two doors on each side—actual wooden doors. "Those two are responsible for spilling more Roven blood than any war." Killien stepped into the last room on the left.

It was more Roven than the downstairs level of the house. Killien walked into the clay room and over to a window where orange drapes sighed in the breeze.

Someone outside shouted out commands and there was a bustle of activity. Killien parted the curtains, his shoulders sagging. "We'll be poor hosts today. At this point I see little hope that we'll be ready to leave tomorrow." He rubbed his hands over his face and gave a tired sigh. "You don't by chance know some foreign magic spell that would pack an entire city, do you?"

Will gave a small laugh that had a tinge of panic. "I'm not really good at magic spells."

Killien turned away from the window and shook his head. "Neither am I." He walked to the door. "Breakfast will be served out back shortly. There are things I need to take care of before then."

Will pressed his fist to his chest and gave the Torch a bow as the man left.

When he straightened, he stared at the empty doorway.

That had been…unexpected. Who knew a Roven Torch could be so…unRoven.

Will put his bag into a corner and dropped down onto the bed. Instead of crunching with dried grass, the mattress cushioned him like…like a mattress. Will lay back with a sigh and closed his eyes. This had to be full of wool. He grabbed the pillow. Feathers. After the restless night, his body sank down into the softness.

Borto must be gone by now, trundling east. At least wayfarer wagons were slow. He'd be four days on the Sea Road before any other large roads branched off. If Will pushed hard tomorrow, he could catch up.

Frustration at being here bubbled at the surface, but underneath, there was a layer of guilt. He had a chance to find Ilsa, and that chance was dwindling. He should have…his mind spun through ways he could have escaped this morning, but none of them would have worked. He probably would have had trouble fighting past Sora, never mind armed guards at the gate. Whatever chance he'd had to leave had disappeared during the night.

The fact that Killien's house was fascinating fed the guilt. How could a stack of books have distracted him from his sister?

Had it? Had he given up a chance to leave just to read some books? Will scrubbed his hands across his face. No. Will had never had a choice. Killien had brought him for entertainment. From the moment Sora had appeared this morning, Will's fate had been sealed.

Will heaved himself up off the bed and walked over to the window. He splashed some water over his face from a small red bowl. The sun had risen and the wide avenue was filling with people. The smell of roasting saltfish filled the street mixing with the ever-present smells of the grass and the ocean. To his left, over the low clay buildings of Porreen, the Southern Sea spread out like a blue carpet speckled with fishing boats.

He pushed aside the guilt. The delay was inevitable and moping about it would make it harder to redeem the day into something valuable. Will picked up the yellow book and sank back into the bed.

In all of Queensland, the Keepers had only found a handful of Flibbet's books, outside the ones in the Keeper's library. The curious little peddler, who used to show up every few years, brought the Keepers new books. He had first appeared one hundred fifty years ago at the top of the tall cliffs above the Keeper's Stronghold. Before that, the Keepers didn't know anyone had ever looked down on their valley from the inhospitable desert above. And yet he had appeared, over and over again, disappearing for two years or five years, then dropping bundles of books filled with strange stories, foreign tales, lost histories down from high above. At least he had until about fifty years ago.

Despite the exotic nature of his books, for some reason Will had never imagined that Flibbet went anywhere outside of Queensland. Yet here was a book the Keepers had been looking for. The Shield would be ecstatic to learn what it said. The leader of the Keepers had a fascination with Flibbet that went beyond normal curiosity.

Will opened the cover slowly. The faint smell of paper and old ink wafted past. He flipped to the first page with a mixture of excitement and hesitation. It had been a long time since he'd committed an entire book to memory. When he'd first arrived at the Stronghold and read all the works Keeper Gerone had assigned him, he'd been faster than he was now. Gerone hadn't expected him to memorize them, but how could he not? He'd read them, and once a book was read, if it was well-written, the words laid out a path in his mind. He could recall them whenever he wanted. The only hard part was remembering the beginning. Once it started, you just had to travel down the path.

Here, at last, was a job he was good at. Probably better than any other Keeper. Alaric wouldn't be able to memorize Flibbet in a morning.

His eyes felt gritty from the long night, but he focused on the beginning and picked up the thread of the swirly blue writing. Flibbet began this book with theories on where the people of the Sweep, Queensland, and the southern countries had come from, positing that they were descended from a common ancestor who had once lived far west over the endless desert.

True to form, Flibbet's words wandered off on tangents and nonsensical tales, peppered by complex diagrams, unexplained symbols, and things that looked like pointless doodles. But somehow the thread ran true through the entire book. There was a special sort of …joy in reading Flibbet. A sort of whimsy and lightness, all anchored to truths that felt as deeply rooted as the mountains.

The original thread of the story thickened into roots, then the thick trunk of a tree, then split off into branches both individual yet similar. The small scattered warlords of Coastal Baylon, the strong central throne of Queensland, the disparate, isolated clans of the Roven. All branches, all related, all somehow the same at their core.

The book was short and the world was still muffled in the quiet of early morning by the time Will finished.

He let the book close, his mind drifting around the ideas, toying with concepts of brotherhood and ancestry and the interrelatedness of everything. The different accents of their shared language feeling suddenly closer than they ever had before.

A spattering of rough Roven voices called to each other

outside his window, and Will pushed aside the drapes to watch a half-dozen people organizing baskets of books into a wide, wooden wagon.

Two children squealed and raced in circles, keeping just out of reach of an older man who kept grabbing for their baskets, while a young woman laughed and herded them forward. It was the right kind of laughter, effortless and free, and he had the sudden urge to join them. He leaned against the windowsill, setting his hands on the cool cob that was familiar, if not comfortable. A little girl ran close to the house and glanced up. Her laughter stuttered and she pointed up at him.

"Dirty fett," the man muttered, loud enough to reach the window. He pulled her away and the game ended.

Will dropped down on the bed.

Flibbet's words were just words.

If Queensland and the Sweep had ever shared a common ancestor, they'd grown too distant by now for it to matter.

CHAPTER NINE

SMELLS of fish and bread wafted through the window.

He took Flibbet, went back down to the main room, and set *Neighbors Should be Friends* back on the shelf. A clatter of activity came from the back of the house.

He walked down a short hall and out into a wide, walled yard scattered with Roven sitting on colorful rugs, eating in a hurried sort of way. A long ledge ran along the back of the house surrounded by people piling plates with prairie hen eggs, red fish wrapped in salted barley flatbread, or butter-yellow avak fruit. Will filled a plate. At the end of the table was a covered clay jar. He opened the lid and smelled saso, Roven coffee. This wasn't the watered-down saso he'd been drinking at out-of-the-way inns. This was rich, full coffee that smelled of roasted nuts and caramel so thick he could almost feel it. He poured himself a cup and breathed in the warm steam.

Will glanced around for a rug on the fringes where he could sit out of the way.

"Come sit, storyman," the enormous Hal called, waving Will over to a large blue blanket. "It's like this every year." Hal looked annoyed as a woman pushed past Will. "Chaotic and rushed. We go to the rifts every year, but no one ever seems ready."

Killien's voice barked something from inside the house.

Hal shook his head. "Every year."

The Torch strode out of the house and toward a blanket with two men and a woman sitting on it nearby. They each straightened and gave the Torch their attention.

"We leave as soon as the horses are prepared, Torch," one man said.

"Take a distress raven with you."

The man's eyes snapped up to the Torch's face. The rest of the group exchanged glances. Even Hal glanced up in surprise.

"We have three messenger ravens already," the woman said.

"Take a distress raven also. And as soon as you reach the rifts, send back a report." The Torch looked around the group, his eyes guarded. "Watch each other."

The back door opened and a burst of *vitalle* rushed into the yard so strong that Will clenched a piece of fish in his hand. Heart pounding, he began to gather *vitalle*, drawing it out of the grass beneath him, his mind racing to think of a protective spell. He hadn't felt that much power since...since he'd been in the Keeper's Stronghold. Not a single stonesteep he'd met on the Sweep had been remotely this powerful.

Lukas, the young man who'd bought the book from Borto, limped out of the house, his thin arms wrapped around a large lumpy leather bag. The rings on his hands glittered in the morning light.

Killien crossed over to him. "Is that the first set?"

The Torch reached into the bag, pulling out a palm-sized yellow crystal swirling with energy. Nodding approvingly, he dropped it back into the bag with a clink, and Will caught a glimpse of more yellow gems.

Will blinked and let the energy he'd gathered drain out of him. All that *vitalle* was from the gems, not the man. These weren't the usual worthless magical talismans found on the Sweep. Whatever those stones held, it was powerful.

"Forty here, and a hundred more promised by tonight." Lukas

smirked at the Torch. "He tried to convince me eighty would be enough."

Killien let out a derisive snort. "Lazy dog. A hundred and forty is already less than half of what he claimed he could make."

The yellow light of the stones lit Lukas's face like he stood over a fire. "After this we shouldn't need him."

Killien nodded and clapped Lukas on the shoulder. "Well done. Divide them into three bags. Make one light enough for Sini, and give Rett the other."

Lukas gave the Torch a quick bow and left, taking the *vitalle* with him. The energy of the stones faded away.

Will turned back to his food, letting his heart slow. The amount of power held in that bag was astonishing.

"What were those?" he asked Hal quietly.

"Heatstones," Hal answered. "For our trip north. I didn't think the stonesteep would deliver."

"I've never met a stonesteep." Will paused, wondering how much Hal would talk about. "I've heard some stories, though. I know a bit about Mallon since he invaded Queensland. He's called Mallon the Rivor there, instead of Mallon the Undying."

"He didn't earn the Undying until after the war."

Will turned in surprise. "But the war ended because of his death."

"No one knows if he's dead. They never found his body."

Hal was unconcerned, but a chill passed through Will at the sentiment. Mallon wasn't dead. At least he hadn't been dead a year ago when the elf Ayda, had showed him Mallon, still alive, but trapped inside his own body, held prisoner by the elves.

Of course it'd been ages since he left the message for Alaric at the palace. The Keepers must have found a way to kill him by now.

"The other stonesteep that comes up often," Will continued, "is Kachig the Bloodless."

Hal raised an eyebrow.

"He's a stonesteep right? I can't get anyone to actually tell me about him."

Hal let out a short laugh. "He's the one who trained Mallon. No one knows which was more powerful, but Kachig was more vicious. He's been dead for ten years, and we still don't speak his name if we can help it."

"Why not?"

"Because we're not stupid."

"Hal," Killien interrupted, heading into the house, his voice sharp. "Get to work."

Hal finished his saso in one long drink. "Every year." He pushed himself up and left.

Will watched him go, torn between curiosity and irritation. Why would people not talk about a dead man?

He finished his fish quickly and headed back inside to Killien's bookshelf.

Children ran in the front door, jostling past Will, grabbing baskets of books and lugging them out to the wagon.

"I've got *Sightings of Dragons*," one called out.

Another peered into his basket and grimaced. "All I've got is barley recipes."

Will stared after them as Killien walked up.

"The children can read?" Will watched them haul the baskets outside. "I've barely met any adults on the Sweep who can."

"Most of the Morrow can read. I like my people to be free. But we're the smallest clan on the Sweep, so we're always in danger. The more we learn, the more we understand the past, the easier it is to decipher the present. And the easier it is to remain free."

Will took these words and let them sink in. "I couldn't agree more."

The Torch raised an eyebrow. "I didn't realize the people of Gulfind valued reading so highly."

Will paused, thinking of the massive amounts of ignorance among the people of Gulfind. The hills of Gulfind were full of gold, all of life was spent on entertainment and paying for guards to protect their wealth.

"I wish the people of Gulfind would value things like history," Will answered. "But it's not entertaining enough for most of them."

Killien straightened the books on the shelf. "How long have you been away from home?"

Will dropped into his usual story. "Almost a year. I spent last summer traveling among some of the northern cities. Last winter I came south to Bermea, Tun and any other cities I could find. Then all the Roven headed north, and I was on my way home. I had reached Porreen yesterday and since you were still here, I stayed the night."

"And why did a storyman from Gulfind come to the Sweep in the first place?"

"I like to travel." Will shrugged. "I didn't intend to get as far as I did, honestly. I started traveling, ended up on the edge of the Sweep, and just kept going."

Killien gave him a slight smile. "That's what the grasses do, they call to you, pulling you on over the next rise, through the next valley."

It hadn't been the grasses pulling him, but Will nodded anyway.

"Have you learned many Roven stories while you've been here?"

"A good number."

"Which is your favorite?"

None. The Roven stories all felt...foreign. Like they had the wrong pacing. Or the wrong ending. There were endless tales of battles between clans, most of which were only told in the victors' clans. He hadn't heard a single one that named the Morrow Clan as the winner. In fact, the Morrow Clan was so small and insignificant, it barely made it into any tales at all.

"Roven tales have a strong sense of...location." Will tried to think of a diplomatic answer. "For instance I heard a tale in Bermea about besting the Tun in a battle. Then I heard the same story in Tun, except with the Tun winning." Will paused. "So I guess I don't know about a favorite story. Every time I find one I like, I discover that it's told differently in the next town."

Killien grinned. "That's the rule of the grassland. The truth changes between hilltops."

"It does seem to." Will paused and glanced around the room. "Lately I've heard a lot of stories about frost goblins."

Killien's smile faded.

"I wasn't sure they were real," Will said, "or that if they were, that they ever came out of the northern mountains, but the Roven I've met in the past weeks seem to believe that the frost goblins could be responsible for raids in the north."

"They haven't come out of the northern ice since my father was a child. That year they came in the fall, killed entire hunting parties and decimated herds. They're more like a hive than like individual creatures. They're not big, no taller than your waist, but they swarm over whatever they're attacking. Often they don't have weapons. They overrun with teeth and claws."

The Torch's voice had a dreadfulness to it that chilled Will, despite the bright morning around him. "That's…unsettling."

"It is," Killien agreed. "They burrow in the ground. They can dig tunnels into deep snow or under the grass almost as fast as you can walk. If they've come onto the prairies this spring…" He glanced around at the people in the room. "So far it's just rumors from clans farther to the west. But the rumors have the ring of truth to them."

"How long will it take the clan to reach the rifts?"

"A fortnight. Maybe a couple days faster, if there's perfect weather. If we encounter any rain storms or, stars help us, a heavy spring snow, it'll slow us down."

Killien caught sight of Flibbet's book on the shelf and turned to Will with an impressed look. "Finished with the book already?"

Will nodded slowly. "Flibbet always manages to both ramble and be concise at the same time."

"I've always thought the same." Killien stepped up next to

Will and ran his fingers along the spine of Flibbet's book. "I can't decide if he's brilliant, or a little touched in the head."

"Or just old." Will laughed. *"Old enough to know that most things are a waste of time. And that wasting time can be a beautiful thing."*

Killien raised an eyebrow.

"He wrote that about himself." Will could still picture the small library in Marshwell where he'd found the skinny volume. "In a book titled *Flibbet's Rules for Life*."

"That is something I would like to read."

"I can write it out for you." The book had been thin, but the pages had been crammed with numbered rules written in a chaos of colors, the words sideways or upside down or spiraling into tiny print.

Killien's other eyebrow rose. "You memorized it?"

Will paused. "I don't memorize it exactly." He was oddly reluctant to explain. "Once I read a book, if I can remember the beginning, the rest of the book just sort of…follows."

Killien studied him. "A useful skill for a storyman."

Will bowed his head slightly in acknowledgment.

"No wonder you're good at your job. Could you tell me everything you read this morning?"

Will glanced back at Flibbet. "Flibbet's always been easy for me. The better written a book is, the easier it is for me to remember. The peddler, even though his books seem disjointed and capricious, somehow has this…thread that winds through his words. They lead to each other. And that makes them easy to remember."

Killien looked at Will for a long, searching moment. "I would very much like a copy of Flibbet's Rules."

Something in Killien's eyes made Will feel exposed. He pulled the edges of his mouth up into what hopefully looked like a smile. "If you have some paper, I'll work on it this morning."

Killien's gaze pinned Will where he stood. "A day may not be long enough to enjoy your company, Will."

CHAPTER TEN

SETTLED with a stack of paper and a new reed pen, Will began writing out Flibbet's rules.

There were simple rules: *Be more generous than you feel.*

There were practical rules: *Never poke a mountain bear.* Or *Never eat blue tunnel beetles.* This one was followed by an adamant, Never.

There were ridiculous rules: *Don't dip your cuffs in the washing water.* Or *Keep an eye on the moon. She'll cause no end of trouble if you don't.*

And tucked amid all these were the ones that Will had read the book for.

Everyone is clear-minded in their own mind.

Too much time alone traps a man in his own mind. Not enough time alone traps him in other's.

It is a terrifying thing to be truly seen—but it is infinitely worse not to be.

There were 213 rules altogether.

When he finished, he had four blank pages left, so he wrote out a short, funny tale from Napon about a serving girl who'd run off to be a pirate.

Then, leaving the papers on the bookshelf, he picked out several history books about the Sweep and sat down to read.

He skimmed dull accounts of obscure Roven battles until the bustle made him feel useless. He offered to help a passing Roven. Everyone in Killien's house seemed to know who he was. Whatever Killien had told them, if he wasn't greeted with friendliness, they were at least polite, which was refreshing.

It occurred to him that he'd never spent so much time with Roven and not been called fetter bait. He spent the next several hours loading wagons with rugs, food, weapons, and leathers, which turned out to be far more educational than the books had been.

He learned that the furniture was left here to wait for their return in the fall. He learned that the wooden wagons had come mostly from merchants who'd brought their wares to the Sweep. Wood was in such high demand, it was more profitable to sell their wagon and buy a new one when they got home. There were enough in Porreen for every four or five families to share one. Unless they were wealthy like Killien, whose household filled three. And he learned that even helping someone with something like packing didn't really earn you trust. Just mild goodwill.

He thought of Borto often, moving ever farther away with whatever knowledge he had of Ilsa, but, as Killien continued to shout at everyone, the clan was leaving at dawn tomorrow. Will would be on his way by then too. He checked on Shadow and found him well cared for and fed, and repeated to himself often that Borto would be easy to catch on the long, lonesome Sea Road.

Killien's slaves and the Roven worked side by side. Will caught sight of Lukas several times, limping along with a pile of books in his arms or patiently directing some children on how to pack them into baskets.

In the end, he found Hal. The enormous man was in charge of the herds of the clan and his afternoon was spent directing people and animals in preparation for the journey north. For the first time in a year, Will began to feel at ease. Hal laughed and joked and complained with utter disregard to Will's foreignness, his voice rumbling over the Roven accent like a wagon crunching along over hard clay.

Hours later Will leaned against the railing at the end of a long porch stretching across the largest building on the main square. He spun his ring, watching the crowd gather.

High, thin clouds reached across the sky like flame-colored fingers. He searched the sky, wondering where Talen had gone. Maybe the little hawk had finally flown off to another part of the Sweep. Feeling surprisingly disappointed at the idea, Will let his eyes follow the trails of light from the setting sun, wishing it was sunrise instead. It would be good to be on his way out of Porreen and off the Sweep, following Borto.

Killien's words from this morning haunted him. *A day may not be long enough.* But this day had been more than enough. Tonight Will needed to tell a story that wouldn't disappoint the Torch, but also wouldn't be good enough for Killien to want him to stay.

He dropped his gaze back down to the square, mentally trimming out parts of the story, making it weaker.

Lukas limped up onto the far corner of the porch, followed by two more slaves. Their grey tunics were as well-made and clean as Lukas's. The first was a large man who towered over Lukas and most of the Roven nearby. He was probably almost forty, with a receding hairline but a full unruly beard of dusty brown hair didn't quite cover his pleasantly distant expression.

The other was maybe fifteen years old, still more of a willowy girl than a woman. The top of her blond head didn't even come up to the larger slave's shoulder. She stood against the railing, talking quietly, but animatedly while both men listened to her with a sort of brotherly patience.

The orange of the sky had tinged the square with a flamelike glow. The clay houses were a dull amber, the packed ground of the square was the color of trampled honey, and the head of every single person was flaming red. An enormous fire of dung patties flared to life in front of the balcony with a smoky, grassy smell, casting a flickering red light into any existing shadows.

Hal leaned against the wall of the house beside Will, peppering him with questions about dwarves.

"Is it true they have a treasure room filled with jewels?"

"I didn't see any, but I imagine they do." Will looked out over the crowd, hoping this would get started soon. "Probably more than one. Any jewels in Duncave belong to all the dwarves and are taken to the High Dwarf. But every dwarf I've seen has jewels on their weapons, on their tools, on thick rings. One had twelve rubies set in the handle of her favorite pitcher. She told me it was a family heirloom. These, for some reason, don't need to be given to the High Dwarf, so you can imagine how many family heirlooms there are."

"Are the walls decorated with gold and gems that sparkle in the torchlight?"

"You're not fascinated with dwarves, Hal." Sora came up onto the porch. "You're fascinated with treasure."

Hal ignored her.

"Actually," Will answered him, "the tunnel walls are mostly earth and stone. And the dwarves don't carry torches. Which makes sense when you think what it would be like to live in caves filled with smoke. They have a moss that puts off an orange glow. It gets brighter if they put water on it, so they carry lanterns made from shallow bowls with moss and water in them. They don't make as much light as a torch, but maybe as much as a candle. And once you've been in the tunnels for several minutes, it's more than enough."

Hal shook his head. "I've never been so envious of any man. You should come north with us and entertain us on the long, boring journey."

Will's fingers tensed on his ring.

Sora raised an eyebrow. "I bet he would love that."

Even without the need to hurry after Borto, the idea of spending weeks traveling with the Roven sounded tortuous. He was spared the pressure of a polite answer by Killien striding up onto the porch. Will hadn't seen the Torch for hours and he gave the man a slight bow. Behind Killien a small Roven woman climbed the steps. She was in the end stages of pregnancy and a slave woman held her elbow cautiously. Will's eyes caught on the slave's dark curls. She bent over, arranging some cushions on a chair for the Roven woman and helped her sit. Then she sat on the porch behind the woman's chair.

She sat forward and something painful clamped down on Will's heart.

The slave was the spitting image of Will's mother. It was his mother's face from years ago. Before Will had left to join the Keepers. Before his father had been killed. Before Ilsa had been taken.

The Roven woman leaned forward, blocking Will's view of the slave and fixed Will with a look that pierced through him. "Fett," she hissed.

Will tore his eyes away from them, his heart pounding so loud he almost didn't hear Hal.

"Pick someone else to stare at." Hal's voice was pitched low but urgent. "That's Lilit, Killien's wife. She doesn't share his... interest in foreigners."

Killien's wife? Will shot a quick glance over. Lilit had turned away dismissively. She was younger than Killien, in her mid-twenties to his thirties. An intricate weave of braids held back mahogany hair that seemed to glow red under the ruddy sky. She wore a dress dyed a vibrant green and stitched with yellow runes along every seam.

Beside her the slave woman, dressed in a simple grey dress, brushed her own loose hair back with a motion that was achingly like Will's mother's.

It couldn't be Ilsa, could it? He tried to match up this face to the last time he'd seen her, terrified, disappearing into the night, his mind grabbing for similarities.

The slave woman smiled at something Lilit said and the image of Ilsa's terrified face blew away like a puff of mist. A different memory surfaced. One he hadn't thought of for so long it had turned brittle, like old paper. His baby sister, smiling and chasing that stupid goat through the grass. That was the face he was looking at. That was the smile.

He wanted to take a step forward, but his legs wouldn't cooperate. His entire body thrummed with a sort of terror. He was desperate for her to look at him, but terrified that she would.

Killien stepped between them to the front of the balcony. Will pulled his gaze away from the slave woman. The world spun and Will put his hand on the railing to steady himself. Killien raised his hand for silence, and within moments the square obeyed.

"Tomorrow the main caravan will leave at dawn," Killien announced. "By nightfall we'll be out of view of Porreen and surrounded by the grasses."

The audience broke out into a loud cheer.

"What about the frost goblins?" A voice called out and the cheers died off.

"We don't know if the stories are true or not," Killien answered. "But it is time to move north. The hay is gone, the herds need the grasses." He paused. "And we need the grasses around us again. The dusting grass has come and the green of the Sweep is waking up. These city walls are starting to feel like a cage."

They roared in approval.

Will risked a glance toward the slave, but Killien's wife blocked his view.

"We have heatstones," Killien continued. Lukas stepped forward, his limp barely noticeable and handed Killien one of the swirling stones. "If there are frost goblins, we will fight them off as our ancestors did, with these burning stones and our swords." There were rumblings of agreement. "But let us hope the tales of goblins prove only to be rumors.

"Speaking of tales, tonight I bring you something different. A storyman from Gulfind has found our clan."

The response to this was more curious chatter than applause. Will bowed toward the crowd. The urge to look at the woman who might be Ilsa was almost overpowering, but he could feel every eye in the square fixed on him.

"Will knows stories from many lands," Killien said. "Tonight he's offered to tell us a tale from Queensland. I know it's easy to think of Queensland as the enemy, as the people who hundreds of years ago took the good land, with rich soil and mild seasons, and left us to the harsher world of the Sweep."

The words cut through the turmoil in Will's mind and caught his attention. Stern faces nodded in the crowd. The Roven thought they'd been forced out of the Queensland? He'd never heard that. Although it would explain the animosity.

"But it is always important to remember," Killien said, "that those we consider enemies are more like us than we think. They have homes and families and worries."

Will held his face neutral as he listened. That was the most humanizing thing he'd heard said about Queensland since he'd come to the Sweep. Was this man actually Roven?

"We must remember our enemies are human," Killien continued, "if we ever hope to defeat them."

Yes. He was Roven.

Thousands of eyes were fixed on the porch. A cool breeze brushed past Will and he breathed it in, gathering the chaos of thoughts and emotions swirling inside him, and breathing them out. The need to follow Borto blew away. That might not be Ilsa, but everything about her was right. The idea of being left in Porreen tomorrow while the clan and this woman went north made his stomach drop.

He threw away all his ideas of how to make his story weaker. What he needed tonight was the best telling of Tomkin and the Dragon that anyone had ever heard. Something so good that Killien couldn't bear to let Will leave.

He resisted the urge to look back, and focused on the tale. It had been a long time since he'd told it. He pulled the beginning of

Tomkin to his mind gingerly, hoping it was still intact. This was the right story to tell. Everyone loved Tomkin.

Would the Roven? A little dagger of ice shot into his stomach. How could they not?

"Much can be learned about a people from their stories." Killien's voice rolled over the whole square. "Tonight, he has agreed to tell us one of Queensland's most beloved tales. A story about a young man and a dragon."

Killien turned and motioned Will to the front of the porch. Something scraped behind him and Will turned too quickly to pretend it hadn't startled him.

Sora dragged a thin stool over. "Nervous?" she said softly enough that only he and Killien heard. "No one is stupid enough to tell stories from Queensland on the Sweep."

Killien studied Sora for a moment, then turned to Will with an unreadable expression.

"Maybe they don't know the good ones," Will answered quietly, taking the stool. "Get comfortable, Sora. Even you might like this."

Killien let out a little laugh and sat down next to a disapproving Lilit. Will caught a glimpse of the slave's shoulder, but turned away. A distracted storyteller was poor entertainment.

Facing the crowd, he pushed everything but the story out of his head. Will did a poor job of many things, but telling stories wasn't one of them. And though there was probably no way to get Sora to like him, by the end of the evening, the crowd would. And hopefully the Torch.

But the faces in the audience were unenthused. This was not a crowd ready for a story.

"I have spent all winter in the Roven cities along the sea." Will stepped to the railing, speaking loud enough that the entire square could hear him, searching for common ground. "But now, when I look north, the land isn't white with snow. I see hints of new green grass growing out of last year's brown."

A few heads nodded.

"Across the Scale Mountains, the seasons change gradually. The snows melt slowly, it takes from one full moon to the next for green to return to the land. But only days ago the grasses here were pale with snow. And then yesterday I saw a hint of green."

The mood of the square rose. "And this afternoon, it wasn't a hint." Will paused. "It was...a flood of it." At the edge of the square, movement caught his eye. Sitting on a porch railing with her skinny legs dangling down, sat Rass, beaming at him. Will bowed his head slightly in her direction. "And I was reminded that the Sweep is enormous and powerful. That everything is born there and everything goes there when it is too old to move." Rass's face split into an even wider grin. "There was a thrumming of life on the hills."

Will let his eyes pass over the crowd, feeling their approval.

Hoping he remembered it right, he took a breath. "Life has returned!"

"We will return!" thundered the crowd in the traditional response, erupting into cheers.

When that faded, Will sat on the stool. "In Queensland, there are men called Keepers who protect stories of the past. I have heard one tell a tale in the hall of the Queen herself." The crowd muttered and Will let the complicatedness of the response grow. "This is one of their favorite stories. It is an old tale, not a sweeping epic. Only a small story meant to entertain." He could feel the crowd's skepticism. He gave them a shrug. "Let's see if it's as entertaining as the people of Queensland seem to think." When the spattering of laughter died, he looked down, not moving or speaking while he waited for the square to quiet.

Once it was still, he began.

"Along the southern border, a company of soldiers surged forward, like the waters of the Great River, battling a deadly foe and performing acts of heroism.

"At his desk, Tomkin Thornhewn sat still, like the waters of a small puddle, shuffling through a pile of paper and only dreaming of such renown."

Thousands of eyes fixed on Will, and he opened himself up to them. The words continued on, building a scene, a question, a dragon. The power of the story drew out the minds of the listeners and unified them into something more.

But this wasn't Queensland. The crowd felt too negative toward Tomkin. It had been a mistake to tell them this was a foreign tale, it separated them too much from it. Will shifted his descriptions of Tomkin slightly, less insecurity, more misplaced determinedness. Less fanciful daydreaming, more shock and indignation at his insultingly poor marriage arrangement. The moment when Tomkin picked duty and adventure over complacency, the crowd stopped feeling foreign. That was the point when they stopped comparing themselves to the story, stopped even being aware of themselves. They fell together into a single entity, amused, leery, fatalistic, or hopeful in turn as Tomkin dug himself deeper into trouble.

The wide, empty, open feeling of the Sweep receded. Will felt only the ruins as Tomkin explored the castle, saw only the orange-red scales of the dragon, imagined himself huddled bruised and cold in the rain.

Stars glittered in a black sky by the time the story drew to its close.

Almost reluctantly, Will spoke the final words, feeling the crowd before him settle into a satisfied pleasure. "I cannot say that Tomkin and the Dragon lived happily to the end of their days, because happiness is trickier than that. They had plenty of hard days, and plenty of sad days, but they did try to be kind to each other. And kindness takes you a long way on the path to happiness. So I think it is safe to say that Tomkin and the Dragon lived, on the balance, happy-ish to the end of their days."

Shouts of approval accompanied the slapping of thighs, the Roven's lower, more rumbling form of clapping. Will stood, set his hand on his chest and bowed his head to the crowd. Thrumming with the triumph and satisfaction filling the square.

"Thank the black queen!" Killien stepped up next to him and

pounded him on the back. Will staggered a bit under the force. "That was the best story I've heard in years."

Will bowed, darting a look toward Ilsa. The slave woman helped Lilit stand. With every movement and every expression, Will became more convinced this was his sister. He'd never imagined she could be this much like their mother.

"Killien!" Hal called out. "I like Will. Invite him north with us. We'd have stories for the entire, endless walk."

Will pressed his fist to his chest, desperately hoping the story had been good enough. When he looked up, Killien's eyebrows were raised.

"Would you like to come north with us, Will?" Killien held out his hand.

"He doesn't want—" Sora began.

"I'd love to," Will interrupted her. He grasped Killien's wrist, feeling the Torch's hand wrap around his own like a vise.

Sora's eyes sharpened.

Killien's other hand clamped down on Will's shoulder and the Torch leaned in close to him, a wide smile spread across his face.

"Welcome to the Morrow Clan, Will."

CHAPTER ELEVEN

A BITE of cold morning air slid down Will's neck, feeling more like the lingering end of winter than the beginning of summer. The sun had been over the Scales for an hour before the wagons had rolled out into the grasslands. He breathed in the cool, placid air, trying to calm the tangle of fury and hope and desperation that had kept him awake much of the night.

Ilsa was here.

He'd wanted to follow Lilit and Ilsa when they disappeared down a wide hallway in the Torch's enormous house. But acting as though he was stalking Killien's wife, even if he was actually trailing her slave, didn't seem like the best way to ingratiate himself with the Torch.

In Will's own room, he'd spent most of the night imagining what he would say to Ilsa, what she would think of his words. And him. The rest of the night had been spent wondering how exactly one went about rescuing a sister from the midst of a Roven clan. Beyond extricating her from the side of the Torch's wife, sneaking past all of the Roven, and somehow escaping across flat, featureless grassland, how would he possibly convince her he was her brother? Every conversation he imagined left him sounding like a desperate lunatic.

If only he knew a story about a man, unskilled in any sort of fighting, who rescued a woman who didn't trust him, from the midst of a traveling clan of Roven. Unfortunately, none of the Roven stories he knew were that interesting.

He'd been left to his own devices all morning and ended up riding near the front of the enormous caravan where he'd tried to stay within sight of Killien and the rangers who surrounded him. Several covered wagons stayed near the front and he watched for Lilit, but he couldn't see her past the Roven that rode between them. More importantly, he couldn't see Ilsa.

Behind him, the Morrow stretched in a long, ragged line that still rolled out of the city of Porreen. Ox-drawn wagons, horses laden down with burdens or pulling carts, herds of sheep and goats. The Roven walked with a sort of contentment. Children ran along the sides of the column, flurries of races or chases sending them skirting out onto the closest hills. Will opened up toward them, feeling a wild freedom.

The Roven were happy to be on the Sweep.

Will let his eyes run over the grass, spinning his ring and trying to match the pale green emptiness he saw with their happiness. But the Sweep was just faded grass and empty sky. The Scale Mountains to the east were dry and rocky, the sea falling behind them to the south was flat and smudgy blue.

Ahead wound the scar left by the Morrow's last migration, stretching north as far as he could see, wide enough for twenty men to walk side-by-side. The serpent's wake, they called it, as though the Serpent Queen herself had descended out of the night sky to lay them a path leading north to their summer homes. He didn't like the imagery. Following a snake that large could lead to nothing good.

He entertained himself by thinking of every rescue story he knew. Out of the countless stories in his head, there must be something helpful to his situation. His favorite rescue story was Pelonia's rescue of her cousins from the marauders. But Will didn't have a sleeping draught to knock out the entire Roven clan. Or a freezing lake. And he doubted he would look fetching enough in a dress to distract his enemy at the crucial moment.

There was also the story of when Petar rescued Taramin from the bandits. But Will did not have Petar's skill with a bow. He rubbed the inside of his forearm where the string had skidded off his skin the one time he'd shot one. That arrow had landed so far from the target, he'd never found it. No, it was safe to rule out any stories that depended on archery skills.

With a sea of Roven around him and Ilsa while they traveled north, escaping would be nearly impossible even if he had Petar himself here. It was best to focus on first steps: getting to know Ilsa and ingratiating himself to both Killien and Lilit.

Above him, a flicker of darkness in the clear sky caught his eye. With a dip of its wings, a hawk plummeted toward him and settled on Will's bedroll, dangling a mouse from its beak.

"I can't believe you found me." Will pulled a piece of dried fish from his bag and Talen dropped the mouse to snatch it up. Will ran the back of his finger down the hawk's impossibly soft chest, feeling Talen's heart patter so quickly it almost vibrated. "And I can't believe how happy I am to see someone familiar." He leaned closer to the bird. "I saw her," he whispered. "She's here."

Talen peered intensely at Will's hand.

"That was the end of the fish." Will spread out his palms.

Talen let out two quick screeches and took off into the sky.

"I'll take that as a display of great excitement on your part." Will flung the mouse into the grass.

A nearby ranger watched Talen leave with a derisive expression. He said something and the rangers around him laughed. They watched him for a few heartbeats, and Will tensed for something more, but they turned away with only a few mutters among themselves.

The absence of the little hawk made the air around him feel empty. The rangers continued to treat him with a cold distance, and the feeling of isolation spread slowly until it surrounded him.

"Do you see the grass?" Rass chirped near midday, running up alongside Will, her dirty face lit up with joy. "It's growing so fast!" She grabbed his foot and tugged him to a stop. "Look look at this blade coming through the dirt. It's brand new!"

Will climbed down out of the saddle and squatted to look at the tiny bit of grass. It was an unearthly green, almost glowing against the dark earth and the pale old grass around it.

"And there are ones just like it *everywhere*!" Rass exclaimed, throwing her arms out.

Will cast out over the nearest hill, almost expecting to feel Rass's enthusiasm echoed back in wild, growing energy from a million newborn blades of grass. But he felt nothing other than the bright energy of Rass herself. Because regardless of the girl's enthusiasm, it was still just grass.

Dirt clung to Rass's little grey shift, and he was appalled again at how poorly the Roven cared for slave children. What was the point of keeping them as slaves if they were going to starve before they were old enough to work? Her body was so gaunt she looked like her own happiness might break her.

An idea struck him. "Rass, do you know many of the slave women?"

She wrinkled her nose. "Do you want your own?"

"What?" The idea was repulsive he drew back. "No! I don't—" She cocked her head to the side like a little bird and Will pressed his mouth shut against all the things he wanted to say about slavery. "I was just wondering if you knew many of the adult slaves in Porreen."

"I don't know any of them." She turned toward the grass again. "So much new grass," she murmured, taking a few steps into it.

"You're welcome to ride with me."

She glanced at the Roven near him. "Not until I'm stronger."

Will bit back a laugh. "When will that be?"

She looked thoughtfully across the Sweep. "Soon, I think."

Will offered the odd little slave girl a hard roll from his bag. "Well, if you need anything at all, come find me."

She considered the roll for a moment, then took it and laughed. "You're funny." She gave Will a little wave and scampered away from the caravan, out onto the Sweep. Her skinny legs flashed as she ran, her head bobbed into the thick, old grass, then disappeared down the nearest gully.

Will mounted Shadow, feeling impotent to help her. The front of the caravan had moved on with Killien's rangers, and the Roven here looked at him distastefully. He trotted Shadow back toward the front. When he drew alongside a handful of slaves, he paused, weighing the risk of asking them about Ilsa.

He opened up to them and a mixture of envy and loathing filled his chest.

"Come to tell us a story, did you?" one of the old men asked quietly. His hair was white and his back bowed beneath his grey tunic.

"He came to offer us that fine horse," another said, "because he doesn't want his elders to walk for a fortnight while he rides up and down the line, whenever he pleases."

"I..." Will stopped, searching for a response.

"Move past, fetter bait," a sharp voice called from past them. A small Roven woman moved through the crowd toward them, her face furious. "The Torch may want your company, but the rest of us do not."

Will bowed his head slightly to the Roven woman, and again to the slaves. He turned Shadow toward the front of the caravan, an odd mix of insult and embarrassment washing over him.

He finally caught a glimpse of Hal and trotted towards him, relieved until Sora rode up as well. Hal greeted him enthusiastically. Sora gave him her usual scowl.

"The Torch ordered you to walk with him," she told Will.

"Ordered me?"

"His exact word was *invite*, but I thought I'd translate it for you. Because you don't seem very bright."

Hal laughed. "He seems bright enough to me."

"He comes to a Roven clan as a foreigner"—Sora's gaze dug into Will—"and then spins stories and lies."

"Sora doesn't like stories," Hal explained.

"You don't like *stories?* Everyone likes stories of some kind or another."

She just looked at him, her face set.

"Did you like the story I told last night? About Tomkin and the dragon?" He hadn't bothered to read Sora after the story ended. Killien had been entertained, Hal and the crowd had loved it.

"You stretched the tale and molded it to manipulate the crowd," she said. "Every word was chosen to do something. Every word was a lie."

A thin claw of fear squeezed Will's chest. The lie part was wrong, but not the rest. He had judged every word, every line, weighing it against the audience, drawing out the parts that pleased the Roven, softening the parts that would feel foreign to them.

He opened his mouth to answer her, to find some sort of defense for it, but Hal spoke first.

"That's the point of a storyman, Sora. If we wanted to hear something boring, we'd ask about your last hunt."

She turned and trotted ahead. "It's not bright to keep the Torch waiting."

Will nudged Shadow to follow her. "This is the second morning you've come to find me. Should I start expecting it? I could have a cup of saso ready for you."

She shot him another glare, the hundredth he'd received that morning. "Unless you don't drink saso." His voice sounded snippier than he'd intended. "Then we could have tea. I know of a red tea from Baylon that would be perfect for you. It's bitter and disagrees with almost everyone."

That earned him the slightest uptick of the very edge of her mouth. She turned into the caravan and led him past dozens of rangers.

The Torch came into view, walking alongside his small fiery-haired wife. Will straightened, looking for any sign of Ilsa. Lilit caught sight of Sora and Will, and her expression sharpened.

"I've brought you your liar," Sora announced.

Killien turned with a raised eyebrow.

Will flung a glare at her. "They're stories. Not lies."

Sora didn't bother to look away from the Torch. "I ride west today." Without waiting for acknowledgement, she rode into the grass.

Lilit whispered something to the Torch that ended with a harsh "fett". Sending a cutting glare toward Will, she walked away.

Killien mounted his horse and glanced back toward her. "I didn't introduce you last night, but that is Lilit, my wife. Flame of the Morrow Clan." He worried his thumb across his lips, watching her walk away, and the burning stones in the rings on his fingers glinted in the morning light. "Carrying our first child. The healers assure me that the child will not come until we reach the rifts."

Lilit walked back to a wagon covered with a tall canopy of undyed wool, colored silks draping the front and back to make fluttering doorways. A hand reached through the silks to help her climb in and Will's breath caught at a glimpse of brown hair. Both disappeared into the wagon.

"Flame?"

"A Torch is not much use without a Flame." Killien squinted back towards her. "She's not happy that I invited you along. I'm expecting you to be so entertaining she changes her mind."

"I could ride with her," Will offered, a little quicker than he'd intended, "tell stories to pass the time."

"That's a terrible idea. Last night she called you a danger to the clan. Thought I should kill you in your sleep. I pointed out that you were a protected guest, she said you weren't her guest, and if she killed me in my sleep, she'd be free to kill you." Killien smiled, but it was a bit strained. "The best thing you can do is stay away from her. Your new goal here is not to entertain the clan, it's to convince my wife to like you. So she stops being mad at me."

The curtains shifted at the front of Lilit's wagon and Will caught a glimpse of movement inside. "I'll do my very best."

"Lilit will come around," Killien said, pulling Will's attention away from the slaves. He did not sound entirely hopeful, "But Sora was right, it's your familiarity with lies I'm interested in."

Will threw up his hands. "A story is very different from a lie."

"Is a rumor? My rangers have found rumors of frost goblins as far west as they've traveled. But since you have been quite a bit farther, I was wondering how far west the rumors went."

"Rumors of frost goblins was the only thing I heard agreed on in every city along the entire coast. They're talking about them in Bermea just as much as here."

Killien blew out a long breath. "That's not the answer I was hoping for."

They topped a small rise and the emptiness of the Sweep felt like a facade. The serpent's wake slithered over the hills ahead of them, dipping into countless unseen valleys. There could be hidden ravines everywhere, full of frost goblins. The earth beneath them could be riddled with warrens.

"Frost goblins aren't a threat to a caravan of this size, are they?"

Killien didn't answer right away. "It's been generations since anyone's seen hives large enough to attack a clan."

"What do they want?"

"Meat and metal. They are especially drawn to silver and gold, but they also gouge out nails, hinges, any metal they find. And they eat raw meat. They'll rip chunks of meat off an animal and leave the rest to rot."

"Do they—" Will hesitated. "—eat people?"

"They seem to prefer animals."

The empty expanse of the sky settled down heavily over the

grass, the wind rippled across one hill and spread onto the next, jostling against them constantly.

"They dislike heat. Usually the spring weather drives them into the mountains, which is why we have heatstones. If you bring a stone near a fire, it'll give off tremendous heat for an hour or two."

Killien turned and gave instructions to a nearby ranger, who rode off down the line.

Pairs of riders cantered out from the main caravan, taking up positions on a perimeter around the main group. Killien gave the riders a brief glance before turning back to Will. "Yesterday you mentioned you'd been to three other clans. How does a storyman from Gulfind end up so well-traveled through the Roven Sweep?"

"I didn't intend to be." When he'd first stepped foot on the Sweep, following rumors of a gathering war, he'd thought it would be easy to confirm or refute. How hard could it be to find a single holy man proclaiming that Mallon the Rivor still lived and calling warriors to his banner? He thought he'd find the old man, figure out whether the Roven were amassing an army, and get back to Queensland within a fortnight. "I was chasing a story, actually. Following rumors of an elderly fellow who claimed a dead man had sent him on a mission." Which was true, from a certain point of view.

"Did you find him?"

"It took a while." A long while. Weeks and weeks of following rumors about the man. "And when I found him, he was a complete disappointment." The old man had been so ridiculous. Will had finally caught up to him in the summer valleys of the Boan Clan and instantly dismissed any rumors he'd heard of the man actually gathering an army. "He was just a doddering old man giving foolish speeches that no one listened to.

"But by then it was late in the fall, and the clans were heading south, so I followed and got caught up learning Roven stories." Especially Roven rumors about wayfarers and whether or not they sold foreign slaves on the Sweep. "It's taken months to work my way east again. I planned to go back to Gulfind before I met you." He kept himself from glancing back at Lilit's wagon. "And your offer was too interesting to refuse."

Killien studied him before nodding slowly. "All my books are in crates, sealed against the weather. But the ones you saw in my house are in a red oilcloth sack at the back corner of the book wagon. I've left them available for you."

Will sat straighter in surprise. "Thank you." The long trip north suddenly felt a bit less grim.

"There is also paper," Killien continued. "Write stories for me that I don't know and we can discuss them as we ride."

Will gave him a bow of acknowledgement.

"Everything you know about Queensland."

Will's bow stuttered before he recovered.

"And don't wander far from the front of the caravan. These are my rangers and won't trouble you. Everyone else in the clan knows the storyman from Gulfind is my guest, but accidents happen to foreigners on the Sweep." He glanced at Will's shirt. "Stay dressed like a storyman. And stay close to me."

Behind them, the line of the Morrow stretched back over the next rise filled with thousands of Roven. "I won't wander."

"Wise choice. The book wagon is that one with the orange oilcloth covering the back."

Will bowed at the obvious dismissal and turned Shadow toward the books.

He hadn't gone far when he reached Lukas riding toward Killien, his face bleak. The slave rode directly into Will's path. "Enjoy wearing the red shirt while you can," he said quietly. "It'll be grey soon enough."

Will reined in Shadow and opened up toward Lukas. A coiled, venomous hatred slithered into his chest.

"The only difference between you and me"—Lukas continued, his voice pitched low—"is that Killien's wayfarer dogs dragged me here, fighting the entire way. You just walked right in."

Will drew back, both from the man's fury and his words. "*Killien's* wayfarers?"

With a last hateful look, Lukas turned his horse away. "The wayfarers may not have brought you," he said over his shoulder, "but Killien owns you all the same."

CHAPTER TWELVE

The rest of the day passed in a vaguely unsettled way, Will's mind gnawing on the problem of how to reach Ilsa. He rode Shadow along the eastern edge of the caravan, keeping Lilit's wagon and Killien in view. Lukas's warning left a knot in his gut and there was something reassuring about being closer to the Scale Mountains than the Roven. Even if only by a handful of paces.

The path of the serpent's wake stretched ahead of them, slithering over the hills, the trail of years of migrations etched into the Sweep. It was strange how a place as vastly open as this could feel so confining.

He kept busy thinking of rescue stories, hoping he'd land on some idea of how to get Ilsa away from the Roven. Keeper Terre had rescued six children from a pack of direwolves, but even if Will had mastered the skill of making trees topple strategically, there were no trees on the Sweep. Knocking over blades of grass was bound to have a less terrifying effect.

It was a much needed distraction when Rass appeared. He dismounted and walked with her for a few hours. She ate the food he offered and chattered at him about the grass or the sky or whatever struck her fancy. It had been such a long time since anyone had talked with him so comfortably, it felt both delightful and overwhelming.

Around midday she ran out into the Sweep and Will found Killien's book wagon, wide with low side walls, open in the back. A burnt-orange oilcloth spread across the bed. The last arm's length of the wagon was open and he climbed onto it, lifting the edge of the oilcloth. Beneath it he found crates of books wrapped tightly in more oilcloth. In the nearest corner sat a red bag holding the books from Killien's shelf, a thick stack of paper, four pens, and a bottle of ink. Sitting on the back of the wagon, he set to writing some innocuous stories from Queensland.

As the sun set, riders came by ordering the wagons to a central location. A haphazard city grew along the top of one wide hill with wagons spilling down into the shallow valleys around it. The entire perimeter of the clan was dotted with fires as well, each with a mound of dried grass and dung next to it, ready to be thrown on if larger flames were needed.

Around him the Roven gathered into small knots talking and laughing and eating together and he sat feeling awkward, wondering where he was supposed to find his dinner. The night cooled quickly and a cold breeze blew across Will's back.

He cast out toward the nearest fire, feeling the *vitalle* blazing up in it. It was too bad Alaric wasn't here. He could pull a blanket of warmth from a fire all the way across a room. *Don't move the heat itself, create a...sort of a net around it. Then pull the net, not the heat,* he'd say.

A net. Will stretched his fingers toward the fire. He gathered its *vitalle*, imagining it forming a close woven net, capturing the heat and pulling it toward him. His fingertips stung, but he felt a wave of warmish air. He sat up straighter.

A net had too many holes. He began again, imagining a cloth wrapping around the heat. Slowly, his fingers starting to ache in earnest, he drew the cloth closer.

The enormous form of Hal stepped between him and the fire,

and Will's concentration broke. The cloth dissolved and the heat escaped into the night.

"What are you doing over here?" Hal said. "Come get dinner. Unless all this wagon gathering is your fault, in which case I hate you."

"I may have had a part in it," Will admitted. "Killien and I talked about goblins this morning. The entire Sweep is worried about them."

Hal glared at the sprawling mass of Roven. "This will cost an hour of travel each night. It'll add at least a day to the trip." Hal motioned for Will to follow him. "You can pay for it by entertaining us with a story. Something about dwarves."

They wound through wagons, Hal keeping up a continual grumble until they reached a small fire near the edge of the clan where he dropped down next to Sora. She offered Will her usual scowl and Will gave her an especially wide smile back.

Hal passed a basket of thin bread and smoked fish before a young girl arrived, asking him a question about a herd. Will ate his piece of salty, dried fish half listening to Hal's herd management, half watching Roven children carrying baskets of food.

Killien walked up talking to some rangers. Neither Lilit nor Ilsa was with him, but he was followed by Lukas and the two other slaves from the porch in Porreen. Lukas and the younger girl swung bags of heatstones off their shoulders and sat a little ways back from the fire. When the big man sat next to them, he clutched his own bag to his chest.

Lukas spread a book on his lap and flipped through the pages before finding a place to read. The girl leaned over and ran her finger along the page. Will stared at the two of them. Did all of Killien's slaves know how to read? They were obviously well cared for. Maybe slavery in Killien's household wasn't as bad as other places. Was it possible that Ilsa's life had been better than he'd feared?

The big slave stared disinterestedly at the fire, relaxing until his bag slouched and two heatstones rolled out, unnoticed.

"Keep them in the sack, Rett," the girl said kindly, tucking the yellow stones back into the bag and cinching the top closed.

"I'm sorry, Sini," he said absently. "I forgot."

"It's alright." She patted his large hand reassuringly with her own small one.

Rett pulled the bag onto his lap, wrapping one hand firmly around the drawstring and his other arm around the bag. With it secure, he lifted his head and looked around with an aimless curiosity. There was a familial type of ease among the three of them.

Sini watched him for a moment, a little crease of worry in her brow. Lukas reached into a pocket and pulled out a small, glowing green stone.

"Don't," Sini pleaded.

But Lukas held the stone out toward Rett.

The large man's eyes locked on the stone and a wide smile crossed his face. "You found one!" He reached out gingerly to take it, then cupped it in his hands, curling his body over it.

"Don't watch it too long." The gentleness in Lukas's voice caught Will off guard. "It'll hurt your head."

Rett nodded and kept his eyes fixed on the green glow, a look of utter contentment on his face.

"I wish you'd stop giving him those," Sini said.

"I've said no for weeks. If he begged you all the time, you'd give in too." Lukas watched the man. "Sometimes I think he needs them."

The little bit of green glow was almost hidden in Rett's hands. He watched it with a desperate sort of fascination, as though if he blinked, it might disappear.

Sini looked down at her hands. "I can't bear how sad it makes him."

"But it makes him happy first." Lukas turned back to his book.

She pinched her mouth into a thin, disapproving line and sat silent for a moment before glancing at Lukas's book. "Did you figure it out? Does it work?"

Lukas shrugged. "Killien won't try it." He shot a glare at the Torch. "He's so fixated that he's missing opportunities."

Sini shushed him and Lukas answered her too quietly for Will to catch.

Two Roven children stepped up to him, delivering more piles of flatbread and fish. During the day, all the children of the clan had romped along the side of the caravan doing as they pleased, but now that the camp was settling, those old enough were busy hurrying about just like the slaves, helping the clan settle down.

"What was it like," Will asked Sora, "growing up with the Morrow?"

She looked away and took a bite of fish.

"You won't get any information from Sora," Killien said, sitting across the fire and reaching for the basket of fish. "She's angry tonight."

Sora didn't acknowledge the Torch.

"Are there some nights she's not?" Will asked.

That she acknowledged with a glare.

"She's especially angry tonight because I didn't send her out with the latest scouting party."

"What's the point of sending out a scouting party when none of them can scout?" Sora asked.

"They're all rangers," Killien said mildly.

"They all wear ranger leathers," she corrected him. "Not one of them could track a black sheep in a field of snow."

"See?" Killien said. "She's angry."

Sora went back to scowling at her fish.

"I didn't know there was an alternative," Will said, feeling a grim, if childish, satisfaction at her annoyance. "This is how she talks to me all the time."

Hal reached for the basket of food. "She can't answer your question anyway. Sora didn't grow up in the Morrow. She's from a mountain tribe."

"Really?" Will turned back to her, several things clicking into place. "Of course, your eyes are green."

Sora looked at him with a stony face. "Your beard is stupid."

Will's hand went to his beard. "What?"

"I thought we were stating obvious things."

Will waved away her comments. "I've never met anyone from the mountain tribes. You live in the Hoarfrost Range year round, don't you? How? In the winter the mountains are so…"

"Cold?" offered Hal.

"Yes, cold. How do you stay warm?"

She gave him an exasperated look but didn't answer.

"Alright, we'll play the 'I make up your answer' game again," Will said. "You live in huge communal buildings and keep fires burning all the time?"

"Yes." She graced him with a flat look. "Because everyone knows the Hoarfrost Range is full of huge communal buildings."

"Good point." Will's mind skipped to other ideas. "Do you build houses out of snow?"

"Good guess, storyman," Hal broke in with a wide grin. "That's how we met Sora. Killien and I were in the Hoarfrost hunting when a blizzard rolled in. We thought we were going to freeze to death." He gestured at Sora. "Until, thank the black queen, an angel appeared."

Sora raised an eyebrow.

"She bossed us into helping her make a snow hut, then crawled inside."

Killien smiled and even the corner of Sora's lips rose slightly.

"We didn't know what else to do, so we followed her. When she learned that we were hunting a snow cat, she looked at us." He nodded to Will. "With that angry, scary look."

"I'm familiar with that one," Will said.

"Then she left."

Will laughed. "She left?"

Hal nodded. "Wasn't even gone long enough for us to decide whether she'd deserted us, when she came back, dragging…a dead snow cat."

Will turned to Sora. "You hunted it that fast?"

Sora started to shake her head, but Hal nodded. "That's when we knew she had creepy magic."

"You do?" Will asked.

Sora let out a long suffering sigh. "I didn't use magic. I hunted it with a bow and a knife. It was dead before I found these idiots."

"So she claims," Hal finished.

Will cast out toward Sora, but there was nothing unusual about her *vitalle*. If she could do magic, she wasn't doing anything right now. Not that she'd have a reason to. He opened up to her as well, assuming he'd still feel nothing. But here, sitting with people she was comfortable around, she had relaxed slightly. Her emotions were still muted, but he found hints of both amusement and irritation. He closed himself off to her, wondering if she ever relaxed enough to let her emotions be fully felt. "So the mountain clans live in ice houses?"

"Caves!" Sora said in exasperation, "Caves large enough to house a village. Wide and clean with crystal clear streams. Rooms. Chimneys. Walls that glitter with silver and gems."

Will stared at her in amazement. "Really?" He glanced at Killien who grinned openly, then turned back to Sora. The mountain tribes lived in caves? Like dwarves? "How big are they?" His mind toyed with the idea, turning it slowly around. "Will you take me there?" The Keepers knew next to nothing about the mountain clans. "You can tell me the tales of your people. Has anyone ever written them down? I'll make you a book of them!"

"Sora's the one you'd want to write stories about," Killien said.

Sora dropped her bread, her eyes thin slits of green, and stood up. "I'm not your personal guide, storyman. I have no desire to travel anywhere with you, and I wouldn't subject my people to your..." Her eyes searched his face for a long moment before she gestured at him.

"My what?" Will demanded.

"Your everything."

Will hadn't even realized he'd opened up toward her until he felt her deep, pulsing anger bloom in his chest. Jaw clenched, she turned and walked off into the darkness. Will took a breath, clearing her anger away until all he felt was the now familiar knot of worry that was all his own. He glanced at the Torch and saw nothing but amusement.

Hal's eyes glinted in the firelight and his teeth shone white through his beard. "She's definitely starting to like you, storyman."

Will let out a laugh that sounded weak even to his own ears. "It seems that way." He glanced at Hal. "Can she really do magic?"

Hal shook his head. "It's just uncanny how good she is at tracking. And it's fun to say because it makes her so mad."

"Never mind Sora," Killien said. "It's time for you to earn your keep, storyman. Tell us a tale."

"Something about dwarves," Hal added.

"Shut up, Hal." Killien glanced toward where Sora had disappeared. "Do you know any about angry women?"

Will ran through the tales he knew from Gulfind and Coastal Baylon. No angry women jumped out at him.

"What about Keeper Chesavia from Queensland?" Killien's eyes were bright. "I haven't heard the entire tale, but from what I know, she was angry."

Will shifted, giving himself a moment. Chesavia was very angry. But it was going to be tricky to tell that story without showing how well he knew the Keepers.

"Have you visited Queensland a lot?" Hal asked.

Will nodded. "I'd venture to say I've visited every country you've ever heard of."

Killien raised an eyebrow. "Have you crossed the Roven Sweep west to the land of the white rocks?"

"No." Past the westernmost Roven cities the grassland turned to desert and continued for days, lifeless and barren. "Have you ever met anyone who has?" Will asked.

"Legend says once a wizard crossed the desert on a dragon."

"Well, if I ever have access to a dragon," Will said, "I'd consider it."

"If I had a dragon," Hal said, "I'd make it hunt for me. And cook."

"If I had a dragon," Killien said, "I would destroy my enemies quickly and utterly. I'd destroy all those who keep the Roven weak and divided. Then I would kill all the Keepers in Queensland so the Roven could take back that land with barely a fight."

Will kept his face mild like a disinterested storyman from Gulfind. "Give me a little warning first. I'd love to learn more of their stories before you wipe them out."

A bleak smile twisted the edge of Killien's mouth. "Agreed."

"One of the times I was in Queensland, I visited the queen's court."

Both Hal and Killien looked impressed.

"The night I was there, a Keeper told the story of Chesavia." This was also true. The first time he'd gone to court, Will had arrived just in time for a feast and Alaric's storytelling. "She lived years ago and had battled a water demon. By the end of the tale, Chesavia's angry. I'll warn you, though, it's not a happy story."

"Most tales with angry women aren't." Killien laughed.

"You can remember the story, after hearing it only once?" Hal asked.

"I don't have many skills in life," Will said. "I can't fight, I can't make anything." *I'm fairly weak at magic and I'm not great at translating old runes,* he added silently. "But I can remember every story I've ever heard, or ever read."

Hal raised his eyebrow. "Every one?"

"If I've only heard it once, or if it was poorly told, I have to work a bit to remember it. This story was told by a Keeper. You may not be fond of them, but they are excellent storytellers."

The small fire in front of them flickered, tossed about by the wind. Will looked into it, considering how well he should tell the story. "The tale becomes interesting the day her childhood friend arrived at the palace, wounded and begging to see her."

Will fell into the story, minimizing the way he spoke of Keeper magic. Killien watched him closely, seemingly hungry for more of the tale, and at the end, he thanked Will and looked into the fire for a long time.

"Do you know more tales about Keepers?" Killien asked.

Will glanced at him, then looked into the fire too. He knew every story of every Keeper recorded in the Stronghold. Dozens of which he had rewritten himself, combining different tellings into complete tales. "A few."

"I want to hear them," Killien said. "As many as you can remember."

"Do you see the grass?" Rass chirped near midday, running up alongside Will, her dirty face lit up with joy. *"It's growing so fast!"*

CHAPTER THIRTEEN

THE SUN DISAPPEARED over the horizon, and the sky pulled the last lingering light up into itself, turning the Sweep into a puddle of darkness. Will tried twice to walk among the wagons where Lilit and Ilsa were, but both times rangers efficiently directed him away. The second time was barely civil. Whatever orders Killien had given them regarding the foreign storyman, Will doubted it would keep him safe if they decided he was paying too much attention to the Torch's wife.

Killien offered Will a place to sleep in one of his wagons along with a pile of blankets. Between a bundle of fabric for a pillow, and wool blankets from the Torch, he had a reasonably comfortable place to sleep.

At least at first. The ever-present wind sent swirls of cold night air jostling around him. His emotions were just as blustery.

First there was Ilsa. All day he'd strained to see her near Lilit's wagon, but in vain.

Then there was Killien. On the one hand, he was more civilized than Will had ever expected. Even his slaves could read. But he *had* slaves, ripped from their homes and brought here. The truth of that was so stark he felt furious and sick at the same time. And just in case Will ever started feeling too comfortable, there was Killien's hatred of Keepers to keep things interesting.

Finally there was Lukas's warning. Was Will fooling himself thinking he'd be free to leave?

Just above the Scales, the sinuous trail of black emptiness rose. A cold darkness crept into Will's chest at the sight of the snake. The Serpent Queen kept drawing his eye back to her utter blackness. As though she were drawing in the whole world. She'd moved halfway across the sky before he fell asleep.

The caravan rumbled to a start as soon as the grasslands were visible. Will walked, trying to work the aches out of his muscles. He stayed close to Shadow, using the horse to block the relentless wind. It wasn't terribly strong this morning, but the constant pushing of it was tiresome. He kept his eye on the covered wagons trailing behind Killien, wondering which one held Ilsa.

He'd remembered a story of a woman who'd rescued her sister from the Naponese blood doctors. She'd disguised herself as one of the servants who disposed of the dead bodies and carted her sister out with the corpses. But unless he and Ilsa could camouflage themselves as a hill of grass, it was unlikely any disguise was going to help them.

Not long after dawn, a noise behind him made Will turn sharply. There was Sora, walking behind him, leading her own horse.

"Is there a reason you're sneaking up on me?" he demanded, his heart racing.

Her eyes took him in, narrowed, and she drew her lips into her usual tight line. "You seem nervous."

He ignored that and took a calming breath. He really shouldn't try to irritate this woman. She was too close to Killien. And now that she was here, he felt the slightest sense of relief. Like he'd been waiting for her without realizing it.

"Does Killien want me?" he asked, hoping he'd be saved from the boredom of walking.

She shook her head. "He's busy."

She came up next to him anyway, wearing the same hunting leathers she had since he'd met her, well-used and plain. Where her arms had been bare yesterday, she now wore a blue wool shirt under her leathers, her shoulders shielded by a flap of chainmail, her wrists covered in thick leather bracers. Her braid lay heavy on her back, catching the sunlight in strands of bright copper. The entire Morrow Clan stretched out around them, but as he walked with her, the two horses blocking out the world around them, it felt almost like they were alone. She didn't seem as annoyed today, so he risked some conversation.

"How long have you been with the Morrow?"

She gave him a long, searching look, as though weighing whether the question was safe to answer. "Almost three years."

A twinge of sympathy caught him off guard. He was exhausted after only one year in the Sweep. "That's a long time."

She turned her gaze back forward. "Not to the Morrow."

"Do they..." He paused, trying to find words for his questions. "Are you still a foreigner to them? Or do they see you for who you actually are?"

Her face tightened a little but she didn't answer him.

"They don't see me either," he said.

Silence stretched out between them. It felt like camaraderie at first. Until the chill of her silence crept in and turned it into just a new form of isolation. Will spun his ring on his finger.

"Why are you here, Sora?"

"I don't trust you." She sounded more thoughtful than hostile.

"The Torch trusts me."

"He doesn't trust anyone."

That was unsettling. "Hal likes me."

She fixed him with her inscrutable look. "I don't trust you, storyman. And I intend to keep an eye on you."

"Well, anytime you feel the need to walk with me, please do.

You're far from the most pleasant person I've ever met, but you are opinionated. And that's entertaining."

Sora stopped and put her hand on his shoulder, stopping him and turning him toward her with one motion. Will's heart lurched as she stepped right up to him. She stood almost as tall as him, her eyes sharp and cold.

"I'm watching you all the time." Her hand weighed like stone on his shoulder. She was so close to him he could see the stark green of her eyes, the dark copper lashes. Will was sure she could feel his heart pounding.

"Are you waiting for a goodbye kiss?" Will whispered.

Her eyes went flat and she dropped her hand. With a withering look she mounted her horse and disappeared into the crowd. Will stood for a moment, letting out his breath, still feeling the weight of her hand on his shoulder.

Will sat on the back of the book wagon and stared dully across the grass. It was the third morning and he already felt like he'd done nothing in his life but trundle slowly northward across the Sweep. He'd wanted to ride among the wagons that held Lilit and Ilsa, but between Killien commanding him to keep his distance and the number of Roven rangers that surrounded Lilit, he couldn't figure out a way to do so. When he wasn't talking with Killien, riding among the other rangers who merely tolerated him for Killien's sake felt awkward and lonely. He'd ended up spending most of the day yesterday and all of this morning near the books. He'd written out four stories for Killien and read a good portion of one of the Torch's books.

His mind continued its useless search through stories for a rescue plan, but he'd thrown out three more ideas. He had neither floating firebrands nor a broken dam, and it would be hard to time his escape during the distraction provided by an attacking gryffon. If any gryffons still existed.

Last night, Will had given in to Rass's pestering and let her put three thin braids in his beard, each sporting a silver bead. She'd pronounced it "much better."

Talen had come and landed next to him on the wagon until he'd eaten all of Will's dried fish, then launched into the sky again and Will found himself wishing the little bird would stay.

The Clans and Clashes of the Sweep lay open on his lap to a page that mentioned the Morrow Clan. "Insignificant... weak... probably the only reason they survived is that they remain relegated to the easternmost margin of the Sweep, and have nothing worth plundering."

He toyed with his braids. The slight weight of the beads felt odd—empowering almost. As though adding those small beads gave him an unexpected measure of strength, or courage.

Sora rode up to the back of the wagon. "Killien wants you."

"Good." He tucked the book into the bag. "I'm terribly bored."

She had a knife strapped to each ankle and a bow slung across her back.

"Expecting me to put up a fight this morning?" Will mounted Shadow.

"Yes. The entire clan is preparing for an attack from *you*."

He let out a short laugh, until a thought struck him. "That's all for frost goblins?"

She leveled a pointed gaze at him. "Do you know of any other enemies nearby?"

"You feel a bit like an enemy sometimes."

This earned him a small smile. She motioned to his beard. "Getting more Roven by the day."

He felt the beads. "Do you like it?"

She raised one eyebrow.

"I mean—" He shifted. "—does it look right?"

She leaned toward him and he pulled back.

"You're a very nervous man."

"I'm not nervous." Even he could hear the petulance in his voice. "You're just scary."

She let out a short laugh. "If goblins attack, I wouldn't have that silver anywhere so easily grabbed."

Will rubbed one of the beads between his fingers. He imagined a bony goblin hand reaching for his face, and shuddered. Sora trotted ahead and he followed.

When he caught up, her armband caught his eye. The wide, dark fabric wrapped around her upper arm, and the claw tied to it with thin leather strips was viciously sharp. Under the band, a white, puckered scar ran down to her elbow.

"What sort of claw is that?"

Sora glanced down at her arm. "Snow cat." Turning away she added, "Killien's just ahead of the wagons," and rode away.

A handful of tall covered wagons, including the one with Lilit and Ilsa, rolled along in a clump. There were fewer rangers around today, and none near Lilit's wagon. Making sure Sora had disappeared, Will turned so he would ride through them to reach Killien. From the back of Lilit's wagon he caught a glimpse of long brown hair and his heart squeezed out several painfully strong beats. Will angled Shadow closer, feeling his pulse all the way down to where his palms gripped the reins.

A horse laden with a tall load of blankets was hitched to the back of the wagon, plodding along after it. Colored silks hung over the back, fluttering in the breeze.

Ilsa stepped out from between them.

She climbed down, grabbed a bundle of blankets, pushed them into the fluttering silks and disappeared after them. Will slid off Shadow and walked toward her, too many emotions churning inside of him to name. He picked up the next bundle, intending to offer his help, but when the silks opened and she saw him, she froze. The sight of her made everything in his chest claw its way up into his throat, and his offer was strangled out into the single word, "—help?"

Her face grew alarmed. "You need help?"

The idea was so wrong he let out a laugh that sounded a bit unhinged, and she drew back. "No." He stepped closer, desperately trying to speak normally. "I was wondering if you would like some help."

She eyed him a little warily, but when he held out the blankets, she took them and went back into the wagon. He wiped his sweaty palms and picked up the next bundle. This wasn't going well.

When she appeared again, he managed a reasonably normal smile. She pulled the silks shut behind her and climbed down, glancing around with a worried expression.

"You shouldn't be here," she whispered. "If the Flame saw you…" Her voice reminded him so much of their mother, but her accent—the rough Roven-ness of it cut at him.

"I'll just help for a minute." He felt as though he were trying to absorb everything about her. Now that he was closer, there was something of their father around her eyes. She looked healthy, and her grey slave's dress was well-made. She reached for the blankets. A line of thin scars from a switch ran across the back of her hands.

"Thank you." She glanced around again before continuing in a whisper, "I liked the story you told about Tomkin and the dragon." Tomkin's name sounded sharper the way she said it. Like the Roven accent could even make bookish Tomkin more savage.

"I'm Will," he whispered, something inside him breaking at the need to introduce himself.

She glanced back at the wagon. "You should go."

A jab of disappointment shot through him at her answer, but he tried not to let it show. There really wasn't any other way this relationship could begin. In her eyes he was nothing but a stranger. A dangerous stranger as far as Lilit was concerned.

"It's just…" He fumbled around for something to say. "It's just nice talking to someone who's like me."

She pulled the blankets out of his hands. "There's not much the same between you and me."

With a flick of silk, she disappeared into the wagon.

Will stared numbly at the back of the wagon until Lilit's voice floated out, jolting him back into motion. He mounted Shadow and wove his way out from between the wagons toward Killien.

Unnecessarily close behind the Torch rode Lukas, with a book spread open in front of him, making small notes in the margins and eating a roll. Nearby, Sini balanced on her toes on the wide saddle, her knees tucked up against her chest and her arms outstretched. She was such a little thing that even balled up she didn't fill the saddle. Her blond hair was busy falling out of a ponytail, her bag of heatstones hung from the saddle, and she chattered at Rett who rode silent beside her. He held one hand fisted on his saddle horn, and when he opened it to peer inside, Will caught a dim glow of green. The stone Lukas had given him last night was fading. Rett looked at it, then clenched his hand closed, his face worried.

Sini glanced over at the big man, a little crease of worry forming in her brow too. "Look, Rett, I'm a bird."

The big man considered her solemnly. "If you fly away, can I come with you?"

"Of course."

"You don't look like a bird, you look like a shrew." Lukas's face was serious, but his voice was light.

Sini dropped her arms. "With wings?"

"Her nose isn't pointy enough for a shrew," Rett disagreed, looking back at his stone with a troubled expression.

"He's teasing, Rett. Lukas is just envious because I have two good legs." Sini wiggled her knees from side to side. "One leg—" Sini balanced on one foot and stretched the other leg to the side. "—two legs." She switched feet and stuck the other out. "One leg, two legs…"

Lukas laughed and threw the end of the roll at her. It bounced off her grinning cheek, and even Rett managed a smile. Lukas glanced forward, catching Will's eye, and his expression soured.

Killien spared a quick glance at Sini and Lukas as he greeted Will. Between the unusual slaves and the nearness of Ilsa, Killien was hard to pay attention to. But the Torch had read the histories

Will had written, and the rest of the morning passed discussing them.

It was irritating to talk to the man. Killien had thought-provoking questions and sharp insights into the minds of other leaders. His thoughts about a historically weak king of Coastal Baylon made Will see the story in a whole new light. Will kept finding himself enjoying the conversation no matter how often he reminded himself not to.

The sun was high in the sky when Lukas closed his book with a snap. Out of the corner of his eye, Will saw him take a bracing breath, set his face into a mask of determination, and ride away.

Not long after, several rangers rode up to Killien, and Will excused himself. There were too many people around Lilit's wagon to even consider trying to see Ilsa, so he set off for the books. To the northwest, clouds were piling up in the blue sky like glowing swells of whiteness, while underneath a dark line sat heavy on the horizon.

When the wagon came into view, Lukas knelt on the back of it, looking into a dark grey sack. Will wove through the crowd until he trailed a little way behind. Lukas pulled out a book, pushed the bag into a crate, and tucked the oilcloth back around the books.

Lukas's brow was drawn, his jaw set. His eyes burned with something jagged. He took a breath and shifted his legs off the back of the wagon. A snarl of pain crossed his face and he pushed himself off, dropping into the grass, one leg twisting underneath him. With obvious effort, he limped to his horse and pulled himself into the saddle.

Will waited until Lukas had disappeared before spurring Shadow closer. He climbed down near the corner where his own red bag was, while the rangers driving the wagon watched him. Will reached into his own bag of books and pulled out a few titles. When the ranger turned back, Will pushed the orange cloth to the side and saw the crate with Lukas's bag. He reached in and pulled out the first book he found.

Methods of Transference.

Will stared at the brown leather cover, his mind tangled up in the odd words. He flipped the book open and his hand froze on the page.

Methods of Transference
based on the stonesteep practices of
Mallon the Undying.

CHAPTER FOURTEEN

Will stared at the name.

Mallon the Undying.

The title Undying was chilling. He was Mallon the Rivor in Queensland. When he'd invaded eight years ago with an army of Roven, the first people to bring a report to the queen were gem cutters, and they called what Mallon did *riving*—cutting a gem so deeply that it became worthless. It was a good description of what he did to people's minds. He cut something so profound inside them that they lost their will to refuse him.

What was unsettling about the Undying title was how true it felt. Everyone in Queensland had thought Mallon had been killed by the elves eight years ago. Until Ayda the elf showed his body to Will, not dead, just trapped.

Will lifted his gaze up to the Scales, as though he could see through the mountains to Alaric and see if the other Keepers had found a way to deal with Mallon.

Will set the book on the back of the wagon and flipped to the first page. Diagrams of stones and energy and animals filled the pages, detailing how to suck the energy out of a living creature and store it in burning stones.

This is what Killien had Lukas reading?

It discussed the sacrifice of the animal coldly, mathematically, as though it was of no importance. The focus was on how the energy, forced into lifeless gems, created the burning stones. Distaste and fascination warred with each other as he skimmed the pages. It was unnatural to put living energy into something not made to hold life. The entire process was ugly. And terribly inefficient. More time was spent on how to keep the energy from fading out of the burning stone than on how to put it there in the first place. Energy did not like to be contained.

A quarter of the way through the book he found pages heavily notated with small, wiry script.

Compulsion Stones

The transference of thought is relatively simple. A gem can be filled to hold an idea with relatively little sacrifice, a cat or other small animal, will provide more than enough.

But the idea in the compulsion stone is only a suggestion. The closer it matches the target's natural inclinations, the more effective the process. While it is occasionally successful with animals, results are not positive in humans. The foreign nature of the idea is recognized too quickly.

Will scanned the rest of the page. This was essentially a cumbersome way to do an influence spell, with similar limitations. An idea that was too foreign wouldn't work. Convincing someone to not notice a single person among a crowd was easy. Convincing them to not notice a single person walking into their room at night was almost impossible.

The rest described how to infuse a burning stone (aquamarine worked best) with a single thought. The process was messy and complicated, with a dozen reasons it could fail. It ended with a comment that Mallon was one of the few who could create compulsion stones reliably, but his methods were unknown.

The scribbled notes on the page were far more interesting.

Not thoughts—Emotions.

Mallon used natural resonance of emotions. Humans inherently susceptible to foreign emotions.

Will ran his finger over the note.

The natural resonance of emotions.

The phrase caught his attention like a glint of light out of the grimness of the book and something profound shifted in his mind. He spun his ring, turning the idea over in his mind.

He'd always thought of reading people as an extension of his other abilities. Emotions weren't exactly like *vitalle*, but he'd always thought of them as a form of energy other Keepers couldn't draw into themselves. But he didn't draw emotions in, he opened himself up and let his own body resound with them.

Resonance fit it perfectly. Because everyone was affected by other's emotions to some extent. A happy friend could lift one's spirits, anger could spread from person to person like a flame. Emotions were contagious.

He spun his ring slowly. Maybe Will's particular gift was that he could isolate others' emotions from his own so he could feel them clearly. The idea sat inside him like a lamp, shining onto other ideas, linking things together that he'd never connected.

Along the very bottom of the page, was scrawled:

Emotions resonate—they do not move. Once the stone is created, transference of emotions, unlike thoughts, requires NO ENERGY.

The lines under the final words were dark and thick and victoriously emphatic.

Will nodded slowly in agreement. It took no effort for him to feel the emotions of others.

He traced the wiry script. Was it Lukas's?

Whoever's it was, this much enthusiasm for controlling people was unsettling. The fact that it reminded Will of the influence spells he'd been using throughout the Sweep made it even worse.

A distant rumble rolled across the grasses. The clouds were closer, climbing high against the blue sky. Their tops so bright white they were almost blinding, and the dark line beneath them as dark as a sliver of night.

"Stow those books, fett," the ranger barked at Will.

Will shot him a scowl and tucked Lukas's book back into its grey sack. He was about to close the bag when he remembered the book Lukas had bought from Borto—the blue one with the silver medallion.

He peered inside, but none of the books were blue.

Grabbing *Clans of the Eastern Sweep* from the bag he was supposed to use, he tucked the oilcloth snugly around everything. Back on Shadow, he took his place along the eastern side of the clan, his mind still toying with the ideas of resonance, and that Lukas was reading books about magic.

Killien didn't have any stonesteeps. He'd paid an outsider to create the heatstones, another to bless the herds. What was Killien planning to do with knowledge he couldn't use? When he didn't come up with an answer, he turned his attention to his own book.

Clans of the Eastern Sweep was short and boring. There were only two tribes besides the Morrow this close to the Scales, the Temur and the Panos. The end of the book was dedicated to the Morrow's history. It was uninspiring.

Always the smallest clan, they were conscripted by whatever nearby clan needed them when infighting broke out in the Sweep. The book ended with Tevien, 17th Torch of the Morrow Clan. It was noted that he had one son named Killien.

A new hand began beneath it.

Tevien, Torch of the Morrow, led his people for 23 years. His goal was to unite the Roven clans. He brought Torches together who had never met in peace.

On Midsummer's Day, in his twenty-third year as Torch, Tevien was summoned to mediate a skirmish between the Temur and the Panos. He was struck by a stray arrow and returned to the grass, giving his life and his strength back to the Sweep.

Killien, 18th Torch of the Morrow, took his father's place at age 18, uncontested.

Will looked toward the front of the caravan where Killien rode. Eighteen was so young.

At eighteen, Will had been seven years into his training at the Keeper Stronghold and just starting to travel Queensland in what would end up being fruitless searching for new Keeper children, traveling through a safe land, and telling stories to small towns. Not exactly the same as becoming the Torch of a small, vulnerable Roven clan.

A raindrop slapped against his neck and Will snapped the book shut and tucked it into his saddlebag just as the real rain hit. Around him, the caravan moved on unperturbed. Hoods were up and heads were down, but every horse, wagon, and person plodded forward, as if nothing was happening.

The storm was fierce and blustery and short-lived. Killien didn't send for him when the wagons stopped, and he jotted stories for the Torch until it was late enough to try and sleep. The boards of the wagon were hard against his back, the chill of the night seeped through his blankets, and the black Serpent Queen snaked through the stars like a stain.

The pale light of morning came too soon. Will rolled himself out of the wagon, toying with the idea of walking until his body loosened up, but weariness won out and he mounted Shadow, riding along the eastern side of the caravan.

They'd barely started when Sora appeared. A fresh wave of exhaustion rolled over him at the thought of talking to her.

"Good morning," he said, without enthusiasm.

She raised an eyebrow. "No unwarranted cheerfulness this morning?"

He didn't bother to answer, and they rode in silence until Talen's tiny form dove down and landed on Will's bedroll.

"Good morning," Will said, ignoring the mouse he dropped.

"I was wondering if I'd get to meet your hawk." Sora looked at the bird with keen interest and ran a finger down its feathers. The hawk fixed her with its expressionless gaze.

"Sora," Will introduced her, trying to sound polite, "meet Talen."

Sora took in the bird's drab, tiny feet. "Talon? Did you name your horse Hoof?"

"My horse is Shadow," Will said, patting the pinto's mottled neck with affection, "because I've always wanted a black horse named Shadow. The Roven wouldn't sell me a black one, so I bought this one instead. And named him Shadow."

Sora fixed him with an unreadable expression. "It's fitting that you would take something as beautiful as a brown and white pinto and, just by changing the words you say about it, think you can change it into what you really want."

Will stared at her. "Do you ever have any fun? Shadow's name makes me happy. And Talen's name isn't 'Talon' like the claw, its 'Talen' like the coin because he was payment for a job. Although whether he was a good payment or not, I haven't decided."

"He's a grass hawk. And he's beautiful."

"A grass hawk? Is anything in this land *not* named after grass?"

Sora shrugged. "The grass is everything here."

"He's not full grown, is he? Because he's too small to hunt anything but mice."

"Just a yearling." She reached out again and ran her finger along Talen's brown and white chest. "But he won't grow much bigger. A female would be half again as big and a better hunter." The edges of her lips lifted slightly. "And faster and smarter and all around more capable."

Talen fluttered his wings and hopped onto Sora's fist—and she smiled a wide, genuine smile at the bird.

It was utterly transformative, like the time Will had seen a brown lizard skitter onto a leaf, and its rough skin had shifted to a vibrant, shimmery green. He was torn between shock and a sudden possessiveness toward Talen.

"Stop seducing my hawk." Will pulled out a bit of meat. Talen hopped back onto Will's saddle horn and snatched it up. "He's small and not particularly useful, but he and I are a good fit."

She sat back, the smile lingering. "Grass hawks are difficult to catch."

He almost opened up toward her. It'd be unusual to feel any pleasant emotions from her. But it felt refreshing to take the smile as enough. He did soften his voice a little. "Don't try to convince me he's valuable. I'm very comfortable with the long-suffering caretaker role I've developed with him."

"He's not valuable, just intriguing."

Talen peered at Will's saddlebag.

Will spread his hands out. "You're going to have to be hawk-like and hunt for yourself if you're still hungry."

Talen let out a whistling call and sped off into the sky.

Will watched him go until he was only a small black speck. He flung the dead mouse past Sora into the grass.

A small crinkle of disgust wrinkled Sora's nose, but it was accompanied by another smile. She kept her eyes trained on the disappearing hawk. "Killien wants you."

Will looked at her sharply. "Why didn't you say so before?"

She shrugged. "He's up near the front." She seemed to have no intention of coming with him. So, spurring Shadow forward, he left her looking thoughtfully after Talen.

As he rode up to Lilit's wagon, the silk scarves hanging across the back fluttered and he caught a glimpse of the Torch's wife lying on a thick bed of blankets. Her eyes were closed, her face set in an expression of exhaustion and irritation. She pressed painfully swollen hands against her belly. The wagon lurched. Her eyes flew open and she hissed something at the driver.

A grey sleeve came into view and laid a wet cloth across the front of her neck.

Lilit's eyes closed again. "I'd sell everything I own for more wet cloths."

"I'll be right back with more water, Flame."

"Thank you," Lilit said.

Will urged Shadow alongside the back corner of the wagon and came face to face with Ilsa. She cast an alarmed glance toward Lilit, who still lay with her eyes closed, and waved him away.

He motioned for her to be quiet, and offered his water skin. She paused, then gave him a begrudging smile which still looked vaguely disapproving. He poured water onto the cloths in her hand until they were soaked.

Thank you, she mouthed, before turning back into the wagon

"I found some," she said to Lilit, spreading another cloth across the Flame's forehead. The Flame let out a long sigh of relief.

Will rode up toward Killien, feeling almost euphoric but trying to school his expression into something less intense.

Lukas rode next to the Torch, bent over a book Killien held. The Torch watched Will, disapproving. With a quick word to Lukas, he shut the book and handed it to the slave. Lukas gave him a nod and glanced back at Will. Whatever he muttered as he rode away made Killien laugh.

When Will reached the Torch, the man glanced back at Lilit's wagon. "Lilit does *not* like foreigners, and she will *not* be pleased if she finds you loitering around her wagon. You don't want to cross that woman, Will. Stay away from her."

Will's buoyant mood deflated. At least Lilit's hostility of foreigners didn't extend to her slaves. "Is she alright? She seems…uncomfortable."

"The healers assure me everything is as expected." The wagon hit a bump and Lilit snapped at the driver. Killien grimaced. "She wanted to stay in Porreen until the child was born."

Will couldn't blame her for that. "Does no one stay behind?"

"Not this year. With the reports of the frost goblins. I couldn't let her come north with only a small guard. She was…not pleased with that decision." Lilit's voice rang out behind them again, scathing. Killien winced. "She's usually not so…"

Lukas had fallen in close behind them, the book spread across his saddle again. A bit behind him Sini talked to Rett, enthusiastically waving her hands while Rett still looked anxiously at the green stone he held.

"Have you been enjoying my books?" Killien changed the subject.

Will nodded. "I read the account of your father yesterday. He sounded like a fascinating man."

"My father led the Morrow with honesty and strength. He said that fear could punish and rule, but never lead."

Will felt a reluctant approval of the sentiment.

Killien didn't continue right away, but his hands tightened on the reins. "What you read is the official version of his death. The Torch of the Panos had refused my father's help several times. But other nearby clans had begun to mend their differences. My father had a way of making people…see each other. Clans who had been enemies for generations were trying a tentative peace.

"Suddenly the Panos wanted help, said they wanted peace. But I think the truth is that my father was uniting their enemies." Killien stared ahead, unseeing, at the serpent's wake that wound ahead of them on the Sweep. "Two reliable witnesses say there was no fighting the night my father died. There would have been no stray arrows. And when he died, all the old feuds were revived."

Killien rode with an unnatural stillness.

Cautiously, Will opened himself up to Killien. A hollow, worn out grief laced with a savage need for vengeance filled his chest. The anguish and anger at his own father's death rose up.

Yes, emotions had resonance.

A tightening in Will's chest shoved the words out without him meaning to. "My father was killed when I was eleven."

Killien turned toward him and Will felt a glimmer of sympathy from the man. He shoved the emotions out of his chest.

"He was murdered." *By one of your wayfarers.* "A man broke into our house..." Will rubbed his scarred palms together. "I could do nothing."

Killien's eyes focused on some unseen point. "You seem like a man of peace, Will. But if you could find the man responsible, what would you do?"

The pressure in Will's chest climbed up into his throat, threatening to spill out. Killien shifted to watch him closely. "I ask myself that often lately...and I never have an answer."

Killien's face was stony. "I do."

They rode for a long stretch in silence while Will battled the anger that filled his chest. Had Killien sent Vahe twenty years ago?

He glanced at Killien. "How long have you been Torch?"

"Seventeen years."

Not Killien then. His father.

Not that it mattered. Killien would have, if he'd been Torch then. Lukas's grey presence behind him felt like a dagger cutting into the afternoon. Spread out behind them, slaves peppered the caravan. So many lives stolen and broken.

"I would like to continue my father's work to unite the clans. But I've become convinced the only thing that will work is a common enemy. I need an attacking army to destroy." He turned to Will, his eyes brighter than they should be.

Will shook his head slowly. "I don't know of any disposable ones."

The Torch turned back toward the grasses with a fierce smile. "A disposable army. That's exactly what I need. With that I could unify the Sweep. I could solve the world's problems."

"Or you could raze it to the ground."

Killien let out a boyish laugh. "No Will, for that, I'd need a dragon."

"I hope you're not offended," Will said, forcing a lightness into his words that he didn't feel, "that I don't share your enthusiasm for the disposable army or the dragon."

Killien grinned at him. "I never expected you to, storyman." The smile slid off his face. "But the Roven need a way to see that they have more in common than they think. And there's nothing more effective than fear to make people see the truth."

Will hesitated before asking, "What happened to your father's words that fear could punish and rule, but never lead?"

"You have to rule them before you can lead, Will."

CHAPTER FIFTEEN

It was days before he spoke to Ilsa again.

Over the next three days Killien summoned him only twice for short discussions about things Will had written. Both times he'd been surprised to find he left thinking better of the Torch than when he'd arrived. Almost worse was how much Will enjoyed the conversations himself. A large part of him hated Killien more each time he saw a grey slave's tunic. But a newer, smaller part of him had formed a firm respect for the man who seemed so unlike the other Roven. He was endlessly interested in other lands and their people, he treated Will with simple friendship, and as far as Will could tell, treated his slaves better than many men treated their own families.

But both times he'd been near Killien, Lilit's wagon had been surrounded by people and he'd had no chance to even see Ilsa.

The days fell into a blur of pale green grasslands. The wind blew constantly out of the northwest. Sometimes a mild breeze, sometimes so fierce it tore away anything not tied down. On warm afternoons, the clouds piled up and rolled across the Sweep with sheets of rain, plunging it into darkness and thunder. And with every day his frustration at not making progress with Ilsa grew. The Morrow would reach their rifts in a week, and if Killien decided he had no more use of a storyman, any chance to talk to Ilsa might be at an end.

To pass the time, Will continued working his way through the books in the red bag and writing out stories for Killien. Whenever he could, he snuck a glance into Lukas's grey bag, but only one book was interesting. Will had enough chances to read *Methods of Transference* to fully understand compulsion stones.

Killien and Lukas were very focused on the idea of transferring emotions or thoughts into someone. Which was troubling.

Most days he spent a portion of the time with Killien, talking about history or stories. Will often found the Torch discussing some book or another with Lukas, but Will's appearance always prompted the slave to close the book and fall back. Although Will was always answering Killien's summons, Lukas didn't bother to hide his feelings about the interruptions.

Most nights Will ate with the Torch. The man continued to request stories from Queensland, and Will felt that each night was spent downplaying his knowledge of Queensland while still satisfying Killien's curiosity. Hal was always there, a constantly friendly face who worked in questions about dwarves whenever he could. Sora joined them if she wasn't out scouting. Lilit too, a scowling, hateful addition to the group no matter how much Will tried to entertain her. But, shadowing Lilit, came Ilsa, who never made eye contact, but seemed to listen with rapt attention. Will found himself tailoring each story to his sister, pleasing Killien falling into a secondary goal.

Killien's other slaves were always close by, but never actually with the group. Lukas, Sini, and Rett sat together a little removed, but usually listening to any story Will told. Lukas watched him with an unrelenting coldness, but Sini and Rett watched curiously.

The nights Will didn't eat with Killien, he sat with Rass in the back of a wagon and let her prattle on about the little creatures she'd seen that day. Each night it got easier to fall asleep on the hard wagon, each morning he rose less sore and less enthusiastic about the walk that was about to begin. Every other day they reached a large cistern dug deep into the ground and covered with a thick metal lid. Will stood on the edge of the first one, looking down into the dark, still water, feeling cool air seep out from it. The well looked endless and the water poured into his canteen tasted stale.

It was the evening of the sixth day before Will caught sight of Ilsa in the crowd near the cistern. He wove his way through the crowd until he reached her.

She met his eye for only a moment before looking away. "I can't talk to you."

"I won't move my lips," he said through a stiff jaw, falling in beside her and looking forward stoically.

She let out a little laugh, then pressed her lips into a straight line again. "You don't have anything to hold water," she pointed out.

Which was true. He searched for some reason he could give her for being there. He wanted to ask her how her life had been. If she remembered her home or their parents. If she remembered him.

He wanted a way to pour all his memories into her mind and show her the childhood she'd lost. A way to figure out how she'd survived here, how hard it had been, who she'd turned into. But those were hardly conversation starters.

Tossing out the first hundred things he thought of to say, he managed, "I just need your help."

Ilsa shook her head, keeping her eyes forward. "If Lilit hears of me talking to you," she whispered, "she'll be furious. She hates you."

True. Will glanced around. "That's what I need help with. Is there any sort of story she would like? Anything that might make her think better of me? Killien keeps asking for things from foreign lands, and with each one, I swear the Flame hates me more."

"She does."

Ilsa was shorter than him by a hand, and she glanced up at him. Being close to her was such a strange combination of familiarity and awkwardness. Such familiar features set in a face he didn't quite recognize. What sort of stories would *she* like to hear?

"Pick something with a powerful woman," Ilsa said. "One who is the driving force of the story."

Will smiled. "That I can do."

"Now go away before you get us both in trouble."

He paused, trying to think of some reason to stay. An idea occurred to him. "Can Lilit read?"

She nodded. "Now leave. Please, Will."

At the sound of his name, his breath caught. For the briefest moment he thought maybe it signified that she knew him. But there was nothing in her face beyond a worry they'd be noticed.

His mother had always teased him that he couldn't resist his baby sister. He'd retrieve anything for her that she couldn't reach, carry her on his back whenever she asked, act out ridiculous stories just to make her laugh. It didn't matter that Ilsa had no idea who he was today. For him, nothing had changed.

He gave her a slight nod and pulled himself away. At least now he had an idea of how to ingratiate himself to Lilit.

When he got back to the book wagon, he pulled out some fresh paper and set to writing out a story with the most powerful woman he could think of. Sable's story was epic enough in proportions to need a whole book, but certain episodes of her life were excellent tales themselves.

He wrote until darkness hid the page, then rose with the sun to finish. By the time the caravan began moving, he had left Shadow hitched to the wagon and woven toward Lilit's wagon.

He reached the side of it and heard a thunk from the back. Moving quickly before any of the nearby rangers noticed him, he ducked around the corner.

"Ilsa," he whispered, walking along with the wagon.

But it wasn't Ilsa sitting there, shifting her weight uncomfortably.

Lilit's eyes flashed in recognition and her lips curled into a sneer. "What do you want with my girl, fett?"

"I don't..." Will almost stumbled. He tried to give her a disarming smile, but it probably looked panicked. He glanced into the wagon, but Ilsa wasn't there. "I have something for you, actually. I thought you might be bored so I wrote down a story for you about a woman named Sable who began with nothing and ended up essentially ruling the world."

Lilit's expression didn't soften and Will held the papers out to her. She glared for a moment before pulling them out of his hand and flicking them to the ground. They fanned out in front of the next wagon, smashed into the grass by the horses' hooves.

Will stared at the trampled pages disappearing under the wagon.

"My husband may see you as some exotic pet," she said, her voice cold, "but I know you're nothing but a field roach slinking in through a crack, spreading disease and filth."

Will opened his mouth to object, but she leaned forward and fixed him with a look of utter hatred. "If you come near my wagon again, Killien will lose his pet."

Will pulled back. So much for ingratiating himself to her. Will gave her a quick bow and turned away. He cast one last glance around, looking for Ilsa, but all he saw was a page of his story fluttering further behind them under the feet of the caravan. Before Lilit could call for any of the rangers, he hurried around the next wagon and headed back toward the books.

The next few days were torturously uneventful. Ilsa stayed at Lilit's side, which was now firmly off limits. Will had failed to find Ilsa near the cisterns when the clans stopped. He'd watched during the days to see if she'd leave the wagon, but he could not catch her alone.

On top of that, some sort of crisis involving an illness among the sheep kept Hal busy and ill-tempered, and Sora spent the days ranging.

The third such morning, he rode along the eastern edge of the caravan, getting some relief from the fact that there were no Roven between him and the Scale Mountains. The flatbread that was breakfast every morning, somehow managed to be both salty and bland at the same time. He ate it mindlessly, bracing himself for another day alone.

A horse trotted up behind him and he almost smiled.

"You missed me, didn't you?" he asked.

Sora pulled her horse up between him and the Scales. "No."

"Good." He felt something loosen inside him. "I didn't miss you either." He took a bite of flatbread.

She rode beside him calmly with her usual distant expression and he studied her out of the corner of his eye.

"Please tell me you're here to either bring me to Killien for a thought-provoking conversation," he said, "or to talk to me yourself. I'll even be happy if you're just here to tell me all the things you don't like about me."

This earned him the hint of a smile. "Killien is busy planning scouting routes with the rangers."

"You're a ranger," he pointed out.

Her leathers were the same as always, plain and well-worn. The morning was as sunny as every spring morning on the Sweep and already warm enough that her arms were bare. The band around her arm caught his eye again, the scar below it white in the morning light.

"Wait..." He took in her leathers and the assorted weapons she wore, "you are a ranger, aren't you?"

Sora shot him an exasperated look. "I don't patrol the way they do. Killien trusts me to pick my own route."

"Ahh. You mean he doesn't want to argue with you."

This time, the side of her mouth definitely lifted as she shook her head. "He knows I'll keep my eyes open and go where I need to go."

"I understand." Will nodded. "I don't like to argue with you either."

She broke into a laugh that rolled across him like one of the breezes rippling across the grass.

He stared at her a minute before realizing he was grinning. He rubbed his hand across his mouth to tone it down. Feeling oddly proud of himself, he ripped off a piece of his flatbread and offered it to her. "If Killien's busy, then you must have come here to talk to me."

She shook her head at the bread and fixed him with a calculating look. "You are usually so clever."

He waited for something more. "…thank you?"

"So why are you so fumbling around Ilsa?"

He stiffened. "Are you watching me?"

"Whatever the reason is," she continued, "stop. First of all, it's the most awkward proposition I've ever seen, and it causes me physical pain to see it."

He stared at her in disgust. "I am not propositioning anyone!"

"Second, it doesn't matter whether you're trying to impress Ilsa or get in the good graces of Lilit. Both are such bad ideas that they'll get you killed and poor Ilsa punished."

Will opened his mouth to object, appalled on so many levels he didn't know where to begin.

A cry rang out behind them and they twisted around to see a Roven ranger trotting up the column leading a young man whose hands were bound to his saddle. The prisoner's bright, wiry red hair blazed like a flame over his panicked face. He was all elbows and knees with a thin, patchy beard. He yanked and thrashed futilely against the ropes.

With a hoarse cry, the man tried to fling himself off the horse. He started to topple to the side, his arms twisted up to the saddle horn. Sora turned to ride up beside him, shoving the man back into his saddle and holding his arm. He hurled himself from side to side, sobbing.

The ranger took up a position on the other side and they

trotted the man forward. He struggled against them for a few paces before his shoulders fell and he curled forward, the sound of sobs coming muffled from his chest.

Will followed Sora, riding with her back straight, her grip on the man's arm never wavering. They slowed when they reached the front of the clan and the ranger sent a child scurrying off to find the Torch.

Killien rode out of the crowd with Lukas flanking him and stopped, letting the rest of the clan pass them by.

"We've found the man who's been spying for the Sunn, Torch," the ranger announced, holding out a small roll of paper. "Arsen, son of Oshin. He was counting the herds. The writing matches the pages we found hidden in the spring shipment of wool for the Sunn."

Arsen yanked his thin arms against the hands holding him.

The ranger untied Arsen from the saddle and dragged him roughly to the ground. He tried to pull away, but Sora climbed down and held him as Killien dismounted. The Torch walked up to the prisoner until he stood only inches from him.

"I've done nothing wrong!" Arsen tried to pull back, but they held him in place.

Will stayed on Shadow, a few paces away.

"Nothing?" Killien's voice was quiet, and the man quailed. "We've intercepted two letters this winter being sent to the Sunn Clan, detailing the Morrow's stores and herds. The one in the wool shipment numbered our rangers. And our warriors."

Arsen's face turned a sickly white. Hal had arrived with a handful of rangers, spreading out in a circle around them. All of their faces were dark. Will barely breathed.

"No, Torch!" Arsen sputtered "I have a cousin in the Sunn Clan, his mother was captured when we were young. We send letters to each other. Just letters. He's a wool merchant, and he thinks that if the clans traded more—"

"You spied for the Sunn." Killien's face was a mask of fury.

"No! We just talked about the two clans, the things we could trade—"

"Why does a wool merchant need to know the number of our rangers? Of our warriors?"

Arsen said nothing, his eyes wide in terror.

"The Sunn have a dragon, and more stonesteeps than the rest of the Sweep put together. They force us to give them our crops, our wool, and our gold. They have no desire to trade with us." Killien set one finger on the man's chest and Arsen jerked back. "You betrayed the clan. You betrayed me."

The words cut through the morning like a slice of icy winter air. Will's hand smashed the flatbread into a lump.

Arsen's mouth opened and closed like a fish, his body quavering and he sank down to his knees. "I didn't...I don't..." His voice fell to a hoarse whisper. "Mercy, Torch!"

Killien stepped back and straightened. He took a long breath and let it out, his face settling into impassivity. His gaze looked through the man and his judgment cut across the Sweep, flat and empty. "Arsen son of Oshin is found to be an enemy of the Morrow Clan."

Arsen's body crumpled forward until he hung from the arms of Sora and the ranger. He began to weep, a bubbling, terrified sound and Will clenched the wad of food tighter in his hand. Desperate for the man, Will looked at Hal, but his face was stony. Every Roven stood severely silent, judgment against the man already cast.

Will opened up toward Killien, looking for any hesitation or pause. A wave of adamant resolve from Killien filled his chest. It was mirrored from the Roven around him.

The man's cries had quieted. Killien, without looking at him again, nodded to the ranger. Another ranger stepped forward with a small knife and sliced two braids out of Arsen's beard, pulling off the silver beads and letting the hair fall to the ground.

When he pulled a silver ring off Arsen's hand, Lukas dismounted and took it. He tilted it in the sunlight, and a watery blue stone glinted. Lukas murmured something to Killien, and at the Torch's approving nod, slipped it into his pocket.

Killien looked past the man. "Take him to the Scales. Don't let his blood fall on the grasses."

Sora dropped the man's arm with grim disapproval. She mounted her horse and rode back into the clan, her back resolutely turned to Killien. Another ranger took her place and they lifted the traitor to his feet. This time he didn't resist as they pushed him away down the caravan.

Will watched them go, straining to see where they took him until they were out of sight behind other Roven. His breakfast sat in his stomach like a stone.

Hours later, when the shadow of the caravan stretched far to the east, Will caught sight of Sora riding out of the column. She didn't say anything, just fell in beside him, her face set in a darker expression than normal.

"What will happen to the man Killien sentenced?" Will asked, his voice low.

She looked straight forward not answering for so long Will began to doubt she would.

"No one who betrays the clan is allowed to live." Her words held no emotion. "The Morrow won't taint the Sweep with the blood of a traitor, though. If one is found while the clan is in Porreen, they're drowned in the sea so their spirit is pulled away with the next tide. Here, they'll have taken him to the Scales to be burned."

"Already?" His stomach sank at the idea of the terrified man. "There's no inquiry? No trial?" One of the southern dukes had been accused of treason not long after Will had become a Keeper. The investigation process had been so extensive Alaric had brought Will to the capital to help with the questioning and recording. It had taken months. In the end the duke had been found guilty of theft, but not treason, and imprisoned.

"You saw the trial."

"But...what if he was telling the truth?"

Sora turned to him, her face unreadable. "Killien didn't believe him, and Killien is the only one that matters. Did you think the Morrow Clan tamer than others?"

The question hung in the air.

Yes, he did. When had that started? Will closed his eyes, shutting out the endless view of the Roven walking next to him, spinning his ring as his thoughts swirled. It had changed somewhere among the books and the conversation and the meals. Somewhere in the midst of discussions with Killien, the Roven had lost their fierceness in his mind.

"You come here from..." Sora paused. "Wherever you come from and think the Roven are like you. You don't know what it is like to live as one. You didn't grow up with the fear of raids and battles and constant war. Don't think that because a few Roven speak to you, that they are like you. No one here is like you. No one here wants to be."

CHAPTER SIXTEEN

ON THE TENTH DAY, from the top of a high rise, a jagged, white mountaintop rose from the horizon in the north. Within hours a handful could be seen, pristinely snowy against the sky. Will strained to see the mountains as they moved up each rise, and watched until they were out of sight as they dropped into each low place, his eyes aching for something to look at besides the grass.

The appearance of the Hoarfrost Range was the only sign that he wasn't trapped in some eternal stagnation. If they were nearing the northern edge of the Sweep, they should be at the rifts within a couple of days, and he'd made no more progress with Ilsa than to exchange quick smiles with her once through a crowd.

He'd always planned to leave the clan when they reached the rifts, but maybe he needed to convince Killien to let him stay. Maybe in the rhythm of normal life he could find more time to spend with her.

Rass found him walking beside Shadow, still stretching out the aches from sleeping on the wagon. The morning was chilly enough that Will had put on a cloak, but Rass wore the same little greyish slave shift as always, her bare feet traipsing over the grass as though it was nothing.

"Why doesn't anyone take care of you?" The words came out harsher than he'd meant them to.

Rass looked at him in surprise. "I take care of myself. And the grass helps, of course."

"Yes, the grass." He ran his hand over his mouth to block all the things that wanted to come out. "Aren't you cold?"

"No," she said carelessly. "Yesterday was so warm I can still feel it."

"I wish I could keep track of yesterday's heat." He handed her the piece of flatbread he'd been saving.

"Can't you?" She took it and squinted up at him. "Not even with your magic?"

"What?" he asked too quickly.

"That magic that you use. Like when I first met you."

His denial stuck in his throat. "What?" he managed again.

She gave him a little exasperated look. "At the festival you did something so the Roven didn't pay attention to you. The magic swirled around you like a sparkly mist."

Will's heart felt like it was being squeezed by her tiny little hands. He opened up toward her, looking for some sense of suspicion, but she was just as cheery and curious as ever. He gathered some energy from the grass reflexively, without any clear plan of what to do with it.

Her eyes widened and her gaze flickered at the air around him.

"You're doing it again," she whispered.

He stopped, staring down at her, his heart pounding against his ribs like it was the wrong size for his chest. He let the energy go, letting it seep out of him and back into the world unused.

Rass glanced around with a disappointed sigh.

"You *saw* that? With your eyes?"

She looked at him, confused. "What other way is there to see?"

There was magic that was visible. Techniques where the *vitalle* glowed as it moved. But he'd just been gathering energy. No one could see that. The Keepers talked about seeing *vitalle*, but usually it wasn't actual sight. It was a sense—like locating something with sound. Another Keeper could have sensed that he was drawing more energy into himself, but he'd never heard of anyone who could actually see it.

A dozen thoughts chased each other around Will's mind.

She could reveal him to the Morrow.

Could she manipulate the energy?

Had she told anyone?

She could *see* it!

His fear kept being shoved aside by excitement. Her light hair, her blue eyes—could she be from Queensland? She didn't look like it. With her wide eyes and her angular face, she looked foreign, even for a foreigner. Could she still be trained as a Keeper, though? She was so young to have any powers.

"Where are you from, Rass?"

She gave a little sigh and looked at him exasperatedly. "The grass."

Will glanced around. The nearest Roven drove wagons and talked to each other, their voices muffled by the creaks of the wheels.

"Do you see magic often?"

Rass shrugged. "The Morrow put it on their ugly dirt buildings. And they wear it on things like rings. They put little bits of it onto their clothes, but that's faded and weak. They don't really have any strong magic." She cocked her head and looked up at Will with her huge eyes the same bright blue as the sky. "I think you might, though."

With a smile she started humming, hopping from one foot to the next.

Will considered her for a long moment, his fingers moving to his ring, spinning it slowly. "Have you told any Roven that I have magic?"

"I don't talk to the Roven."

"Not ever?"

"They don't like me."

They walked along for a few breaths in silence. "Thank you. For not telling them."

She looked at him curiously. "Where did you learn to do magic?"

"At my home. There are other people there who can, and they taught me."

"Is there anyone there like me?"

Will shook his head. "Me and a bunch of older men. But we've been looking for someone like you for a very long time."

"Are you as good at magic as you are at telling stories?"

"Not really."

"Why not?"

Will thought back to Keeper Gerone's constant prodding. "My teacher thought I had a motivation problem."

"Stories are a good thing to be good at," she assured him.

"Rass, can you do anything with magic?"

She opened her mouth to answer. Before she could say anything her brow dove down into a frown. "The mean lady is coming."

Sora rode down the caravan toward them and Rass scampered off into the grass. Will watched the little slave girl go with a strange mixture of worry and fondness. She looked stronger. Her legs and arms had lost some of their gauntness. But as she left, it felt like she pulled something away with her, leaving him feeling more vulnerable.

Will mounted Shadow as Sora came up to him.

They'd fallen into a pattern of sorts. Usually not long after the caravan had started, while the duskiness of dawn still spread across the never-ending grass, she would come by and either bring him to Killien, or ride beside him. If she hadn't arrived by the time the sun was completely above the Scales, Will knew she wouldn't come. Some days she would answer questions about the Roven, but he'd given up asking her any personal questions days ago. Those were met with biting sarcasm.

It was the days where every question was met with a silent

scowl that he didn't know what to do with. Because on those days she would ride beside him for hours barely speaking, showing no interest in him, but not leaving.

He'd asked if she was on some sort of guard duty, sent by Killien to keep track of him, but she only responded with a scathing remark about not being Killien's guard dog. On those days Will pulled out a book and read, letting her stew in silence and trying not to think about her too much.

But during the days she was gone Will found himself watching for her, and this morning he felt a surprising amount of pleasure as she rode up.

"Good morning," he offered, testing the waters.

Her face was grave and she nodded absently to him. "Killien wants you."

Will motioned for her to lead the way. "Did you find anything interesting out ranging?"

A flicker of something distasteful crossed her face, but she didn't answer.

"Are you still looking for signs of frost goblins?" The urgency of the search had faded from his mind. It had been days since he'd heard Killien mention it, and while the Roven still built fires around the edges of the caravan at night, most of them seemed to be out of habit, not fear.

"No," she answered dryly. "We thought we'd just stop looking and pretend we'd never heard reports of them."

"I just...no one seems worried about them anymore."

"Anyone intelligent is."

Will looked out over the grasslands. "Have you found any?"

Sora gave a single nod.

"How many?"

"Three."

Will stared at her. "Were you alone? Are you alri—?"

"I don't want to talk about it," she interrupted his fumbling questions.

Will closed his mouth and looked around the Sweep, feeling suddenly exposed on the wide open grass. "Should I be worried?"

Sora gave a short laugh. "We should all be worried."

She didn't elaborate, and Will didn't push. He watched Lilit's wagon as they passed near it, and while he could see movement within, the interior was too shadowed to see if it was Ilsa.

When Killien came into view, Will turned to Sora. "How come you stay with the Morrow?" He pitched his voice low so only she could hear.

Sora started and looked at him as though she'd forgotten he was there. Her eyes flickered away from him and rested on the Torch, her face unreadable. "Killien pays me well."

Surprisingly, he couldn't sense any sarcasm in her answer. "That's very mercenary of you. But wouldn't your own people benefit from your skills?"

"My people have enough hunters."

"So, what?" The irritation from her terse answers rose to the surface. "You're here because you're not special enough among your own tribe?"

Sora let out a harsh laugh and turned her horse away. "That was never the problem."

He watched her ride off, wondering why he'd bothered to ask.

Turning back toward Killien, he tried to push her out of his mind. The man had been growing more irritable lately. He'd stayed distantly polite to Will, spending a few minutes questioning him about a Baylonian duke Will had written about. But he'd been short with the rangers who reported to him and snapped at Lukas for riding too close. Sini and Rett had taken to riding a little farther back.

Today, though, when he approached, the Torch was in an animated discussion with Lukas, both their faces bright as Killien clapped the slave on the back, and Lukas closed up a book. Even making eye contact with Will didn't totally dampen Lukas's spirits, and he fell away from the Torch, leaving room for Will to approach.

Killien greeted Will with an enthusiasm that was almost overwhelming. "Will! I don't feel like I've properly thanked you for all the writing you've done for me on this trip. Thank the black queen you showed up in Porreen when you did."

Will gave him a bow, his fist pressed to his chest. "It's been my pleasure. I should thank you for the books you've shared."

Killien waved off his thanks. "No, you deserve a gift. Tell me, what payment do you want? A book?" He motioned to Will's hand. "Another gold ring?"

Something glinted blue on one of Killien's fingers—the ring they'd taken from the traitor sat between Killien's other rings, and the light from the blue burning stone in it was visible even in the sunshine. He could see *vitalle* in several of his rings, actually. Maybe Killien's actually held magic.

Will shook his head and opened up to the Torch. A wide undercurrent of satisfaction and pleasure flowed into Will. Whatever Killien was happy about, it was strong.

"There must be something you'd like from the Morrow."

Yes. Will kept his eyes away from Lilit's wagon.

"There is one thing." Will paused. "Would you consider selling me one of your slaves?"

Killien raised an eyebrow. "I didn't take you for a slaveholder."

Will forced a smile. "We all have our secrets."

Killien let out a short laugh. "We do. But you haven't done nearly enough writing for me to earn a slave." He looked calculatingly at Will. "It would take three month's wages for most Roven to buy a slave, and that only gets them a mediocre one." He paused. "Although if you're talking about that tiny girl you seem so fond of, we could come up with a less expensive agreement."

Killien knew about Rass?

Will's pulse quickened.

It wasn't freeing Ilsa like he needed to do, but freeing Rass was a good first step. "Her name is Rass." He tried to keep the disgust out of his voice at the next question. "How much would she cost?"

Killien rubbed his thumb across his lips, watching Will closely. "Do you read ancient runes? I have some I need translated, and that would be worth quite a bit to me."

You've got the wrong Keeper for that. "I'm familiar with some runes, but I'm not an expert."

Killien considered this answer. "Where did you learn them?"

"When I was twelve, I moved to a place with a library." The first time he'd stepped into the library at the Keepers Stronghold, it had taken his breath away. Floor after floor of books. "The man who kept the books had some with ancient runes"—which Gerone had constantly and unsuccessfully tried to get Will interested in—"which he loved, but I was never terribly good at."

"How big was the library?"

"To my eyes, it was enormous." He glanced at Killien. "You won't like this, but the largest library I ever saw was the royal library in Queenstown."

Killien's brow darkened. "How big is it?"

"The main room is as big as the Square in Porreen."

The Torch's eyebrows rose.

"And there are a dozen smaller rooms off of it, all filled with books."

Killien was silent for a long moment. "That would be something to see."

"You should come there with me, we'll take a trip into Queensland." Will motioned to the notch in the Scales that was almost next to them. "It's only two or three days past Kollman Pass."

The Torch laughed. "Even a library that big isn't a strong enough draw."

"Is there a particular reason you hate Queensland more than other countries?" Will tried to keep his tone merely curious, while he focused on Killien's emotions. "I've never totally understood the Roven's animosity."

"Queensland drove us out of our homeland and forced us to live on the Sweep."

He chose his next words as carefully as possible. "That happened a very long time ago. When you talk about Queensland, the animosity feels...fresher."

A jab of irritation lanced across Killien's satisfaction, and he studied Will for several heartbeats.

"If that was too personal of a question," Will said, "I apologize."

"It's hardly a secret. You know that the warriors of the Morrow went with Mallon when he attacked Queensland?"

"I heard a story about it my first night in Porreen. I remember there was a giant."

"Yervant tells the story every year because their company only lost one battle during the entire war. And they were winning that one too, until a Keeper showed up."

"How many men did the Morrow lose?"

"Many." A sharp grief cut into Killien's emotions. "Among them my uncle, Andro, who had been my closest advisor, and my cousin Adaom, who was like a brother to me." Killien turned a hard gaze toward the Scales. "They were the only family I had left. And a Keeper burned them alive."

Killien's grief and vengeance flowed through Will's chest and he almost shoved them out. But the emotions were so familiar, he let them stay, mirroring his own losses, resonating in the deepest part of himself.

"Adaom was Lilit's older brother. She idolized him. It's why she hates you so much." Killien looked slightly apologetic. "And why she always will. You look too much like you're from Queensland for her to see anything else."

They rode in silence until Will felt Killien's emotions settle. That at least explained Lilit's animosity. And why a peace offering of a story wouldn't be nearly enough. Maybe nothing would be enough. How would he ever get Ilsa away from her?

Needing something else to think about, Will asked. "Why did Mallon attack? To Queensland it seemed unprovoked. Did they do something I'm unaware of?"

Killien looked at him in surprise. "Because it was personal." At Will's blank look, he added, "Mallon was from Queensland."

CHAPTER SEVENTEEN

Will's mouth dropped open. "What?"

Killien's gaze turned piercing and he nodded slowly. "Mallon came to the Sweep as a child, ten years before my father was Torch. His father had debts, and to pay them, the duke sold his children to the Sweep."

Will stared at him, stunned. "Sold? They don't do that in Queensland. It's unlawful to sell slaves."

Killien let out a laugh. "And so you think it doesn't happen? Mallon was sold to the Morrow, in fact, when my grandfather was Torch. He was with us for two years and already training to be a stonesteep. Already promising to be stronger than any we'd seen." His face sobered. "Before Kachig the Bloodless took him from us."

Mallon was from Queensland?

"You thought Mallon was Roven?" Killien asked.

Will nodded. "Everyone does."

"He had black hair," the Torch pointed out.

"That does seem like a clue right now," Will admitted. "Although until I came to the Sweep, I didn't know *every* Roven had red hair. I just thought a lot of you did. I've never heard from anyone that Mallon wasn't Roven."

An idea snagged in Will's mind. "How long ago did Mallon come to the Sweep?"

"Fifty years ago."

Will's grip tightened on the reins. The fact that there were no Keepers younger than Will wasn't the only gap. Historically Keepers were born every five to ten years. Between Will and Alaric was a twelve year gap, but that length wasn't unheard of. The bigger question had always been that between Alaric and Mikal, who was seventy-one, the gap was over twenty-five years. The space between them was generally thought to have belonged to at least two Keepers who, it was assumed, had died during childhood, before their abilities were awakened. But if Mallon was born fifty-some years ago, and came from Queensland, with powers like he had—he would fit in that gap.

Mallon should have been a Keeper.

The thought struck an odd note. Keeper Mallon, puttering around the Stronghold with the other old men, browsing the library, wearing a black robe.

It was too far-fetched. What were the chances that the one child of his time who should've ended up a Keeper had been enslaved to the Roven?

Still, the Keepers hadn't known of any children born during that time with abilities.

Until now.

"Someone in Queensland knows," Killien scoffed. "The people in power know. The Queen. The Keepers."

Will clenched his teeth down on the answer that he was positive they didn't.

"They're just keeping it quiet," the Torch continued. "They wouldn't want their people to know it was one of their own trying to kill them. Better to blame the nomads, right?"

"He came with an army of Roven."

"We didn't have a choice," Killien objected. "Mallon gathered the clan Torches together and told them he was going to conquer

Queensland and required our warriors. He said if we helped, he'd give us some of the land."

"Did anyone refuse?"

Killien looked at him incredulously. "You understand what he was capable of. No one refused who valued their lives or the lives of their clans. We were commanded to gain the support of our people and send all our troops."

"All of them?"

Killien nodded, his face dark. "Every man between fifteen and sixty. And to send weekly shipments of food and supplies."

Will looked away from Killien, letting his eyes run over the Scales. An uncomfortable level of sympathy for Killien vied with an illogical guilt that Mallon was from Queensland. Will shifted his cloak, pulling more of it around himself to block out the little fingers of cool morning air wriggling in through the gaps.

A half-dozen rangers appeared over a rise to the east and Killien studied them for a moment. "I'll send Lukas with the runes I'd like you to translate," he said. "When we reach the rifts, we'll discuss the little slave girl again."

Will took it as a dismissal and left, conflicting thoughts about the Roven and Killien and Mallon butting against each other in his mind. And the idea of buying Rass's freedom was bittersweet. Certainly he'd love to take her away from the Roven, but she was small enough he could have snuck her out. It was Ilsa he needed to get to.

When he reached the book wagon, he found Rett driving it. Will gave the slave a friendly nod and the man nodded back. There was a general sadness about him this morning.

"Looks like a big storm is coming." Will nodded toward the clouds piling up on the horizon.

"I don't like thunder." Rett kept his attention forward. Ahead of them was another wagon, loaded with baskets and sacks. And ahead of that one, another. The clan moved forward doggedly, each person and animal and wagon following the one ahead of it with no real need for thought. But Rett concentrated anyway, his hands gentle on the reins, his eyes determined and sad. Next to him sat his lumpy bag of heatstones.

Will couldn't quite figure out the man. He was older than Will by a few years, and his mind didn't seem slow as much as... distracted. As though there was too much going on and the simplest tasks required enormous concentration.

"I'm Will."

Rett glanced toward him. "I know."

"You drive the wagon well, Rett. Some of the others aren't careful about what they're doing."

Rett shook his head disapprovingly. "The Torch's books are very important."

Will agreed, and when Rett kept his focus forward, he rode around to the back of the wagon, and dismounted. Walking behind it, he moved the oilcloth out of the way and opened the red bag of his books. He pulled several out, laying them across the back of the wagon. He'd already read most of them. The only two left were genealogies, and he couldn't quite bring himself to commit the rest of the day to reading something that boring. Stuffing them all back in the bag, Will tugged at the leather straps cinching the bag shut.

The wagon creaked over the uneven ground and the bag and the boxes shifted haphazardly, making him feel slightly off balance. Will glanced up at Rett, but the man was facing forward, his shoulders slumped. He pushed the oilcloth farther to the side and opened the bag with Lukas's books, slipping out *Methods of Transference* again, even if there was nothing left to learn from it.

A rumble of thunder came from the storm clouds and Will flipped the book closed. He shoved it back into Lukas's bag and put it back where it belonged.

He was setting his own bag back in its place when the wagon wheel nearest him slammed into a hole and the entire wagon jarred to the side. Rett's bag of heatstones tumbled to the side. The wagon jolted forward again and the box in front of Will slid, its edge tipping off the back of the wagon.

Will grabbed for the box, staggering forward with the wagon hearing the thunks of dozens of heatstones falling next to Rett. Will shoved at the box, trying to push it back into place, but his own bag of books toppled down into the space where the box belonged.

Shoving his shoulder against the box, Will stretched around it with his other hand, grabbing a handful of the red bag and yanking it out of the way. He'd almost cleared it when the bag jerked to a stop, the leather strap snagged on something he couldn't see. With a curse, Will wrenched the bag toward him. The wood cracked and the bag slid clear. With a shove, he pushed the box into its place.

A rumble of thunder rolled from the dark clouds piling up to the north and Will climbed up on to the wagon to see what he'd broken. In the front of the wagon, Rett was focused on picking heatstones up and tucking them back into his bag.

A jagged piece of wood was caught in the straps of the red bag, and behind the box, one of the boards of the wagon bed had split, leaving a gap two fingers wide in the bottom of the wagon. He grabbed the broken sliver of wood and stretched around the box to put it back in place. It wouldn't be fixed, exactly, but he couldn't just leave a hole in the bottom of Killien's wagon. Just before he placed the wood in, a flash of blue shimmered from the hole.

Will glanced up at Rett, but he was looking forward. Will leaned farther over the box. There, just visible through the crack was a piece of grey oil cloth.

Why put oilcloth under the books? A bit of it stuck up through the hole and Will tried to stuff it back in. The cloth shifted and he caught a glimpse of blue leather, glimmering with silver letters.

Will's hand clutched the sliver of wood.

It was the book—the one Lukas had bought from Borto behind the wayfarers' wagons.

He pushed the cloth out of the way, the jagged edge of the

wood cutting into his finger until he could read the title. *The Gleaning of Souls.*

He pulled the board farther, feeling the wood groan, and leaned over. Just at the edge of the shadow he saw the author.

Kachig the Bloodless.

In the center of the cover, where the silver medallion had been, there was only a darker blue circle of leather, rough and scarred. Will stared at the disfigured cover, confused for a moment before realizing Killien had pulled the metal off the book to keep it safe from frost goblins. Will tested the boards next to the broken one, but nothing moved. The book was well sealed in the base of the wagon.

Thunder rumbled overhead again. The round pile of clouds were surging closer, like some kind of flower that kept blooming, swell after swell of whiteness piling on top of each other. And underneath the whiteness, the Sweep was cast into dark shadows slanted with distant rain.

"The books should be covered," Rett called back to him, worried.

Will let the board fall back into place, then shoved the box of books back on top of it before covering everything with the oilcloth. His fingers itched to pull it all back apart and grab the book. Instead, he climbed down off the wagon and mounted Shadow again.

The reins stung against his hand and he looked down to see a gash in his finger from the wood. Will cast out to the Sweep. The *vitalle* of the grass was no longer little pinpoints of energy, it now covered the ground with thin strands, like humming, shimmering fur.

He found the rough edges of his cut by the tangle of his own *vitalle* crowding around the wound, beginning the long, slow process of healing, which it would work at for days. The sheer amount of energy expended in healing made anything more than small cuts nearly impossible to heal quickly. Funneling the energy from the grass into his finger, he pressed it toward the cut, bolstering the healing, drawing the deepest part of the gash back together, working his way toward the surface until new skin spread across his finger in a slash of paleness.

He rode behind the book wagon for the next several hours, reading and pondering ways to get Kachig's book out of Killien's wagon.

It wasn't Lukas who brought the runes for him to translate around midday, it was Sini.

When she appeared, Rett stood up in the still moving wagon and started to climb down. "Where are you going? I'll go with you."

"No, Rett." She pulled up alongside him, speaking gently. "We'll sit together at dinner. You need to drive the wagon and keep the books safe."

"Oh." He stopped and sat down slowly. "I forgot. Thank you."

She gave him an encouraging nod and once he was seated, rode back toward Will, carrying a roll of paper. Her face lost the serious expression it often carried around Rett and settled into something curious, but cautious as she got closer.

"Is Rett…?" Will began quietly, looking for the right words.

Sini glanced back at the big slave, her face turning pensive. "There was an accident a long time ago. They say he almost died. I don't think he remembers it, but he has trouble remembering a lot of things. He's always distracted by things inside his head."

"Do you take care of him?"

She shrugged. "He doesn't need much care, just reminders sometimes. And he's funny and kind." She brushed a bit of blond hair back behind her ear, nervously. "We like the stories you've been telling at night. Both of us knew the one you told in Porreen, about Tomkin and the dragon."

"Where did you hear it?"

"We're both from Queensland," she answered.

Will tried to ignore the complicated surge of pity and anger that thought evoked, and tried to find something to say.

But she didn't seem to need a response. "How many stories do you know?"

"I could tell you a different one every day until you turned a hundred."

She gave him a dubious look. "There aren't that many stories in the world."

"There are enough stories in the world that each of us could hear a different one every day until we turned a hundred, and we still wouldn't run out."

She considered this, biting her lip. With an almost absent expression she held the rolled papers out towards Will. He took them with thanks.

She lowered her voice and glanced around. "I'm glad you're telling stories from Queensland." With a quick smile, she turned her horse away.

Will watched her go, a convoluted tangle of emotions crowding into him. Killien might give him Rass if he could read these runes, and he'd find a way to free Ilsa, but how was he going to walk away and leave a girl like Sini here? She should be at home with her parents, growing closer to adulthood every day, complaining that they didn't give her enough freedom. Not trapped here with no hope of it. It didn't matter whether she seemed to be treated well or not, she was still a slave. The list of people he wanted to rescue from the Roven kept growing.

He unrolled the papers and his stomach sank for a completely different reason.

He'd been hoping that when Killien said "ancient runes," what he'd really meant was "old fashioned runes." A more decorated version of modern ones. But these runes were old. The deep, original-magic-workers-creating-a-language-to-hold-power old. The Keepers had plenty of books that used them. And all the Keepers could read them. To some extent.

For Will, that extent did not include being able to do more than narrow down their general meaning to a marginally more-narrow meaning.

Will's eyes trailed over the page, sliding past the precisely written, highly complex shapes.

The topmost rune was something watery. Yes. Watery.

Will tilted the paper slightly to the side.

The next was definitely something about death. Except the corner of it was odd.

The third had entirely too many pieces. He pulled it closer, trying to make out the thin lines of extra strokes drawn into the bottom.

Chicken.

It said chicken.

Will let the paper fall back against the saddle.

The translation was "dead water chicken."

That seemed unlikely.

He scrubbed his fingers through his hair, scanning the rest of the page. There were a dozen different runes. Each complex, each nonsensical.

Will closed his eyes.

If Rass's freedom depended on this, she was never going to get away from the Morrow.

The day dragged inexorably on. Will returned, time and again to the runes, dissecting them, rearranging them, turning them on their heads. None of it was comprehensible.

The Morrow crept slowly north through the brownish green pelt of the grasslands, the sun moved slowly west through an empty, faded blue sky, and Will made no progress at all with his translations. Which began to tie his gut into a small knot of worry.

Rass appeared briefly, tugging on his foot to bring him down so she could show him the chain of flowers made from stalks and little blooms with greenish-yellow ray-like petals.

"I made it for you," she said, seriously, holding it out toward his head.

Will leaned forward and let her set it on him. When he straightened, she nodded approvingly. Her face was so much less gaunt, her arms less skeletal. She'd lost the hollow sort of look in her eyes.

He reached into his bag and pulled out a wide salt flat and handed it to her. She must have been eating almost nothing before if the little food he was able to share with her was making such a difference. She grinned and took a big bite.

"Do I look kingly?" He lifted his chin and gazed over the grass ahead of them.

She giggled. "Like the King of the Grass." And with that she ran off, stopping occasionally to yank something out of the ground.

Will watched her run, the knot of worry growing. There was no way he was leaving her here.

Ahead of him the peaks grew taller, connecting with each other until the entire northern horizon was blocked by the imposing wall of the Hoarfrost Range. He found himself staring at them more and more often, spinning his ring. His mind avoiding the impossible runes, avoiding thinking about Ilsa and Rass and Sini.

The sun wasn't remotely close to the horizon when the caravan stopped. There didn't seem to be a cistern, and Will was caught between wondering why they'd stopped and if he could come up with a good enough reason to go near Ilsa when he heard the news that Lilit's time had come. There was no reason in the world that would get him close to Ilsa tonight. Will settled down on the back of the book wagon, glad to be able to sit still during the daylight and write for Killien.

The sun had sunk low in the west when Sora rode up next to him. He hadn't seen her since that morning, and her mood had not improved. She sat down beside him on the back of the book wagon with a curt nod. He waited for a minute or two before leaning over and whispering, "Are you mad at me? Or someone else?"

A small smile cracked through her scowl.

"Good." He sat back. "It's nice when you spread your anger out among other people."

This earned him no response at all.

"Have you been doing something more riveting than walking north through grass?"

"Helping Killien." She didn't look toward him, and by the way she said the Torch's name, Will didn't have to wonder who she was angry with.

Will fiddled with the page of the book a moment, waiting for her to continue. She didn't and he let the silence go as long as he could. "Did you finish whatever he needed?"

"Yes." The word came out as almost a hiss, and Will leaned back slightly to be farther from her line of sight.

"Sometimes you're terrifying," he said.

She closed her eyes and let out a tired sort of laugh. When she opened them, her face was weary. The sun was low enough that the air had turned golden, and the copper of Sora's braid caught at the light, reflecting strands of dark red.

"Why don't you go home, Sora?" he asked. "Get out of these infernal grasses. Leave the Morrow to whatever Roven things they want to do, and go do something…anything else?"

She sank over against the wall of the wagon. "Because it's never that simple."

Will couldn't argue with that. "Well then don't go home. Go somewhere else." He paused for a moment. "Come with me when I leave."

She turned to him with an incredulous look. "And go where?"

Will shrugged. "Off the Sweep. There are a lot of interesting countries just over those mountains."

"When is it that you're leaving?" Her face was back to being unreadable.

"Once we reach the rifts, I suppose." Or he freed Ilsa. And Rass. He felt a cold doubt in his stomach at Lukas's warning that

Killien already owned him. But a sudden realization struck. "Can you leave?"

"Of course I can." The scowl was back on her face.

"Does the work Killien asks you to do usually make you this mad?"

"No. This was a first."

She stopped talking and Will let the conversation end. The gnaw of doubt that had crept into his stomach was still there, and he tried to push it away.

Several minutes passed before Sora glanced over at him. "You have dead flowers on your head."

Will laughed, pulling off the crown. The dried stalks of the flower chain broke where he touched it, and one of the little blooms, which had curled in on itself into a brownish cage of withered petals, snapped off and rolled down his leg and into the grass.

"I'm King of the Grass." The whole dry chain crumbled and fell.

Her mouth quirked up in a smile. "You should get a better crown."

Will brushed his fingers through his hair, dislodging bits of dead flower. "I should get a better kingdom."

Sora didn't seem inclined to talk any more, so Will went back to flipping through the book, before the last of the daylight trickled away. When it was too dark to see the page, Will flipped the book closed and pointed out that if they didn't find Hal soon, they might not find any dinner. Sora gave a "hmm" that sounded like an agreement and mounted her horse, turning it in to the clan. Will climbed up on Shadow to follow when shouts rang out from somewhere nearby. A rider tore toward them.

It was Ilsa.

"Sora!" she cried. "Killien needs you! The baby has come, but the Flame—she's bleeding and it won't stop. She is losing her strength. The Torch begs you to come!" Her face was drawn, her eyes worried.

Sora's horse danced away from Ilsa's mare. "What does he think I can do?"

"He asks..." Ilsa hesitated, her eyes flashing toward Will for just a breath before facing Sora again, her brow creased with uneasiness. "For your blessing."

Sora's face hardened into stone. "He's a fool."

"She's dying, Sora." Ilsa voice was quiet, pleading.

Sora pressed her eyes shut.

"The Torch begs you."

With a growl torn from somewhere unbearably deep, Sora spurred her horse forward. She and Ilsa raced toward the front of the clan. Shadow, jolted into action by the others, raced after them.

CHAPTER EIGHTEEN

SHADOW GALLOPED after Sora and Ilsa to a small tent near the front of the caravan.

What did Killien think Sora could do that a healer couldn't?

Ilsa swung off her horse and hurried into the tent. Sora sat still in her saddle gripping the reins.

Killien rushed to her. "Please!" He stood at Sora's knee like a supplicant.

"You know I can't help her," Sora hissed at the Torch.

"She's dying." Killien reached up to clench the bottom of her shirt. "It can't hurt to pray."

He wanted her to pray? Will leaned forward trying to see Sora's face, trying to understand what was happening.

A low, torn moan came from inside the tent and both Killien and Sora flinched. With a curt nod, Sora shoved his hands off her and swung down from her horse.

Fixing the Torch with a look of pure hatred, she whispered, "You and I are finished."

Without waiting for a response, she ducked into the tent.

Killien sank to his knees and dropped his head into his hands. Will sat awkward in the saddle, unable to make sense of either Killien's request or Sora's response.

Another low moan tore through the night and Killien shuddered. Will cast out toward the tent and felt three people's *vitalle* blazing like watchfires. A low, smoldering form lay at their feet.

Lilit had very little time left.

Will waited to see if Sora did anything with *vitalle* in the tent, but nothing happened. He climbed quietly off Shadow. Skirting around Killien, Will drew in some energy from the grass and wrapped it around himself like a cloak, infusing the influence spell with the idea that he was not worth noticing.

Will reached the tent door, and when none of the Roven at the nearby fire objected, he stepped inside. A lantern cast dim light on Sora and Ilsa kneeling next to Lilit's still form. Sini leaned over a basin of red water, washing blood off her arms. Tears traced tracks down her cheeks, and she dashed at them with her shoulder.

He cut off the influence spell, letting it dissolve and Sora gave him a quick, surprised glance.

"The healers gave her mutherswort," Sini whispered to Sora, "but she still bleeds from somewhere deep inside." Her voice broke. "It's too much to stop."

"The child?" Sora asked softly.

"A healthy boy."

All the fury was gone from Sora's face. With her jaw clenched, she shifted the blanket covering Lilit's legs. Beneath them, everything was soaked with blood. "Find some clean blankets," she said firmly to Ilsa, who hurried out of the tent without glancing at Will. "And fresh water," she added to Sini with a tight smile at the girl.

Sini nodded and left.

"What does Lilit need?" Will whispered.

"Strength she doesn't have." Sora gently lay the blankets back down.

Sora sank back, her hand resting on Lilit's stomach. She bowed her head and began whispering words Will couldn't understand. He cast out toward her, waiting for…something.

The words rolled out of her mouth rhythmic and heartfelt.

Killien brought her here to pray?

Will knelt down next to Lilit's head, setting a hand on her damp forehead and casting out. Her *vitalle* lay weak and thin, like tired coals of a dying fire. The little energy she had surged against the tattered edges of a tear deep inside her womb. She was weak enough that the blood flowed through it slowly.

He drew all the energy he could find from the grass beneath them. It wasn't nearly enough. If he took from the grass past the tent, it would leave a difficult to explain, enormous dead spot, and it still might not be enough. Casting out farther, he found the blazing energy of the fire and drew in as much *vitalle* as he could. It poured into him, and he felt the fire growing dim. Someone outside called for more fuel for the flames. Hopefully it would come soon, because this wouldn't be enough.

As gently as he could, he set his hands on the sides of Lilit's head and slowly funneled the energy into her, offering the *vitalle* her body needed to heal itself. Will leaned down near her ear. In a low, calm voice, he began.

"The night the nineteenth Torch of the Morrow Clan was born, the winds of the Sweep blew like a dragon, flattening the grass and driving evil omens before it."

A sound near the door caught his attention. Killien stood there, watching Will sharply, a dangerous glint in his eyes. Sora was still bowed, whispered words pouring out of her in a rhythm like a prayer. Lilit groaned quietly.

"Lilit, Flame of the Morrow," Will continued, pressing more *vitalle* into her, "had fought and bled, until her strength was almost spent."

Slowly the wound drew together. He drew in more from the fire, funneling everything into Lilit's body.

"But the Flame of the Morrow was not like the grass, she did not bend and bow before the wind."

Lilit took in a deeper breath and Killien sank down past to her feet, shrinking back from the horror.

"She reached down into the Sweep," Will continued, "down into the grasses, into where the power of her people lay."

Lilit opened her eyes and a spasm of pain flashed across her face. Sora placed both her hands on the Flame's stomach and continued whispering. Will cast out toward Sora, but she still did nothing more than pray.

"The Flame of the Morrow reached into the place where all life begins," he whispered. "Into the place where all life goes when it is worn out with living."

Lilit grimaced and shifted. The wound was almost healed, the blood barely flowing, but the fire was almost out. "She reached that place," he said, offering some of his own energy while casting out desperately to find more, "and she found the strength to fight on."

Killien stayed drawn back, his eyes locked on Lilit's face.

She was pulling energy from Will too quickly. He couldn't quite stop the bleeding. The blood kept wanting to push the tear open again. He cast out toward the grass past the tent. It would be impossible to hide a huge swath of dead grass, but he didn't see another choice.

Outside the tent the fire flared with new fuel and Will grabbed the *vitalle* from it, pouring it into Lilit.

And finally the last of the wound closed.

He waited a moment, but everything held. She was terribly weak, but the immediate danger was over. Lilit groaned and twisted and Will let his hands fall off the sides of her head.

Sini returned, bringing an armful of blankets. She lifted the filthy one off Lilit and began to clear away the soaked ones. Will sank back, his palms aching.

Sini grabbed Sora's arm. "The bleeding—" She shoved blankets out of the way and called for clean water.

Killien scrambled forward, clinging to Lilit's hand. "The bleeding stopped?"

Sora shoved herself up and stepped back, her face white. She pressed a trembling hand to her mouth, staring at Lilit. She looked at Killien, her eyes wide, shaking her head quickly. "I didn't..."

Without finishing, she spun and shoved her way into the night.

More healers rushed in, and Will slid back against the tent wall. Killien bent over his wife whose eyes were cracked open. Her *vitalle* was still more like embers than flames, but it wasn't pouring out of her any longer. Will slipped outside.

The wind whipped against him. The world had fallen into darkness and the fire burning near the tent, now blazing, lit only a small area. His feet dragged against the ground and his arms hung limp and heavy at his side. Shadow's saddle horn stung against his sore palm as he heaved himself up and headed toward his own wagon.

The stirrings of the clan woke Will the next morning while the sky was still a faded yellow-grey. He pulled the blanket up over his face and stayed in the darkness, the rough wool warm against his face. His arms were heavy, and his eyes felt like someone had poured sand into them. He stretched his hands experimentally, but his palms were only slightly sore.

A voice called out, proclaiming the son of Torch had been born. The Roven around him let out cries of celebration, and Will shoved himself up, waiting to hear anything about Lilit. But the red-bearded man announced the caravan would move at midday, and moved on.

As the morning wore on, the ramifications of the night before grew heavier. The clan was abuzz with the news of the Torch's son, Sevien. He heard enough to know that Lilit lived, although she was weak. But did Killien know what Will had done? The Torch had focused only on Sora. What had he thought she'd done?

Questions spun tumultuously in his mind and his stomach

hardened into a cold knot. Someone must have noticed what he'd done. A trio of rangers trotted toward him and Will's heart slammed into his throat. But they rode past without a word.

He scrubbed his hands through his hair. If Killien knew he'd done magic, Will would already be busy explaining himself. Which meant Killien had a new baby, and a wife who had almost died, and Will hadn't come by to show he'd even noticed.

Will pushed himself up and trudged toward the Torch. When he reached Lilit's tent, he found Killien surrounded by Roven, holding a small bundle. There was no sign of Sora or Hal or Ilsa. Will worked his way through the crowd until he reached the Torch, his heart pounding so hard in his throat he could hardly swallow.

Killien turned and Will's chest clamped down on his heart until the Torch's face broke into a grin. "Come see the future Torch!"

A scrunched face with a shock of red hair peeked out of the blankets.

"He's definitely Roven," Will said, leaning closer and trying to look calm. The baby was asleep, his brow drawn in a little scowl as though he were put out by all the activity.

"He is indeed," Killien said. "He's got a cry that will wake the dead."

"Congratulations. He looks like a fine boy." Will tried to keep his voice calm for the next question. "How is your wife?"

Killien's smile faded slightly. "She's weak. But the healers think she is out of danger. They say it is safe for her to ride in the wagons. We reach the rifts in a couple days and she'll rest better then."

Will nodded and breathed out a long breath. "Good."

"Last night in the tent, I heard you telling her that story," he said, and Will tried not to flinch. "I appreciate what you did." Killien set one hand on Will's shoulder. "Lilit doesn't remember your words, but I do. And I think they gave her some strength."

Will pressed his fist to his chest. "If I helped in any way, I am glad."

When he looked up, Killien was still studying him. With a curt nod, he said, "The little slave girl you wanted, when you leave, you may take her with you."

Will stared at the Torch. "Really?"

"But I'd still love to know what those runes say," Killien added, turning to a healer who'd just arrived.

Relief washed over Will. He could take Rass with him. And Killien had no idea what he'd done last night. He watched the Torch walk toward Lilit, wondering what he thought had happened in that tent.

There was no sign of Ilsa, so he headed back to his wagon and collapsed back down.

The day passed in an uncomfortable sort of loneliness. Will fell asleep in the wagon, which helped curb some of his exhaustion, until the caravan rolled out around midday. He caught one glimpse of Hal riding toward the herds, but no glimpses at all of Sora.

Huge storm clouds built up along the western horizon dropping the Sweep into an early shadow that night. He wrapped his cloak around himself, but the rising wind tugged at it like greedy fingers.

"This storm will be big," a little voice said behind him.

He turned to see Rass, and a blaze of affection rose in him for the girl. She looked...healthy. Still too thin, but healthier. He found a pile of flatbread and dried meat at a nearby fire and sat on the wagon, Rass's bare feet dangling down as she chattered at him.

"Rass," he said when she had quieted for a moment, "You know I'm not staying with the Morrow forever."

She looked at him and let out a little sigh, but nodded.

"When I leave..." He stopped, feeling suddenly nervous. He glanced down at her hands, stained brown with dirt. "Is there really no one here who takes care of you?"

She heaved an irritated breath. "I can take care of myself."

"I know," he assured her. "I just..." He rolled a piece of the flatbread between his fingers until it formed a snake. Taking a breath, he pushed the words out. "When I leave, would you like to come with me?"

Rass looked up at him, her eyebrows shooting up higher than he'd ever seen them. She didn't speak and something very much like terror clamped down on Will's chest. She tilted her head to the side. "Would you like me to?"

Will nodded, although the motion felt awkwardly wooden. His mouth felt dry and the next words rushed out. "I have a home, of sorts. It's a big stone tower. And you could come there with me." The idea of bringing this little, eccentric girl to the Stronghold made him grin. "The people there would love you." He leaned close to her and whispered, "They know about magic too."

She gave him a small smile, but her brow was still creased. "You'd leave the grass, though. Wouldn't you?"

Will looked out into the darkness of the Sweep. "I'd leave *this* grass, but then we'd go places with other grass. My tower is surrounded by it." He gave her a smile. "It's hard to find places with no grass."

Rass looked away, and he couldn't see her expression for an excruciating handful of heartbeats. When she turned back, though, she smiled up at him and nodded. "I think I'd like to go with you."

Will let out a long breath and wrapped his arm around her shoulders. "That makes me very happy."

She leaned against him. "You're funny, Will."

Her shoulders were definitely less boney. The idea nagged at him as he let Rass fall into her normal chatter. He'd known her less than a fortnight. And while he'd shared his food with her, he was hardly feeding her a lot. But there was no doubt she was gaining weight. Her face was filling out too, although not exactly how he'd expected. She was gaining some roundness to her cheekbones, but the rest of her face was still thin. Her chin was still pointed and long. She looked less and less like someone from Queensland, and more like...someone more exotic. She reminded him of something he couldn't quite place.

Rass's eyes flew open wide and she scuttled behind Will.

Sora strode over, her face thunderous. Will leaned back from her fury.

"You did something," she hissed, pointing a finger in Will's face.

He batted her hand away, his heart pounding in his chest. "What are you talking about?"

"You did something to the Flame." Her voice was low, but sharp enough to cut through the Sweep itself. "Killien thinks it was *me*." The word ripped out of her throat.

Rass grabbed the back of his shirt and pressed herself up against him.

If Will had ever thought he'd seen Sora angry, he'd been wrong. Her body shook with rage, her eyes dug into him as though she could rip his heart out with a thought.

A different sort of fear jabbed into his gut. "What is Killien going to do to you?"

"Do to me?" she asked, incredulous. "Probably build me a shrine." She leaned close again and Will forced himself not to pull away. *"But I didn't do it."*

Will stared at her at a complete loss. She was angry about getting credit for healing Lilit? He could understand a reluctance to accept it, but not this level of rage.

"Stay away from me," she said slowly, biting off every word, fixing Will with a look of pure hatred, "or, I swear by the black queen, I will tell Killien everything I know about you and you'll be dead by morning."

"Why would he build a shrine to you, but kill me?"

"Because you and I are nothing alike. Stay away from me." With a last look that threw daggers, she spun and stalked off.

He stared after her. A gust of wind tumbled around him

bringing cool, stormy air and a vacant sense of waiting. Thunder growled through the clouds, and the smell of rain whipped past.

Rass peeked out around his shoulder and looked at Will with wide eyes.

"Don't wander too far away," Will told her, spinning his ring, watching the direction Sora had gone. "We may be leaving the Roven sooner than I'd thought."

CHAPTER NINETEEN

THE STORM CHARGED CLOSER like an attacking army, smashing into the clan with breathtaking force. Will and Rass copied the other Roven and huddled under the wagon, still pelted by raindrops shot under it like arrows. Lightning stabbed down from the clouds in a chaos of blinding flashes and howling darkness. The wind howled like a creature out of a nightmare, but it whipped the storm quickly past, driving it away to the south.

Rass ran into the grass to sleep, and Will lay watching stray clouds chase after the storm, troubled by Sora's unaccountable fury. He could understand frustration or awkwardness at getting credit for something she hadn't done, but Killien merely thought her prayers had been answered. What was so terrible about that? Of course, the question as to why Killien begged her to pray in the first place was equally unanswerable. Killien's desperation he could understand, but Sora had never given any sign of being religious.

The blackness of the Serpent Queen hung overhead, clouds scuttling across her, seeming to spread bits of her darkness across the sky. Is that who Sora had prayed to? The monster set on devouring the stars? His mind circled back on the questions, not finding any answers.

To distract himself he ran over every interaction he'd had with Ilsa. It didn't take long. The urgency to talk to her again was growing, but with Lilit needing so much attention, he doubted he'd have a chance to see her before they reached the rifts in a few days. And then, would Killien let him stay longer? At what point was the Torch going to tire of his new storyteller? All the thoughts spun in his head like a second storm.

He finally slept, but the next day turned out to be just as agonizing. Hal was busy, Killien didn't summon him, and there was no sign of Ilsa, and no sign of Sora. Although that last thing wasn't bad. Will watched Lilit's wagon, but if Ilsa was there, she was staying inside.

The caravan had just stopped for the night, and Will was sitting down to some dwarf-talk with Hal, bracing for another meal of flatbread, when a rider arrived from the north, cantering down the serpent's wake. She carried sacks of bread baked in the rift and the Roven crowded her, eagerly grabbing fresh loaves.

The ranger reported that the caravan should reach the rift the morning after next, and the news along with the bread worked a sort of magic. Will sank his teeth into the thick, spongy bread with relish, hoping he never saw flatbread again. From their spot a little away from the fire, Lukas sat with Rett. When Sini arrived Lukas handed her a small loaf with a flourish, and she squealed with happiness and sank down in between them.

Before he'd even finished eating it, another ranger raced up from the west. He galloped toward Killien, his horse staggering to a stop, its sides heaving.

"Shepherds killed, Torch, three hours hard ride west. Three Roven from the Panos Clan, and four dozen sheep."

Will felt every person near him tense. Killien's face turned stony. "Cause?"

The ranger's eyes flicked to the people around the Torch. "No sign of weapons. The meat was ripped off the sheep. The carcasses left to rot."

Murmurs of "goblins" rippled through the Roven.

Will stretched out and felt fear growing in people. A spot of coolness appeared as Sora stepped up next to Killien. Will drew back when he saw her, but she didn't even glance in his direction.

"And..." The ranger paused, his eyes wide and slightly wild. "There've been fresh signs of goblins in every ravine I've passed."

Will focused on Killien and felt a growing dread in the Torch.

"How many?"

"Dozens." The ranger twitched a nervous half-shrug. "Hundreds, maybe."

"How long ago were the shepherds killed?" Sora asked.

"Within the past day."

Sora sent a girl running to fetch a horse. "Landmarks?"

"Between the white bluffs and that rift with all the bones."

Sora fixed him with the exact same gaze she always gave to Will. "It's getting dark. Can you be more specific?"

The ranger shifted slightly. "A bit closer to the bluffs, I think. There's not much to see out there."

"Not if you don't open your eyes."

Killien looked out over the Sweep to the west, his eyes scanning the emptiness. "Word from any other rangers?"

The man shook his head. "I haven't seen anyone since I left the rift yesterday."

"Take someone with you," Killien ordered Sora.

"They'll slow me down. I'll be back by dawn."

The girl ran back with a horse, and Sora swung into the saddle. For once Will could pick out her emotions strongly enough to tell them apart from the Torch's. She was angry, which seemed to be directed at Killien, but she was also filled with a roiling fear. Feeling Sora lose her tight control was far more frightening than the ranger's report.

"Sora," Killien said, his tone dangerous. "You are not going alone."

She shot him a furious glare and galloped across the grass.

Killien's fury and sharp fear matched Will's as he watched

Sora's shape shrink into the vastness of the Sweep. The Torch barked orders, sending Roven scattering.

"Hal," the Torch called, "get the wagons in tight circles tonight, the children and elderly inside. Split the animals into as many groups as you can build fires around. As much fire as you can. Form a line along the western side. Everything done before dark."

Sora's silhouette disappeared over the first ridge, outlined for just a moment against the red sky.

The dark came long before the frantic activity of the clan subsided. The wagons were drawn into wide circles around tight knots of children and elderly, protected by a ring of Roven with campfires. Hundreds more Roven lined the western edge of the clan, their own fires well-stocked.

North of the clan sat wagons loaded with all the metal they could find, including Will's three silver beard beads. Around the metal wagons, a wall of grass and dried dung bricks were stacked, ready to be turned into a ring of fire. The only metal left in the clan was in the weapons they'd need to fight.

The flurry of activity settled into a quiet nervousness.

And nothing happened.

Will lay on the ground at the edge of one of the circles of wagons and actually missed the hard wood of his wagon. The brooding Serpent Queen worked her way up the sky and he spun his ring, waiting, straining for any sounds of goblins in the night. The ground was uncomfortable, and no matter how he adjusted the wool blanket, cold air crept in somewhere.

The knife he'd been given felt awkward in his hand, too long, the blade weighted oddly. It was sharp though, so there was a chance his wild, unskilled hacking would turn out to be an effective fighting strategy against goblins.

He was forgetting something he should have done by now. He just couldn't figure out what.

Part of it was that he had no idea where either Rass or Ilsa was. A cold wind slid over him, sneaking down inside his blanket. Two Roven sat at a fire not far from him, and Will looked at it enviously.

He gathered in some *vitalle* from the flames. He focused on the air above it, bending it into a cloth, gathering up some heat and drawing it closer. His fingers tingled with the effort, but it reached him with a rush of warmth lasting for three or four breaths before it cooled.

Will gathered in a little more *vitalle* from the grass, an idea forming. If he created a tent of cloth from the fire to himself, then the heat would just roll along the tent continually. Slowly, starting near himself, he constructed the idea of the tent, pushing *vitalle* into it, ignoring the tingling in his hands.

He pushed the tent forward until the end of it was over the flames. The first bit of warmth rolled over Will's skin and he smiled. The warm air wrapped around him, warming his blankets and his clothes. When he was thoroughly warm, he cut off the *vitalle* and let the warm air rise into the dark sky. It didn't take long before the cold seeped back in.

He was forgetting something. The feeling nagged at him. But the harder he tried to think of what it was, the more his brain offered up the wrong answer.

You forgot to take the silver beard beads out, his brain offered for the hundredth time. He heaved a sigh. He had done that. He'd searched his bag three more times to make sure there was no metal left in it. Still the thought niggled at him. What had he forgotten?

Beard beads, his brain offered.

He pressed his face into his hands and growled. He opened his eyes and between his fingers he could just see the flicker of the nearest small fire glinting off his ring.

His wide, gold ring.

"Idiot!" he hissed, trying to work the ring off his finger. The edge of it dug into his knuckle.

He squeezed his way out of the circle between two wagons and paused at the sight of the long line of Roven warriors. Surely the goblins wouldn't attack something this large? The Morrow Clan looked prepared for an attacking army. Firelight glittered off hundreds of weapons and suddenly he felt foolish for worrying about one small ring.

Past the line of Roven, the Sweep lay still and dark. For the first time, the grassland didn't feel empty. It felt full of...nothing. Which sounded the same, but felt very, very different.

Will was jogging by the time he reached Killien at the far northern end of the clan. Hal stood by his side, huge in the dim light, a wide sword slung across his back. Farther north, separated from the clan by a hundred paces, sat the wagons holding all the metal.

Killien had a well-used, common looking sword hung at his belt. Slung across his back was another, more rustic one. It took Will a minute to recognize it as the seax Killien had been given by Flibbet the Peddler.

"Come to join the fight?" Hal asked.

Will held up his knife. "If this is the sort that needs two swords, definitely not."

"Only one sword for fighting." Killien shifted his shoulders under the scabbard on his back. "This is just for safe keeping. Svard Naj doesn't sit in the metal wagon with the common things, unprotected."

"Speaking of metal wagons..." Will held up his hand with the ring. "I forgot to take this off. But now that I see how much metal is still among the clan, does it matter? There are metal weapons everywhere."

"The weapons aren't gold," Hal pointed out. "Goblins love gold. You should get that far away from you."

"I'll get a runner to put it in my chest." Killien motioned to the wagons set fifty paces away across the grass, his voice tinged with irritation.

Will opened his mouth to explain that he couldn't get it off, when a faint horn blast cut through the silence of the night. A single fire flared larger near the sheep herds. Another horn rang out three sharp notes and other fires flamed up.

A spot of blackness raced down the nearest hill toward them. Another burst of a horn called out, this one long, and a handful of Roven rushed out in a wedge, swords drawn, facing out into the Sweep to offer protection to the rider. More fires flared, painting the rise of the Sweep in flickering orange, turning the grass to a dim, mottled red fur.

Will's stomach dropped.

Sora raced toward the clan, calling out something he couldn't hear.

The wedge opened and she galloped in, the Roven collapsing back in after her, re-forming the line.

A low growl seeped out of the ground itself.

The hillside shifted.

A wide section of the grass slid sideways, then disappeared, falling into deep blackness. It widened into a gaping, hollow maw. Another appeared beside it.

A scrambling stream of dark, ill-formed shapes vomited out of the ground. The Sweep trembled from the charge. Grating, piercing shrieks split the night.

"Heatstones!" Killien shouted and the command was echoed down the line.

Hal dropped a heatstone close to the fire. Inside it, a kernel of light like a candle flame appeared, spreading and brightening. When it was almost as bright as the fire, Hal kicked it between his fire and the next one. The stone glowed with a searing yellow light, looking almost molten. A rush of heat washed across Will, like he stood in front of an oven.

Down the line, blazing yellow spots appeared, one after another.

To the south, goblins broke through the line and reached a herd. Terrified squeals from the sheep mixed with the shrieks of the goblins. The animals panicked, crashing into each other like waves trapped in a roiling sea.

A heatstone flew in a bright arc, disappearing into the stream of goblins. Screeches rang out and the goblins scattered away from it, into the path of Roven swords and knives.

"Get that ring out of here," Killien shouted at Will, pulling two long knives out of his belt and pointing one at the seat in the front of the nearest wagon. "And then get up on something high."

The Torch turned toward the approaching goblins. Hal stationed himself by the fire, his enormous sword drawn. Will scrambled toward the metal wagons, yanking at his ring.

A long line of bonfires and heatstones edged the clan now, stretching down the Sweep like blazing teeth. Outside the line, the first row of grass hills was visible, and streaming from the wide holes came goblin after goblin. They rushed out in an endless stream a half-dozen goblins wide.

The creatures pooled along the fireline, rushing closer, their eyes reflecting back the firelight in wide, white orbs. The small, hunched goblins scrambled forward in a chaos of green, wiry legs and arms.

"More heat!" Killien called.

Whenever a fire flared up, the goblins pulled back. The stream of goblins had stopped flowing out of the hill, leaving the two holes gaping like hollow eyes.

Will wrenched at his ring, drawing in some *vitalle* from the grass to heat the gold up, hoping it would stretch. The goblins outside the fireline surged past him in a swarm of limbs and eyes and hunger. But the heatstones seemed to be working and the creatures held back a dozen paces. Roven archers shot into the horde, felling goblin after goblin. But every time, another vicious face appeared, its open mouth edged with thin, sharp teeth.

Ahead of Will, a more guttural cry rang out and the swarm raced toward the metal.

Flaming arrows shot toward the wagons, setting the ring of grasses around it into flame and Will slid to a stop, letting his hand fall from his still tight ring. Creatures raced toward fire-encircled wagons. The goblins in the front screeched and scrambled against the mob, trying to stay back, but the mass moved forward like a wave. When the first goblin touched the fire, it let out a piercing scream. Two more were shoved forward into it, then the flames were smothered below burning bodies, and goblins poured through, clawing over each other to reach the metal.

Will turned and ran back, climbing up on the wagon near Killien. The goblins swarmed against the line, screeching like birds fighting over a carcass. The Roven cut into their numbers with brutal efficiency. But they were falling too. One Roven for every twenty goblins.

There were not enough Roven.

Killien strode down the line, calling out commands. Hal stood between the nearest fire and a heatstone, his huge sword sweeping through the frost goblins like a scythe.

Will's heartbeat pounded in his ears like a drum underneath the screaming and fighting.

The goblins swarmed over the metal. The Roven retreated, re-forming a line between those wagons and the clan, hacking any goblins that chased after them. One of the Roven stumbled and a gap appeared between Will and the creatures.

A single goblin face turned toward him, eyes glinting like two flat moons. It raised its nose into the air as if catching a scent. With a hideous grin, it dropped to all fours and raced toward him, tearing into the earth.

Will's feet scrambled back against the wagon floor. He drew in *vitalle* from the ground, from the fire blazing nearby, from anything he could find, his mind scrambling for an idea of what to do with it.

Then Sora was there, stepping between the wagon and the

racing goblins, two long knives in her hand. Her long braid was disheveled, her leathers glinted dark and wet.

A different level of fear wormed into him as the goblin raced closer to Sora.

Another goblin peeled away from the swarm and ran toward them. Then another.

Will cast about desperately for some way to stop them, some protection he could throw up in front of her. He opened up toward her and felt a swirl of fear wrapped in resolve and surrounded by cold, calculated waiting.

A bright glint of yellow near his foot caught his eye.

A heatstone.

He spun around. He was standing on the book wagon where Rett had spilled his heatstones. A new fear gripped him. He'd brought his gold ring to the books.

Will grabbed the stone. The goblin was halfway to Sora, more and more veered out of the main group to follow. She stood alone. At the sight of claws and teeth rushing toward her, he yanked some *vitalle* out of the grass and shoved it into the heatstone. The stone lapped it up and began to glow, the surface blossoming with heat. He threw it between Sora and the goblins.

Sora drew back from it. Will needed a way to focus the heat on the goblins—needed something like a tent of air.

No, something stronger. Thick, like the walls of an oven.

He molded the air around the heatstone into the idea of clay walls. Reaching toward the nearest fire, he drew energy in one hand, singeing his fingertips, and out his other hand until those fingers hurt as well. He wrapped the walls around the heat on three sides and over the top.

In a breath, the cool night air brushed against his skin as the heat from the stone was channeled away. From the side of the stone facing the goblins he pushed out the idea of a tunnel of clay, funneling all the heat in that direction. Thankfully, the fire near the wagon was burning strongly and he pulled more energy from it, strengthening the walls. His fingers burned from the *vitalle* pouring through them.

The heat hit the first goblin and the creature twisted back away from it, with a shriek of pain. Will pushed the heat forward and more goblins cried out in pain, drawing back. The wave of heat pushed them all the way to the metal wagons before they stopped running and sank down, their white eyes glaring towards Will.

Sora spun around and stared at him.

His fingers ached, but this wasn't enough. He needed so much more heat.

Will dropped to his knees and looked under the wagon seat. A half dozen heatstones lay shoved in the corner. Will grabbed them all, tossing them down onto the blazing one.

Sora cried out and dove away from the pile.

The heatstones exploded into searing yellow light and Will flinched back, but the clay wall held and no heat reached him. Will drew even more *vitalle* from the nearby fire, pouring it into his air-walls. The tunnel rippled with heat, rushing toward the goblins in a narrow river, flattening and searing grass in a long line before widening out into a wave of air so hot that the goblins shimmered through it.

The creatures shrieked, pulling back.

Seeing the goblins' hesitation, the Roven attacked with renewed fury, cutting at the edges of the swarm. A few Roven reached into the line of heat and spun away, crying out and cradling singed arms. Will turned his palm out instead of just his fingers, letting more and more *vitalle* flow through him to shape the walls. The energy pushed clay walls farther, wrapping the heat around the goblins until it herded them back out of the Roven lines.

Will followed the retreating goblins with his wall, pushing the heat after them. The skin on his palms blistered. He squeezed his eyes shut, shoving away the pain, and cast out again, this time searching for all the fires and all the heatstones. He visualized another long, tall wall of clay along the inside of the fire line, growing up and bending out over the tops of the fires, reflecting all the heat out at the goblins on the Sweep.

With a sharp slice of pain a blister on his palm burst, then another. Will bit back a cry and focused his mind on the wall.

The goblins paused, then with a twist like a flock of birds spinning in flight, they turned and darted toward the openings in the hills. A cry went up from the Roven and hundreds of arrows shot into the air, dropping goblin after goblin to the ground.

In moments the Sweep was empty. There was a shudder of the ground and the entrance of the goblin warren quivered and sank, turning the hillside into a mass of torn up earth.

Will cut off the flow of *vitalle*. For just a moment the clay wall held, then the air relaxed into itself and a wave of heat rolled off the heatstones next to him, burning the skin on his cheeks and sending searing pain across his burned palms. He ducked down onto the seat of the wagon, cradling his hands on his lap.

He'd never controlled that much *vitalle* before. The thought was dull and heavy. He stretched his fingers and pain lanced across his hands. Raw, red skin filled his palms, covered with blisters, some taut and shiny, some split open, dripping. His hands blurred as a wave of exhaustion rolled over him.

Celebratory shouts from the Roven echoed around him as though they came from far over the Sweep. He heard Hal bellow something incomprehensible. Will's body melted down against the wagon, his head falling back against the hard wood wall.

The earth was spinning, falling. There was nothing but the sharp pain in his hands.

Will closed his eyes.

The pain in his palms was excruciating. He closed his eyes and cast out toward his hands, feeling the energy from his own body pressing against the inside of his skin, beginning the long process of healing. Burns were much harder to heal than cuts. Instead of drawing skin back together, this required growing new skin across both palms.

Maybe he could dull the pain a little. Will cast out toward the grass below the wagon. His mind worked sluggishly, and when he reached for the *vitalle*, it dribbled through his grasp like water. His eyes slid shut and he lost focus. His arms rested heavy on his lap like two dead weights.

A crack split the night and Will's eyes snapped open. Sora stood at the side of the wagon, her knife jabbed down into the wood of the wagon seat. The brightness of the heatstones cast her face into stark light and black shadows.

Her eyes glittered with an icy coldness he hadn't seen before and her voice cut through the night like a blade. "What did you do?"

CHAPTER TWENTY

Sora stood by the wagon, her face livid, but he was too exhausted for it to cause more than a thin thread of fear. And he was far too tired to open up to her and deal with her anger.

Will closed his eyes again and the wagon beneath him spun slowly. All he wanted to do was sleep. But Sora shifted, and the movement sounded angry.

She was always so angry.

Will had just saved her life. He, Will, the least useful Keeper in the history of Keepers, had just fought off a horde of frost goblins and saved dozens, maybe hundreds of Roven lives. He cracked one eye open and worked to focus on Sora. She stood stone-still, her glare sharp enough to cut.

If only it was Alaric standing there, not Sora. He'd appreciate what Will had done. How far had that wall reached down the line? He grinned. *Yes, Gerone,* he thought, *I had a motivation problem.*

The palms of his hands were hurting worse by the moment, but he didn't care.

"Stop grinning like an idiot," Sora hissed. "Do you realize—"

"Sora," he interrupted her, "why are you always so angry?"

"I'm angry," she hissed, "because you keep doing stupid things and I have to save your life."

He pushed himself up. "*You're* the one who got me into all this, by telling Killien about me."

She leaned over the edge of the wagon, her hands gripping the side, her voice furious. "Killien knew about you before you finished telling your foreign story at the festival. He already saw you as a threat. I came to see if you were as dangerous as he thought."

"You hid in my room and threatened me!"

"Killien had men set to take you when you left the city. I told him he should see if your stories were worth hearing.

"I was going to help you escape while the clan packed. It's not my fault you decided to play bosom friends with the Torch."

"He likes foreigners," Will objected. "He knows more about foreign people than anyone I've met in this wasteland. Everyone else jumps straight to the sword. Killien realizes not everyone outside his clan is an enemy."

"Not everyone. Just you."

A rock fell into his stomach. "I'm a storyteller."

"Stop it." Her face was taut and her shoulders tense. He opened up toward her and, for once, felt a rush of emotions. She was mad and scared and exhausted. She looked at him for a long moment, suspicion fighting with something else in her expression.

Leaning closer, she whispered, "You're a Keeper."

The word hit Will like a punch. He opened his mouth to answer her, but found nothing to say.

At his silence she shoved herself away from the wagon.

"Killien isn't opposed to magic." He shook his head, desperation growing. "He's studying it."

"He's against Queensland. And Keepers." She turned away from him and rubbed her hand across her mouth, looking uncharacteristically nervous.

To the east, the top of the Scale Mountains were visible as a dark wall beneath the stars. "What do I do?"

She looked away from the mountains. "Tonight, after first watch, I'll slip you westward into the grass. There are some small rifts that are almost impossible to find. You can hide until the Roven are gone, then you can get yourself off the Sweep."

"West?"

"Killien wouldn't imagine you'd go farther into the Sweep. He'll think you ran home."

"I want to run home. I'd run home crying if I thought it would get me there faster. What I don't want to do is go farther into the Sweep and hide in the exact places where frost goblins frequent."

She rolled her eyes. "I know. And Killien will be counting on that level of…"

"Cowardice?" Will offered, glaring at her.

"…inexperience. He won't send trackers west. He'll send me. And I'll take all the best trackers with me. When we can't find your trail, we'll blame it on your evil, deceiving magic. We just need to keep you away from him for the next few hours."

Will stared at her for a long moment. "You're very sneaky for someone who disapproves of deceiving people."

The clan spread out around him, and he had no idea where Ilsa was. Or Rass.

"I can't leave."

Sora turned a disbelieving look on him. "Why not?"

There was a loud laugh nearby and she glanced behind them and swore. A flare of anger, harsh and new blazed up. Killien's voice came from nearby and Sora raised hers at Will. "You deserve to be burned if you were stupid enough to pick up a glowing heatstone."

The Torch stepped around the end of the wagon, his eyes sharp. Two thin lines of blood slashed across a bandage near his shoulder. With a glance he took them in, his gaze coming to rest on Will's hands. Will fought the urge to hide them.

"What happened?" Killien demanded.

I saved your entire clan. Will thought. He could feel the tightly controlled fury of the Torch, and beside it, Sora's towering fury, which had risen a hundredfold as Killien approached. But she kept her glare burning into Will.

"I found some heatstones," he began. He stretched up to see over the edge of the wagon at the pile of heatstones still shining painfully bright. "I heard people calling for more heat. And the goblins were coming this way. And"—he lifted his hand to show Killien the ring, still firmly on his finger—"I couldn't get the ring off." He looked back at the heatstones. "So I heated up one stone, then threw the rest on top of it."

This was a stupid story. It explained nothing.

"And your hands?" Killien never took his eyes off Will's face.

"One of the heatstones rolled toward the wagon." The lie was so stupid he didn't need to feign embarrassment. "All the books were here..."

"So he picked it up," Sora finished for him.

"I thought it was going to reach the wagon." It felt good to snap at someone. "And I don't like the idea of blazing hot things near a pile of books."

"Enough," Killien said quietly. The fury Will could feel from him was unabated, but none of it showed up in his face.

"If the heatstones are ruined, I'll pay you for them." Will lifted his hand again. "Would this ring cover the cost? It's currently burned onto my finger, but once it heals..."

Killien let out a little huff of amusement, and Will felt the fury subside the smallest amount. "No more resting. It's time for a celebration. And for that we need stories."

Will worked a smile past his exhaustion. "Everything's better with stories."

Sora made an irritated noise, but Killien kept his attention fixed on Will. "It's a good night, Will. We're almost to the rifts. No more watching out for monsters...no more wondering what is hiding right next to us."

Will ignored the implication and heaved himself up, climbing out of the wagon and following Killien. The Torch was splattered with dark goblin blood, the sword at his hip grimy with it.

Across his back, the sword from Flibbet still hung looking unused.

"Tell me, Will, are there monsters where you live? Creatures that hide close by, lulling you into the false sense that you are safe? When all along they're just waiting for the opportunity to destroy you?"

The sharp suspicion he felt from Killien cut through him and he shoved the Torch's emotions out of his chest. "No. Just people trying to live at peace with each other."

Will couldn't shake the fuzziness of exhaustion from his mind, but the conversation continued, Killien asking probing questions in his light, unconcerned voice, Will dancing along the edge of the truth in his answers. They reached a large fire surrounded by rangers. A handful of healers wrapped wounds, and children scuttled through carrying food and wineskins.

Lukas pushed his way through the crowd holding a thick roll of bandages. The slave's grey shirt was splattered with blood, but none of it looked to be his own. The blood on Killien's arm had spread and the Torch offered Lukas his arm.

"Have the healer see to your burns, storyman." Killien winced as Lukas pulled a bloody dressing off his arm.

Lukas gave the Torch a quiet apology, examining the two long, ragged gashes that ran down his arm.

Killien kept his eyes on Will. "Stay at my disposal tonight."

A slave bandaged a ranger's leg nearby, and Will sat down to wait his turn. A knot of dread sat in his stomach. He watched Sora take a seat behind the other Roven around the fire. There was no sign of Lilit or Ilsa, but he heard enough conversations to know that there'd been no injuries away from the front line of fighting.

The healer spread a thick poultice across his palms and wrapped his hands, leaving his palms pleasantly numb and Will turned his mind to which story to tell. There were several stories from Coastal Baylon that painted Queensland in a bad light, and he was tempted to use one of them, but felt reluctant even to bring his homeland up. Instead he sorted through the stories he knew that mentioned neither Queensland, nor magic, nor anyone in disguise, and most definitely not any stories where traitors were put to death.

Which left him with a surprisingly limited repertoire, and ruled out most of his favorites.

He settled on one about a shrewd merchant trapped in the garden of the indulgent Gulfind god Keelu. The fast talking merchant was funny, and hopefully no one would draw too many parallels between a trapped merchant and a trapped storyteller.

The lump of foreboding growing the longer he sat there, and when Killien finally stood to address the Roven around the fire, Will's gut was in knots.

"Our storyman," Killien announced, standing near the fire and motioning Will to join him, "is here to entertain us."

There was a general murmur of approval from around the fire, and Will stepped up next to the Torch, clasping his hands together behind his back in case they started to shake. The fire lit the closest of the faces, but the back of the group, where Sora sat, was lost in darkness.

"Our enemy in Queensland have their own magic men." Killien's voice rolled over the crowd. "They call them Keepers."

Will's blood turned icy, his entire body felt too long, and too awkward.

"The Keepers do not put their magic safely into rocks, though. They pull what they use from the world around them, then twist it to do their will."

Muttered disapproval rose around the fire.

"So they do not share their magic with the people. Here on the Sweep, our stonesteeps infuse stones with power that are available to all. They ward our houses against disaster, guard our children against illness. Give us heatstones for protection. The magic on the Sweep is used for the good of all the Roven.

"But in Queensland, the Keepers hoard all the magic to themselves. They hide away in a hidden tower, leaving only to consult with their ineffective queen."

The mutters of the group turned angry.

"You've been to Queensland, Will. Tell us a story about their Keepers." Killien's eyes were flat in the fire light. "Tell us whether they're as terrible as we've heard."

Will gave the Torch a bow, the motion stiff. A story about Keepers? That narrowed it down to hundreds of tales. None of which he was stupid enough to tell here. "In Queensland they don't have the same view of Keepers as you. The Keepers are..." He paused again. This was awkward. "The Keepers are honored there, revered even. The people there think that the Keepers protect their land and their history."

Killien's eyes glinted in the candlelight. "And what do you think of them, Will?" His voice was pitched low, but the crowd was listening so quietly that Will knew every one of them had heard.

"I think Keepers are known for preserving as many stories as they can. And in my mind, anyone who has that much respect for stories"—he nodded to Killien—"can't be all bad."

The Torch didn't move.

Will's heart was pounding alarmingly fast. He couldn't tell any of the stories he knew. They all treated Keepers like heroes, or great leaders, or brilliant strategists. They were all spoken of irritatingly well, actually. He rubbed his fingers over the bandages on his hand. Tonight, faced with the fact that the only impressive thing he'd ever done as a Keeper was about to get him killed, and would never be told to anyone, he found himself wishing for more stories about Keepers that didn't glow with adoration. Like that story from Coastal Baylon blaming one for a drought.

He bit back a grin. It was perfect.

"Queensland cannot be trusted to say anything but good about their Keepers," he began. "Whether they do so out of fear or respect, I do not know. But no group of men can be as pure, as noble, and as faultless as Keepers are supposed to be." He felt the truth of it growing in him, the need to say all these things building and gaining momentum. "They are just men. And men are not so uncontaminated.

"A person can rarely see his own people clearly. His mind is so entrenched in his own way of thinking, he can't even see where he's blind. To truly see the Keepers, let's step away from Queensland, with their prejudices and myths, and go to their neighbors, where men are not blinded by loyalty."

He told of the terrible drought that had plagued Coastal Baylon for two years after a skirmish involving a Keeper. He told of the rumors of a curse. The slow, starving deaths, the dusty, barren fields. He told of the superstitious farmers and the desperate lords needing someone to blame. How their prayers for rain were shoved away and their cries for vengeance grew. He told of the hatred that burned toward the Keeper, the oaths taken by those who vowed to bring him to Baylon and spill his blood on the ground he'd laid to waste.

"And so they went, leaving the bodies of the ones they loved behind. They climbed through barren hills into Queensland, moving toward the town where the Keeper had been.

"Their eyes had seen nothing but drought and death for so long, they didn't notice the shadows they crept through were cast by bare branches, and their footsteps were cushioned by dust and despair.

"When they found the Keeper, he lay in the corner of a cottage. His black robe, tattered and greyed with dust, was wrapped around a child. Their starved bodies clinging to each other in death."

The whisper of the fire was the only sound among the Roven.

"The vengeance and hatred they'd brought into that place breathed its last, and crumbled to dust. The Baylonese went home empty, drawing out again their brittle, neglected prayers for rain and holding them gently on their parched tongues."

The Roven before him were still. Will let the silence hang in the air, refusing to offer any more closure to the tale. He pressed his fist to his chest and bowed to the listeners, then to Killien. The

Torch stared at Will with unreadable eyes. Not bothering to open up toward him, Will sat down.

Killien sat in the silence and looked at Will for a long moment. "Well," he said, "the storyman knows how to spin a tale."

It took a moment before the sounds of approval began. Exhaustion rolled over Will again as Killien called for more wine and the group around the fire dissolved into smaller conversations. Sora walked by, fixing Will with a look dripping with displeasure.

Hal moved over next to Will. "That was the most depressing story I've ever heard." He handed Will a basket of bread and cheese.

Killien came over, passing small wineskins to Will and Hal. "That was quite a tale."

Will shrugged. "You're the one who asked for something about Keepers. I had something much more upbeat planned."

"Next time let the storyman pick," Hal said, taking a huge bite of bread. "I'm so depressed I can barely eat."

"Agreed," Killien said. "Next time he can pick. For now, let's celebrate. We're still alive." He held up his wineskin toward Will. "And you put on quite a performance."

"A performance depressing enough to lower even the spirits of the victors," Hal agreed raising his wineskin.

"To the victors," Killien said with a thin smile.

Will raised his as well, and took a drink. The wine slid down his throat bitter and rough while he watched the Torch walk away.

"What'd you do to piss off Killien?" Hal asked around a mouthful of cheese.

Will took another sip of his wine to give himself a moment to come up with an answer. "Maybe he didn't like the story."

Hal grunted. "No one liked that story." He lifted his skin toward Will for a salute. "Tell something better next time. Something about dwarves."

Will laughed. Starting the story of the dwarven princess who was so ugly she'd frightened a troll, he set about passing the time until the first watch changed and he and Sora could leave.

But before he'd reached the part where the trolls showed up, his eyes grew heavy.

"Don't fall asleep on me," Hal protested, shoving Will's shoulder.

The big man slid out of focus.

"Will?" Hal's voice came from a long distance away.

Huge hands shook his shoulders, but everything spun off in strange directions and his shoulders didn't feel particularly well attached to the rest of him. The edges of the world began to turn black and Hal's words grew more insistent.

The last thing Will heard was Killien coming closer.

"Hal," the Torch said, his voice distant and cold. "Stop shaking the Keeper."

CHAPTER TWENTY-ONE

THE WALLS, the floor, the very air was drenched with orange, like he lay inside a flame. Will's tongue filled his mouth, thick and dry. When he pushed himself upright, a groan scraped out of his throat.

He sat on a clay bed stuck to the clay wall, which curved up around him like a beehive. A cup and a bowl full of water sat below him on the floor. He grabbed for it and the tepid water felt like life rushing down his throat. He filled the cup three times before letting it fall from his fingers. A small window punctured the wall, showing still more orange clay. The tiny room was perfectly empty besides the cup, bowl, and bed.

He heaved himself to his feet. The world leaned to the left for a moment before pulling itself upright. Ducking through a low archway, he found another room with a wicker table and two chairs. Through the open doorway, bright sunlight raked down a cliff wall.

Will stumbled to the door.

Outside was nothing but stone and more clay. Across a thin path, no farther from the door than Will could reach, the ground dropped off sharply into a gully. Up the other side, barren cliffs rose at least three times his height. Behind him, another cliff jutted up toward a weak blue sky.

He was in a rift.

He stood at one end of it, on a path that wound past three more huts on its way to the far end where it zigzagged its way up the cliff to a pair of guards. Will cast out through the rift, but didn't find a single hint of *vitalle*. There weren't any living things closer than the guards.

He turned back, looking for the water and events of the goblin attack came back to him. He stretched his fingers and his palms ached, but not as terribly as before. They had begun to heal. A thin trickle of fear dribbled down his back. How long had he been here?

When he reached his room, a small lump at the foot of his bed caught his eye—a dead mouse. Talen knew where he was, for whatever that was worth. He sank onto the floor next to the water.

Killien knew he was a Keeper.

The thought thudded dully in his mind.

He let his head sink back against the bed. This felt...expected. As though it was the only way this could have ended.

His eyes slid shut.

A scraping noise jolted him awake. Sharp pains ran down the muscles in his back as he jerked awake.

"Hello, Will."

Will flinched at the calmness of the voice. Killien leaned against the wall relaxed, his face blank. Will opened up toward him and felt a surge of dark anger boil into his chest, dark and somehow cold.

"How do you like your accommodations?" Killien glanced around the room. "We call it the Grave."

When Will didn't answer, Killien ducked into the other room and sat at the table next to a plate of bread.

Will heaved himself up, suddenly ravenous. Three Roven guards stood at the outer door. Will sank down in the other chair, and a guard stepped behind him. None of them looked familiar. Or friendly.

"Why feed me if you're just going to kill me?"

Killien pushed the plate closer to Will. "I wouldn't have gone to the trouble of dragging you here if I was going to kill you."

Will picked up the bread, his fingers clumsy around the bandages. It crumbled a bit with staleness, but no bread in the history of the world had tasted this good.

Killien settled back in his chair. "A Keeper. Right here in my clan."

Will paused with a piece of bread halfway to his mouth.

"Sneaking and lying, right at my own table, right alongside me. For days."

"What exactly would you have had me do?" Will dropped the bread onto the plate. "Introduce myself as a Keeper? That might have dampened our friendship."

Killien's face darkened. "We never had a friendship."

The words struck deeper than Will expected, immediately followed by irritation that they had. "Would you have talked with me about books? History?" he asked, refusing to acknowledge the man's words. "Would you have told me about your father?"

"I would have killed you," Killien hissed, leaning forward. "And left your body to rot."

"Then you can hardly blame me for lying." Will picked up the piece of bread again. "If you're so keen on killing me, why am I here?"

Killien sat back, drawing in a breath, visibly trying to calm himself. "I've been reading your books."

Will stiffened.

"You've been spying on the Roven for a year now. And you learned a lot from us…" Killien nodded to a guard who brought over a book. "Now I want to learn from you."

The Gleaning of Souls glittered in silver across the blue leather.

Killien flipped open the book. Runes filled the page, similar to the ones Sini had given him. "Translate this."

Will shook his head. "I can't."

Killien grew still, his eyes dangerous.

"I'm not saying that I won't," Will clarified. "I'm saying I can't."

"Queensland and the Sweep use the same written language, and the same runes."

Will pointed at the runes. "These aren't normal."

"They're ancient."

"No. Ancient runes I can read." He paused. "Sort of. These are different. I've never seen any like this."

"I thought Keepers were brilliant scholars." Killien's voice was harsh.

"Most are. You captured the wrong one. But even if I could, I wouldn't translate something called *The Gleaning of Souls* for a power-hungry Roven Torch." Will shoved the book away. "So go ahead and kill me or whatever you have planned. Because I'm not helping you."

"You do not understand—" Killien clenched his jaw. When he spoke, his calmness sounded strained. "I could kill you. But contrary to what you think, I'm not thirsting for the blood of my enemies. I'm looking for the quickest way to peace."

Will let out a sharp laugh. "You won't find that in a book by Kachig the Bloodless."

When Killien spoke, it was quiet, spilling out onto the table like shards of ice. "I thought you might need convincing." He motioned to the door and a guard stepped aside.

Ilsa walked in.

CHAPTER TWENTY-TWO

ALL THE AIR left the room and Will's body froze.

Ilsa gave the Torch a small bow and carried Will's bag over to the table, never lifting her eyes off the floor. Her hair fell in a curtain across her face. Will opened up toward her and her nervousness rushed into his chest.

She set the bag down next to the table. Her eyes flicked up to Will's face for the merest second, and he leaned toward her. She flinched away from the movement and his gut turned to ice at the spike of fear she felt. A guard took a threatening step forward.

"Thank you, Ilsa." Killien waved her away, his eyes burning into Will.

Will started to rise, but the guard shoved him back down. Ilsa kept her head down and backed up against the wall.

"You'll have to excuse Ilsa's nervousness." Killien spoke calmly, like he was discussing the weather. "Imagine her surprise when she found out she'd spoken several times with a Keeper. She's relieved she didn't anger you. She says you often seemed agitated."

Will dragged his gaze back to Killien. "How…?"

"I told you that your books made fascinating reading," Killien said.

Of course. His search for Ilsa had been written in his books starting long before he'd met the Morrow. She moved quickly back from the table and Will searched her face to see if Killien had told her, but she didn't look like someone who was worried about anything as complicated as having a new brother. She was looking at him more the way one might look at a snake that might be poisonous.

Killien set his hand on Will's bag. "They gave me so much insight into why you were on the Sweep. What you've been looking for all this time. I thought about keeping them for myself, but I've decided to let you have access to them, in case they are helpful to you while you work."

Killien stood, leaning on the table until Will had to look up to meet his gaze. "Translate those runes, Keeper, or…" He let the threat hang unfinished.

Killien walked out the door, followed by Ilsa and the guards.

Will dropped his head into his hands. It felt heavy, his arms hollow and shaky.

Killien had Ilsa. The thought stopped every other thing in his mind.

Whatever hope he'd had of freeing her from the Morrow crumbled to ash.

The gnawing fear of what Killien could do to her forced his head up. He pulled Kachig's book closer.

The silver medallion was back on the cover, a drip of hardened resin running along the edge. Four daggers split the disk into quarters. Intertwined around the blades were strings of runes connected with thin, snaking lines. Or maybe they weren't runes. There was something odd about them, something ominous. In the very center of the medallion, in a small square formed by the hilts, there was just smooth silver. Except it didn't reflect light right. It was somehow both silver and dark at the same time, and that darkness made the emptiness into something horrible.

Will leaned forward, his gaze drawn along a path of the symbols. It pulled at him gently, but persistently. None of the runes were recognizable, and the daggers themselves were part of the path. A shadowy sort of haze fell over his mind and he wrenched his eyes away and flipped the book open.

The strange runes covered the page in faded black ink. There was no way he was going to be able to read this. He scanned the page, looking for anything he recognized. Each time he found one, *age, exhaustion, coldness, death,* there was something wrong with it. As though it had been broken and put back together with too many pieces.

Something scuffed outside and Lukas limped in the door, followed by Sini. She carried a large pitcher to the table.

"I don't suppose that's saso?" Will asked.

She shook her head, with a little smile and pulled a stack of small papers and a jar of ink from her pocket.

"Prisoners don't get saso," Lukas said. "Back away from him, Sini."

"It's alright, Lukas." The girl added a short stub of a candle to the table.

"I'm not going to hurt her." Will worked to keep his voice even.

Lukas set a book on the table and Will picked it up. It was a dictionary of runes. Lukas took a step and his leg twisted awkwardly. He grabbed the chair, a grimace crossing his face.

"I might be able to help with the pain—" Will stopped at the look of undisguised hatred Lukas shot him.

"Ah, the great Keeper will fix everything." Lukas's knuckles whitened around the back of the chair. "You're fifteen years too late to help me."

Will lay the book down on the table, guilt snaking into him. "The wayfarers took my sister twenty years ago, but we thought it was an isolated event. No one knew they were still taking random children. If we knew—if the Queen knew—"

"Can you translate the runes?" Lukas interrupted.

Will fought against all the other things he wanted to say, before letting the topic of the wayfarers drop. "I'm working on it."

"I for one, don't think you'll be able to." Lukas turned and limped toward the door. "Which means Killien will kill you soon. I just hope it's before I have to walk all the way out here again. Come on, Sini." Without looking back, he left.

Sini gave Will a smile, half apologetic and half worried, and followed.

Queensland had failed these two. The Keepers had failed them. The wayfarers had been taking children all this time. He dropped his head into his hands, fury and impotence clashing against each other.

When he got home, he was taking this to the queen.

If he got home.

He forced himself to focus on the book again, and on the next page, one of the runes looked familiar. Grabbing his own bag, he unwrapped his books and flipped through one of them, searching through his writing for a specific page. Someone else's handwriting caught his eye. Will had recorded what he knew about the death of Killien's father, but underneath, in bold strokes, new words had been added.

Tevien, Torch of the Morrow, was betrayed by a man he trusted.

A man who lied about everything he was and everything he wanted.

A man who befriended him to sneak and spy and destroy.

Will let out a long sigh and flipped to a page with six runes he'd drawn down the side, each formed in the same sort of odd way as the ones in Kachig's book. He'd seen them months ago embroidered on a robe worn by a stonesteep in Tun. Will had walked behind him for ages memorizing the shapes so he could record them. Next to them were written guesses at their meaning, but they weren't good guesses.

There was a flutter at the window as Talen flew in and landed on the table, a mouse hanging from his beak.

Will ran a finger down the hawk's neck. "Good morning. How

do you like our new home?" He pulled his bedroll out of his bag and took it over to the bed. "There."

Talen flew over to the blanket and picked at it with his beak.

"Have you seen Shadow?" Will sat next to the bird. "Or Rass? I haven't seen her since..." Before the goblin attacks. A little knot of worry for the little girl sat in his stomach. "Or have you seen Sora? She's sharp enough to stay safe from Killien. Right?"

Talen let out a loud squawk.

"I wonder if I'm ever going to stop wishing you could talk to me." Will slumped back against the wall. "This place is so...lifeless. I'm surprised you came back."

Talen turned and launched into the air, flapping out the door of the hut, and soaring up into the sky.

Will stared after him for a moment. "Although I suppose this place isn't as bad when you're free to fly away."

He trudged back to the table. There had to be a way to read these runes. He rubbed at his face, trying to push away his frustration and focus on the book.

Talen came back three times, bringing with him beakfuls of dead grass. The third time, Will followed him into the bedroom. Talen stood next to a neat little nest, looking at Will expectantly.

"I have no food." Will brushed the back of his fingers down the hawk's chest. "You know what would be useful? If you brought back something that had energy in it. Like living grass. Or better yet, a tree."

Talen leaned down into his nest and nudged the stalks of grass around with his beak.

Emotions resonate. They don't move.

Will considered the bird. He'd tried in the past to push emotions toward Talen, but maybe there was another way. He opened up toward the hawk and felt a nebulous pleasure that seemed to be focused more on the nest than anything else.

His finger froze against Talen's chest.

Talen felt pleased *about the nest*. Because emotions were focused on something.

Will fanned his own emotions, trying to make them strong enough for Talen to notice, willing them to resonate in the little bird.

"Or you could find Sora. Because if anyone could get me out of this, it'd be her." That was very easy to want. He let his need for her help grow until it filled his chest. "I need Sora."

Talen shifted his weight and Will held his breath. The hawk twitched his head toward the other room and launched into the air. Will, stunned that it had actually worked, watched the hawk flutter to the next room—and come back with the dead mouse. He dropped it onto Will's blanket.

"Or you could just keep bringing me mice." Will leaned back and closed his eyes, exhaustion washing over him.

Talen let out a short, self-satisfied squawk, and Will heard him rustling in his nest.

The wall and the bed spun slowly underneath him. His body felt hollow except for a gnawing fear. He considered the fear for a moment, wanting to believe it was all for Ilsa. But it wasn't. A healthy chunk of the fear was for himself. Because as sure as Talen was going to bring more mice, Will was never going to figure out these runes.

With a quick screech, Talen took off and flew out of the hut rising effortlessly out of the rift. Will had never wanted to fly so badly.

But Killien had Ilsa. Will pushed himself up.

Laying out some paper, he studied the first rune. *A page of runes is like a story*, Alaric liked to say. *Each symbol interacts with the ones next to it, altering it slightly, changing the shape of the tale.*

Except runes were nothing like stories.

He copied rune after rune, hoping to see something that made sense, but copying them was awkward. The lines were all too crowded. He flipped one rune upside down and found...something vaguely like *tree*.

This wasn't getting him anywhere. It seemed unlikely that Kachig wrote something-like-a-tree, maybe-upside-down. Or why it sat between the almost-rune for winter, and the backwards—and embellished—rune for fish.

Will paused, studying that last one. Fish or disease?

Talen flew back in the door, and winged into the bedroom.

Will shoved himself away from the table. There was no way he was going to get even a single rune translated. He walked to the door and leaned against the wall, staring up at darkening sky.

Runes are like stories.

Will let his head fall back against the hut. No, Alaric, stories were a series of events that took you someplace. Runes didn't go anywhere.

He pushed himself off the wall. The *rune* didn't move, but the *pen* did.

The room had fallen into a dark orange gloom. He set his finger against the wick of the candle and gathered a bit of *vitalle* from himself.

"*Incende.*" The candle flickered to life.

Talen had fallen asleep in the bedroom, his head turned backwards and tucked into his back, leaving him looking morbidly headless.

Will looked at the first rune. Instead of looking at the completed form, he focused on how the pen must have moved. There were two possible starting points. He picked one and drew the rune from there. A line down, more pressure at the top, lifting to gentle thinness at the bottom. A slope up to the right, a slash across. When there was no obvious next stroke, he lifted his pen, ignoring the rest of the marks.

Empty.

Clear as day, it said *empty.*

Or *hollow.* Or *void.* He couldn't quite remember the nuance between the three.

That wasn't important. At least not yet. He started on the lines left in the original rune. They began at the left, curled across and down before thinning again to a spidery line that connected to an accent mark.

Soul.

Will stared at the words, then back at the original rune. Kachig had intertwined *soul* with *empty*. The runes were stacked.

The empty soul?

No, *empty* wasn't descriptive, the rune leaned to the side—an action. *To empty.*

To empty the soul.

Will moved to the next. It split into four. *Stone, require/must, be chained, fire.*

He split the next rune, and the next, until the page was full. When he finally put down the quill, his hand was shaking.

Absorption Stones

To empty the soul, the fire must be chained in a stone. Drawing out (or washing out?) the fire (life?) leaves _____ (possibly 'kill', but more like 'unmaking' than 'killing'.)

It went on, describing death and power and stones.

Will leaned back in his chair. This was what Killien wanted? Absorption stones.

And how could he possibly do it? There was no way he had a stonesteep with these skills hiding in the Morrow.

The candle sputtered out hours later. He stood and stretched, walking outside the lump of a hut. A swollen half-moon sat atop the cliffs, casting dim silvery shadows through parts of the rift and leaving most of it in blackness. Rising out of the east, the Serpent Queen's shadow stretched up into the sky. Her shape seemed to grow out of the darkness of the rift itself, leaving him with the eerie impressions that this rift was something she'd already devoured.

A scuff sounded just behind him. He spun, casting out. The bright *vitale* of a person stood only paces away.

"It seems I should have snuck you away from the Morrow a little sooner," Sora said from the darkness.

CHAPTER TWENTY-THREE

"Sora!" he snapped, his heart slamming into his chest. "Why are you creeping around in the dark?"

"You're not supposed to have visitors," she said mildly, her voice almost agreeable. "Can we go inside?"

He blew out a long breath, trying to calm himself. "It makes me nervous when you talk nicely."

When they'd stepped inside, she pulled a cloth off a small bowl in her hands and a dim orange light filled the room.

"You have glimmer moss?" He leaned closer. A small bundle of the luminescent moss sat submerged in water. "I've never seen any outside Duncave."

"My people live in caves, Will," she said, exasperated.

Despite everything, he grinned at her. "There's your real voice."

The moss glowed dimmer than candlelight, more diffuse and gentle. She studied him with a small wrinkle in her brow. "I thought you'd be dead by now."

"So did I," he admitted, sitting down. "How'd you get past my guards?"

She raised an eyebrow. "You think I can't get past two lazy, distracted boys playing ranger in the dark?"

"Could you get me out?"

She bit her lip to hold back a smile. "I've heard you walk through the grass, Will. They could be unconscious and they'd still hear you."

He tried to smile, but he couldn't muster a real one. For a heartbeat, he considered the idea she'd been sent by Killien. But he couldn't imagine her feigning friendship like this. With more than a little surprise, he realized he trusted her.

He took a deep breath. "Killien has my sister."

She sank back in her chair and nodded. "He told me." At Will's surprised look, she added, "He doesn't suspect I knew you were a Keeper. So far all of his anger is focused exclusively on you."

"I just need to make sure he keeps it focused on me, not on Ilsa." Will sank back in the chair. "I don't *think* he's told her yet. At least Ilsa didn't seem to be trying to decide if I am her long lost brother."

Sora gave him a half-smile. "I've known Ilsa the entire time I've been here. I haven't been around her often, mostly because Lilit never warmed up to me, but we've spoken several times, and I like her. Lilit always has too, if that makes you feel any better. As far as I know, she's been well-treated." Her smile turned to a smirk. "And now I feel a little better about how horribly awkward you were around Ilsa all the time."

Will ran his hand through his hair. "I needed to talk to her without scaring her."

She raised an eyebrow. "I doubt she was scared, but she might think you're a lunatic." She sat back in her chair. "I can't figure out how to get her away from Killien, though. Any more than I can figure out how to get you away from him."

He pushed the next question out. "Does he have Rass too?"

Sora shook her head. "No one's seen the girl since the attack."

A wave of relief washed over him until he realized what she'd said and jolted forward.

"I don't think she was hurt," Sora said quickly. "There were a lot of injuries, but only twelve deaths, and all of that happened along the front line."

Twelve dead. "Did they have families?"

"Most of them." She paused. "Killien will never say it, but he knows the only reason there aren't more is because of you."

Will dropped his head down onto his fingertips, staring at the table without seeing it.

Sora shifted, and Will felt her hand on his arm. "We should have lost many more, Will. No one has ever heard of that many goblins on the Sweep." She pulled gently but persistently on his arm and he lifted his head. "The only reason the clan wasn't massacred is you."

"Twelve dead." He shook his head. "I should have done it sooner. I could have pushed the heat toward the holes in the ground as soon as they appeared, chased them back in."

She dropped her hand from his arm, leaving a cool spot in the shape of her fingers. "Why didn't you?"

He couldn't look up at her. The goblins had come so fast, like a flood.

"You didn't know you could do it, did you?"

His gaze flicked up to her, expecting her usual sharp contempt, but she was solemn.

He rubbed his hands over his face and let out a laugh. "I've never done anything remotely like that."

"Will," she said seriously, "you need to give Killien whatever it is he wants from you. I've never seen him this angry."

The blue book sat heavy and undecipherable on the table.

"I can't."

"Do something magical"—she waved one hand in the air, fluttering her fingers—"and give Killien what he wants."

Will stared at her. "I can't just *do something magical*."

"You can make a wall of heat. You can walk through a crowd and have no one notice you're there."

"Congratulations." Will glared at her. "You've named the two *magical things"*—he wiggled his fingers at her—"that I know how to do."

She sat back in her chair, looking at him in disbelief. "You can't do anything else?"

"Not anything worthwhile. Gerone, the Keeper who spent years trying to train me, says I have a motivation problem. Which maybe is true, because I just mastered the not-being-noticed thing since coming to the Sweep, and I figured out how to move the heat while the goblins"—it had been the goblins racing toward Sora. She'd looked so exposed in the face of their viciousness—"Ran toward us."

"Are most Keepers better at magic than you are?"

He gave her an annoyed look. "Yes, but it matters less than you'd think. We do a lot of reading, and writing, and research. Most of the Keepers are elderly and never leave the Stronghold. I'm the youngest. Alaric is next. He's the court Keeper. He's decently good at magic, and he could decipher these runes in his sleep."

She looked at him curiously. "Sounds irritating to have someone who's better than you at everything."

"He's not better at storytelling," Will corrected her. "And he's not irritating. He's been like a brother to me since I was ten."

She looked at him for a long moment. "If he was the court Keeper, what was your job?"

"I traveled around Queensland telling stories and learning stories and looked for new Keepers. When a child develops the ability to do magic, around the age of ten, their family brings them either to court, or to the nearest Keeper. For poorer families that can't afford to travel, it's nice if there's someone close."

"But you're the youngest."

"I was looking for new ones, not finding them. There should be at least two younger than me. The gap between us is usually less than ten years."

Sora gave him a long, probing look. "Is it true Keepers can sense people they can't see? And suck the life out of them?"

Will let out a laugh. "We're opposed to things like sucking the life out of people. But living things are full of energy—*vitalle*, and we can sense it when it's nearby."

Sora's face grew taut and she sat perfectly still.

"Grass and plants have a little *vitalle*," he continued, uncomfortable at her rapt attention. "Humans have a lot." He cast out through the rift finding only Sora, blazing bright in front of him, and the compact energy of Talen, nestled in the other room. "You, Talen, and I are the only ones in the rift."

Sora nodded slowly, her eyes losing their focus. Will waited for some sign of disbelief, or doubt. But she sat still, her eyes unseeing and her head slightly bowed.

"People are usually surprised to learn that I can do that."

Her gaze flickered up at him, more uncertain than he'd ever seen her. She was almost frightened.

Several disparate ideas he had about her clicked into place.

He leaned forward. "You can sense it too."

She flinched at his words.

Will stared at her for a long moment, then burst out laughing. "You can! Hal's right! You have creepy magic. No wonder you can —what did Killien say? Find a mountain hare in a snowstorm?" He leaned closer, grinning. "You have magic."

The edge of her lips curled into a reluctant smile.

"How much can you see?" he asked.

"It's not like seeing. It's more like a smell...or like feeling the temperature. I can tell when something is alive nearby, but not what direction it's in. I just have to move and see if it gets stronger."

"Fascinating! I've only met two people who had the ability to sense *vitalle*, but not manipulate it, and they were both in Queensland. It's unusual for people to have abilities like you."

"Can all Keepers sense things the way you do?"

Will hesitated. That was a complicated question.

"Can they sense *vitalle* as clearly as you?" she prodded, testing out the word.

"Yes. They can all sense *vitalle*."

She waited a moment, her eyebrows raised expectantly. "There's a but coming. Do they do it like I do? Without knowing really where it is?"

"No, we all send out a…wave of sorts, searching for energy, and it echoes back to us where things are."

Her brow knit together. "So what can you do that they can't?"

"I can…" He'd never told anyone this outside the Keepers.

"I don't really talk about it," he said.

She leveled a gaze at him, her face incredulous.

"And you don't talk about your creepy magic either," Will said. "Right." He rubbed his hand across his mouth. "I can feel people's emotions."

One of her eyebrows shot up. "Feel them?"

Will nodded. "Right around here." He pointed to the left side of his chest.

Sora was silent, pondering this. "Can you tell what they're thinking?"

Will shook his head. "It isn't like that. You know how if someone's angry, it can make you feel angry? Well I can feel that anger as strong as they do, but still separate from my own emotions."

"Can you read me?"

Will laughed. "I gave up trying to read you ages ago."

Her brow dove down and she looked at him, insulted.

"I've never met anyone who keeps their emotions as clamped down as you. When I try to read you, all I feel is…emptiness."

She considered him for a moment. "How many times have you tried?"

"At the beginning, a lot. You were terrifying. And finding out you had no emotions made it so much worse."

She looked satisfied by that answer. Then her eyes widened. "That's how you tell stories so well. You feel the audience. You change your story to please them."

Will shifted in his seat. "Well, it helps, of course. But all storytellers do that. They watch expressions and notice when attention starts to wander. I just have…a little more information. And I like to think that my success lies in the fact that I have some storytelling skills."

She shook her head, smiling. "I was right about you, storyman."

"In the most negative way possible."

"Let's see if I can control how much you feel. I'll try to open up." She leaned forward expectantly. It was strange to see her face so pleasant. The slight smile in her eyes was distracting and he closed his eyes before opening up toward her.

Emptiness bloomed in his chest and he shook his head. She kept her emotions too tightly controlled. As though she didn't want to feel them herself, never mind let anyone else know they existed. But then he felt a hint of…something.

"Curiosity," he said, "and a bit of worry, or fear."

She made a noise that sounded like agreement.

He focused and found the current of seething anger that he'd felt in her a few times before. It was so deep-rooted and so…foundational.

"What else?" she asked.

"You're angry," he continued, keeping his eyes shut so he didn't have to look in her face. "It's down below everything else. Like it's fundamental to everything you are."

He waited, with his eyes closed, listening and feeling for a reaction to his words.

Her silence filled the room, and there was no change in her emotions.

He was just about to crack an eye open to see if she was glowering at him when he noticed a thread of something else. Something…

"Happy."

He focused on the tiny bright feeling that was intertwined with the worry and the curiosity that floated above all the anger. It was definitely happiness.

He snapped his eyes open. "What are you happy about?"

She looked at him and laughed.

An odd thought struck him. "Are you happy to see me?"

She raised an eyebrow.

"Or are you happy to see me *captured*?"

She rolled her eyes and stood up.

"Or are you happy that you were right about me all along?"

She ignored his questions. "Killien's not a patient man, Will. Figure out a way to get him what he wants." She picked up the small cloth and draped it over the glimmer moss bowl, dropping the room into darkness. Her feet crunched softly on the hard floor as she left.

He peered into the blackness after her from the doorway. He couldn't see a thing, but he cast out toward her and felt her *vitalle* moving slowly down the path.

"What are you happy about?" he whispered after her.

Nothing but a little ripple of laughter came back to him.

CHAPTER TWENTY-FOUR

Morning sunlight barely dribbled over the edge of the rift, leaving it a dim honey color. Will's back felt like it had hardened overnight. Lying on the hard clay was even worse than the wagon.

He pushed himself to his feet and splashed some of yesterday's water onto his face. He tried a sip, but it tasted like clay. Outside, nothing had changed. Aside from the two guards at the top of the rift, it was empty. He sighed, sat down at the table and pulled Kachig's book towards him, his palm stinging slightly.

He cast out and felt the *vitalle* pressing against the inside of his palms, working to grow new skin. It would take more energy than he could possibly find to heal them. It had always seemed stupid that Keepers couldn't heal burned palms, when it was one injury they were almost guaranteed.

Will picked up the last page he'd translated. It was a list of gems with notes as to which held more souls, which damaged them, which tainted them.

Topaz, apparently, was what you wanted when trying to suck someone's soul into a stone.

He dropped the paper. He couldn't give this information to Killien, but before he could decide what he should do with it, footsteps sounded outside his door. He snapped his attention to the door, but it was only Sini, followed by a guard.

"I told Killien that you might work better with some saso." The girl held up a clay pitcher and a cup.

"You're amazing." Will shoved his work aside so she could set it down.

She pulled another stack of paper from a bag slung around her shoulders. "In case you need more."

He poured himself a steaming drink and the smell of dark roasted caramel filled the room.

"I told Killien I had faith in you." She picked up a page of split-up runes, holding it upside down and frowning. "You *are* figuring it out, aren't you?"

Will held the saso in front of his face for a long moment, breathing in the scent. Nothing good could come from this book. Even though Killien had no way to perform this level of magic, Will couldn't translate it for him. But he couldn't risk what Killien would do to Ilsa if he didn't.

"I thought I was on to something," Will said, taking the paper back from her and tossing it onto the others. "But it turned out to be nothing."

Sini's brow creased. "Killien will be back this afternoon. I've never seen him so angry."

"People keep saying that."

The girl hesitated, fidgeting with the papers. "That's because it's true."

She didn't continue, and Will took another drink. "I thought Lukas said prisoners don't get saso. Does this mean I'm not a prisoner anymore?"

Sini gave him a small smile. "It means that Lukas hates you."

Will sat back. "Yes. As subtle as he's been about it, I'd picked up on that. What I don't know is why."

"He doesn't hate you personally, he hates what you represent."

"The Keepers?"

She shrugged. "All of Queensland. He feels like the entire country betrayed him because it let Vahe take him." She looked down at her own hands. "It's easier than blaming his family."

The thought sank into Will, thick and bitter.

"Lukas's not as bad as you think. His hip hurts him a lot, but he still tries to be nice—to everyone but you. I was only twelve when I came to the Morrow, and he took care of me. He spent weeks letting me trail after him, introducing me to the nicest of the Morrow, helping me learn the skills that would make me useful to the Torch." She stared unseeing at the table. "He and Rett are like brothers. Lukas created a place for me here until it began to feel like home." She flickered a glance up to Will. "Not a home like my real home, maybe, but still a home."

Will set the saso down. "How long have you been here?"

"This is my third summer."

"I'm sorry..." He stopped, not knowing how to possibly say everything that needed saying.

She tapped the papers into a neater stack, not raising her eyes. "It's not as bad as I thought it'd be. The Torch treats us well. And there's always enough food. My family lived outside Queenstown, in a shed behind an inn. I used to slip into the city and steal food for us, but I had five younger brothers. There was never enough."

Queenstown. She'd been surrounded by so many people who should have protected her.

"When Vahe came to take me, we hadn't eaten in two days. My father barely put up a fight."

"Vahe?" Was he the only wayfarer who ever took children? Or was he the only one who delivered them to Killien?

She nodded, but a mischievous grin spread across her face. "He had three money bags, so, while my father tried to stop him, I tore one off and tossed it to my mother. They should have had food for a while."

Will grinned at her. "Too bad you couldn't get all three."

The guard cleared his throat loudly and Sini flinched. Will shot him a scowl which was utterly ineffective.

"Good luck, Will." The girl turned and hurried out of the hut.

Will stared at the empty doorway. Sini, Lukas, and Ilsa, all brought *here* by Vahe? Why them? And how many others had he brought?

CHAPTER TWENTY-FIVE

WILL PULLED out a new piece of paper and separated out a new page of runes, translating two more pages. "Translating" was too strong of a word. There were too many runes he wasn't sure about. The more runes he deciphered, the more chilled he felt. The human soul was nothing more than a commodity in this book. Something to be taken, stored, and used.

He couldn't give this information to Killien.

He needed to get it back to the Stronghold. The Keepers could study it, understand how Roven stonesteeps used stones for magic.

What he wanted to do was set this book on fire. He set his finger against the corner of the book and began to gather in *vitalle*. It felt deeply right to destroy something this evil.

Except he couldn't.

As evil as it was, there were things here the Keepers didn't understand. There must be more copies of this book. Destroying this one wouldn't keep the world from having the knowledge, just the Keepers. He let the energy dissipate, not entirely happy with his decision.

Still, he couldn't give this to Killien. He picked up the pages with the real translations and grabbed his own books out of his pack. He tucked his translations into empty spaces among his other writings. Thankfully his books were eclectic enough that phrases scattered about didn't seem too out of place.

When he finished he wadded the pages into balls and set them around the pitcher. It would be nice to have some warm saso. There weren't enough to surround it, so he grabbed two more blank sheets from the pages Sini had brought.

Writing on one caught his eye.

We're not random.

The letters were round and smooth. Was this from Sini?

He thought back over their conversations. He'd mentioned something being random…What was it?

His hand tightened on the paper. It had been with Lukas. Will had said no one knew that wayfarers were still taking random children.

Were Lukas and Sini not random? Had they been taken for a reason? Did that mean Ilsa had been too?

He crumpled the paper and tucked it next to the others, mulling over the idea. Gathering some *vitalle*, he set them on fire. Flames licked up the side of the pitcher, the paper turned to ash, and he still didn't know what Sini meant.

With a warm cup of saso, he set to creating useless pages for Killien, runes turned this way and that way, his best guesses at their meaning scribbled, scratched out, and rewritten.

He had fifteen pages "translated" when Killien showed up.

Killien walked in with a slight smile on his face, and for the briefest moment, he looked like the friendly, interesting man Will had talked to so often.

The three guards took up their positions around the room. Killien walked over to the table and picked up a few pages, he raised an eyebrow at Will's work and thumbed through the other pages, then looked around the room. When he saw the ring of ashes around the saso, his hands curled into fists, crushing the paper. He pressed his eyes shut, and loosened his hands, letting out a small laugh.

He set the papers down and sat in the chair across from Will. His voice was unnaturally light. "It doesn't convince me of your friendship if you start destroying the work I want to see."

Will's chair felt hard beneath him and he tried not to shift his weight. Around him the guards were attentive, but relaxed and Killien leaned back in his chair like an old friend come to visit. "Sini saw your work this morning. None of us had realized the runes were stacked."

Will's hand tightened on the quill. She'd both spied for Killien, and left Will that note? "I hadn't thought Sini was that sneaky."

"The translation should move along quickly, now. I considered taking the book and doing it myself. Lukas and Sini could help. They've spent a good deal of time learning to read runes. Sini, in particular has a knack for them. She's only been learning them for a short while, but she's picking it up quickly. Still, we wouldn't be as fast as you, Will."

The book sat heavily between them. Will almost opened up toward the Torch, but he decided he didn't want to have to face what the man was feeling.

"What do you want this book for, Killien? There isn't enough death and fighting with normal means? You need to add in more?"

"There is too much death." Killien tapped his finger on the book. "Which is why we need this. People respond to nothing but power. If the violence is going to end, it has to be crushed by something stronger."

"This—" Will stabbed a finger at the book. "—is not the answer. It speaks of dark things, Killien—things worse than killing people. Are you going to do this to Roven? Suck the life out of them and trap it in a stone? What happened to wanting to unify them?"

"I'm not going to actually *use* it." Killien's face was so intense Will pulled back. "You don't have to use such force against people, Will. What's important"—his voice dropped to a whisper —"is the *threat* of power."

For the first time since he'd been captured, Will actually looked at the man. There was no lightness, no fairness or interest in his face. The Torch's eyes were shadowed with exhaustion, his face strained. He looked driven, haggard. Angry. Like there was so much anger in him, it might rip him apart.

Something about Killien had come unhinged. Will searched the Torch's face, as though he'd find the answer to why written across it.

"The threat of power doesn't work," Will said, "unless you're willing—and able—to use it. If you had to hire someone to make heatstones for your clan, you can't have anyone skillful enough to do this."

Killien brushed off the words. "Your concern for my success is heartwarming. I'll worry about what to do with the translation, you just focus on giving it to me. You're off to an excellent start, and I think that's worth celebrating." He motioned to the guard in the doorway.

The guard moved and Ilsa walked in, carrying wine, some cups, and a plate of cheese.

Will's hands clenched. Part of him wanted to open up toward her, but too much of him was terrified of what he'd feel. He forced his hands to relax and dragged his gaze back to Killien, funneling as much hatred as he could into it. "Last time you offered me wine, it didn't go well."

Killien laughed, and it sounded slightly crazed. "There's nothing in this. I promise." He poured dark red wine into each cup and slid one close to Will. "To our…" He raised his glass and gave Will a complicated smile. "Partnership."

Will left his cup sitting on the table. "That isn't what this is."

"Relationship, then." Killien shrugged, taking a long drink of the wine. He stretched over, picked up Will's cup, and took a sip.

"See? It's just wine. Very good wine, actually. One of three bottles I bought from a Baylonian merchant last summer. Cost a fortune."

Will thought about refusing, about tossing the wine at Killien's face and hurling the bottle across the room. But the saso was cold and stale and his water had run out earlier. When he picked up the cup, Killien's smile turned almost genuine.

"I have only shared this wine with one other person. And that was the stonesteep from the Sunn clan who was kind enough to tell me the location of Kachig the Bloodless's book."

Will lifted the cup to his mouth and took a sip. It was delicious. Rich and simple and effortless.

"Best wine you've ever tasted?" Killien watched Will with a curiosity that was both eager and guarded.

Will set the cup down slowly. He stared at Killien's face, wondering how he'd missed the ruthlessness there for so long. "It's almost as good as what's served at Queen Saren's table."

The flash of ire in Killien's face was utterly satisfying.

The Torch took another drink, and when he set his cup down, his face was a mask, as cold and inhuman as the clay walls. Will's gaze flicked to Ilsa where she waited against the wall, her arms wrapped around her stomach, her eyes fixed on the floor as always.

"I think Will's done with the wine, Ilsa." Killien's eyes bored into Will.

She started slightly at his attention, then moved quickly across the room to gather his cup off the table.

"Thank you." Killien's voice was kind but his eyes never left Will's face. "Ilsa's served my wife for years, but only recently have I realized how valuable she is."

Ilsa smiled, timid and pleased. Both parts of it gouged at Will's heart. He opened up to her and her gratitude toward Killien bloomed in his chest, cutting into him like knives.

The Torch fixed Will with a smug look. "I keep finding more and more reasons to keep her near me." A streak of viciousness from Killien cut into Will.

A shiver of unease wriggled through Ilsa's pleasure and her hand tightened on the wine. A silence, taut and rigid, filled the room. Ilsa stood still, her breath shallow and quick, her apprehension growing the longer the silence stretched.

"I've done what you asked for." Will kept his eyes fixed on Killien.

"You burned what I asked for," Killien corrected him.

If Killien knew how to decode the runes, there was no point in keeping it from him any longer. Will's hands tightened into fists. "I'll write it out for you again. You'll have what you want."

"And you think you deserve a reward for doing such fine work?"

Will didn't look at Ilsa. "I'm the only one you have anything against."

Killien cocked his head to the side, he gave Will an easy smile that was stabbed in the back by the savagery in his eyes. "What exactly are you asking for?"

Will's own anger drowned out Ilsa's shrinking pleasure and Killien's cruelty.

"Leave her out of it," he whispered.

Ilsa glanced at them, her brow drawn in confusion.

"Ilsa," Killien began, leaning back in his chair, "Will has developed a bit of a…fascination with you."

Will felt a dart of fear worm its way through Ilsa's emotions and she stiffened.

"No—" he started to deny it, turning to look her full in the face.

She shrank back away from him.

"Don't speak, Will," Killien interrupted. The guard behind Ilsa shifted closer to her, unsheathing his knife.

Will dragged his gaze back to Killien, fury and impotence threatening to explode out of him.

"It's understandable," Killien said, a glint of viciousness in his eyes. "Ilsa is a lovely young woman, and you've been lonely a long time."

"That's not—"

Killien raised a hand sharply to stop him. The guard loomed

grimly behind Ilsa, who held her arms close to her side. Will kept his eyes fixed on Killien's face, he pressed his fists down into the table.

"I'm sorry, Ilsa." Killien nodded to her. "I didn't mean to make you uncomfortable. Thank you for your help. You may return to your other duties."

With the tiniest glance at Killien, filled with gratitude, she bowed to the Torch and hurried from the hut.

Will turned back to Killien, furious. The sound of Ilsa's footsteps drew farther away, tearing a part of Will out with them. He slammed himself closed.

"You see, Will, you're not the only one capable of making people like you."

"If you hurt her," Will said, his voice unsteady.

"I admit I had my doubts she was your sister. Obviously you do not."

In blind fury Will cast out, found the *vitalle* of Killien and the guards, and snatched at it, not caring if it killed them. Not caring that the guards would kill him for it. Only caring that he had enough time to destroy Killien.

Nothing happened.

Drawing in the *vitalle*, was like grabbing smoke.

He stretched his hand out toward Killien. The man was a flaming beacon of energy, even the ring he'd taken from the traitor wrapped around his hand with a blaze of energy, but Will could move none of it.

Will grasped at it again. He'd never had *vitalle* be so elusive. "What did you do to me?"

The guard behind him grabbed his shoulder again, pulling him back in the chair. Each person in the room was a towering pillar of energy that Will could not touch.

"You don't think I'd walk in here and put myself at the mercy of your powers, do you?" Killien asked. "If I were you, I'd stop trying to fight, Will. Every guard has orders concerning Ilsa if you try anything…unpleasant. At the moment she knows nothing about you beyond that you are a Keeper. She hasn't suffered anything on your account. If you cooperate, she won't have to."

Will let his hand drop to the table, a coldness spreading through him and he felt more exposed than he ever had on the Sweep. Why couldn't he touch the *vitalle*?

Killien considered Will for a moment. "How old were you when she was taken?"

Will almost didn't answer, but he couldn't see what it would matter. "Eleven." Will pushed the word out between clenched teeth.

The Torch seemed to find that answer amusing. "And did you use your magic to try to save her?"

Will clenched his bandaged hands on the table, his anger burning like searing hot coals in his chest.

"Ah." Killien nodded. "But it obviously didn't work. And even though you were only eleven, you still blame yourself."

Will stared at the man's face, pouring all his impotent rage into the look.

"Ironic," Killien said with a slight exhale of laughter.

The word caught Will off guard. "Why?" he demanded.

The Torch looked at Will with an odd expression. "Just think how different things would be today if they'd gone differently that night." Killien heaved himself out of his chair.

"But you're right about one thing. You have given me what I wanted. The beginnings of it anyway. And if you want Ilsa to stay as safe and happy as she currently is, you'll continue your translations.

"Tonight," he continued, "as a little celebration, I'm letting you out of the Grave. Not for good, of course, but for a short time. I have visitors from the Sunn Clan here. One of them is the Torch's own nephew. For the first time in ten years, the Morrow will be invited to the enclave of Torches."

Killien's face split into a broad smile. "The Sweep is being reshaped. The smaller clans are banding together and things will change, beginning with this enclave."

Knowing it was useless, Will still cast out and tried to grab at some of Killien's *vitalle*. It slipped through his grasp. Will stared at the man who'd become a stranger.

"I need the storyteller from Gulfind to impress my guests tonight, Will. Of course Ilsa will be there. I wouldn't want to deny you the pleasure of seeing her. You have a few hours to come up with a story." He walked to the door and paused. "If I were you, I'd make it something spectacular."

CHAPTER TWENTY-SIX

WILL WENT TO THE DOOR. As Killien and the guards topped the path and disappeared, the flat blue sky settled back down like a glass lid, clear and empty.

A smooth shape glided over the edge of the rift and toward him, Talen's white chest glinting against the sky. Will held his arm out and leaned his head away as the small bird flapped onto his shoulder. "You're getting better at landing."

A thin green shoot swung from Talen's beak, its roots still entangled in a clod of earth.

"And that's better than your usual offering of a mouse." Will let out a long sigh. "Let's take it to your nest."

Will cast out toward the bird and found the coil of energy. Even when Talen rested, he was poised to burst into flight. Gently he took hold of the *vitalle* in the little hawk. There it was, solid, malleable. Will could have drawn it out, shifted it, anything.

Whatever Killien had done to keep him from manipulating energy, had ended. Will thought back over his time with Killien. Had he ever tried to use any *vitalle* when he was that near the Torch? Maybe one of Killien's rings had the power to stop him. He'd read people's emotions. He'd used *vitalle* to heal Lilit, but

Killien hadn't been as close. He'd been down near her feet, too worried and broken to come close.

Will opened up to Talen, searching for the bird's emotions. But the hawk had only a slight sense of anticipation.

"It seems like I should find some sense of loyalty. Or companionship." Will settled Talen on back of one of the chairs. "You're free to leave this charming place, and yet every day you come back."

He reached out slowly and ran the back of his finger down the front of Talen's wing. "Things don't seem to be going well. If you come back and I'm not here…" Talen's heartbeat thrummed against Will's finger. "I'm sure you'll find plenty of mice."

He sat down in the other chair. "If you get a chance, will you keep your eye out for Rass?" He tried to push the idea of the little girl at the hawk. To resonate his desire to know where she was, but he could sense no change in the little bird. "I doubt anyone's taking care of her." Talen turned his golden eyes toward Will, then with a rush of air, winged out of the door, and out of sight.

Will stared at the empty door. "I didn't think so."

He dropped his head into his hands. It really didn't feel like a night for storytelling. He needed something impressive, but easy enough he could tell in what was bound to be a stressful situation.

Sable would be a good choice. An orphan who'd joined a traveling theater company, she'd grown famous and wealthy. She'd left that life, not entirely by choice, and managed to save her people from a terrible enemy.

Yes, Sable was long enough to feel epic, intriguing enough to keep his attention even with Killien and Ilsa there. And since it was older than Queensland, there'd be no way to trace it to the current country. Yes, Sable would do nicely.

The rest of the afternoon passed in excruciating slowness while Will translated runes for Killien. Talen didn't return. Neither did Sora. Or Killien. Even Lukas's hateful glares would have relieved the boredom.

Eventually the shadows inched their way up the rift walls and the sky darkened to black, except for a reddish glow to the west. The wind tore across the Sweep, sending clouds racing past the earliest stars. To the west, the red in the sky brightened. Had they lit a bonfire? The glow stretched wider across the sky and a smudge of darkness covered the stars.

Not a bonfire. A grass fire. The smoke grew, piling up in malevolent shadows, glowing with a red-blackness. The guards still stood at the top of the rift. Will took a step toward them, wondering if they'd let him see the fire.

A small figure stepped out from the shadows next to Will. He froze, opening up and a burst of excitement exploded inside of him.

"Will!" a little voice whispered.

"Rass?"

She grabbed his hand. "Come. There's a big fire near the other rift, you can sneak out."

He almost laughed, but she sounded so serious. "The guards are still there."

"Not that way. I have a rope. Hurry!" She tugged him.

He held back. "Wait, I need my bag." He ran into the hut and grabbed it, tucking Kachig's book in it too.

He let Rass pull him around the hut and press a rope into his hands. He gave it a hard tug, and it stayed firm. Gripping it sent a thousand tiny daggers of pain into his palms, but he set his foot on the cliff wall and started to climb. With each step his feet crumbled away part of the wall. The rope was strangely textured, more like a braid of smooth vines than normal cord. Almost like—

"This is grass!" he hissed down at Rass.

"Of course it is."

It was unhealthy, that's what it was. It was unhealthy for a people to have this much of a love for grass. And this little girl was the worst. "How'd you make this?"

"I used *grass*. Hurry up."

They climbed above the height of the hut, and the guards stood clearly outlined against the reddening sky, focused by the fire. If they turned, Will and Rass would be clearly visible on the cliff.

Will pulled himself up, inch by crumbling clay inch. It took a lifetime to reach the top where the thin rope spread out into a wide net stretching up onto the Sweep. Will clawed his way over the edge and threw himself down. Wind laced with smoke and ash rolled past him and he covered his mouth with his arm.

A low line of rust-red flames spread across the ground to the west, like an army of fire demons dancing across the Sweep, the wind whipping them closer.

Will felt along the netting of grass, trying to find what the rope was anchored to. He found nothing. It merely spread out and tangled with the blades growing out of the earth. Rass climbed nimbly out over the edge.

"Rass, how did you—?"

She grabbed at Will's hand. "Hurry!"

"Wait. Where is the rift where the Morrow live?"

Rass pointed at the wall of flames. "Past the fire."

He took a few steps toward it. In the chaos, could he get to Ilsa?

Rass pulled his hand. "The fire is coming fast. We need to run!"

Will paused another moment. "I have to go back."

"After the fire!" Rass yanked at him. "You can't go that way!"

The line of flames spread unbroken to the north and south. He'd never get past it. With a growl of frustration, he nodded. Pulling two shirts out of his bag, he tied one over his nose and mouth, and the other around Rass's tiny head, then motioned her to lead the way.

The Hoarfrost Range sat to the north, close enough to touch. She ran toward a particularly jagged peak, far enough past the smoke that the snow on its peak glittered moon-white. Will ran after her, his bag bouncing against his back and his legs complaining before they had gone more than a dozen steps. The smoke whipped past them in fits, interspersed with cool night air and the fire rumbled like distant thunder.

He was utterly exhausted and the mountains seemed no closer when the wall of flame reached the nearest hillside, fingers of black and red thrashing wildly into the sky.

Rass stopped and whirled toward the flames. "It's going to catch us."

The flames flew toward them faster than they could hope to run. He spun around, but the fire was stretched out across the whole world to the west. There was no escape. Past the thick line of flames, the Sweep was black and charred. They'd be safe on the other side, but they'd be burned alive before the flames passed them.

Stepping forward, Rass closed her eyes and dropped her head down. Her hair fell over her face and she spread both her hands toward the grass between them and the approaching fire.

She was tiny and insubstantial in the face of the fire and the smoke.

"Rass!"

The flames crackled and roared like the rush of a huge waterfall, or a crashing surf. He took a step toward her and stretched out his hand, desperate to pull her away, but she flicked up her hand in a commanding gesture and he stopped.

His breath was hot and damp under the shirt, the sting of smoke burning his throat. There was no going back. The fire was already between them and the Grave. He waited a breath, then another.

A swirl of flame spun up from the grass in front of them, like a demon tearing out of the earth, showing Rass in stark relief. She clenched her hands into claws, rotated her palms up, and like a giant heaving a mountain, she hurled her hands toward the roiling sky.

The ground in front of them exploded.

CHAPTER TWENTY-SEVEN

DIRT AND GRASS thundered into the air. Will spun away, throwing his hands over his head and crashing to his knees. He grabbed Rass, pulling her back, leaning over to shield her from the earth crashing down around them.

When dirt stopped pelting him, he looked up.

A swath of turned earth cut through the leading edge of the fire. Strings of grass wafted down through thick, swirling dust.

The two of them sat in a gap of darkness. Flames blazed past on either side, driven east by the wind. A wave of heat rolled by, and they were behind the fireline, kneeling in a world of blackness and soot. All around them thin trails of smoke rose like wind whipped spirits.

Rass shifted, sinking back against his chest. Her eyes were closed and her shoulders heaved with thick, heavy breaths.

He cast out across the wasteland, but there was nothing left living but roots. No plants above the ground, no animals, no people as far as he could sense. The line of fire racing eastward was a gash of bright energy.

Rass's shoulders slowly settled down into regular breathing and she pushed her dusty hair out of her face. She looked like a creature made of earth. The shirt around her face was caked with dirt, and the skin by her eyes was rough with more. Bits of grass stuck out of her hair.

Will pulled the shirt down off his face and stared at her.

"You're not just a little girl."

She pulled her own shirt down and quirked a curious smile at him. "I'm a pratorii."

Will waited for her to say more.

"I have no idea what that means."

"Pratorii. I am the grass." She tilted her head as though considering the words. "Or the grass is mine."

A memory triggered in Will's mind.

What are the elves? he'd asked Ayda during the weeks he'd spent in the Lumen Greenwood.

We are the trees. She'd spun and thrown her arms out. *The keepers of their souls.*

Will touched a lock of Rass's dirt-caked hair. It was thin and straight and stiff. Like grass. "You're an elf?"

Rass considered this for a moment. "The tree elves are our cousins. They are silvii, we are pratorii."

"So…a grass elf?"

Rass grinned up at him. "Yes."

It seemed so obvious. She didn't look like she was from Queensland. The wide eyes, the sharp chin, the cheekbones: she looked like a smaller, wilder version of a tree elf.

Will stared at her, stunned. "Why didn't you tell me?"

Her smile faltered. "I thought you knew."

"I didn't even know grass elves existed." He gestured to her little grey shift. "I thought you were just an odd little slave."

"Roven slaves don't live in the grass."

"I know, that was part of what was so odd." He frowned at the fabric she wore. "Don't tell me that's made of grass."

She plucked at the edge of it. "The veins that run down the grass blades can be woven together into anything."

Will shook his head and laughed. "It all makes perfect sense, now that you say it. Are there many grass elves here?"

She nodded. "There's a lot of grass."

"You know, I have spent a lot of time over the last few weeks imagining rescue scenarios. Never once did I include a grass elf."

Rass puffed up a bit and gave him a proud smile.

Will looked at the long line of fire, a hundred questions circling in his mind. "Does the fire hurt you?"

She let out a small laugh. "Only if we're foolish enough to be in its path. Fires are as good for the Sweep as rain and sunshine. It burns away the ghosts of the old grass and feeds the new shoots. But most fires are small, and easily avoided."

The gap of flame that had passed around them had closed, and raced eastward unimpeded.

Will cast a sidelong glance at Rass. She was an elf. The idea was both shocking and utterly fitting.

"That was well done." He pointed to the upturned earth.

Rass pushed herself up and shook her hair out, dislodging dirt clods and small bundles of grass. She set her fist on her chest and gave Will a small bow before breaking into peals of laughter. A swirl of smoke enveloped them and her laugh turned to a cough.

"We should keep going," she said.

Will hesitated. "I need to go back. I need to get someone."

Rass shook her head. "The entire clan will be on guard. If you need to go back, wait until the fire's out. You'll never get close without being caught again."

Will knew she was right, but it was still frustrating to tug the shirt back over his face and follow her north. They'd find somewhere safe to regroup, then he'd figure out how to get back for Ilsa.

With the fire racing away, the world sank into blackness. His boots kicked up ash. All of the grass was gone. Will glanced down at Rass walking silent beside him. "Are you...alright?"

She looked up at him, her brow drawn down questioningly.

He waved his hand at the wasteland around them. "The grass," he began, not knowing exactly what to ask.

"Last year's grass was dead. The fire passed quickly and the roots are fine. New grass will grow soon."

Question after question popped into his mind. "Can you talk to it?"

She considered the question for a moment. "The grass talks to me."

When she didn't continue, Will bit his lips closed to keep from laughing. "What does grass have to say?"

"It tells me about the weather and where the herds are. If the ground is wet enough. How hot the sun is. Where the Roven are."

"How much of it can you hear?"

She looked at him as though the question made no sense.

"Can you hear the grass near your feet? The grass on an entire hill?"

"All the grass is one."

Will stared at her. *"The roots of each connects with the others, so the whole world is an endless living thing,"* he quoted her from the first day they'd met.

Her eyes wrinkled in pleasure. "You remember."

"It was very story-like." He stared at this tiny girl, trooping along next to him, just as she had for days. "You can hear the entire Sweep?"

She shrugged. "The grass is one. But I can't hear anything where it's scorched. The roots never speak."

The night dragged on endlessly, each step charred and crunchy. The fire continued off to their right, but all around them, as far as they could make out, there was nothing but burnt grass and ashes.

The thought of Ilsa haunted him. Would Killien punish her because Will had left? He almost turned back three times, but he couldn't figure out what good it would do. Putting himself back at Killien's mercy would change nothing. The book by Kachig the Bloodless sat in Will's pack. It was a strong bargaining chip. Maybe he could find a way to trade it for Ilsa.

It wasn't quite midnight when they reached the end of the burned grass. They continued north through the Sweep until the ground rose into the first slopes of the Hoarfrost Range. The sun was just rising and the wind had died. Far behind them where the Sweep had burned, lines of smoke rose up like thin grey reeds out of a black swamp.

"We need a place to hide before the sun rises." Will headed uphill until the trees grew into a proper forest. The smell of evergreen filled the air, clean and fresh. It smelled like the woods at the Keeper's Stronghold, and a sharp pang of homesickness hit him. Sunlight slanted through the trunks brightening patches of the trees and tufts of bright green grass. He breathed in the air, letting the height of the forest wrap around him. For the first time in a year he felt right. If it wasn't for Ilsa, he would never step foot on the Sweep again.

Ilsa. He glanced back toward the Sweep. Killien wouldn't do anything to her, would he? Maybe Will should have done something besides run. But even as he thought it, he knew there was no way he could have even found Ilsa in the chaos, never mind convinced her to come with him.

Rass walked along next to him, looking around at the thin sprinkling of grass with a slight pucker in her brow. The forest ended and the ground sloped up to their left across a bare patch of earth, toward a rock wall. Rass scuffed her way up the slope, her shoulders slumped, but he was struck again with how healthy she looked compared to when he'd first met her. It had been less than a fortnight.

The reason was so obvious he laughed. "You're getting stronger because it's spring, aren't you?"

She nodded. "I always get thin in the winter."

"I thought it was my food."

She wrinkled her nose. "I like the bread, and the avak. But the dry meat is too hard to chew."

"You never actually lived with the Roven, did you?"

"I hadn't been near them in ages. I only came the day I met you because I do love hearing the stories from the colored wagons."

It was astonishing how many wrong ideas he'd had about her. "If you live in the grass, what do you eat?"

"Worms and grubs. But in the winter, those burrow lower than the roots of the grass, and I can't find them. There are plenty around now, though, if you're hungry."

Will tried not to let his revulsion show on his face and dampen her offer. "No thank you."

He was about to collapse with exhaustion when he saw a shadowed spot above two large boulders. He scrambled up and found a small cave. He spread out his bedroll and the two of them collapsed on the floor in a patch of warm sunlight. Using shirts for pillows, they both lay down. Will's mind searched for ways to get back close to Ilsa, but he hadn't thought of any before he sank into sleep.

He woke no less tired. He lifted his head to look outside, and the muscles in his neck cried out in protest. The woods were silent and empty in the afternoon light. He heaved himself up. The cave was high enough that he could see through the tops of the trees down to the grasslands. In the distance he could see a wide swath of blackened Sweep.

Rass came to his elbow, looking out across the Sweep, her face untroubled by the destruction.

A thought struck him. "Did you start the fire?"

"No. I wouldn't have started it where it would try to kill us."

"Good point." Will thought for a moment. "Where did it start?"

"West of the rift where the Morrow live. There were people near it when it first flared up."

Will's gaze traveled over the endless black. "Who would start a fire like that?"

Something thumped in the cave behind them and Will spun around.

Two rabbits lay on the floor of the cave, and Sora climbed in after them.

"The first person most people blamed," she said, "was you."

CHAPTER TWENTY-EIGHT

WILL STOOD CAUGHT between fear and relief. The smallest smile curled up the edge of Sora's mouth. "I think this is only the second time I've made you speechless. It's nice." She leaned to the side so she could see Rass. "Are you hungry?"

Rass peeked out from behind Will. "Yes."

Sora slung off her pack and pulled out some dried meat.

Rass wrinkled her nose. "I'm gonna find something for myself." She scooted past Sora, giving her as wide a berth as she could.

Sora sat down, stretching her legs out in front of her. "This is one of my favorite caves. I'm mildly impressed that you found it."

Will grabbed a piece of meat. "Are more rangers coming?"

"Not any time soon. I told them you'd run back toward Queensland as fast as your lumbering legs could carry you. We'll rest until dusk. We need to find somewhere safer to hide, but it'll be better to move after dark."

Rass scrambled back in and scurried back over next to Will, offering him one of the four squirming grubs in her palm.

Sora peered into Rass's hand. "The darkish blue ones are the best."

Rass looked at her in surprise, then smiled. "They are."

Will held up a piece of meat. "I've got plenty."

Rass considered Sora for a moment before shyly offering her the grubs. At Sora's refusal, Rass popped a thin, pink one into her mouth.

Sora watched the girl closely. "I expected you to be alone, Will."

"Rass is the one who got me out of the rift," Will said. "And saved me from the fire."

Rass swallowed the last grub. "All we needed was a rope. And a little grass ripped up so the fire would go around us."

Sora glanced between the two of them. "I saw the torn earth. I thought Will had done that." She leaned closer to the little girl, taking in her wide eyes and her angular face. "How did you—" Her eyes widened. "You're a pratorii."

Rass elbowed Will. "*She* knows what pratorii are."

"Yes. She's very wise."

Sora looked at her in wonder. "I've never met one before. I think I've caught glimpses of a couple, but was never sure. You look more human than I expected." Her gaze flicked to Will. "Why are you spending time with him?"

"Because I'm likable," Will protested.

Sora ignored him and turned back to Rass. "I've never heard of a pratorii spending time with people."

"Will isn't a normal person."

"Agreed." Sora picked up one of the rabbits and began to dress it. She glanced at Will. "Someone should take first watch."

Will nodded and started to rise, but Rass grabbed his hand. She cast a nervous glance at Sora. "I'll do it." Without waiting for an answer, she scooted out of the cave and settled into a little nook in the rocks.

"It's a good thing she's a pratorii." Sora pitched her voice low. "Because unless you have some capable wife stashed somewhere, I can't see how you're going to take care of a little girl."

"I would have done just fine. Besides, Keepers don't marry."

Sora looked up at him. "Ever?"

"Not often. We spend all our time studying and traveling. It doesn't leave much time for a family. The last time one married was sixty years ago."

"Hm," she said in a tone impossible to read. "Can you hand me some pine needles?"

A thick layer of pine needles crowded along the edge of the cave floor. He ran his fingers along the floor and scooped up a jumble of needles, their dry tips jabbing into his fingers. "We don't have wood for a fire."

She fixed him with an annoyed look. "Why would I make a fire on a clear day while the entire Morrow Clan is looking for us?" She set half of the pine needles in a pile on the floor and pulled a heatstone out of her bag. "I just need a small flame. Be useful. I know you can start this with your finger."

"Don't you have anything to start a fire with?" Will asked. "If you've misplaced your tinder, you could just give it one of your flinty looks."

"I like to save those for you. And I have several ways to start a fire. One of them is your magic finger. And since you don't have much else to contribute…"

"Fine." Will set his finger against the needles. He hesitated just a moment, at the fear that he wouldn't be able to move the *vitalle* again. But Killien wasn't here, and neither was whatever he'd done. The energy flowed easily out of Will's finger and the needles lit.

It burned for only a handful of breaths, but the heatstone began to glow with a rich, yellow light. Heat poured out of it and Will backed up.

"Why didn't you tell Killien about my magic finger the night you met me?"

"I don't know."

She rigged the rabbit up to hang over the heatstone and offered no further answer.

There was something different about her. She didn't smile, but her face was…content, her movements relaxed. She was comfortable here, in a way she'd never been on the Sweep.

He leaned against the wall, his body heavy with exhaustion. Sora's eyes were shadowed, and for the first time it occurred to him that she had been up all night as well, and probably hadn't had the luxury of sleeping all morning.

"Any chance you have anything useful in your bag?" she asked.

He dragged his pack over. "I think it's useful, but you're going to be disappointed. I have some clothes, some avak pits I'm taking back to Queensland, and I have books."

"Books. How shocking." She picked up the second rabbit, pulled out her knife and sliced into its skin.

"That is both disgusting and fascinating."

She answered him by yanking off the rabbit fur in one, quick wrench.

Outside the cave, Rass laid her head against a wide boulder next to her and hummed a catchy little tune.

"Your hawk brought me a clump of grass," Sora said.

"Of course he did. Because what people need on the Sweep is more grass. Although grass is better than dead mice."

"You didn't send him to me?"

"No. Why wou—" He sat up straight. "When did he come to you?"

"Just before I saw you in the rift."

Will's mind spun. He pointed at Rass. "Talen found her while I was there, too."

"Maybe he's in the market for a better owner."

"Or maybe," he said, "he *listened to me*.

"The first day I told him it'd be useful if he could bring me something with energy, like a tree." Will leaned forward. "And he *did*. It was barely a shoot, but the roots still had dirt in them. I'd thought it was for his nest—but he didn't take it to his nest, he brought it to *me*."

"I'm not sure a shoot counts as a tree."

"A very small tree for a very small hawk. But then I asked him for what I really needed—you."

She drew back slightly.

He gave her a wide smile. "Although it turns out all I needed was Rass."

The hint of a smile appeared on her face. "I hadn't decided yet whether you were worth rescuing."

Will sank back against the wall. The sky was a bright, clear blue, without a single speck of hawk to be seen. "I can't believe Talen did what I asked."

"How'd you get him to?"

"Emotions resonate." Was it really that simple? "I think I... shared my emotions with him. My need to find you."

"You're not making sense."

"I think I am," he said slowly, sitting back and unwrapping his bundle of books. Had Talen really found Sora? And the tree? And Rass?

"What is that?" Sora pointed at the blue book.

"Killien's book. It's about fairly horrific magic by Kachig the Bloodless. And Killien is probably very angry that I have it." He opened one of his own books, starting his usual check for dampness and mites.

Sora watched him. "What could you possibly have to write down that takes up that many pages?"

"Mostly stories I've learned on the Sweep. This one's from the Temur Clan about an old woman who lives in a cave, chases the ripples of grass across the hills. And sends bats to terrorize the clan."

"What is the point of recording something like that?"

Her tone was so sharp that Will glanced up at her.

"Why write down useless, harsh things about a woman who has probably suffered her whole life as an outcast? Do you know what story might actually be worth writing down?" She leaned toward him, pointing her knife at the book. "That woman's story. She was someone's daughter. What happened to her that she ended up banished and shunned? That"—she sliced the knife viciously into the rabbit—"would be a story worth writing down."

Her face was furious and she sliced strips of rabbit meat off the creature with a frightening efficiency.

Will flipped to the next page. "It's right here."

Sora's knife stopped and she lifted her glare from the rabbit to Will's face.

"It took me three days to find her." The stench had been awful. The wind had blown past, hollow and uncaring.

Sora sat utterly still, leaning as though she might explode off the ground toward him at any moment.

"She was dead." The woman's body had been curled up in the corner of the cave. Grey hair wild and matted, gaunt cheeks, bone-thin wrists.

Sora leaned closer and Will shifted it so she could see his sketch. The cave had been scattered with clay tools and dishes. There had been goat droppings everywhere and a rickety cage along the back wall with a chicken, also dead.

"She'd had a goat, and a chicken, a small bucket, a cup, and an assortment of things made out of woven grass."

"Any bats?"

"No sign of them. The cave was covered in filth." He stared at the page unseeing. "Except for the basket her body was curled around." Her arms had held it so tightly, he'd had trouble removing it. "The rim of it was woven with withered flowers, and inside lay a set of neatly folded clothes, small enough for a young child."

Sora ran her hand over the drawing, looking at Will's notes, silent for a long time.

"But why write it down?" She spoke so quietly Will had to lean closer to hear her. "There's nothing left to do."

"I buried her." She'd been so light Will could have carried her all the way back to the Temur village. "And then I made a copy of what I'd found, describing as much of her life as I could figure out, and delivered it to the biggest gossip in the Temur clan."

Sora looked at him with raised eyebrows.

"The entire clan must have known about it in a matter of days." He paused and flipped back to the story the clan had told him about the woman, with all its meanness and fear. "I also copied this, word for word as I'd heard it, on the same sheet of paper."

A small smile curled up the edge of Sora's mouth. She nodded in approval before busying herself with the rabbit again.

"But in some ways," she said, "your story is just as bad as theirs. You wanted them to feel something about the woman. So you made your story to fit it." She looked up at him. "How you tell a story changes everything about it."

Will nodded. "There are all sorts of stories in the world. Theirs was full of fear and contempt. My story was a reminder of her humanity. Of her weakness and struggles and isolation. And ultimately of her death, neglected and shunned by them." Will stopped and flipped through the book again, phrases of fear or hope or pain jumping out from each page. "We tell stories about everything. We can't escape them. It's how we interact with each other, it's how we keep the things we value close. It's the fearful stories, the ones that strip the humanity from everyone but ourselves that cost us nothing to spread. It takes a lot of searching to find the true stories, the ones that reveal people's humanity instead of crushing them beneath the weight of hatred."

Sora was silent for a long time. "Stories are too powerful. The ones people told about that woman defined her life."

"Which is why they're important." He flipped back to the page with the sketch of the cave. "Her name was Zarvart."

"Zarvart," Sora said quietly.

Will nodded. "Names are important too."

She considered the picture for a long moment, then piled strips of rabbit onto a piece of leather. Pulling another small heatstone out of her bag, she set it next to the rest of the pine needles. She wiggled her finger in the air and looked expectantly at Will.

Leaning forward, he lit the needles. The heatstone glowed and Sora used her knife to roll it up on top of the rabbit meat. The meat sizzled as she wrapped up the leather, trapping the meat against the hot stone. She bound it with some twine, soaked the entire bundle with water, and tied it to the top of her pack.

The other rabbit cooked over the first heatstone, little drops of fat sizzling onto the stone and the hot floor of the cave next to it. Sora lay down and Will traded places with Rass at the entrance to the cave who then curled up in a corner and went straight to sleep. The next several hours passed in boredom watching nothing at all happen in the forest below.

It was late afternoon when Sora came and sat next to him. "Let me see your hands."

His bandages were grimy and shifted out of place, showing the angry red edges of his palms. Sora pulled out a small bottle from her pack and a ball of bandages.

He raised an eyebrow. "You put a lot of thought into rescuing me."

"Remembering food and medicine isn't exactly high level planning."

Will looked up at the wide blue sky. It was unaccountably comfortable here. The floor was hard, there wasn't much to eat, and if he stayed too long, Killien would find him and kill him. But somehow in the midst of all that, it felt homey.

The sky was a rich blue like home, and Queensland felt almost within reach. The Keepers' Stronghold, book after book after book, stories that made sense and had all the right feelings. A place where being comfortable wasn't restricted to one small cave, a ranger, and a grass elf.

Sora unwound a dirty bandage slowly, revealing the ugly burn on his palm.

"Do you think Killien will hurt Ilsa?" Will pushed the question out quickly before the fear behind it overpowered him.

It took her a moment to answer. "I don't."

"Are you just saying that to make me feel better? Or do you really think Killien is that decent of a man?"

"No and no. I used to think Killien was a decent man. And maybe he is, but lately he's so angry. He's done savage things when he thinks the clan is in danger. But Ilsa is the only leverage he has against you. I don't think he'd give that up. He was certain we'd find you and he needs something to control you with." She let out a long, slow breath. "It's my guess he'll do what he can to ingratiate himself to her. Because the more loyal she is to him, the more it will hurt you." Sora finished unwinding the bandage and he stretched his hand a little. She bent over his hand, inspecting the burn.

Will looked up again at the patch of right-color-blue sky outside the cave and let it call to the deepest parts of himself. The parts he'd been trying not to think about for a year. He wanted to go back home so much he almost couldn't breathe.

"I can't leave her there. You need to take me back to Killien."

CHAPTER TWENTY-NINE

Sora's head snapped up.

"If you take me back," Will said before she could argue, "Killien will still trust you. He probably expects you to be the one to find me anyway. Maybe you'd get a chance to help Ilsa escape."

"I'm not taking you back." She dribbled some water on his palm and rubbed at the dirty ridge of crustiness along the edge of his burn.

"There's no other way that Ilsa's ever going to get out of there."

Sora dropped his hand and looked up at him in exasperation. "If you go back, he'll kill you. Then he'll have no reason to keep her alive." She picked up the jar of salve and spread some across his palm and wrapped a new bandage around it before starting on his other hand.

She was right. He stared across the forest. There had to be a way.

Sora worked quietly, and he was struck again with how comfortable she was. He tried to pinpoint what was different. She wore the same leathers she'd been wearing ever since he met her. Her arms were bare of anything but the wide cloth band around her upper arm. The long white claw was still there, tied on by strips of thin leather, and the long puckered scar beneath it ran from her shoulder to her elbow. Her boots were worn leather, her hair hung over her shoulder in its thick braid. And every bit of it looked…at home.

"You love the mountains, don't you?"

She looked up at him sharply, as though expecting some sort of teasing. "I do."

"Why did you leave?"

Her face hardened and she picked up the salve to put on his palm. "I'm not interested in talking about my life with someone I know almost nothing about."

Will felt a flash of irritation at the return of her coldness, but his retort died on his lips. He deserved that. "You're right, you don't know much about me. What do you want to know?"

She narrowed her eyes at him.

"Alright, I'll start at the beginning. I was born outside a small town a half day's ride south of Queenstown. You already know I have a younger sister Ilsa, although I haven't seen her since she was a baby. My mother's name is Marlin. My father's name was Tell."

"Was?"

He nodded. "We lived on a small farm. I wasn't much help, I'm sure. Neither the chicken nor the cow was much trouble, but we had this goat, Tussy, who was the bane of my existence."

Will flexed his fingers slightly and saw the puckered red and white outline of his old scar, almost covered up by the new burn. "The first time I ever did magic it was because of that stupid goat."

Sora sat perfectly still, her eyes wide, searching his face. He dropped his gaze back to his hand. It had been twenty years since he'd told this story to the Keepers when he'd first joined them. But now that he started, the words pressed up inside him, and after only a short struggle, he let them out, telling her everything about Vahe and Ilsa.

"How old was she?"

Will pressed his eyes shut against the image of Ilsa's terrified face. "Two."

He felt a touch on the edge of his palm. Sora's finger brushed over it, feather light on the edge of his healthy skin, blanking out to nothing over the scar.

"All I wanted was to stop him, but after everything, he still killed my father and took my sister. And I almost killed my mother."

Sora set her hand across his palm, blocking the scar with her own long fingers.

"How old were you?"

"Eleven."

Sora said nothing, but picked up the jar of salve and began to spread it across Will's palm.

"When I was born," she said quietly, "stars flew across the sky."

The memory of his parents dissolved at her words. She focused on his hand, spreading the cool cream over the blisters, filling the air with the scent of mint and sulphur.

"A star shower?"

She nodded. "Not unusual, except this one came from the mouth of the Serpent Queen."

"Do the mountain clans think of her the same way the Roven do?"

Sora shook her head. "Among the Roven the Serpent Queen is a shadow that is devouring the heavens. But to my people she is Tanith, a serpent moving thorough the stars, giving meaning to the blackness between them. She searches out paths in the darkness and leads those lost in the night."

"I like your version better."

Sora didn't look up at him. Her face was distant as she picked up a new strip of bandage and wrapped it around his hand. "But she is not all good. She is still full of darkness, and when dark things must be done, she is the one to do it.

"The night I was born they say a hundred stars flew out from her mouth, scattering across the sky." Her hands paused for a moment. "And one gave life to a child."

"They think you came from the Serpent Queen?" Will let the idea take root and grow, seeing the effects of such a belief rippling outward, shaping all of Sora's life.

Her expression, when she looked up, had a tinge of desperation. "Everything I did," she continued in a whisper, "they said was a sign from the Serpent Queen. If I was near a sick man and he recovered, Tanith had deemed him worthy to live. If I passed a man who died soon after, I had brought the queen's judgement on him.

"For as long as I can remember, they brought people to me. Wanted me to touch the sick, bless pregnant women and hunters. And whatever happened, they claimed it was because I had doled out the will of the Serpent Queen."

"Did they blame you?" Will asked. "When things went wrong?"

"Never to my face. To speak out against me was the same as speaking out against Tanith. But they kept their distance, unless they were desperate. The other children stayed away, afraid they might anger me." She twisted the last bit of bandage in her fingers.

"It wasn't you," he said, reaching forward to set his hand on hers, stilling them. "None of it was you."

Her eyes flicked up toward him, a hollow bright green. "It didn't matter. Everyone believed it. The story shaped everything."

His hand tightened on hers. "And that's why you hate stories."

She dropped her eyes again, brushed his hand away and finished tying his bandage. Her next words were so quiet Will had to lean forward to hear her. "My mother tried to protect me from it, but the clan was relentless. I witnessed births. I sat by sick beds. The dying, in an effort to seek Tanith's mercy, confessed to me." She squeezed her eyes shut. "Terrible things. Things a child shouldn't hear."

Sora sat silent, and Will felt a deep anger growing at the thought of the small girl alone, wading through the darkest parts of people's hearts.

"The cave system we lived in was enormous. I had free range of it all. No one dared upset me, never mind hurt me. But wherever I went, I was watched. So I learned to sneak out.

"I learned to stay quiet in the woods for hours at a time so that none of the rangers or hunters would find me. I learned what sorts of things the animals did. Where they lived, what they ate.

"That's when I realized I could sense them before I saw them." She glanced up at Will. "I didn't know other people couldn't until I watched hunters walk right by some brush with a hidden deer.

"So I started to hunt."

"And they all thought you hunted so well because you were blessed."

Sora nodded. "It was nice to be outside, though. When I hunted with others, I brought them to larger herds in the mountains. There was no point in telling them the way I found things. It would have just convinced them more strongly that I was different."

"I finally understand why Killien asked you to come to Lilit."

She nodded. "He knew why I'd left the mountains. I stayed with him because he didn't believe it."

"Desperate people believe a lot of things." Will paused. "I also understand why you were so upset that he thought you healed her. I'm sorry."

She waved off the apology. "I'm a little sensitive to people thinking I did something miraculous."

"Are other people born with talents like yours in the mountain clans?"

Sora's brow knit. "The holy men and women claim to have powers. I don't know if they're real, though."

"I'm surprised they didn't try to make you a holy woman."

"They did." She ran her finger down the long claw that was tied around her arm. "Did you know the snow lynx is the enemy of the Serpent Queen? It's a creature that only hunts at night, but it is all white. It camouflages itself in white places, whereas the queen hides in the darkness. And it hunts the mountain snakes. It's supposed to be a great snow lynx that keeps Tanith up in the sky.

"I was with a hunting party. I'd chased a small hare away from the others." Sora wound up the rest of the bandage and tucked it into her pack. "I don't know why I didn't notice the lynx. But it was on me before I could do anything.

"It sliced down my arm"—she nodded to the scar that ran under her armband—"but I had just enough time to stab up into it with my hunting knife. The other rangers found the lynx lying on top of me, blood soaking the snow around us.

"For a moment I couldn't get my breath enough to call out to them."

Will let out a laugh and she looked up sharply. "I can only imagine what they thought."

A smile spread across her lips. "One of them cried out *'We are ruined! The lynx has killed the queen!'*"

"Who says things like that?"

Sora's smile widened and a short laugh escaped her lips. "I was covered in the cat's blood. It was so disgusting, and so heavy, I shoved it off with all my might."

"What did they do?"

"About fell down and worshipped me. I tried to tell them the stupid cat had leapt directly onto my knife, but no one listened. In the official story, I rose 'like a shadow of death, black against the winter snow, flinging the corpse of the lynx aside like a rag.'"

Will grinned with approval. "Dramatic."

She looked down at her hands, the smile fading off her face. "After that, things changed. They gave me the pelt as a cape. They replaced the eyes with black river stones. It sat on my shoulder and stared at anyone I talked to."

"I think I'd like to see you wear that."

Sora rolled her eyes. "I wore it once, at the ceremony where they gave it to me, then told them something that sacred should be kept in the presence of the holy woman."

"Did they give you the claw instead?"

Sora looked at her arm band. "I was terrified to step outside again. I felt too vulnerable.

"My mother went to the holy woman and claimed the claw as a trophy." Sora's lips curled up in a slight smile. "She wrapped this band around the wound, and told me it was a reminder that it wasn't Tanith who'd saved my life, it was me."

She raised her eyes to Will's face and in her eyes he could see a spark of defiance. "It was the first time I ever felt I'd done something myself. I wasn't just a tool of some great power."

Her face was set with something mutinous and despite himself, Will let out a short laugh.

"Sora, you are the most independent, competent person I've ever met. It is incomprehensible to me that anyone would think you were only a tool."

She looked at him earnestly. "They believed because of the stories they were told."

"Your people need to hear the real story of who you are. One that shows a woman who is just as human as the rest, who has been misused by the people who should have protected her, and has grown into a capable, perceptive, strong person despite it all."

Sora snorted and turned away, but Will grabbed her hand. "This is why Keepers seek out stories. Because if the truth isn't told, people are hurt."

She looked at him for along moment, before pulling her hand away. "Then I wish there'd been a Keeper in my clan."

They got a little more rest before the shadows of the mountains stretched far to the east and Sora announced it was time to leave. Will roused Rass and packed up his things while Sora cut thick pieces of rabbit for everyone to eat.

Will was packing his books when Sora came up next to him. She held a roll of leather in her hand, fiddling with the straps that tied it closed.

"Do you think Talen will find you again?"

"He's found me everywhere else."

"Then maybe you'll have a use for this." She pushed the leather towards him. "It adjusts small, so it might fit Talen...If you ever need something like this."

Will unwrapped it to find a falconry glove and a small leather hood. He slid his hand into the glove. It was darkly stained, thick leather, the fingers blocky and an extra thick layer of leather blanketing the wrist. The hood was a tiny, bulbous piece of soft leather with straps in the back and a braided tassel perched on top.

"You bought these for me?" He held up the glove, fisting his hand.

"I bought them for Talen," she corrected him. "If he stays with you long enough, I have no doubt you'll bring him to inappropriate places, like the queen's court, and the poor bird deserves to be protected from the chaos."

"Ah." He pulled the glove off and wrapped it back up with the hood. "Then Talen thanks you for such a thoughtful, and unexpected, gift."

"I like that hawk," Rass piped up.

Sora looked up at the darkening sky. "We can leave soon."

Will's body ached with exhaustion. "I can't leave Ilsa. But Killien's book..." He scrubbed his hands across his face, rubbing at the weariness. "That book should definitely get off the Sweep."

"There's no way you can get to Ilsa, Will. And even if you could..."

He sank down next to his pack. "She might not want to come with me."

Sora's face was sober. "It would be strange if she did. She doesn't know you."

He shoved the rest of his things into his bag. "I know you

think I should leave. But I can't. And it's not just Ilsa. Rass is free—"

Rass raised an eyebrow at this.

"I didn't know you've always been free."

She grinned at him and rolled her eyes. "I'm going to find some grubs. Do you want any?"

"I'll be fine with the rabbit," he assured her, and the little girl slipped out of the cave.

He cinched his bag shut with a yank. "What about Sini? How can I just walk away and leave—"

He stopped. That note Sini had left him…

"Is there something unusual about Sini and Lukas? Sini said they weren't random slaves."

"Of course they're not. They're Killien's because they're training to be stonesteeps."

Will stared at her, his hand clenched on his bag.

"Maybe Lukas already is one, I don't know. Killien spends a lot of time with the two of them, but keeps their training secret."

"They can do magic?"

"Lukas does…"—Sora's face turned distasteful—"*things* for Killien. And Sini can heal people. That's why she was in Lilit's tent. She's getting better at it all the time, but Lilit was far too much for her."

The cave around him spun slowly and he set his hand against the floor. Lukas and Sini were from Queensland. And they could do magic. "Sini's fifteen…How old is Lukas?" The question came out in a whisper.

"Around twenty-five. Why?"

The truth sank into him.

They filled the gap almost perfectly. Keepers appeared every five to ten years.

Lukas was about six years younger than Will.

Sini ten years younger than that.

"Killien has the next two Keepers."

Sora's brow crinkled in doubt. "How could he?"

"Vahe found them. He must have a way…"

The fire. Vahe had thrown that fire over the crowd, and when it had reached Will, it had done…*something*. The air around him had sparkled, and right after that he'd shoved closed Tussy's gate with magic. Vahe had somehow woken his powers.

"Vahe brings Keepers to Killien."

"But Ilsa can't do any magic," Sora said. "At least I've never seen her do anything unusual."

A rock dropped in Will's gut. "She can't. It doesn't run in families like that." He could see Vahe's face in the window, reaching for him. The man's fury when Will hadn't come.

"He wasn't there for Ilsa," Will whispered. "He was there for me."

Vahe had taken Ilsa only because Will had refused. The truth felt so obvious, he couldn't believe he'd never seen it before.

All this time he'd felt guilty because he hadn't fought hard enough to save Ilsa. When in reality, his fighting had been the reason she was taken.

Will pressed his eyes shut, finally understanding Killien's comment in the rift. "Ironic," Will whispered in agreement.

He stood. "We need to find a way back into the clan."

She threw up her hands in exasperation. "We can't—"

"Will!" Rass shrieked from below.

He scrambled to the entrance.

Hal stood in the barren clearing below the cave. His huge hands held Rass's tiny form in the air at arm's length while she thrashed around, her legs flailing and her arms pinned to her side.

Sora stood next to Will perfectly still, her knife in her hand.

"You're in luck, Will," Hal said. "Bringing you back to the clan is exactly what we're going to do."

Sora's eyes narrowed and her lips tightened into their usual line. "You seem nervous."

CHAPTER THIRTY

"Come down. Sora first." Behind Hal a ranger stepped forward, an arrow nocked and aimed at them.

Will cast out, but the *vitalle* of the nearest trees was too far away and the ground from the cliff to the forest was just dirt.

"Anything your magic fingers can do right now?" Sora asked him under her breath.

Will shook his head. "And there's no grass nearby for Rass."

Sora waited a breath before shoving her knife back into her belt and flinging her pack onto her shoulder. Will searched for anything to do, but came up empty. Sora started down the rocks and Rass went limp at the sight. Hal lowered her until she stood on the ground, but kept this hand clamped around her little arm. When Sora reached the bottom, she dropped her pack and the ranger stepped forward, keeping his bow trained on Sora until the last moment, when he grabbed her and tied her arms roughly behind her back. He gave a sharp yank and Sora grunted in pain.

"I confess I'm a little surprised to see you here," Hal said to Sora. "When Killien said not to trust you, I doubted him."

Sora fixed him with a furious look. "You know Will doesn't deserve what the Torch has planned for him."

Hal motioned for Will to come down. "Will is a Keeper, who

can suck the life out of us at any moment. Who traveled with us for weeks, and lied to us the entire time. What confuses me, Sora, is that you spent most of those weeks trying to convince us he was a liar. Then, when he proves it, you're suddenly friends with the man?"

"Of course he lied," Sora said, squeezing her eyes shut as she shifted her shoulders, pulling against the ropes.

Will climbed down while Sora's feet were bound, the truth of their situation gaining more of a stranglehold on him the farther down he went. Before he reached the ground, the ranger took Rass from Hal, gripping her shoulder with one hand and holding a long, wickedly curved knife in the other. Rass's face was set in a little mask of fury.

"Hello, Will." Hal clapped his hand on Will's shoulder and pushed him to his knees several paces away from Sora.

Will shoved against Hal's hand. "Let Rass go."

"I have no intention of hurting the girl." Hal looked at Rass with an apologetic face. "Are you thirsty?" He nodded to the ranger who, after the slightest hesitation, offered her a drink from his water skin. "She's too young to be held responsible for her terrible taste in friends."

Will cast out toward the trees again, but they were just too far away. Hal pulled a leather package from his pocket and unwrapped a long chain holding a blue stone. He slipped it over Will's head and it thunked against his chest. A crushing wave of exhaustion rolled over Will.

He cast out for any *vitalle* he could find from the trees or even Hal, but it dribbled through his grasp like water. His mind worked sluggishly. His eyes slid shut and he lost focus. His head felt like dead weight, and his body pressed heavily down into the ground.

"The compulsion stone will only work for a few hours." Hal crouched down in front of Will, studying him. "But I think the exhaustion should keep you too tired to work any magic. It's too bad we don't have a stone that could keep you from lying."

The ranger came over to Will and wound ropes around his wrists, tight and scratchy.

Will shook his head, trying to clear the fog. "The only thing I didn't tell you was that I was a Keeper." Will shifted his shoulders, trying to relieve some of the pressure in his arms.

"And that you were from Queensland, you sit on the queen's council, and you wield magic."

The ranger gave one last, sharp tug on the rope and a shooting pain sliced up Will's arm to his shoulder. With a few quick loops his feet were tied together too.

"I don't sit on the queen's council," Will muttered. "That would be my friend Alaric. He's the one who talks to the queen. And he's quite a bit better at magic than I am. Actually, he's better at translating runes too, so he's the one Killien should have captured."

"Is he nearby? I'd be happy to bring him to Killien also."

Will let his eyes slide closed. "He's too smart to come to this barbaric, ugly land."

"Ugly land?" Rass sounded sleepy too.

"Lukas made the compulsion stone you're wearing. We weren't sure it would exhaust a Keeper to the point where they couldn't perform magic, but it looks like it's a success. Which means I didn't really need to use my backup plan."

The world beneath Will spun slowly and he forced his eyes open. "If it was Lukas, I'm surprised he didn't make it something deadly."

"Lukas isn't that bad," Hal said. "Although I have noticed he doesn't like you much."

Rass swayed slightly on her feet and the ranger sheathed his knife. Will's heart lurched and he leaned toward her, but Hal held him back. Sora strained against her bonds.

"What did you do?" Will demanded.

Rass's eyes sank shut and her knees buckled. The ranger caught her and lay her down on the ground.

"Rass!" Will called, pulling against Hal's grip.

"Just an added measure of security," Hal said. "She's sleeping. Would you like a drink too? It's the same concoction Killien put in your wine the night of the attack, although a much lower dose."

Will glared at Hal, hopeless fury rising in his chest. Hal pushed Will over and he crashed onto his side, landing heavily on his shoulder. The ranger rested his knife on Rass's sleeping chest.

"I don't want to hurt her, Will, but if you give me trouble, I'll do what I need to do."

Hal opened Will's pack. "The Torch will be pleased that you still have his book." He went to a pack sitting near the trees, wrote something and tinkered with a cage. A small raven flapped out and soared out toward the Sweep. "That should let Killien know where we are." He crossed over to Rass's limp form and gave the ranger some orders. After a last check of Sora and Will's bonds, the ranger struck out down the hill. "There are rangers spread out all across the Hoarfrost looking for you. Reinforcements will arrive soon, and we'll all be on our merry way back to the rift."

Will let his head sink down on to the hard ground and watched the ranger go with a sick feeling in his stomach. Maybe it was better this way. Maybe if he could get back to Killien, he'd convince the Torch to let Ilsa go.

There was no hope in the thought.

"Let Sora and Rass go," he said to Hal. "I'm the one Killien wants. He doesn't even know Rass is here, and you can say Sora got away. He'll believe it."

"When Killien finds out that Sora helped you, he's going to want her too." He leaned back against a boulder. "Let's all just sit tight for a bit. Shouldn't take more than an hour or two for the nearest rangers to get here." He glanced at Sora. "We didn't really follow your orders, of course. We're spread all across the Hoarfrost and the Scales to catch our Keeper no matter which way he ran." He gave her a look more regretful than angry. "Killien liked you. He never likes foreigners. And yet he brought you in, trusted you, paid you better than any of the rest of us—"

"I'm better than any of the rest of you."

"—and despite your constant superior attitude, Killien still put up with you. What made you take up with this traitor?"

"I am not a traitor!" Will threw the words at Hal. He shoved his elbow against the ground, trying to push himself back up to a sitting position, but his strength gave out and he just rolled to the side, sending dust into his own face.

"Killien was generous to you, too." Hal turned on Will. "He shared meals with you. I heard him tell you his dreams of peace for the Roven."

"Oh yes," Will said, spitting out dust, "he's an amazing, benevolent leader."

Hal looked at Will as though he'd spoken in a foreign tongue. "You think that because you lied to him and he got mad, that it negates all the good he does?"

"No. I think Killien is actively searching for knowledge that only leads to tyranny and death."

"What are you talking about?" Hal asked, irritated.

"Killien has a book by Kachig the Bloodless."

Hal's eyes narrowed.

"It describes how to—how did you word it? Suck the life out of someone. And use it for your own power."

"Sounds like it should have been written by a Keeper."

Will clenched his jaw. "A Keeper would never do that.

"Ahh, you didn't deny you can."

"Yes, I can pull the energy out of you. But you don't need a compulsion stone, or to sit there threatening a sleeping girl, to keep me from doing it. Keepers believe that the energy in a person is sacred. We would never take the smallest bit from you unless you wanted us to. If we need energy for something, we pull it from a fire, or from plants. Or from ourselves." He looked at Hal, and the hardness in the man's eyes felt like knives. "You've never had anything to fear from me."

Hal's expression didn't soften.

Will shifted his arms against the tightness of the rope. "Whatever Killien wants with that book, nothing good can come of it.

No matter what he's told you about wanting peace and wanting to unite the Sweep, there is only war and death in this book. And magic beyond anything Killien has the power to do. The magic in this book would require advanced stonesteeps from the Sunn Clan."

Hal's jaw clenched stubbornly. "If Killien is trying to read it, he has a good reason. Everything he does is for the good of the clan."

"So that makes it ok? Sucking life out of people is fine as long as they're not *your* people?" Will snorted. "You're lucky I don't feel the same way."

"Killien wouldn't do something like that." There was a note of finality in Hal's voice.

Weariness washed over Will again and he let his retort go.

"Who set the fires?" Sora asked.

"Our visitors from the Sunn Clan."

Sora's mouth dropped open in shock.

Will let his head sink down onto the ground. "I thought they were coming to invite Killien to some enclave."

Hal sank back against a boulder and blew out a long breath. "So did Killien. It's been ten years since he was invited. But he's been in communication with so many of the other Torches that when the Sunn wanted to visit, he thought…"

Will fought to keep his eyes open. There had to be a way out of this. He watched Sora, hoping she was working on her bonds, but he couldn't tell. "What happens at the enclave?"

"The powerful clans make demands." Hal made an irritated face. "And the smaller clans agree to them publicly. But Killien thinks that if the smaller clans can band together, they can have a voice. Together the Morrow, Panos, and Temur clans would make the third largest group on the Sweep. Both the Panos and Temur have been in talks with Killien all winter. Right now the struggle for power on the Sweep is caught between the Sunn Clan with all their stonesteeps, and the Boan with their huge army. Killien's determined to change that.

"Over the winter he managed to settle a longstanding dispute between two of the western clans over a river. It made enough of an impression across the Sweep that last night the nephew of the Sunn Torch was supposed to be coming to invite Killien to the enclave. And probably demand his support."

Sora snorted. "Killien wouldn't support the Sunn in anything."

Hal nodded slowly. "Twenty Sunn warriors hid on the Sweep and started the fire before Avi, the nephew of the Sunn Torch, had time to talk to Killien about it. So I'd say they didn't expect him to."

Sora considered this for a moment. "They attacked Killien too? With him dead, there's no good choice for another Torch in the Morrow."

"They tried. Killien hadn't trusted the little weasel, so he'd had guards in the back room. Little Avi didn't even get his knife close to Killien before they'd caught him. We killed twelve of them and captured the rest, including Avi. The man's a weasel but some say he'll be the next Torch of the Sunn. So Killien has a powerful bargaining chip."

Sora looked at Will, uneasily.

Will looked between the two of them, understanding dawning. "Killien can get stonesteeps from the Sunn, probably enough to do whatever magic he's trying to figure out."

Hal shook his head. "The Sunn have more stonesteeps than blades of grass, but most of them aren't worth the cost of feeding them."

Sora turned her head slowly, looking over the Sweep with wide eyes.

Will's mind was too sluggish to follow. "What else does the Sunn have that Killien would want?"

Neither Sora or Hal answered, but the truth hit Will like a stone in the gut. "The dragon."

"Killien was still composing the ransom letter when I left. But, yes, he's demanding use of the dragon."

"How do you use a dragon?" Will asked.

Hal pulled his hand through his beard. "The stonesteeps of the Sunn Clan control it, so whatever Killien wants it to do, they'll have to agree to it. I don't know what he has planned. But he was very pleased about the opportunity."

"He told me once," Will said, glancing up at the sky as though expecting to see an enormous creature flying across the Sweep, "that all he needed to solve the world's problems was a disposable army and a dragon." He looked back at Hal. "So he's not invited to the enclave?"

"No." Hal leaned his head back on the rock. "And even if he were, among the Sunn attackers we found three from the Panos Clan."

Will let out a long breath. "Who were supposed to be Killien's allies."

The three fell silent. Will's shoulders ached from his hands being tied behind him, his wrist chaffed from the ropes. He lowered the side of his head down to the ground again, shifting his wrists back and forth. The ropes felt as though they might be getting looser.

A very small bird soared across the sky and settled high in a nearby pine. Relief and alarm vied for control as Will glanced toward Hal to see if he'd noticed Talen's arrival, but the huge man had gone back to spinning the knife point in the ground.

Will cast out toward the hawk and felt his little coil of energy. Talen was far enough away that Will couldn't feel any emotions from the bird. What had he done before? When Talen had listened? He'd sort of pushed the idea of them, the longing for them at the bird.

Will gathered all the strength he could, firmed up the image of Talen sitting on the branch in his mind, and infused it with the feeling of contentment. He pushed the idea up toward the hawk.

Stay there.

Talen's wings flared, and for a heart-stopping moment Will thought he would dive down. But the hawk merely shifted his feet and settled down on the branch.

Rass stirred. She stretched and opened her eyes to look around groggily. Hal set a hand on her arm.

"Are you alright?" Will asked her.

Her tiny arm looked like a stick grasped in Hal's enormous hand.

She blinked at the sunlight and peered at Will, then turned to Hal with a thunderous face. "Did you make me sleep?"

Hal laughed. "I did, little fiery girl. I see why Will likes you."

She tugged against his grip, but she couldn't even jostle his arm.

Hal sighed. "If you don't want to be put back to sleep again, stop fighting. Look at Sora and Will. We've got a nice, calm afternoon going here. No problems, no fighting, just some friends chatting on a mountainside."

Rass glared up at him. "You should let us go."

"Why's that?"

"Because Will is a mighty wizard and Sora's smarter and faster and braver than you. They're letting you sit here for now, but you can't win against them."

Hal's eyebrows rose and he let out a long, rolling laugh. The first real laugh he'd given all day. He glanced at Will. "This girl is a treasure."

Past Hal, Sora stiffened. Her gaze snapped uphill, searching.

The rangers couldn't be back so soon. Will cast out and his stomach dropped. Two people were approaching from behind him higher up the slope. And up past them waited two more.

They were out of time. He strained against the ropes at his wrists, desperation returning.

Sora's eyes, still staring up the hill, widened in surprise.

"Treasure?" a gruff voice called out from behind Will. He spoke with a rough brogue. "There's no treasure here. We've searched it before. Nothing here but rocks."

Will twisted, trying to see behind him, and caught a glimpse of the two people he'd felt. It wasn't Roven rangers.

Stumping down the side of the rockslide were two dwarves.

CHAPTER THIRTY-ONE

Hal's mouth dropped open at the sight of the two dwarves. Will shifted for a better view.

They came down the slope with heavy steps, thick leather boots crunching against the ground. Their long beards covered their chests and tucked behind their belts. Their leather armor was darkened with age and use, and scarred blades of their battle axes sat behind their shoulders looking ruthless. Only glittering eyes were visible in their faces.

"I don't see any treasure, cousin." The darker of the two studied the group from under black, wild eyebrows.

Hal stood, pulling Rass up with him.

"Patlon," said the other dwarf, stroking his own copper beard. "We've found nothing but a bunch of humans in the midst of a disagreement."

Hal stood unmoving, his hand wrapped around Rass's thin arm, his expression caught between stunned and thrilled.

"If the giant man says they're treasure," Patlon said, "we should take them, just to be sure."

Hal's face darkened. "You're not taking anyone."

The two dwarves glanced at each other and Patlon pulled his

axe over his shoulder. The shaft was a dark, glimmering purple. Sora watched the two with narrowed eyes.

"We didn't introduce ourselves," the copper-bearded dwarf said. "I'm Douglon, this is my cousin Patlon." He gestured to Will, Sora, and Rass. "I've recently started collecting needy humans, and I'd be happy to take these off your hands."

"No." Hal stepped forward, holding out the small hunting knife. "You won't."

Will heaved himself onto his back. Sharp pain shot across his shoulders and his head fell back, heavy. "I'm a Keeper from Queensland. I've been to Duncave before, visited King Horgoth's court. Even spoken to the High Dwarf himself."

The dwarves gave him their attention.

Will opened up toward them and curiosity and amusement poured into his chest. "He has a brilliant mind for strategy and is a keen negotiator." The amusement soured.

"If you keep talking about Horgoth like that," Douglon said, "I'm going to leave you with the giant."

Will glanced between the two. "I promise you, I'm a friend of the dwarves."

"Don't trust his promises of friendship," Hal said.

"Cousin," Patlon warned as Hal took a step forward.

Douglon sized up the huge man and slid his own axe out of its sheath with a glint of fiery red. "I suppose, being a Keeper," he said to Will, keeping his eyes fixed on Hal, "you are useless when it comes to using a weapon and have moral qualms about fighting with magic."

Will opened his mouth to protest, but Sora spoke first.

"It's like you already know him."

"I feel like I do." A grin flashed out from his beard. "You, on the other hand, look as though you could take care of yourself."

"Against Hal? Just cut my feet loose. I won't need my arms."

"I like her." Patlon stepped closer to Sora and pulled a small knife out of his belt.

"Stop." Hal's voice echoed off the rocks.

Patlon paused and raised an eyebrow at the enormous man.

Hal stepped forward again and Rass took the chance to wrench her arm out of his grasp and skitter out of reach. Hal grabbed for her, but she was too quick.

"Hal," Sora said, "this isn't a fight you're going to win. You couldn't take one of these dwarves, never mind both. And despite the fact their axes are"—she glanced at the two axes, the shafts shimmering with purple and red—"colorful for dwarven warriors, they seem well used."

Hal clenched his jaw.

"She likes my axe." Patlon twisted the purple shaft, catching the evening light in a deep violet glitter.

"She likes *my* axe," Douglon corrected him. "She thinks yours is stupid."

Patlon's teeth flashed from behind his beard in a grin. Rass scurried over behind Sora and Patlon tossed the knife near her. Rass grabbed it and ducked down behind Sora.

"Hal," Will said. "You don't want to be killed by dwarves. Not after you've waited so long to meet some."

"You were overpowered by a superior force." Sora rubbed her wrists. "Killien can't hold that against you." With a flick of the knife she cut the rope around her feet and came over to Will.

Hal's expression sagged and he dropped his knife by his side.

"He loves dwarves," Will explained to Douglon and Patlon. "Under most circumstances this would be the best day of his life."

"What's not to love?" Patlon asked.

Will felt the cool side of the blade against his arm, then with a quick yank, the ropes loosened and he pushed himself up with a groan. Bone-deep aches filled his shoulders, as he took the chain with the blue stone off his neck and threw it at the ground near Hal. The exhaustion that had been plaguing him blew away like smoke on a breeze.

Sora handed him the knife for his feet, and grabbing some rope, went over to Hal. She barely came up to his shoulder, but when she held out her hand, he only hesitated a moment, glancing at the dwarves before handing her the knife.

"You won't have too long to wait," Patlon told Hal. "Your ranger friends should be here before dark."

When Hal was tied up, Douglon turned uphill and gave a long whistle. Will cast out up the mountain and found the two other people.

"I met a dwarf at court once." Will watched up the hill for the others. "His name was Menwoth. He was…funny."

"Stop talking," Patlon advised.

Douglon glowered at him. "Menwoth? Slimy, fawning toad."

Despite the look on the dwarf's face, Will laughed. "He was fawning."

Douglon's face mollified a bit.

A wave rushed over Will and he snapped his gaze back up the slope.

It hadn't been a wave of anything in particular. Almost a wave of nothing, if nothing could surge like an ocean swell, and pass through you.

But it was a nothing he recognized in the foundational way he recognized home.

"Alaric!" he called.

A man stepped around one of the huge rocks.

At the sight of the black-haired man wearing the black Keeper's robe, the isolation and weight of the last year loosened.

"You were easier to find than I thought you'd be." Alaric looked pleased.

"Easy?" Patlon fixed Alaric with an incredulous look, "You've mobilized half of the dwarven outposts for the last four days!"

The sheer familiarity of Alaric was fortifying. His black hair had been cropped short, but his eyes were scanning the group exactly the way he studied every new situation. Will could almost see the questions stacking up in his mind. Seeing a face as familiar as his own broke away the last of the crust the solitary last year had built around Will.

"I have never"—Will strode up to Alaric and wrapped his arms around him, crushing Alaric to his chest—"been so happy to see anyone in my life."

Alaric laughed and patted Will on the back. "It's good to see you too."

A woman came out from behind the rock as well, walking up to Alaric.

Will stepped back, but kept his hands on Alaric's shoulders. "I'm so happy to see you."

Alaric raised an eyebrow. "You mentioned that."

Will let go of Alaric's shoulders, rubbing his hands over his face and letting out a breath. "It's been a long year."

"Long enough to grow a beard," Alaric said.

Will scratched at it. "They're popular on this side of the mountains."

"And under them," Douglon said.

"I like it," the woman said.

She smiled at Will with a hopeful sort of smile, but her green eyes watched him nervously. Blond hair hung around her face, working its way out of a braid. In contrast to the dwarves, she didn't look particularly fierce. She wore traveling clothes, simple pants and a light brown shirt, and carried no weapon besides a small knife at her belt. She stepped up to Alaric, so close that their arms almost touched. Will glanced at Alaric, waiting for an introduction.

Alaric gave him a nervous look. "Will, I'd like you to meet Evangeline—"

Will gave her a small bow as Alaric leaned against her shoulder.

"—my wife."

Will's bow stuttered to a stop. "Wife?"

Alaric's smile turned self-conscious and he nodded. He stayed pressed against Evangeline's shoulder, his expression somewhere between worry and entreaty.

Will shoved aside his surprise at the news. "Congratulations!"

Alaric's smile widened and Evangeline's shoulders relaxed.

"I'm Will. Obviously. And you married a great man. He's been like a brother to me since I was ten."

Sora stepped up next to Will. Before he could introduce her, Alaric grinned. "Did you find a wife too?"

"No!" Sora pulled away from Will her face shocked.

"Um," Will started. "It's not..."

Alaric laughed. "That's too bad. You should find one."

Sora fixed Alaric with a scowl.

"This is Sora," Will introduced her. It was nice to see her irritation focused on someone besides himself. "And despite that expression, which she wears a lot, I owe her my life. Several times over."

Sora crossed her arms, still scowling.

Will glanced up the hill. "Why were you hiding behind the rocks?"

"Because," Evangeline answered, "he is ridiculously overprotective of me."

Alaric shrugged. "With good reason."

"We need to move somewhere less exposed," Patlon said.

A glint of blue from the ground caught Will's eye, and he picked up the necklace, careful not to touch the stone. He considered putting it on Hal before deciding it would be more interesting to study it. He shoved it into his pack.

He looked up to the top of the pine where Talen still perched. He pulled a bit of rabbit from his pack and held a slice up toward the bird. Talen dove off the branch and sped down, flaring his wings at the last moment to land on Will's outstretched arm.

"We have less than an hour until the other Roven come back." Patlon pointed out.

Will nodded. "I didn't leave the Morrow on the best of terms. We should be gone by then."

"Kollman Pass is being watched," Sora said.

Alaric nodded. "We don't need the pass. There's an entrance to Duncave up the slope."

Sora's eyebrows rose and she nodded. Then she glanced at Talen. "This is a perfect example of you taking Talen somewhere inappropriate, Will." She stepped up behind him and reached into his pack. "But he'll lose track of you if we go underground." She pulled out the little hood. "Keep him calm."

Will opened up toward the hawk and pushed the idea of peace toward the creature.

Talen stilled and Sora slipped the hood over his head in one smooth motion and tied a thin strap of leather to his foot. Talen tensed, but stayed on Will's arm. With some shifting Will got the glove on and Talen settled on it while Will held the end of the strap, keeping the idea of calmness pressed into the bird.

Will felt Rass behind him, peeking around him at the new people.

"This is Rass," Will introduced her. "She's a *pratorii*, a grass elf."

"Really?" Alaric leaned to get a better view of her.

Douglon moved toward Rass and Will tensed. The dwarf, although his head only reached Will's chest, looked like a towering giant next to the tiny girl.

Sora took a step closer to the dwarf, loosening the knife in her belt.

Alaric raised his hand toward her. "It's alright."

Douglon looked at Rass like she was some sort of rare sparkling rock. He dropped down on one knee so their faces were even. "Hello."

She reached forward tentatively and touched a braid hanging from the bottom of his copper beard. "I've never met a dwarf before."

"I've never met such a tiny elf."

"Have you met tree elves?"

The dwarf stilled before nodding. "One."

Will looked up at Alaric in surprise. The other Keeper gave a small, sober nod.

"I hope I get to meet one," Rass sighed.

A heavy silence fell over the others. Something raw and broken flashed across Douglon's eyes before he closed them.

"There aren't any more," he answered.

Will's gaze snapped to Alaric's face, but he was watching the dwarf with a grave expression.

"We should go." Alaric turned up the slope.

Will and the others started after him, but Rass hung back.

"I don't want to go into the tunnels. They're too dark and quiet."

Douglon paused. "They're not quiet. The rocks talk."

Rass fixed him with a dubious look. "No they don't."

He shrugged. "I didn't used to think trees talked, but they do." He glanced over at the pine trees closest to them. "They talk so much, I wish they'd shut up."

Rass giggled. "I thought dwarves only liked rocks."

"I did, until I met that elf."

Rass looked up at him with wide eyes. "What was she like?"

Douglon's gaze traveled back to the edge of the forest. "Crazy as a bat." He turned back to Rass. "Maybe I can teach you to hear the rocks."

Rass looked doubtful.

Douglon stopped and held out his hand, "I know the tunnels are different from out here, but they have their own beauty. I'd be happy to show you. I never had the chance to show Ayda."

"Ayda?" Will asked quickly. "The elf?"

Douglon nodded, still facing Rass.

Rass studied his face for a minute, taking in his coppery beard, and his dwarfish face. His eyes were a rich, earthy color, and there was something broken in them. Whether Rass saw it or not, she set her tentative hand into his thick one.

"The rocks don't chatter like the trees. They have slow, ponderous thoughts. But there's great truth there to be heard." Douglon leaned closer to her. "It turns out, there's great truth in many different places, if you just know how to listen."

He started uphill, Rass stepping along beside him.

Will glanced at Alaric. "That's an unusual dwarf."

"Crazy as a bat." Patlon stumped up the hill after Douglon.

Will turned to Hal where he sat against a boulder, and the man fixed him with a glare. Unlike Sora's glares, which had lost much of their power from overuse, the expression on Hal's face felt like a knife in Will's gut.

"I'm glad I met you, Hal. You were the first Roven I ever thought that, if things were different, we could have been genuine friends."

Hal let out a short, humorless laugh and turned his face away, looking out over the Sweep. The setting sun cast the Sweep into a golden haze. It was past time to go. Will shifted his pack on his shoulder.

"Goodbye, Hal." He paused a moment. When Hal didn't respond, Will turned away to follow the others.

He'd only taken a step when a surge rolled over him. This time it wasn't a surge of nothing. This was a ripple, a taste of a power so vast that Will was merely a candle flame before it, about to be snuffed out.

Sora flinched and snapped her attention to the hills, her gaze raking over the slopes around them, her face pale.

Alaric spun around and the wave of his casting out ripped past Will just as he cast his own. He searched through the trees and over the rocky slope, searching for any movement.

The casting out returned nothing for a moment.

Then, high above the Sweep, a blazing inferno of *vitalle* burst out.

Cold, sharp fear clenched around Will's chest as he spun.

Glinting blood red in the setting sun, tearing straight toward them, hurtled a dragon.

CHAPTER THIRTY-TWO

"Dragon!" Will choked out the word over the fear gripping his chest.

Still far out over the grassland, the shape was etched against the clear sky. Wide, jagged wings growing larger by the moment.

Around him, everyone spun to face the grass.

"What is it with Keepers and dragons?" Douglon shouted down to them.

"Will!" Hal's voice was taut. He yanked against the ropes tying his hands and feet.

Will ran to Hal, calling for Sora and her knife, yanking on the ropes around his ankles.

She was at his shoulder in a breath, slicing Hal's feet free.

"You'd better run, Hal." She grabbed one arm of the huge man and Will grabbed the other, hauling him to his feet.

Alaric, Evangeline, Douglon, and Patlon ran up the hill. Rass waited, her eyes flickering between Will and the dragon. Sora reached her and grabbed her hand, pulling her up after the others.

The dragon streaked toward them, growing larger and faster than Will's mind could grasp.

"Looks like you get to see Duncave, Hal. Come on."

Will ran, Talen gripping his arm. Hal's heavy steps thundered after him as they chased the others up the hill. Will caught a glimpse of the dragon and the cold fear clamped tighter in his chest.

Ridged, thin wings, spread wide across the sky, striated with tendons snaking like veins in a leaf. The sunlight shone off its scales, glinting a deep, biting red.

Voices called out and Will pushed himself faster, stumbling over loose stones. The two dwarves shouted at him, waving him up to a thin crack in the side of a huge rock.

Will's legs burned from the climb, his ankles aching from being tied up, and fear coursed through him, making his limbs clumsy.

The others reached the dwarves and Patlon slipped inside with Rass. Sora paused at the door, shouting down toward Will to hurry. Her face was terrified and a detached part of Will's brain realized he had never seen her scared before.

Without stopping or turning, Will cast out.

The massive surge of *vitalle* soaring toward them almost knocked him off his feet. The creature blocked out a huge section of the sky. With a roar that shook the earth, the dragon shot out a long spray of fire, setting trees alight and covering the ground with a churning sea of flames.

The *vitalle* released with the fire and knocked Will forward to his knees. Talen flapped his wings, panicked, but Will shot a burst of calmness at the bird. The ground trembled beneath him and the crack of rocks splitting filled the air.

"Get up!" Hal stopped in front of Will, holding one of his still-tied hands awkwardly behind him. Will grabbed it and pulled himself up, shaking his head to clear the shock of so much power. He looked up and saw Alaric bent over too, grabbing onto Evangeline for support.

Smoke poured around him, tinged red with firelight, swirling until he could barely see Hal right in front of him.

Will took a step. An overwhelming anger slithered into his chest. It wasn't human anger. It was old and savage.

He slammed himself shut, trying to close it off, but the emotions plowed into him. A desire to burn and kill and destroy. The glory of the sky, the strength of wings that ruled the wind.

And a gnawing, driving hunger to burn *someone*. A single, mindless goal.

Will dropped to his knees again, trying to shove them out, but the emotions filled him until there was nothing else—only power and strength and greed.

Talen screeched, but it sounded distant. Voices called to him, but they meant nothing. The world meant nothing.

Rough hands grabbed him, trying to pull him to his feet. Someone shouted. Will squeezed his eyes shut.

"Will." Sora's voice cut through the noise and he opened his eyes to see her face right in front of his, pale and frightened. "Will, you have to *run*."

The rush of power filled him, drowning out everything else, and Sora's face glowed red in the light from the dragon fire. Heat seared against his back.

Sora ducked down, leaning against him and pulling his head down against her shoulder. He could feel her trembling as the whole world shook. He caught a glimpse of the rocks behind them glowing like molten copper. The forest blazed with red flames, black smoke billowed around him, hiding the beast.

The dragon broke through the smoke above him and swept past. His wings stretched over the treetops and brushed the cliff, a jagged sheet of red tipped with spikes. The dragon's belly glittered dark red, reflecting countless glitters of firelight. One clawed foot tore out a huge pine and flung it down the slope.

Uphill, the others raced for shelter, and the tiny part of Will's brain that could think stared at them in horror, waiting for the flames to envelop them. But the dragon launched up into the blue sky, dwindling to a small shape and the tide of emotions receded.

"Will, please get up."

He shoved at the emotions of the dragon, but it was like pushing back the ocean.

"Will," she pleaded, pulling on his arm.

Will tried to focus on Sora's face through the chaos. For the fleetest moment he felt an emotion of his own—envy at the fact that she would never feel this.

His mind snagged on the idea of her coldness and hollowness. He grabbed her arm, squeezing his eyes shut again and instead of pushing at the swirling mass inside him, he opened himself up to her. There was none of her normal emptiness. There was only cold terror. But it was a human terror that fit inside him. Something he could understand.

He gulped in a breath. The taste of melting rock stung his throat. He opened his eyes and saw Sora.

At his look she sank down in relief. "There you are."

Talen flapped agitated on his arm and he pushed the best semblance of peace he could at the bird. The hawk quieted somewhat. Sora pulled Will to his feet and he stumbled forward. Alaric and Douglon had started down the slope toward him, but now they turned and ran back. Douglon waved them on, his face turned up to the sky. The dragon, so high he had shrunk to a small silhouette, gave one last beat of his wings and with a lazy arc, rolled over into a dive. Straight toward them.

Sora craned her head up. "That dragon is after you!"

"Me?" he demanded, his breath ragged. "Maybe it's after you!"

She spared him the shortest glare and raced forward.

They reached the entrance to the tunnel, no more than a crack, barely wide enough to fit through. Douglon stood at the entrance with his axe blocking the door, shouting at Hal.

"Let him in," Alaric yelled.

Douglon glared at the enormous man before yanking his axe out of the way and giving Hal a shove.

Evangeline stared up at the dragon, a puzzled look on her face.

"Go!" Douglon yelled.

"Evangeline," Alaric called, grabbing her hand and pulling her toward the door.

"I know that dragon…" she said, bemused.

Will glanced at Alaric, but he looked as surprised as Will at the words.

"You don't know any dra—" Alaric snapped his head upwards. His eyes widened. "You might know it, love, but it doesn't know you. Please come." He pulled at her hand, drawing her toward the rocks.

She shook her head and blinked. The two of them ran into the darkness. Sora slipped through after them and Will pushed between the rough sides of the crack, holding Talen near his chest and hearing Douglon's feet behind him. A rush of power flared outside and flames licked into the tunnel.

Douglon heaved something and the opening slammed shut, blocking out the flames and dropping them into complete darkness.

"Farther in!" Douglon cried. "Run!"

The ceiling above Will gave a low crack, and spreading his hand out to feel the walls, he ran into the darkness.

CHAPTER THIRTY-THREE

A LOW RUMBLE shook the tunnel walls. Will's heart pounded, thrumming down even into his fingers as he ran. His eyes stretched open in the blackness, aching for some light, flickering from one formless bit of black to another.

Talen perched on his glove, still calm, but Will curled his fist closer to his body, afraid he might crash the bird into some unexpected rock. There were no unexpected rocks, though. The tunnel had the finished sort of feel that came from dwarven skill, as if any irregularity in the wall was a decision of style. The floor beneath his feet sloped gently downwards.

"Not far." Douglon's words echoed from behind. "There's an outpost just ahead."

Another resonant crack of splitting stone sent a shiver through the walls, but weaker than the last, farther behind him. Proof that they were making some progress in the black.

A dragon. Killien had sent a dragon after him.

A dim burnt-orange glow outlined Sora, and a flicker of fear shot into Will that it was dragon fire, before he realized it was only glimmer moss. Will's eyes latched onto the light and he stood straighter, seeing the vague outline of the arched tunnel.

In half a dozen steps it opened up into a wide cavern too

much like a room to be called a cavern. It was domed, rising smoothly to a wide medallion carved out of the rock in the center of the ceiling. Shelves lined one wall, stocked with small crates and casks. A long table filled the middle of the room. Three maps were set out along the middle, their corners pinned by smooth black rocks. A trickling noise echoed around the room and the mosslight caught on a thin line of water sparkling down the far wall. Piles of sleeping furs were rolled against another wall.

Patlon leaned against the table watching everyone run in. Rass sat huddled next to him, looking like a little snip of grass that had gotten terribly lost. Alaric wrapped his arm around Evangeline, a bit off to the side. The naturalness of it was almost more jarring than the fact Alaric had a wife. Sora walked along the shelves, looking at the supplies. Hal stood over near the bedrolls, his hands still tied behind his back.

Douglon jogged into the room. "How often are you Keepers attacked by dragons?"

"Before this one it had been a hundred and twelve years since any Keeper saw a dragon," Alaric protested.

"This is the second one in a matter of weeks." Douglon dropped his axe on the table with a crash. "And that feels too often to me."

"But this was the same dragon as the last one."

Douglon shook his head. "It tried to kill me twice. Counts as two. You Keepers should focus a little of your study time on how to fight them. Because you're useless."

"It's a dragon!" Alaric said. "Everyone is useless against a dragon."

"Not everyone," Douglon said.

"I think you only get to count one," Evangeline said. "This dragon wasn't trying to kill you. I think it was trying to kill Will. Or maybe Sora."

"There were dragon flames shot in my direction," Douglon said, sinking down onto the end of the bench. "I'm counting two."

Alaric turned to Will. "Evangeline's right, it did seem to be after you."

"It might have been," Will answered. "I may have made Killien, the Torch of the Morrow Clan, a little angry. And he may have recently come across an opportunity to use a dragon." He explained about Killien and the attack by the Sunn Clan. "I knew he was mad." He shook his head and admitted, "I didn't realize he was send-a-dragon mad."

"Good thing the dwarves were here to save you," Douglon pointed out.

"He'll know the dragon didn't kill you," Hal said. "He'll keep sending more rangers. It's only a matter of time until he finds these tunnels."

"No one finds dwarf tunnels," Patlon said.

"Who would want to?" Rass's voice came muffled from her arms.

Douglon walked over and sat next to her. "It's not that bad." He pulled a tiny, bright red gem out of a pocket and set it on the table in front of her. "Under here there are all sorts of treasures."

Rass picked up the stone and examined it, turning it, letting it glimmer in the light of the moss.

Will settled Talen on a long wooden peg at the end of the shelves. "How'd you find me?" he asked Alaric.

"That's also thanks to us," Patlon answered.

"The dwarves had been monitoring the movements of frost goblins this spring," Alaric answered, "because they'd been more active than normal. Then about a week ago they saw the goblins attack a clan."

"The Morrow," Will agreed.

"And it seemed the frost goblins were magically forced back, chased into their warrens by something the dwarves couldn't see." Alaric dropped his gaze to Will's wrapped hand. "When their reports came back, we were in Duncave clearing up some"—he shot an annoyed look at Douglon—"misunderstandings, and the report made me worried there was some unusually strong stonesteep traveling with the Morrow. King Horgoth agreed to have the dwarves watch the clan, and imagine our surprise when they overheard two Roven rangers talking about a Keeper." Alaric paused and looked at Will expectantly.

"I was..." Will glanced at Sora who was watching him with an expressionless face. "Invited to join the Morrow on their migration north after Killien learned I was a storyteller."

"From Gulfind," Hal pointed out. "We wouldn't have invited a liar from Queensland."

"There may have been some subterfuge," Will admitted.

Alaric grinned. "You infiltrated a Roven clan?"

"Yes," Hal answered.

"That sounds more planned than it was," Will said.

"The dwarves followed the Morrow north," Alaric continued, "and saw you imprisoned in a small rift. We were working on how to get you out when the Sweep caught fire and one of the scouts saw you escape. It took us a full day to find you, but the dwarves have entrances to their tunnels all over the Hoarfrost. Once we figured out where you were, it was pretty easy to get to you." Alaric paused, then leaned closer. "What did you do? To drive off the frost goblins?"

Will felt a smile growing. "I took the heat from the fires and the heatstones." At the questioning quirk in Alaric's brow, he said, "I have to tell you about heatstones. Anyway, I took the heat and pushed it toward the goblins."

Alaric's eyebrows rose. "With a fire net? That wouldn't hold enough heat."

Will's smile turned into a grin. "With a fire *wall*."

Alaric's head tilted to the side and his eyes flickered unseeing around the room as he thought through it.

"A clay wall, like an oven."

Alaric stared at him. "That's brilliant. Show me."

Will held up his bandaged hands. "Maybe someday. Last time it hurt. A lot."

"Where's that gem you picked up?" Patlon asked Will.

Will pulled the blue necklace that Hal had put on him out of his pack. "It's a compulsion stone holding a spell that will exhaust you if you touch it."

Patlon pulled back the hand he'd been reaching.

Alaric peered at the stone. "Do the Morrow use a lot of magic?"

"No, but Killien is actively trying to change that. He has a book that talks about burning stones like this. It's based on the magic Mallon used."

"Mallon the Rivor?" Alaric exchanged glances with Douglon.

Will nodded. "The thing he seems to be studying the most from that book is how to transfer thoughts and emotions into others. They're called compulsion stones, but I don't think he's figured out how to use it."

"He definitely knows how to transfer thoughts," Sora said.

"Really? Lukas's notes said it wasn't sophisticated enough to work on humans, and he seemed to lose interest. Seems like it was meant to control beasts."

Sora nodded. "Like frost goblins."

Will tucked the blue stone back in his pack. "If Killien could control frost goblins, why didn't he drive them away from the clan?"

Sora let out a derisive snort. "He's the reason they attacked."

CHAPTER THIRTY-FOUR

"What are you talking about?" Hal demanded.

"On the trip north," Sora said, "Killien ordered me to bring him a goblin. Two days before the attack, I was able to capture one alive." Her mouth tightened with distaste. "He put a blue stone around the creature's neck." She stopped and stared unseeing at the bowl of glimmer moss on the table. "The goblin went mad. It was bound, but it thrashed around, trying to move toward the clan.

"It had almost torn its own hand off when Killien gave the order to kill it. When I touched it, I had this idea of a box of gold nearby, and suddenly I wanted it. I don't think I've ever wanted something as much as that."

Her hand gripped the hilt of her knife. "I pulled the stone off its neck and threw it to the ground, and the idea disappeared. But the creature didn't calm. If anything, it fought harder." She dropped her hand from the knife. "In the end, there was nothing to do but kill it."

"Killien gave a goblin the idea that there was metal nearby?" Will asked. "That's insane."

"It was more than an idea of metal," Sora said. "It was a desire for it."

Will nodded. "That makes sense. He's not trying to transfer a thought, he's transferring emotions. Lukas discovered that emotions were easy to share."

Hal shook his head violently. "That doesn't mean that Killien brought the army of frost goblins."

They had poured out of the ground like a single creature, like a hive of drones. Swarming toward the metal.

"He did. They're all connected," Will said. "Like one creature, or like a thousand spiders sharing a web. What one senses, they all sense. Killien didn't just give one goblin the desire for metal near the clan, he gave it to every goblin it was connected to."

"And they all came," Sora finished.

Hal fixed her with a look too complicated to describe, still shaking his head. "Killien caused the attack?" He sounded half angry, half appalled.

"At least now I know what Killien did that made you so mad at him." Will almost asked her why she hadn't told him, but the question felt like it presumed more secret-sharing than they'd been in the habit of. At least before today.

She nodded. "And after all of that, he has rangers trying to capture more."

"Why?" Hal demanded.

"Because he's obsessed with gaining power for the Morrow Clan," Sora said. "And he is increasingly violent about it."

Hal looked like he wanted to object, but there was something in his expression that agreed with her. "I've never seen him like this." He sank down on the bench. His next words came out slowly. "He told me nothing...about any of this."

"I'd like to see that book about Mallon's magic," Alaric mused.

"I have something better." Will pulled *The Gleaning of Souls* out of his pack and the book fell to the table with a thud. "Or maybe worse."

Alaric leaned over and drew in a breath. "Kachig the Bloodless."

"You know the name? I hadn't heard it until I came to the Sweep."

A flicker of something dark crossed Alaric's face. "The blood doctors in Napon speak highly of him."

Will glanced up at him. "You've spoken to blood doctors? In Napon?"

Alaric's eyes were dark and angry. "I don't recommend it." He sat next to Will on the bench and reached out toward the medallion on the cover. His finger paused above it. "I've seen something like this before."

"That thing is dark." Will pulled his eye away from it. "It describes how to make something called absorption stones."

Alaric nodded and opened the book. He ran his fingers over the stacked runes, tracing the lines. "They've put runes inside each other."

Will watched Alaric's finger slide over the page, heard him muttering the words. Laughter started to bubble up inside him, foreign and shocking. Like something that hadn't happened in years. It burst out and Alaric looked up in surprise.

"You're just"—Will gestured to the page—"reading it. Like it's nothing."

Alaric smiled and pointed at one complicated one. "This is fascinating. They stacked four of them here. *Fire, escape, capture, and...*" He tilted his head to the side and leaned closer. "*Broken.*"

Will leaned forward. "I thought it was *empty*."

Alaric shook his head. "This line draws it into the past, referring to a cause. The end result would be *empty* but the rune itself is talking about the brokenness that emptied it."

Sora let out a laugh too, a rippling, free sound that filled the room. "I thought you were being mopey. But you really are bad at this."

"I'm bad at everything that goes into being a Keeper."

Alaric glanced up at him in surprise, his finger set on one of the runes. "You don't believe that. Do you?"

"Name one thing I'm good at."

"People," Alaric answered, as though it was too obvious to be worth saying.

Sora sat down across the table from them, her eyes shifting between Will and Alaric, utterly amused by the conversation. Will shot her a glare before answering.

"People. That's your answer? I'm a Keeper who's fairly useless at magic and terrible at reading." He stabbed his finger at the book. "It took me over a day just to figure out those runes were stacked. And I'm not even going to let you see my attempts at translating them."

Alaric looked at Will as though he were speaking a different language.

"Could anyone but Alaric read them this quickly?" Evangeline asked.

"Probably not," Will answered. "Your husband is irritatingly good at everything. And he's freakish about runes."

Her eyebrow rose.

"No offense," he added.

Evangeline laughed. "That's my point. Alaric's obsessed with runes. He has notebooks color coded based on region of origin, but organized by meaning. And there are three extra notebooks cross referencing it all."

Alaric shrugged. "Runes are like puzzles. Like there's some enormous game going on and everyone uses the same pieces, but not always the same rules." He turned to Will earnestly. "They're like a story."

Will groaned. "No. They're not. They're nothing like a story. I want to think it's weird that you're this studious, but really, it proves that you are just better at all things Keeper."

"Except people."

"You're good at using grass," Rass piped up from where she sat, munching on a piece of hard bread Douglon had found her.

Will shot Rass an irritated look and received a cheerful grin in return.

"People?" Will demanded of Alaric. "What does that mean?

The Shield sends you to court because you're the one who's good at talking crazy noblemen down from weird schemes, at giving the queen rational, useful council. That all involves people."

Alaric let out an annoyed breath and cast around the room. He jabbed a finger at Hal. "Why is he mad?"

Hal, still stood near the bedrolls, his arms still tied behind his back. The giant man's eyes were smoldering with anger, and Will could see his jaw clenched even through the bushy beard.

"He's mad," Will began, pulling out the most obvious reason, "because he just found out that the man he's been friends with his entire life endangered everyone they both love in the pursuit of power."

Hal's gaze snapped over to Will's face.

"And he's angry because he would have done anything for that man, and now he doesn't know if that's been a mistake. He's mad because all this time he thought Killien was being honest, and now doesn't know how much he's been hiding."

Hal glared at Will and turned away.

"And he's still mad at me," Will continued, quieter, "because he thought we had a friendship before all this fell apart. So that's two friendships he's afraid have never been real to anyone but him. If I were him," he finished, "I'd be mad too."

The cave was silent for a long moment.

"See?" Alaric turned back to the book. "I would have said he's mad because no one's bothered to untie him yet." He ran his finger down the page again. "You effortlessly understand people in a way I never have. In a way maybe no Keeper ever has."

Will scowled at the side of Alaric's head. "I have an advantage in reading people."

"Were you using it?"

"No."

"Then you had no advantage. The Shield has said more than once that having you be the Keeper the world meets might be the best thing that's happened to us in a hundred years." Alaric leaned closer to one of the runes, squinting at it. "Understanding people is considerably more complex than understanding runes."

Hal glared into the corner of the room. Will nodded to Sora's unspoken question, and she cut Hal's ropes.

"I know Killien thinks I'm his enemy," Will told Hal, "but I'm not. I used to think that he and I might work together toward some kind of peace, but lately…"

Hal rubbed at his wrists and nodded. "He's changed," he admitted.

"You're not our prisoner." Will motioned toward the entrance the dragon had attacked. "I don't think the way we came in still exists, but at the next exit we find, you're free to leave."

For the first time since finding them, the anger faded off Hal's face, and he looked Will in the eye. "Thank you."

"There's an exit an hour east of here," Douglon said. "The rest of us can continue back over to the Scales. A day and a half from now you can be on your way down the other side of Kollman Pass into Queensland."

"We can take supplies from here." Patlon went over to the shelves and started rummaging. "Torgon keeps up the western storerooms and he can be counted on to keep things stocked. We'll have plenty of supplies."

"I can't leave the Sweep," Will said.

Everyone turned toward him.

"Killien has Ilsa."

There was a breath before Alaric's eyes widened. "Your Ilsa?"

Will nodded. "And there's more. When she was taken, the wayfarers were actually trying to get me."

Alaric's expression clouded. "Why?"

"Because I was going to be a Keeper. The Morrow Clan has been sending wayfarers into Queensland for over thirty years, searching for children who have the ability to do magic, and bringing them back to the Morrow to be the Torch's personal slaves. They tried to get me, but when I wouldn't go, they took Ilsa.

"And they've found others. Killien has two slaves, Lukas and Sini, who are both from Queensland and can both do magic." He turned to Hal. "And Rett too? That would explain why Killien has him."

Hal hesitated, then nodded.

"Three?" Alaric sank down onto the bench. "They found three Keepers before we did?"

"I don't care if he did it for the good of his clan," Will said to Hal. "Killien abducts children and keeps them as his own personal slaves because they have powers he wants. *Three children*, Hal."

The giant man looked down for a long moment. Then his gaze flickered up toward Will's face, troubled. When he spoke, it was almost too quiet to hear.

"There used to be four."

CHAPTER THIRTY-FIVE

The room fell into silence as every head turned toward Hal.

Will took a step toward him. "What do you mean, 'used to be'?"

Hal met his gaze for a breath before looking down at the floor. "It was before Killien was Torch."

Will opened up toward Hal. An old, worn out mix of sadness and anger rolled into his chest.

"Killien's father, Tevien, was the one who started trying to bring people with powers to the Morrow. He knew Mallon was from Queensland, and he turned out to be more powerful than any of our stonesteeps."

Alaric watched Hal with narrowed, searching eyes. "Mallon was from Queensland?"

Will nodded.

"Tevien learned about Keepers," Hal continued. "Thinking they would bring the Morrow power, Tevien spent a fortune on stones able to recognize people with powers, and sent them to Queensland with some wayfarers.

"The first time they brought anyone back, it was twins."

Alaric shot a questioning glance at Will. There had been three sets of twins in the history of the Keepers. The latest pair, Matton and Steffan, were nearly a hundred years old and so identical that Will had given up trying to tell them apart years ago. Since they were never away from each other, there really was no need.

"Rett was big, even for a twelve year old. His sister Raina was average sized, but it was hard to remember that because she looked so small next to her brother." Hal fixed his eyes on the floor, his voice low. "The twins were the same age as Killien and I, and we spent a lot of time with them. Raina was quick and funny and brave. And Rett was stronger than me, by a lot. The two of them were inseparable. Raina told me once that she could almost hear Rett's thoughts, that she could catch a shadow of them." He let out a small laugh. "They were constantly trying to read each other's minds. Killien was half in love with her, although he hid it well from his father."

Hal shifted his shoulders. "Tevien became obsessed with training Rett and Raina into a pair who would be more powerful than any stonesteep. He wanted them to try something from a book years beyond their training. It involved both of them putting a bit of themselves into a stone, and storing it there. Rett thought it would never work, but Raina wanted to try."

He blew out a long breath. "I think she thought that if parts of each of them were really connected, they'd finally be able to speak into each other's minds." He pressed his eyes closed for a moment, and when he opened them, they were flat. "Raina went first. The stone glowed this eerie green and when she touched it —" His voice caught.

"It happened so fast. She started screaming, and it just pulled everything out of her. She went from laughing and talking and living...to nothing.

"Rett went crazy. He tried to rip the stone out of her hands, but as soon as he touched it, it started to take him too." He squeezed his eyes shut again, twisting away from the memory.

"It was Killien who stopped it. He wrested the stone away from them both. But by the time he did, Raina was dead and Rett was...empty. He still had some abilities, but there's nothing left of *him*." He drew in a deep breath, and blew it out. "Killien and I have never been able to figure out if he even remembers who Raina was."

"That's why Rett likes glowing green stones, isn't it?" Will asked.

Hal let out a growl. "Lukas gives him those... Something in him must remember because he watches those stones like he's waiting for something. And when the green light fades, he's heartbroken."

"Is Lukas trying to be cruel?"

Hal shook his head. "Rett begs him for them and sometimes Lukas gives in. And while they glow, he's so happy, it almost feels like the right thing to do."

"How did Killien save him?" Alaric asked. "Why didn't the stone just take him too?"

Hal closed his mouth.

"Because magic doesn't work around Killien," Will said. "Does it?"

Hal clenched his jaw, but didn't disagree.

"That's why I couldn't do anything near him." Will turned to Alaric. "He was sitting at a table with me. I could feel the *vitalle* from everyone around us, but when I tried to grab it, it just slipped through my fingers. I don't know what kind of magic he has in one of those gems he wears, but I couldn't do anything near him."

Alaric's hand felt absently for something at his chest that he didn't find. "Could you touch the *vitalle* at all?"

Will started to shake his head, then paused. "It was like smoke. I knew when I had reached it, but there was nothing to hold."

Alaric turned his eyes up to the ceiling. "Fascinating."

"What's fascinating," Hal said, his face dark, "is that after all your protesting, Will, you obviously did try to use magic against Killien."

"Once. After he'd drugged me, imprisoned me, forced me to

translate an evil book, and threatened to kill my sister. After all this, you can hardly expect me to give Killien the high moral ground."

"What happened to Raina and Rett is why Killien is the way he is," Hal fired back. "Why he studies everything as extensively as he can before he does anything. Why he spends the Morrow's money on as many books as he can find."

"Like this?" Will pointed to Kachig's book. "What we need to do is free Lukas. Then Killien won't have the power to do anything."

"You can't do that to Lukas," Hal objected.

Will stared at him. "I think he'd be in favor of being freed from slavery."

"He won't leave Killien. His limp isn't from a normal injury. A few years ago he was attacked by a stonesteep. The healers fixed his leg, but the pain never went away. It's driven by some sort of magic because if Lukas is close to Killien, it stops."

Will sank back. "That explains a lot." The closeness to Killien. His foul mood anytime he was away from the Torch. How his limp seemed to change in severity. "Why doesn't Killien just give Lukas one of the gems that stops magic from working around him? Is it in one of his rings?"

Hal fixed him with a look that clearly said Will didn't know what he was talking about.

A thought struck Will. "Unless it's not in a gem. It's something about Killien himself."

Hal scowled more deeply.

Alaric's eyebrow rose. "Killien can nullify magic?"

Will shrugged. "I only tried to move *vitalle* around him once, but if it's like that all the time, I'd say yes, he can nullify magic."

Both Keepers looked at Hal questioningly. Hal's shoulders sank. "I don't know how it works," he admitted, "but no magic works near Killien. He's been like that since we were boys. So Lukas stays near Killien as often as he can. Even at night. The room he sleeps in shares a wall with Killien, and that's close enough."

Alaric's eyebrows rose more. "He can do it through walls?"

Hal nodded.

Alaric eyes were bright with curiosity. "Fascinating," he repeated.

"If Killien nullifies magic, why does he wear all the rings and have the runes on his leathers?" Will asked.

"Only a handful of people know he has the ability. He thinks it's more valuable if he keeps it a secret."

"This is all very interesting," Douglon interrupted, hefting a crate off a shelf and bringing it over to the table, "but if we're not leaving the Sweep, where are we going?"

"I need to go where Killien has Ilsa," Will said.

"He's in the rift," Hal said. "We were supposed to leave for the enclave tomorrow, but after everything that happened, I'd imagine he's waiting impatiently for us to bring you back."

"How are you going to reach her?" Sora asked.

Will scrubbed his hand through his hair. "I don't know, but I can't leave her there."

"It's gonna be tricky sneaking Queenslanders and dwarves into a Roven rift," Patlon pointed out. "We don't blend in."

That was true. It would be stupid to take this group into the Sweep. Will dropped his head into his hands. There was no way any of them were going to get anywhere near the rift, never mind Killien's own house, without the Torch finding out.

The room was silent for a few breaths while Will searched desperately for an idea. It was Hal who broke the silence.

"I can take you in."

CHAPTER THIRTY-SIX

Will looked up at Hal sharply. "Somehow I don't think walking into the rift with you will work out much better for us."

"We'll go in the back entrance. There's a tunnel that leads from the Sweep directly into the back of Killien's house." He ran his fingernail along a groove on the table. "Ilsa's been helping Lilit recover since the baby was born. That's where she'll be."

"Who knows about the entrance?" Sora asked.

"Killien, Lilit, Me. Lukas." Hal turned to the dwarves. "Do you have an exit closer to the rift?"

"There is one," Douglon answered. "Only a couple hours away."

"Cousin," Patlon warned. "The High Dwarf isn't fond of foreigners in the tunnels."

"I don't see Horgoth here, cousin."

"He's going to be furious."

"That's hardly new."

"Can we get into Killien's house without being seen?" Will asked.

"If we go during the night," Hal answered. "We'll have to avoid rangers, but we'll have Sora with us."

"And me," Rass said. "Rangers stomp around so much you can hear them long before you can see them."

"The hours before dawn would be the easiest," Sora said. "But what if we run into Killien before we find Ilsa?"

"Trade me for her," Hal said.

Will glanced at Sora. "Would Killien make that trade?"

"Hal's family owns half of the herds in the Morrow Clan. Killien would be stupid not to. But if we run into Killien, we won't be in a position to trade."

"Then let's not run into Killien." Will turned to Hal. "Are we going to be able to find her?"

"The tunnel comes out in a back storage room near the slave's quarters. Killien's sleeping room is one floor up. If we're quiet, we can go in, talk to Ilsa, and leave before Killien knows you're there. I'll find a different way back into the rift once it's daylight."

Sora's face was hard. "Why are you helping Will?"

Hal ran a hand through his hair. "Ilsa's served Lilit for a long time, and she seems like a good person." He glanced at Will. "And the Torch hates you with a ferocity I haven't seen before. I don't think Ilsa should be a pawn in that. You're letting me go. Killien's letting her go. It's fair."

Sora's mouth pressed into a reluctant acceptance, before she turned back to Will. "And what if Ilsa doesn't want to come?"

Will's stomach tightened at the words.

"Will you be able to leave her there?"

"I'm not taking her against her will." He pushed aside the memory of how she'd flinched away from him. "But when she hears the truth, I hope she'll come."

Sora leaned on the table and fixed him with an expression that told him how likely she thought that was. "You're following a man who's angry with you, into the home of a man who hates you, to try to convince a woman who's terrified of you, to leave everything she's ever known."

Will shook his head "You're telling the story all wrong. A Keeper is journeying through the night, using a secret tunnel shown to him by a friend, to reach the house of...an old friend, in order to save an innocent girl from slavery, and possibly death." Her expression didn't change and Will gave her a hopeful smile. "And he's taking the greatest ranger on the Sweep with him, so that counts for something."

"Changing the story doesn't change the truth."

"The truth is complex enough for more than one story."

She shook her head and stood up, walking over to where Evangeline and Patlon were discussing supplies. Will glanced at Hal who was running his thumbnail pensively along a groove on the table.

"Is my horse alright?" Will asked.

Hal nodded without glancing up. "Killien made him a workhorse in the barley fields. He'll be cared for."

Will sighed. "I liked Shadow. Although I suppose he'd probably have been eaten by a dragon by now if he was here, seeing as how he wouldn't have fit in the entrance to this tunnel."

He watched Hal run his hand along the grain of the table. "I am sorry that I lied to you about who I was."

The big man paused for a moment. "Telling us you were a Keeper would have been a death sentence."

"Does it make it any better to know that it wasn't long into knowing you that I regretted the fact that the lie existed?"

Hal grunted noncommittally and Will let silence fall between them for a moment, wondering if there was a better way to ask his next question. "Are you sure you should be helping us?"

Hal didn't answer immediately. When he did, he sounded reluctant. "I've spoken to your sister several times, and I like her. I don't think it's right, Killien using her like this."

Will thought back on the past few weeks. "I've never seen you with a slave. Do you have any?"

"My father did. I grew up with some of them. One was a girl just two years younger than me. She was...like a sister." Hal ran his fingers through his beard. "And one day my father traded her for a breeding ram." In the dim light, Hal's eyes were hard.

"When my father died, I took all our slaves to Kollman Pass and sent them off the Sweep."

"You set them free?"

Hal nodded. "Never sat right with me, owning people like that."

"But you're friends with Killien, and he has plenty of slaves."

"If I kept my distance from every Roven with slaves, I'd have no friends at all," Hal answered. "Killien and I have been friends our entire lives. I love him like a brother even if we don't agree on everything."

"Won't he see this as a betrayal?"

Hal ran his hand through his beard. "Maybe. But there's a lot of what he's done lately that feels like betrayal as well. I can't believe he did that with the frost goblins, and still wants to capture more. Also, he already knows how I feel about slaves. I've tried to convince him more than once to free his."

"How did he take that idea?"

"Not well. I don't think Rett would know what to do with freedom, but Sini and Lukas deserve it. Sini is too fun and happy to be kept as a slave. And Lukas is bright, he could probably do anything he set his mind to."

Except be pleasant. "Well, thank you. I appreciate the help."

Hal gave Will a hard look. "When I met you, I thought you'd make my journey north more enjoyable. Instead you've made my life much more complicated."

"I introduced you to dwarves," Will pointed out. "And brought you into their tunnels."

A smile showed behind his beard. "True. Maybe that's the real reason I'm helping you. And I do like the stories."

"Maybe after we eat I can tell the one about a dwarf princess who was so ugly she was mistaken for a rock."

"I've never wanted to hear anything more."

Down the table, Alaric leaned close to a page in Kachig's book, squinting at a rune and muttering.

"What we need," Will said to him, "are the more elementary

books on how to do magic with stones. All the books I've read expect a familiarity with a process we don't know anything about."

Alaric cleared his throat and smoothed his hand across the page. "I may have figured out a little bit of it."

"When?"

Alaric glanced at Evangeline, then began the story of how she was poisoned and how he drew out her *vitalle* into a Reservoir Stone to keep her alive.

Will stared at his old friend, stunned. "That sounds like the absorption stone that Killien's book talked about, drawing the life out of someone."

"Very much like it." Alaric told of the long, painful search for the cure, and how it led to the discovery of a wizard named Gustav who planned to awaken Mallon.

"He was the reason the dragon attacked us the first time," Douglon said.

"How did you fight it off?" Will asked.

Douglon looked away and took a bite of his bread.

"Ayda did," Alaric answered.

"Ayda the elf? I underestimated her," Will said.

"Everyone did."

Will looked back and forth between them. "I followed a wizard onto the Sweep because he claimed he was going to wake Mallon. I found him, eventually, but he was just a doddering old man. His name wasn't Gustav, though. It was Wizendor."

Alaric laughed. "That's him. His full name was Wizendorenfurderfur."

"The Wondrous," Douglon added.

They seemed perfectly serious. "That's ridiculous."

Douglon shook his head. "You can't even imagine."

"He was a master of influence spells." Alaric's distaste of the idea was obvious. "He fooled all of us."

Will shifted. "Influence spells can be useful when you're surrounded by enemies."

Alaric raised an eyebrow, but after a moment's thought, gave a nod of agreement. He explained how Ayda had been the last elf, and held the power of all the others, how she'd used it to help destroy Mallon and Gustav.

"But you said before there are no more elves." Will looked at each of their somber faces, not wanting to ask the next question. "Did destroying Mallon kill her?"

Alaric shook his head. "No, that came later."

Douglon let out a long sigh and pushed away from the table, going to rummage through another crate on the shelf.

"Douglon," Will whispered, "and Ayda?"

Alaric nodded.

"That's…" Words failed him.

"It is," Alaric agreed. "When we got back to Evangeline, she was far too weak to revive. Until Ayda…"

Evangeline looked pensively at her own hands.

"She was tired of being the only elf, tired of carrying the weight of her people. She'd done it long enough to see Mallon destroyed, and she was done."

Will sat back, taking in the whole idea. "So there really are no elves?" The idea felt so hollow. Granted he had only seen a handful of elves in his life, most of which were polite but distant emissaries at court, but elves always felt like a breath of life in the world. He'd often thought of returning to the Greenwood to find Ayda again. "Is that how you knew the dragon?" he asked Evangeline. "Whatever Ayda put in you recognized it?"

Both Alaric and Evangeline nodded.

"She put some of her memories into me," Evangeline explained. "It's like when you're doing something and you have that feeling that you've done it all before. Sometimes I see something, or Alaric says something, and I know about it. But it's like a dream. If I think about it too much, it all goes away. So Alaric's taken to slipping things into conversations to catch me off guard."

"You would not believe the things I've learned about the elves," Alaric said. "It's fascinating. And depressing."

"We should go." Douglon pulled some squash and onions out of the crate. "There's a cavern not far from here with a chimney. We can cook and get a few hours sleep before we need to head to the rift."

"I thought we'd just sleep here." Alaric glanced at the bedrolls.

"Trust me." Douglon shoved the crate back onto the shelf. "You want to get to the other one."

Patlon poured water into cup-like lanterns. As he did, each one began to glow with a faint orange light.

Sora pulled her own glimmer moss lantern out of her bag, and using a bit of Patlon's water, set hers glowing a ruddier color. Patlon peered into her lantern and grunted. "Frostweed?"

"Mixed with crushed tundra lichen."

Patlon gave her an approving nod. "You may be the most competent human I've ever met." He motioned her toward the tunnel. "You're going to like where we're headed."

Sora walked into the tunnel next to him, the sound of Patlon's voice dropping to muffled echoes. Everyone else followed.

The world shrank to the size of their group. The lanterns cast four patches of orange light. Bits of the ceiling and walls slid through them. A nagging discomfort began to plague Will that they weren't actually moving. That they were doing something like treading water. A peal of laughter echoed back from Sora, and Will craned around Hal to see her. She talked animatedly, outlined in the dim light of Patlon's lantern. It felt partly reassuring, partly irritating that she was so at ease.

"You can't listen with your ears," Douglon's voice came from behind him. "Listen with the part of you that understands the permanence of the stone. The part of you that knows that life should continue, that *you* should continue, that dying goes against what should be. The part of you that understands eternity."

Will glanced back to see Rass reach out tentatively toward the wall. "When I talk to the grass, it is always growing and dying and growing again. There is nothing lasting about it." She let her fingers trail along the rock.

"Don't think about the voice of the grasses. Think about the voice of the Sweep, lying still and strong and unmoved for a thousand years."

Rass's brow furrowed and she pressed more of her hand against the wall, dragging her whole palm along it. She shook her head.

"Give it time, wee snip," Douglon said. "The rocks speak slowly."

They walked for more than an hour. At some point, Patlon began to hum a deep, thrumming tune. The melody echoed off the walls mixing with new strands of the song. Douglon joined in, humming from the back of the group, and the echoes became more layered and rich, the pulse of the song rang through the mountain like a drum.

Eventually the darkness paled and the tunnel, which had run reasonably straight, twisted sharply to the left. Will squinted into the hazy light that filtered around another turn not far ahead. The tunnel continued in the excessively serpentine way for four more turns, each growing gradually brighter before Hal mentioned it to Patlon.

"It's giving your eyes time to adjust," the dwarf answered. "You'd have been half blinded if you just stepped into what's ahead."

Even so, when the tunnel turned the last time, Will could barely open his eyes. The air was saturated with a blue-tinged light, as though they had stepped out into the middle of the shimmering sky. After the closeness of the tunnel, the cavern gaped open taller than pine trees and wide enough that the other side was lost in hazy brightness. The faint smell of trees and earth wafted past, but everything looked like sky.

"Move in," Douglon grumbled from behind them.

Will took a stunned step forward along with everyone else, and the floor beneath him shot out fierce glints of light, flashing reflections of the glimmer moss like specks of blazing fire.

"It glitters everywhere!" Rass's little voice skipped off the walls and echoed through the chamber.

The floor itself was a pale blue, but glitters of orange from the mosslight skittered across it with every step, like infinitesimally small fairies flitting by faster than he could see. On the rough walls, the lights tripped from crevice to ridge, scattering like shattered glass.

"Welcome to Hellat Harrock'lot." Douglon's words echoed as well, deeper and richer. "The Cavern of Sea and Sky. You may be the first foreigners to set eyes on it."

"Another thing the High Dwarf is going to love," Patlon muttered.

The cavern wasn't as large as Will had first thought. His eyes adjusted and revealed the far side of the oblong cave only a hundred paces away. Four tunnels branched off, dark mouths opening in the blue-white walls. The ceiling was just the continuation of the walls, arching over them in a low hanging dome. Near the far side, the ceiling was cut by a gash letting in a trickle of light.

"We're close to the surface," Douglon said. "It's only a short climb up that shaft to an outcropping of rock on the mountainside. Judging from the light, it's close to sunset. Thanks to that little chimney, we can have a fire and a proper meal. We can get a few hours sleep before we need to leave."

In a wide, flat area there was a circle of ash on the floor and a small pile of wood stacked up against a nearby wall. Patlon lit a fire, and the flames sent millions of tiny shards of light reflecting across the cavern. Sora took out the rabbit that had been wrapped around the heatstone. The stone had stopped glowing, but the entire package was still warm. The strips of rabbit were hot and dripping with juices, and they were divided up and eaten within moments.

Will set Talen on a thin piece of firewood and ripped off small bits of rabbit, feeding them to the hawk who seemed perfectly content to sit on his perch in his hood.

Everyone gathered near the fire except Sora, who faced out into the cavern. He walked over to her, watching the floor glitter and flash below his feet, like he was treading on the stars. "Have you ever seen anything like this?"

She shook her head.

"A place like this makes me understand why you like caves."

"Everyone loves places like this. But it's the small, common caves that feel like home. The tunnels that wander through the mountains."

He thought about the passageways they'd traveled through all day, the darkness, the silence, the lifelessness. There was nothing homey about them.

"You think I'm crazy," she said.

"No, I think you're scowly," he answered, "and have an odd definition of homey."

With a small shake of her head she strode across the cavern. "Come."

He let her walk a few steps before following. "I also think you're bossy."

CHAPTER THIRTY-SEVEN

He followed Sora to the nearest tunnel mouth. She paused at the opening, and with a disapproving grunt, she walked to the next.

"This one." She stepped in and turned a corner out of sight. Her voice came back in an echoey, hollow way. "Come."

Will followed her. Around the first turn, the tunnel dimmed and he found her waiting, arms crossed. The corners of the floor were lost in blackness, and shadows filled more spaces on the wall than seemed reasonable. "What are we doing in here?"

"You are going to see what tunnels are really like." She turned and disappeared around another corner, proving this was just as serpentine as the one from earlier.

"What if we get lost?"

"It'll make a great story," she answered. "Hurry up."

In two more turns the darkness crept out of the corners and seeped into the air itself. He could barely make her out in front of him. "Not to sound like a frightened child," he said, letting his hands run along the wall as he walked deeper into the darkness, "but I'd be thrilled to find out you had a bit of glimmer moss tucked away somewhere."

She turned back towards him, and he was almost certain she

was laughing. She took one of his hands and started walking again, pulling him along.

"Not much farther."

One more turn and the tunnel straightened out. His eyes stretched wide, but there was nothing to see but blackness. He could feel Sora's hand in his, but there was no way to pick her out from the dark.

She walked a dozen paces more and then stopped. He tried to hold her hand loosely, fighting the urge to cling to it. The darkness was so thick it felt like a thing in itself.

"Do you hear that?" she whispered.

There was nothing at all to hear. Beyond Sora's slow, measured breathing and the unnerving sound of his own heart pounding, which he was sure she could feel through his hand, there was utter and complete silence.

"No," he whispered. "I hear nothing."

"That's what you're supposed to hear." Her words slid through the darkness, calm and pleased. "The tunnel is like a cocoon, like the walls of a fortress so thick that nothing can get through them. Not noises, not armies, not other people's expectations, not even the Serpent Queen."

Will closed his eyes and tried to find what Sora felt. "It all feels too heavy. Like the rocks will crush us."

"You're thinking of the mountain as an enemy. It's life and shelter and warmth and endless, timeless permanence."

Her words almost made a difference. For a breath he felt the solid mass of the mountain above him like a shield. But it grew heavier until it was ready to smash down and flatten them all. His grip tightened on her hand.

"You're not seeing the mountain for what it is, Will. You're imagining what it's capable of, but you're not seeing what it is now, what it's been for thousands of years. When you walk through the forest, you don't imagine it will burst into flames at any moment, do you?"

"No," he admitted.

"This tunnel is more permanent than the trees. Think about what the rocks are, what they do. Wind and storms that terrify us don't affect them. Nothing is indestructible, but the rocks are close. They're…" She gave a short growl of irritation. "I can't explain it. Here, feel what it's like for me."

Emotion surged into his chest. Contentedness, security, belonging. Like he was a child again in the years before Ilsa had been taken, tucked under a wool blanket, lying in his bed in the dark cottage, alone but safe. The walls of the cottage surrounded him, blocking out the foxes and packs of little brush wolves that roamed the forest. All the dangers were outside the walls and inside there was nothing to fear. Just the endless night, a black backdrop waiting to be filled with imaginings.

The freedom in that moment was liberating. Freedom he hadn't noticed as a child.

The sensation drained out of his chest and he ached with hollowness in its wake. He gripped Sora's hand in the darkness of the tunnel and he understood. The tunnel walls stood solid around them, holding off the mountain, holding back the sky. The Sweep and its politics, Killien and his plans, Queensland and its responsibilities, all those things were outside the walls. And in here there was just the silence of endless years of stillness. Nothing rushed, nothing expected.

"Oh," he breathed.

"Now you see?" Her voice was quiet, low enough that he almost missed it.

"Yes."

They stood in silence for a breath and Will realized his shoulders were relaxed. He breathed in the stillness of the tunnel.

A jarring question broke through the quiet.

"How did you do that?" He wished he could see Sora's face. "Your emotions are always so tightly controlled, I can barely find them. How did you make me feel that?"

"I just did what we tried in the rift. I tried to let you feel my emotions."

"But *I* wasn't trying." He hadn't been, had he? "I have to... open up to someone. It doesn't just happen. I have to want to feel them."

"Maybe you want to know what I'm feeling more than you think you do." There was a note of amusement in her voice.

"I don't—that sounds like I'm stalking you."

Her laughter echoed off the walls, bouncing back on itself into a jumble of sound. "Do you really think that if I were trying to get away from you, you could stalk me?"

"That's not exactly what I meant."

"Shall I leave you here in the tunnel and you can try to track me?" Her fingers loosened on his hand.

"No!" He turned and brought both hands to clench hers and she laughed again. He cleared his throat. "I mean, maybe some other time. Right now, I just want to stay here and absorb all this comforting silence you just showed me."

"Of course you do." Her fingers wrapped around his hand again. "Because there's nothing better than being deep in the mountain."

The stillness of the tunnels became a palpable thing again.

"Living with your people was so bad that you won't go back? Even for this?"

She didn't answer. All he heard was the sound of their breath and the silence of the mountain.

"There was another thing my clan believed about me…"

The words trailed away, absorbed by the mountain.

"When I was twelve, Lyelle, the daughter of the holy woman, fell ill. They brought me to her and she recovered. From then on she was allowed to play with me." A wistfulness crept into her voice. "It wasn't just that Lyelle was my only friend, she was exactly the sort of girl I would have picked. She was funny and smart and brave.

"The other children never left the cave without adults." The wistfulness was gone, replaced by something Will couldn't name. "The mountains are too wild. But she wanted to sneak out with me. We went out twice with no problems, and she grew more eager to do it again.

"The third time we went..." Sora's voice stopped and her hand trembled. "By the time I sensed the wolves, it was too late. They were too close."

The horror of the idea stole his breath.

"I climbed up on some boulders." The words sounded like they were spilling out of their own will. "But Lyelle wasn't tall enough to get up. And I wasn't strong enough to pull her..." Sora's hands clenched his. She drew in a shuddering breath. "It was over so fast. I didn't..."

They stood in the darkness while she took several breaths. When she began again, a coldness had crept into her words.

"I was too young to understand why the holy woman didn't blame me."

The truth of it hit him like a fist in the gut. "She needed the people to believe everything was related to your power."

He took her silence for agreement.

"She quoted some ancient text claiming to court the friendship of the Serpent Queen was to court death. The next winter I fell sick, and in caring for me, my mother did as well.

"I wasn't even fully recovered when she died." The ache in her voice dug into Will's chest. "Terra told the clan that she'd been a good mother, but it had always been only a matter of time. Because to draw too close to the Serpent Queen brought nothing but death."

"None of this was you," Will whispered to her, pulling her hand to his chest. "None of it."

"I know." She paused. "At least most of me does. But there's a part that's still twelve, watching them take away my mother's body." She let out a long breath and her grip loosened. "So no, Will. Not even the tunnels could draw me back. Because the farther I am away from home, the easier it is to remember that I'm not twelve, I have no power, and I'm not cursed to kill everyone I love.

"Or it was. Until Lilit was dying and Killien demanded the same thing from me. I was that girl again."

She pulled gently on her hand and he let her pull it away from his chest, but didn't let go of it.

"Killien was desperate," Will said. "But still, he should have known better."

Sora didn't answer him.

"There's an easy solution to Killien, though." He felt Sora waiting. "You should curse him."

She smacked him on the shoulder with her other hand, but he heard her laugh. "If I curse anyone, it's going to be you."

Will drew in a breath of the cool tunnel air. "The stories the holy woman told about you aren't you. She doesn't have the right to choose your story. She's stolen some power over you, but if you take it back, there's nothing she can do to stop you. She's twisted and controlled the entire clan. What they need is the truth. If you tell them, if you claim your own story and stop letting her control it, you'll be free of her. And it will loosen her control over your entire clan."

When Sora didn't answer, he let the subject drop. "I see what draws you here." Will's voice echoed off the wall beside him. "But you forgot to mention the best part."

She waited in expectant silence.

"This would be a great place for storytelling. Can you hear the little echo? So dramatic. I heard a tale once in Napon about a young woman who was chased by trolls into the hill caves—"

"Will," Sora interrupted with a laugh, "let's just enjoy the silence."

"Right."

The story pushed at him, begging to be told, but he squeezed his mouth shut.

Next to him Sora shifted. "It's killing you not telling me, isn't it?"

A voice interrupted his reply, calling down the echoey tunnel to announce the soup was cooked.

"Of all the reasons to have to go back to the rest of the world," Sora said, "hot soup is one of the best." She turned and walked back the direction they'd come, and he fell in beside her, running his free hand along the wall beside him as they turned into brighter and brighter sections of tunnel.

After several turns Sora paused. He could see her clearly now, looking attentively ahead of them. He opened his mouth to start the troll story again, when she tightened her grip on his hand and motioned him to be quiet.

Voices floated down the tunnel.

Evangeline's voice bounced off the walls, jumbling with itself, "Thank you for coming with Alaric. He's relieved that you came."

"Can't expect the Keeper to get out of any troublesome situations on his own," Douglon answered. "And I didn't have anywhere else to be."

There was a long pause. And Will took a step forward, but Sora stopped him.

"Why are we stopping?" he whispered.

"Don't interrupt this." Sora's voice was firm.

"Interrupt what?"

"Do you hate me?" Evangeline's words came out in a rush and Will felt a jab of awkwardness.

He leaned close to Sora. "We should not be listening to this."

"I know." She started backing down the tunnel and Will followed, but he could still hear Evangeline clearly.

"Do you hate me because I'm alive, and I'm the reason she…" She paused. "The reason Ayda isn't?"

Will's gut tightened at the question. He set his foot down as quietly as possible, backing away and barely breathed during the silence that followed.

"At first it was hard," Douglon answered. "But Ayda was exhausted. And with her people gone, she was utterly alone. In a way no one could fix." The dwarf's voice stopped and Will held his breath. "In a way I could never have fixed."

"I'm so sorry." Evangeline's words were almost lost in the tunnel.

"I'm luckier than most," Douglon answered. "When someone you love dies, you usually have nothing but memories. I have something…more." The stillness of the tunnel waited for him to continue. "Sometimes…when I listen to the trees…I can almost hear what she would say to them." His voice was soft, but the longing in it caught at Will's chest. "Almost."

"Does it make it better? Or worse?"

Douglon let out a long, jagged breath. "Both."

"I'm grateful for everything, of course, but…" She paused for a moment. When she spoke again it was determined, as though she was forcing out a confession. "Having all the knowledge from Ayda makes me somehow more equal to Alaric. He's always known so much, and I was just an innkeeper."

Douglon's answer was kind. "I don't think Alaric has ever thought of you as 'just' anything. He was ready to tear apart the world to save you. We even had to talk him out of sacrificing himself."

She murmured something to him, and there was a long, awkward pause. Will and Sora took another step backwards.

"If my cousin's finally finished cooking," Douglon said louder, "we should get there before Hal eats our portions." There was a shuffling noise. "Do you like the cavern?"

"It's amazing," Evangeline answered.

Their voices faded away.

Will let out a long breath. "I feel like I just invaded a private conversation."

"We did." Sora dropped his hand and walked forward again. "But it was that or interrupt, and she's been working up the courage to ask that for a very long time."

"How do you know?"

"We walked together earlier. What do you think we were talking about?"

Will stared at her. "You've walked for hours next to me without saying a single word."

"Maybe," she said with a smile, stepping out into the cavern, "I was waiting for you to tell me a story."

Will stopped. "Really?"

"No." She laughed. "I walked quietly with you because you let me. There's not a lot of people who will."

The cavern scattered splinters of reflected firelight across the floor.

"I thought if I talked to you," he said, "you'd leave."

"I probably would have."

"Well, that would have been a shame," he said. "Seeing as you were about the only person I was sure didn't want to kill me."

"Oh," she said, "there were plenty of times I wanted to kill you."

The soup was more delicious than a watery concoction of old vegetables had any right to be. Will told the story of the dwarf princess who was as ugly as a rock with a good deal of clarification from Douglon and Patlon. The sparkling cavern echoed with laughter and even though they'd have to wake soon, the fire burned to ashes before anyone settled for the night.

CHAPTER THIRTY-EIGHT

It felt like Will had barely fallen asleep before the dwarves roused everyone and they headed back into the tunnels. Will paused, taking in the cave again before stepping out of the cavern. After the glittering brilliance, the tunnel was dismal. Only the dwarves and Sora seemed to find any enjoyment in them.

An hour later, a small room opened off the side of the tunnel. Shelves lined the walls again, holding supplies, and a small table almost filled the middle of the room. Will and Sora put their packs on the table. Sora slung her bow and a thin quiver of arrows across her back.

Douglon looked at Will critically, then offered him a knife. "I'm sure you don't actually know how to fight with that, Keeper. But maybe you'll need to cut a rope or something."

Will took it and put it on his belt.

Patlon went to a wide, flat rock at the far end of the room and after a small click, it shifted and a breeze swirled in. There was a breath of freshness to the air and Rass lifted her face. "I can smell the grass."

Talen shifted his weight on Will's shoulder and Will ran a finger down the hawk's chest. "Almost out."

"The rift is a short walk southeast." Patlon set his shoulder against the rock and shoved. Slowly it swung open, revealing a slightly grayer blackness than the tunnels. The wind squeezed through the opening, humming and blustering its way in. "We'll be watching for you."

Rass hurried through the gap with Sora, and Hal followed.

Will looked through the opening with a sinking feeling in his gut. The tunnels were dark and close and lifeless. But through that door lay the exposed Sweep. He'd be shoved about by the wind, surrounded by endless nothing and endless Roven.

He turned to Alaric. "If we're not back in a few hours…"

"We'll find a way to get you out," Alaric assured him.

Will nodded and ducked out into the open night.

Huge boulders crowded around him beneath the sky. Wind swirled past him, pushing at his clothes, saturated with the scent of trees and grass. The ground rolled away in front of him, down to the vast Sweep.

A heavy moon sat low over the western horizon, washing out all but the brightest stars and spreading a stark grayness across the grass. A little east of them it turned black where the charred grass began. The wind blew in chilly, fitful gusts, twisting and pushing at the grass, whipping the Sweep into constant motion.

Talen fluttered and shifted his weight. Will pulled the hood off the hawk's head and Talen shot off his shoulder in a burst of wings.

Will cast out, but the only people he could find were Sora, Hal, and Rass. The tiny elf hurried down the hill toward the edge of the grass, her feet fairly flying across the ground. Sora stood at the end of the boulders and Will stopped next to her.

Hal stood a little away from the rocks, spinning slowly, facing up the slope, taking in the peaks behind, their snowy tops a cold white in the moonlight.

"It's that way." He pointed a little to the east. "The back entrance is not far."

Sora watched him as he headed down the slope. "Do you trust him?" Her voice came quietly through the wind.

Will pulled at the end of his beard, pushing down the fear that had been growing for the last several hours. "I think so. At least he believes he's going to help us."

The feeling of exposure the Sweep always caused wrapped around him.

"And if he changes his mind?" she asked.

"Then you'll have to use your amazing ranger skills and I'll have to use my amazing magical skills to execute a heroic escape."

The moonlight traced strands of her braid in silver and caught just the edge of a small smile. It was enough of a smile to draw out a little of his fear and let the wind snatch it away.

"Thank you for coming," he said. "Thank you actually doesn't come close to conveying how grateful I am."

"I don't trust Hal. And even though he's not much of a fighter, he could take you easily enough."

"I'd have been fine," he protested.

She shot him an incredulous look.

He wiggled his fingers at her. "Keeper."

She sized him up for a moment, then turned back toward the Sweep, the smile peeking back out. "If it was a Keeper we needed, maybe we should have brought Alaric."

Will grinned at her. He pulled his eyes away and tried to focus on the blustery motion of the Sweep ahead of them, searching for whatever Hal could be aiming for. "Maybe, but he seems a bit preoccupied with a woman."

"And you're not?"

Will snapped his attention back to her, an uncomfortably tight feeling in his chest. "I—" The moonlight etched her amusement in silver and shadows and he tried to meet her eyes, but he couldn't quite get his own to cooperate. "I'm not..." He trailed off weakly.

She laughed. "She's your sister, Will. It's alright. We'll get her out. But we should move faster."

Sora sped up, heading down after Hal. Will watched her for a moment, an awkward tangle of emotions smoldering in his chest. He blew out a long breath, hoping to push them away.

Rass waited for them at the edge of the grass. "There's no one nearby." She ran her hand across the top of the old brittle grass, then bent down and pulled a new blade of grass through her fingers. "The closest people are near the rift."

"We don't need to go that far." Hal hunched closer to the grass and set out southeast across the Sweep.

It took half an hour to reach a little pile of scrub brush and some rocks piled in the middle of the grass, only stopping once when Rass motioned them all down as a ranger passed by them to the east. They hadn't quite reached the fireline yet, but it wasn't far off. The jagged edge of the rift was easy to see here. It was wider than Will had expected, stretching away southeast from them. At the scrub brush, Hal reached under the edge of a large rock and lifted. It hinged open and thumped back with a distinctly unrocklike sound, revealing a black hole beneath.

Rass leaned forward and sniffed the air and drew back. "I'll wait here and make sure no one comes."

Hal nodded and climbed down into the hole and Sora followed.

"Be careful," Rass whispered to Will.

"You too."

"I'm in the grass. No one can hurt me." She shifted back and forth, her bare little toes digging into the soil.

"There's nothing unexpected going on nearby?"

She shook her head. "Three Roven spread out far on the other side of the rift, the one who passed us earlier is still heading south, and there's a herd of sheep with two shepherds grazing so far to the south you wouldn't be able to see them, even if the sun was up."

"You're amazing," he said, tousling the top of her head. He sat at the edge of the hole and felt along the wall until he found the rung of a ladder.

She smiled at him, then turned and tilted her head slightly. "That dragon isn't home."

Will stopped.

"He's usually down by a city that sits on a bay, with a big cliff below it."

"That's Tun," Will said. "That's the city of the Sunn Clan. They are the ones with the dragon."

"The grass goes all the way to the edges of the cliff and he lies there, looking at the ocean," Rass said. "But tonight he's much closer. Not near any cities or any people. He's just lying in the grass."

The wind shoved through scrub brush around him, shaking it against the sky. The heavy moon was almost low enough to touch the horizon, and the stars bright enough to brave the moonlight glittered clearly. Will scanned them, his mind kept offering the silhouette of wings in any dark spot. "How close?"

"It would take you more than a day to walk to him. But why didn't he go home?"

"I'm not sure, but keep track of him. We'll be back soon. I hope."

"I'd like to meet your sister," Rass whispered to him. "I hope she's happy to come."

"Me too." He grabbed a handle on the lid. It swung easily, and Will pulled the not-rock down into place. A dim orange glow illuminated the base of the ladder.

At the bottom, a rough dirt tunnel ran off to the east. Hal hunched his head down to avoid the rough ceiling and the thin roots that hung down from it. The air was damp and earthy but not as stale as Will had expected. He blew out a long breath, trying to slow his heart. Somehow being here, below the empty Sweep, was worse than being under a solid mountain. The tunnel left him feeling trapped and vulnerable at the same time.

Sora held a bowl of glimmer moss ahead of her as she peered down the tunnel.

Hal dipped his finger into another one that sat on a rough shelf. "It's wet. Someone's been in this tunnel recently."

Will cast out, but besides Sora, Hal, and the ceiling of grass above them, there was nothing living larger than a worm. "There's no one in the tunnel, and Rass says no one's nearby."

Hal frowned at the bowl before turning and heading down the tunnel. Their feet made no sound in the soft earth, and the silence and the unwavering orange light made everything feel dreamlike. And not the good kind of dream. Will had the irrational fear that this tunnel would never end, or worse—lead him to that horrible barren rift.

The tunnel ran relatively straight. When Hal held up his hand to stop, Will's fear that the tunnel wouldn't end was instantly replaced by the fear that it had, and that he was about to sneak into Killien's house. Hal motioned Will to come up with him. Will put his hand on Sora's arm as he passed her and could feel her tension. He squeezed up beside Hal and found himself looking at the back of a piece of fabric.

"Anyone there?" Hal whispered, almost noiselessly.

Will cast out past the fabric, but found no one. He shook his head and Hal pulled back the fabric and stepped through. With his heart pounding loud enough to shake the Sweep, Will followed. Sora came through with the glimmer moss and lit the small room with orange light. The wall to their left held shelves packed with books, candles and paper. Hal let the fabric fall back and Will could make out that it was a wall hanging with the image of the Serpent Queen stretching darkly across it. Most of the fabric was darkish in the dim light, but the form of the queen, which slithered over mountain peaks and coiled around the moon, was utterly black. He reached out to touch her and his fingers ran across soft, thick fabric that caught slightly at his fingertips. Pulling his hand away, he wiped it on his pants to erase the feeling.

There were other wallhangings too, overlapping on the walls. On one shelf, a pile of gems glittered dully in the dim light. Off to the side, two greenish stones glowed with a watery light, like blades of grass under a stream. In the far corner, a set of leather armor hung, silver buckles glinting in the light. Sora walked closer, holding the glimmer moss up to it, revealing intricately tooled leather with runes covering most of the surface.

"Killien's ceremonial armor," Hal whispered. "I've only seen him wear it once, the day the clan named him Torch." Hal turned toward the door and stopped so abruptly that Will almost walked into his back. He stared above the door at two empty wooden pegs.

"Killien's sword." Hal turned back to the armor, then spun slowly around the room. "Svard Naj, when we're in the rifts, it's always here. Killien never moves it. He's almost superstitious about it."

"Maybe he took it to show his new son," Sora said, irritated. "We should move."

Will looked up at the empty hooks. The seax Flibbet the Peddler had given Killien. The one the Torch had said was "too serious for a mere fight." The empty hooks looked black and slightly ominous in the mosslight.

With one last frown at the hooks, Hal pulled open the door. It squeaked and Will's heart slammed up into his throat. They all froze for a moment, but when no sounds came from the house, Hal stepped in to the hall. He led them to the right, and stopped near the end of the hall. Three doors sat closed ahead of them. Will cast out. There were two people, one behind each of the doors on the right. He told Sora and she nodded.

"Any idea which is Ilsa?"

Will shook his head.

"Stay here," she whispered. She handed the glimmer moss to Hal and walked to the first door. Easing it open, she slipped inside. She was back quickly, and with a shake of her head, moved to the other room. In moments she was out of that one as well, shaking her head again. Will sank back against the wall. He cast out again, but there was no one else on this floor. Upstairs he could just sense someone, but there was no one nearby.

Hal motioned them back to the room with the armor and they crept quietly back down the hall.

"If she's not here," he said once they'd closed the door. "She could be anywhere."

Will sank against one of the shelves. The fact that she wasn't here loomed in front of him like a blank wall.

Sora paced back and forth down the room. "You have to have some idea, Hal," she whispered.

He shook his head. "At the other end of this hall a door leads to the kitchen. Upstairs is a gathering room and Killien's sleeping quarters."

Sora froze, spun slowly around and fixed Hal with a dangerous look. "You better not be suggesting Ilsa is in Killien's quarters."

"No," Hal said quickly. "He wouldn't."

A flicker of anger pushed past the fear and Will stared at Hal. The big man turned to him and held his hands out toward Will, his face earnest. "Killien and Lilit are inseparable. And since she almost died, he barely leaves her side. He wouldn't."

Will pressed his hands against his eyes, blocking out the dim light of the moss. Sora's footsteps paced quietly, Hal let out a long, slow breath, and the fear that had been growing in Will turned icy. Where had Killien put his sister?

"I'm going upstairs." He pushed himself away from the shelves. "Killien is going to tell me where she is."

"No you're not." Sora stepped between Will and the door.

"I'm not leaving here without knowing where she is." Will stepped forward, but Sora didn't move.

"If anyone goes upstairs, it's going to be me," she said calmly.

Will stared at her incredulous. "Absolutely not. Killien will kill you."

One of Sora's eyebrows rose the smallest bit. "I wasn't asking your permission."

"And I wasn't asking yours. If my sister is here, I'm going to find her."

Sora took in an irritated breath, then froze. Her eyes flew wide and she spun toward the door, sliding the knife from her belt.

Will cast out and felt the blazing *vitalle* of someone directly on the other side of the door. He swore under his breath. Killien.

Except this person was too small. He clutched at a strand of hope. Ilsa?

The door began to swing open and the three of them backed up. Will cast out again looking for *vitalle* to draw in, but found nothing but people. He reached for the knife Douglon had given him, gripping the hilt to keep his hand from trembling.

"You'll be looking around the rift for a long time if you're expecting to find Ilsa," a woman's voice came through the opening.

The door creaked the rest of the way open and the dim orange light of the glimmer moss barely reached the face of Lilit.

CHAPTER THIRTY-NINE

"Hello, Hal," Lilit said lightly, looking down at the bundle in her arms. "Sevien was restless, so I thought a little walk would help him. But maybe he's a blessed child. Maybe he could sense rats in the storage room." When she looked up to consider them, her face was stony. "Sora," she acknowledged coldly, "and Will the Keeper."

The bundle she carried gave an irritated, tiny grunt and Will pulled his hand off his knife. "Where's my sister?"

Lilit stepped into the room, stopping underneath the empty sword pegs. Hal took a step back away from her, his hands held out to the side, unthreatening. Sora stood her ground, letting her knife fall to her side, but not putting it away.

"I had expected you two to return as Hal's prisoners." Lilit's eyes were cold and flat. "Not as his companions, sneaking into my house like thieves."

"We were his prisoners briefly," Sora said when Hal didn't answer. "And then he was ours."

"He wasn't our prisoner," Will said. "He was merely restrained momentarily so we could make our escape."

"And then your husband sent the dragon," Hal said, "and I

would have been a charred lump on the mountainside if they hadn't saved me."

"That's very touching," Lilit said. "Which part of that compelled you to show my husband's enemies the hidden entrance that leads into our very home?"

Hal dropped his hands to his side. "Did you know it was Killien who brought the frost goblins to the clan?"

Lilit stood perfectly still, her eyes fixed on Hal suspiciously.

"It's true," Sora said.

Lilit was quiet for a long moment before she breathed out something between a laugh and a curse. "He called an army of goblins."

"Where's my sister?" Will asked again.

Lilit shifted to face him, bouncing the baby in her arms and considering him, distaste mingling with frustration on her face. "I know you were there, with Sora in the tent. The night Sevien was born. I remember your words." Her eyes closed. *"But the Flame of the Morrow was not like the grass...She reached down into the Sweep... and found the strength to fight on."* She opened her eyes. "But it wasn't the Sweep that gave me strength that night, was it?"

He considered denying it a moment, then shook his head.

"I felt it come through your hands," she said.

"Does Killien know?" Sora asked.

Lilit shook her head. "I wasn't sure it was real." She looked down at Sevien and blew out a decisive breath. "Killien has left, taking several slaves with him, including Ilsa."

"Where?" Will asked.

Hal looked up at the empty sword pegs on the wall. "He went to the enclave." He turned back to Lilit, his face incredulous. "He took the seax, and went without being invited. They're going to kill him."

Lilit's shifted the baby and her head twitched in a nod.

"What's he going to do? How many men did he take?"

"No one, aside from the slaves. He wouldn't tell me his plans, but I think he's going to kill Torch Ohan. It was the Panos who attacked us and betrayed their word."

"He went alone?" Hal shook his head. "He's gone mad."

The baby fussed and she dropped her face down to kiss his head, bouncing him gently. When she looked up, it was at Sora. "Go after him."

Sora stepped back. "There's nothing we can do."

"They'll kill him." Lilit turned to Hal. "You have to bring him back."

"He's not going to listen to us," Hal said.

"If he kills Ohan at the enclave, they'll execute him. If he dies we have no strong choice for a Torch. The clan will be overrun. And I—" Her voice caught and her hand tightened on Sevien's blanket. "He can't die."

"He's impossible to stop once he sets his mind to something," Hal said.

"Then tie him up and drag him home." Lilit's words cut through the room. She spun toward Will, the coldness of her face cracking with desperation. "You saved my life when you had no reason to. And you have no reason to save Killien now, but stop my husband from getting himself killed and I promise you, you will have your sister and your freedom."

"Why did he take Ilsa?"

She bounced the baby for a breath before answering. "Because she's the only leverage he has against you. And he wants to make sure you don't steal her away."

Lilit clung to the baby. She was angry, but she was genuinely scared.

"How far is it to the enclave?" Will asked.

Sora blew out a frustrated breath.

"We can't get in," Hal objected. "They meet in a cave. The other clans bring legions of stonesteeps and their best warriors, all of it spread across the front of it, guarding the entrance. No foreigner could ever walk into the enclave. And even if the

Morrow were invited, they wouldn't let me into the mountain unless I was with Killien."

"He left hours ago," Lilit said, ignoring Hal and walking over to a wallhanging mapping the northern half of the Sweep. She pointed at a single mountain that jutted out into the grass. "The enclave is here. It won't begin until tomorrow night. Killien will have to ride far south of the Panos and Odo rifts to avoid being seen. He'll be lucky if he reaches the mountain before the enclave begins."

"Can we get to him before that?" Will asked Sora.

She scowled at the map. "Maybe."

"You must," Lilit said.

Will nodded and Sora shot him a glare before giving Lilit a curt nod and pulling the fabric away from the tunnel opening.

"There is no way this will work," Hal grumbled, following her.

Will pressed his fist to his chest and gave Lilit a short bow. She gave him only a nod in return.

The wind shoved into the far end of the tunnel as Will climbed the ladder. Rass greeted him, peering eagerly down the hole behind Will.

"She's not there."

Her face fell as he explained.

"Can you feel them anywhere nearby?"

Rass shook her head. "This close to dawn there are more people out. Small groups of rangers and hunters are spreading out everywhere."

The wind shoved past with long gusts and fleeting moments of calm. The moon was so low it grazed the horizon, sending a thousand golden fingers dragging through the fur of the giant creature that was the Sweep.

Sora turned to him. "Was she lying to us?"

Will shook his head.

"Did you read her? Or whatever you call it?"

"I didn't need to. It's hard to fake that sort of desperation."

Sora looked unconvinced.

Hal sat on a low rock, his eyes fixed on the mountain peaks stretching to the west. "If Killien's going to the enclave, he's not going with a handful of slaves."

Sora nodded. "He's planning to call the frost goblins."

Will turned to Rass. "Can you tell if there are goblin warrens under the grass?"

"If they're not too deep." She knelt down and ran her hand along the new grass that reached a handbreadth out of the ground. "There are some, but they are small and feel…unused. There are none like the night the goblins attacked the clan."

"Makes sense," Will said. "He won't call them until he reaches the enclave."

"Which means"—Hal pushed himself to his feet—"we need to get to him before he gets there if we have any chance at stopping him. Does anyone have any idea how we're going to do that?"

"Did Patlon tell you how far west the dwarven tunnels go?" Will asked Sora.

"Not exactly, but I think a good deal farther than we are now." Sora's gaze trailed along the Hoarfrost mountains. "I had no idea the dwarves had tunneled so far from Duncave."

"Neither did I," Will said. Did they have an equal amount of tunnels stretching along the northern end of Queensland? Burrowing through the Wolfsbane range? Did their tunnels stretch down the Scales to the sea?

"We're running out of darkness," Sora pointed out.

The jagged top of the Scales cut a crisp purple line across the indigo sky, and Hal led the way back toward the dwarf tunnels. Will cast out across the Sweep, as though he'd find Ilsa and Killien walking over the next rise instead of hours away already. He found Hal and Sora, two pillars of energy moving steadily ahead of him, and the bright burst of life that was Rass, gamboling through the endless carpet of *vitalle* made by the spring grass. There were bright bits of energy from small animals scurrying across the plains and some bird soaring off to the south, but no other people.

The sky over the Scales glowed a serene blue by the time they reached the boulders at the dwarves' tunnel. Will peered at the dark lumps of rock, none of which looked like the entrance. Patlon called to them from off to the right and they wound their way to the tunnel entry. The pale sky above them was empty of any little hawk-shaped specks. Will cast out, and even though he found nothing, he lingered an extra moment before squeezing his way back into the small room.

He sank into a chair at the table while Patlon closed the entrance. The wind whistled through with a final, loud protest before it swung shut and the mountain closed around him like a shield against the vulnerability of the Sweep.

Will dropped his head into his hands. Everything was so much worse than it had been a few hours ago. The room around him was silent until Hal explained what had happened to Alaric, Evangeline, and the dwarves.

"I know the mountain you're talking about," Douglon said. "The tunnels will take us almost that far."

"Cousin." Patlon's tone was hard. "Escaping a dragon was one thing—although I'm not sure even that's enough for Horgoth to forgive us for bringing outsiders into the tunnels. We can't take a band of humans and an elf on a tour to the western end."

"You don't have to come," Douglon answered.

"Horgoth," Patlon answered, speaking slowly and clearly, "is going to kill you."

"He's wanted to kill me for years." There was a rustling of paper and Will saw the edges of a map spread out on the table and Douglon let out a short laugh. "This is one of the first times he'd actually have a reason to. Makes the relationship feel more…complete."

Patlon let out an irritated breath and dropped onto the bench.

"You with me, cousin?" Douglon asked.

"I'm always with you," Patlon grumbled.

"Excellent. The route we'll take will lead us here..."

The sound of Sora, Hal, and the dwarves discussing their route filled the room with echoing murmurs and Will stared at the table through his fingers. Killien was going to attack the enclave with an army of frost goblins. The truth of it tasted sour. He wanted to shake the man. To drag him back south on the Sweep, back to when he was rational. To break through the obsession that drove him to make the Morrow powerful. No, not obsession. Fear. The fear that if he didn't strengthen the Morrow, the Roven would destroy what he loved. And now he was going to kill hundreds of people, bringing even more violence to the Sweep.

Were all wars started from fear? He turned the idea over in his mind. Perhaps. Fear that sank so deep that it grew up in the forms of anger and greed. Anger that the fear existed, and greed for anything that would stop it.

Was he here on the Sweep because of fear? Will spun his ring slowly, pushing away the immediate refusal of the idea and forcing himself to consider it. He'd first come because he'd been afraid Queensland was in danger. But after that, what had driven him the entire time, if he really looked at it, was fear. The fear that had been planted the night Ilsa was taken, the night Vahe had stepped into his life and murdered and stole. The night when the sense of safety he'd always lived in had shattered.

Alaric leaned over the map and asked the dwarves a question. It was such a familiar sight, Alaric in his Keeper's robe, poring over some book or map. Whatever he'd asked, Douglon and Patlon both paused and considered the map before nodding. Will rubbed his hands across his face, scrubbing at the exhaustion. That was familiar too, Alaric asking the right question at the right time.

It didn't take much soul-searching to see that the last year had been fueled by another fear, more recent than Vahe. Will ran his fingers along the cuff of the greyish robe he wore. The fabric was thin and the stitches along the edge were irregular. It was simple, basic fabric with no pressure and no expectations. A small hole had formed next to the seam, and he worried at it with his finger.

The bench shifted next to him as Sora sat down. She glanced down at his hands. He tried to smile at her, but somehow the effort fell flat. He pushed his finger at the hole, widening it a bit.

"I can lend you a needle and thread," she offered, the hint of a different sort of question in her voice.

Will dropped the cuff from his fingers and ran his hands over his face again. "This isn't really worth mending, is it?"

She considered him for a long moment, her eyes dark green in the light of the glimmer moss. He spun his ring, pushing aside the edges of the bandages to get at it.

"Do you think you'll ever go home?" he asked her. "Could you ever go back and just be you? Somehow not tangled up in the expectations they have for you?"

"I don't know." She pulled his hand over toward her and began to pick at the knot on his bandage. "You shouldn't need these anymore." She picked at the knot in silence for a minute and Will watched her hands. Her nails were rimmed with dirt. Scratches and thin scars nicked her skin.

"Even with the Morrow," she said quietly, "there were expectations. They saw me partly as a ranger, but mostly as a foreigner." She worked the knot apart and started to unwrap the bandage. "But they had those expectations because it's what I gave them. If I wanted the Morrow to see me as more, I would have had to have shown them more."

She pulled the last layer of bandage off and picked up his hand, tilting his palm toward the glimmer moss. The skin was red and shiny. Sora ran her finger over the edge of where the blister had been and he flinched at the sharpness of the sensation. She raised an eyebrow.

"It's sensitive." He opened and closed his hand. There was a jolt when his fingers touched his palm, but not exactly pain.

Sora gave an approving nod and motioned for his other hand. "You're the first Keeper I've ever met, Will. I don't have any idea what a Keeper is supposed to be like. But I've seen you do some astonishing things."

"You wouldn't be impressed by pushing heat toward frost goblins, or starting candles with my finger if you'd spent time with other Keepers."

"I'm not talking about that," she said, nodding her head toward where Rass sat nestled in a corner, braiding together a wide, complicated band of grass. "It's more like what you did with Rass."

Will let out something between a laugh and a snort. "I'm never going to admit to Alaric that I knew her for weeks and thought she was just an odd little girl." He watched her fiddle with the grass, picking a new piece off the floor next to her where she had a small bundle, and weave it into the rest. "Until she exploded the ground in front of me, I had no idea she was anything else."

Sora shook her head. "You saw her as a little girl, when everyone else saw her as…nothing. No one else even noticed her."

"She came and talked to me," Will objected. "The first afternoon I was in Porreen."

"And what did you do then?"

"I talked back, Sora," he said, trying to to hide his exasperation. He shifted, wishing she'd hurry up so he could have his hand back.

Instead, she stopped and looked him in the face. "And you fed her an avak."

Will drew his hand back in surprise until her grip stopped him. "How do you know that?"

"I told you I was watching you. Your stealthy creeping around had caught my attention."

"I obviously wasn't stealthy enough."

"I hadn't noticed Rass before that." She pulled his hand closer and picked at the stubborn knot. "And I notice a lot. You set the avak on the bench and drew her out. Then you talked to her, just like she was anyone else."

"She was better than everyone else. She was the only safe

person in the entire festival."

"And then somehow you convinced a *pratorii* to trust you. To walk with you, to eat food she'd never eaten." The knot came loose and Sora began unwinding the bandage. "To leave the Sweep with you."

"I didn't do anything…special to make that happen."

"I'm not saying you did. I'm saying it happened because of who you are. And it wasn't just Rass who trusted you. Hal did too." She pulled the last of the bandage off and lifted his palm to examine it. When she rubbed her finger across his palm, he almost kept it still.

Hal was over by the shelves helping Patlon sort through some supplies.

"He's never going to believe I didn't do something to trick him."

"Maybe not, but I believe you. And I believe you did nothing to trick Killien into trusting you either. Nothing more than seeing him. Seeing past the expectations that everyone else puts on him, past the expectations that he's built up around himself. And befriending what you saw."

"You don't know that." He spun his ring. It was so satisfying after not being able to reach it for so long.

"Yes I do." She let go of his hand.

He rubbed his palms together, trying to press out the weird sensitivity. She kept her eyes focused on his hands.

"Because you did it to me too."

Will's hands froze and something hitched in his throat. She started gathering up the bandages.

"So, from the little I know about Keepers," she said, "if I were in charge of choosing them, you're the sort of person I'd want to pick." She wrapped the bandages into a bundle.

He reached out and put his hand on hers to still them. Her skin and the jumbled edges of the bandage shot a painfully strong sensation across his hand.

"Come with me to Queensland."

CHAPTER FORTY

THE WORDS SHOVED their way out before Will could stop them.

Sora's eyes widened. He squeezed her hand, ignoring the sharp twinge in his palm. "Once we've found Ilsa, will you come back with me? Not forever, if you don't want to, but for a little while. I can't stay here. I'll have to take Ilsa home."

She stared at him, speechless.

"You don't have to tell me now, of course." He let go of her hands, pushing down the regret that threatened to drown him. "But if you're willing, I'd like to show it to you."

Alaric cleared his throat from behind them and Will turned to see him watching Will with a wide smile. "We should get going. The way the mountains run, if we move quickly and make tonight a short night sleep, we think we can beat Killien to the enclave." Alaric raised an eyebrow toward him and Sora. "If you two are ready."

Sora pushed herself up and walked over to her pack. Will watched her before shoving himself up from the table. Alaric stepped up and slung his arm over Will's shoulder. Evangeline asked Sora a question, and the two stood with their heads close together, looking in Sora's pack.

"I see a new future for the Keepers," Alaric said with a grin.

Will spun his ring. "That future is terrifying."

Alaric laughed. "It gets better." Then he paused. "But also it stays terrifying."

They walked for hours through the dwarven tunnels, the blackness barely ruffled by the bowls of glimmer moss they carried. Douglon led with Rass. Evangeline and Sora went behind them, talking in low voices while Will and Alaric followed behind them. Hal brought up the rear, peppering Patlon with questions about the dwarves.

"Do you think there's any chance we're going to find Ilsa?" Will asked Alaric when the featureless walk through the darkness began to feel as though it was all they'd ever done.

"I don't think finding her is going to be the problem." Alaric pulled a cord out from under his shirt with a glitter of yellow light. "The problem is going to be getting to her. The mountain where the enclave is held isn't terribly big, and the Roven are camped only on the southern side of it. Hal has been there a number of times. There's a network of tunnels near the front of the mountain. The ones that head toward the back are barred and locked to keep people from doing what we're doing, sneaking in. Patlon believes the humans tunneled all the way out the back side of the mountain, and that the locks shouldn't be a problem. The dwarves and Hal seem fairly hopeful that we can find a back entrance and get in without having to walk through an army of Roven."

"That would be nice."

Lunchtime passed, noted only by Douglon passing along a sack of hard rolls that tasted of honey and pine nuts. Sora contributed some sticks of dried meat, and they kept walking.

The day was a strange mix of tedious walking through darkness, gnawing worry about what lay ahead, and pure enjoyment of talking with Alaric. The dwarves kept up the humming song as a backdrop. Will had to stop himself from talking too fast, asking too many questions. His mind felt awake in a way it hadn't been in ages. There was something inside him that was free, reveling in the fact that there was nothing to watch out for, nothing to keep hidden. By the time Douglon called back that they were close to where they'd stop for the night, he felt more normal than he had in ages. Which considering he'd spent the day in darkness, was saying a lot.

This cave was nothing like the ones with the scattered lights. This was merely a room hollowed out of the side of the tunnel with a flat floor and more darkness. Will finished his cold meal and closed his eyes. The cave spun beneath him. It had been two days since he'd had a real night's sleep. The others murmured around him, all their voices enveloped by the silence of the cave. He leaned back against his pack. Even the stone floor wasn't enough to make him uncomfortable.

There was mention of several more hours of tunnels tomorrow, speculation on how they'd cross the open Sweep between their exit and the enclave mountain, and a debate between the dwarves about the likelihood of human tunnels actually reaching the back of the mountain. But Will couldn't get his mind to focus on any of it. Soon there was only the feeling of his body sinking down against the hard floor and the mountain wrapping around him like a cocoon.

The next morning Will discovered Rass curled up next to him.

"I'm tired of tunnels," she groaned when he roused her.

"I'm a little tired of them myself," Will said, "but I don't think it's too much farther."

"How long until we're back near living things?" Will asked Douglon.

Douglon considered Rass with a small frown. "It's not far to the grasses now." He reached down and lifted her up. "Just a couple hours."

"I can walk," she objected. "You can't carry me for hours."

"You're just a wee snip of a thing. The only fear is that I'll drop you and not even notice."

She made a petulant little noise, but wrapped her arms around his neck and dropped her head onto his shoulder. Douglon walked back into the tunnel and began to hum. Patlon grabbed some glimmer moss and everyone followed.

The hours dragged on. To pass the time, Will told one story after another, first just to Hal and Alaric, but soon Sora and Evangeline had moved close enough to hear too. He'd told four reasonably long ones and was convinced the walk was never going to end when they spilled out into a small storage room. Patlon ordered everyone to wait, then moved to the far wall and shoved at a large rock. He disappeared through a gap while sweet, fresh, clean air rushed in and swirled through the room. Rass lifted her head from Douglon's shoulder and looked around sleepily.

In a few moments Patlon was back. "There's no one nearby. But come out slowly, it's bright."

Will filed out with the rest of them. The wind brushed across his face and the clean scents of pine and earth revived him with an almost magical power. He stepped out into a shadowed, rocky gorge with trees stretching up around them, but still, the light was painfully bright. Rass sat in a wide patch of bright green grass, squinting and beaming and running her fingers back and forth through the blades.

The grassy slope they were on angled down, interspersed with bushes and pines until it flattened out onto a wide swath of grass that lay between them and the lone mountain that held the enclave.

Mountain was too big of a word for it, really. Large hill. Oversized outcropping. Whatever it was, it sat detached from the rest of the range, surrounded by a moat of grass.

Off to the south on the far side of the enclave, smoke from dozens of campfires rose into the air. Small bands of rangers roamed across the grass between them and the mountain, and as far out into the Sweep as Will could see. The sun hadn't reached midday, and if Lilit had been right, Killien shouldn't reach the mountain for hours.

Of course, they weren't going to reach it any sooner.

The sky above them was a clear, empty blue, and Will scanned through the trees around them for Talen. Not that there was any way the little hawk could know where he was. A twinge of sadness rippled through him. He cast out into the sky, but found nothing beyond the slow, ponderous energy of the pine trees. He thought of the little bird's mind and threw an image toward it of where he stood.

The idea faded away, doing nothing. With another look across the empty sky, Will pulled his focus back to the others around him.

"You really think you can find entrances on this side of the mountain?" Alaric asked Douglon.

The dwarf nodded. "Hal says there are tunnels that come this way."

"I see three places with possible entrances," Patlon said, pointing out rocky sections of the mountainside. "What does the front of the mountain look like?"

"There's a huge cave," Hal answered. "Fifteen mounted men could easily ride abreast each other through the opening. Inside the cave is a lake that's fed from somewhere under the mountain, and it pours out of the mouth in a waterfall down to another lake down on the Sweep."

"How high is the cave?"

"A third of the way up the mountain," Hal answered.

"That makes the top entrance unlikely," Douglon said. "Unless someone just really liked digging uphill."

"I think the bottom one is too low," Sora said. "If there's water in the caves where the enclaves meet, anyone stupid enough to tunnel down would have been flooded."

"Agreed." Patlon tugged on his beard and nodded.

Sora turned to Alaric. "We're headed for that reddish cliff face about halfway up."

"You don't seem worried that there are doors blocking all the passages that lead to the back of the mountain," Hal said. "And they're locked. The Temur Clan controls the mountain. They're the only ones with keys. If there even are keys any more."

"Locked doors aren't a problem," Patlon said. "Wide open grassland is a problem."

"We'll be seen by a half-dozen scouts if we try to cross here," Sora agreed. "Most of the clans are here. And each will have their own rangers on the lookout for anything unusual."

"Good thing there's nothing unusual about this group," Patlon muttered.

A pair of Roven rangers rode slowly across the grass between them and the mountain.

Rass gave a small sigh. "We could go under the grass."

"There are no more tunnels," Douglon told her.

"No more dwarves tunnels. But"—she wrinkled her nose—"the frost goblins have tunnels all over down there."

No one answered for a moment.

"We can't go into a goblin warren," Hal said. "We'll be ripped apart."

"Only if goblins come," Sora said.

"The one thing we know," Hal answered, "is that Killien plans to call goblins to the enclave. And when that happens, I really don't want to be standing in the way."

"I can tell if they're coming," Rass said.

"From how far away?" Will asked.

She set her hand on the ground. "The closest ones are far to the west of here. There are none under the grass close by."

"How can you tell?" Hal asked.

"The roots of the grass reach down to the warrens. And when the goblins brush past them"—she shivered—"the grass knows."

"Can you tell if they're under the mountains we're on?" Douglon asked her.

Rass shook her head uncertainly. "I don't think they tunnel in the mountains. They can't get through rock, just the soft earth of the Sweep."

"I agree," Sora said. "In the mountains they travel above ground, I've seen their tracks."

"Can you lead us through the warrens?" Will asked Rass.

She wrinkled her nose and nodded, pushing herself up. "The closest one is this way."

The mouth of the warren sat at the bottom of the slope, gaping open just as the grassland flattened out. A few trees straggled out into the grass, and a small finger of bushes ran almost to where the warren started. When there were no Roven rangers in sight, the dwarves clambered down into the hole and disappeared. In a matter of breaths they were back.

"Filthy worm hole," Patlon said, brushing clods of dirt from his head.

"It's not pleasant," Douglon agreed, "but it looks stable. Rass is the only one of us that's going to be able to walk upright, though."

A hoarse screech echoed off the rocks behind them and Talen dove out of the sky. His wings faltered slightly and there were gaps in the feathers of his left wing. He landed hard on Will's arm with a weak chwirk. Feathers along his neck were disheveled and wet with blood.

Sora came over and ran her fingers gently down his neck, smoothing the feathers. Talen flinched once. Will opened up to the little hawk and felt a tangle of fear and exhaustion.

"A larger bird must have attacked him." Sora pulled out a piece of dried meat and offered it to Talen. The hawk snatched it up, his feet unsteady on Will's arm.

"You have bad timing," Will said to him. "We're about to go into another tunnel. But we'll be out soon, over on that mountain." He walked over to a nearby stump and set his arm next to it. "I'll leave you some food, and you can meet us over there."

Talen's claws tightened on Will's arm. Will rolled his forearm toward the stump, but the little hawk turned his head away from it and grabbed Will tighter. A spike of fear flashed across Will's chest.

"Ok, you can come with us, but that means the hood again."

Sora helped Will slide the leather glove on his other arm and the hawk willingly stepped onto it. Talen didn't move at all as Sora put the hood on him.

"Can we go?" Douglon asked. "Or are we going to collect any other animals that have no right to be underground?"

Will waved him on, offering Talen more meat.

"You're sure there are no goblins?" Patlon asked Rass.

She nodded and, although no one looked happy about it, the group dropped down into the hole, one at a time.

The hole was wide enough for two people to walk next to each other, but even the dwarves had to duck to avoid the ceiling of loose dirt and dangling roots. Will held Talen close to him and stretched his other hand out to run along the wall. His feet sank into the soft churned up earth on the floor and the wall crumbled off beneath his fingers while he hunched over and took a few steps into the gloom. The walls and ceiling were gashed from the scrambling mass of goblin claws that had burrowed through. The smell of the earth mingled with the fetor of rotting meat.

The tunnel ran straight ahead as far as he could see, past the stooped forms in front of him, and the dwindling light lasted long past the point when his back began to ache from bending over. Roots brushed past his head and down his back, pellets of dirt showered down on him, crumbling and rolling down his neck.

Their feet sank silently into the soft earth, so the only sound was the breathing of his companions. Something from the wall tangled wetly in his fingers and wriggled across his palm. He flicked his hand and the squirming larva gripped his finger for a breath before flinging off.

The warren dimmed to the point where the orange glow from the glimmer moss was visible, tinging the dark earth a bloody red.

Time stretched on interminably. Will's back and neck ached from hunching over and the rotten stench had settled into a sour taste in his mouth. The arm holding Talen had developed an ache that demanded he shift position. He stretched his shoulder and elbow, trying not to alarm the bird.

To pass the time he concentrated on the little hawk. It could have just been his imagination, but when he cast out toward Talen, the bird felt dimmer. Gently, Will funneled bits of *vitalle* into him. Letting it seep up from his arm through Talen's legs. Inside the hawk were three different injuries. The cut at his neck, and two slashes on his wing. Will drew in *vitalle* from the roots brushing over him as he walked and fed it into Talen, directing it toward where the little bird was healing. Slowly Talen's grip relaxed. Will offered Talen the last piece of meat, and the little hawk gobbled it up, standing straighter than before.

"We're halfway." Rass's voice trickled back, muted from the front of the group. She walked next to Patlon with her arm stretched above her head, trailing her fingers through the hair-thin roots that hung down.

Alaric fell back next to Will, holding glimmer moss up near Talen. "How did you get the hawk to come?"

"I'm not sure." Will ducked under a low-hanging clump of roots. "I sort of threw the idea of where I was out at him."

The edges of Alaric's eyes tightened in such a familiar way, Will laughed. "I know that doesn't tell you anything." Will explained the connection he'd built with Talen.

"More interesting than that, though," Will said, "is that Sora can...push her emotions at me, and I feel them when I'm not trying to."

Alaric's eyebrows rose. "Did you know that was possible?"

Will shook his head. "Gerone spent all his time developing ways to close myself off to people. We never got to the point of experimenting with anything else. And outside the Keepers, Sora's the first person I've told that I can feel them."

"The first?" Alaric said mildly. "Interesting."

"Can we stay on topic? The important part here is that she was able to do it. To show me how her childhood memories made her feel."

"Is that really the important part?" Will could hear the grin in Alaric's voice.

Will shook his head. "Evangeline has changed you."

Alaric laughed. "You have no idea." He was quiet for a moment. "Can you push your emotions into me?"

Will searched for a good emotion to share. What was the last strong emotion he'd felt? There was the conversation with Hal, but that was too complex. There was the dark tunnel with Sora, but that was even more complex.

The dragon.

Will focused on the memory of the dragon, plummeting down toward them, the flames licking the trees next to them as they ran. The rush of air from the wings, the glint of red scales. His heart quickened at the memory of being utterly defenseless in the face of such overwhelming power. He gathered that feeling and pushed it toward Alaric.

Alaric's breath caught. "I feel…scared? It's small, and distant. Like the echo of being terrified."

Will cut off the push of emotions with a surge of triumph. "The dragon."

Alaric let out a long breath. "Yes, that's what it felt like. Both times. He gets no less terrifying upon the second meeting. How have we never tried this before?"

"I don't know if I could have done it before. In Queensland I did nothing but try to close people off. It wasn't until I came here that I was nervous enough to need to read people around me. I've gotten so much better at it. I can pick out individual people in a group and filter out only their emotions. And I can feel people from much farther away."

Smaller warrens branched off to the sides, but Rass led them on without hesitation. Alaric and Will continued to test what Alaric dubbed Will's trans-emotive skills. Thankfully they soon spilled out into a slightly larger warren and there were groans and grunts as the group stretched slightly taller.

"Not far now," Rass called back over her shoulder. "This warren runs—"

She spun around. "Goblins!" she hissed.

"Where?" Patlon yanked his axe out of its sheath and turned.

"Behind us. They're pouring into the warren."

"Can we get out before they get here?"

Rass shook her head, her face terrified. "They're coming!"

"Get us out of this main warren," Will called up to her.

She nodded and ran forward, her hand dragging along the roots. She paused and pointed to the side, and everyone poured into a wide but short side tunnel.

Douglon and Patlon took up positions facing the main warren, kneeling so they could be upright, their axes out.

"This isn't going to stop them from finding us," Sora pointed out.

"We have enough metal to call an entire horde down on ourselves," Patlon agreed.

"Rass," Douglon said, "Can you collapse the warren between us and them?"

"Not without burying us too."

"So buried alive or torn apart by goblins," Patlon said. "I think I preferred the dragon."

"How many are there?" Sora asked, kneeling next to the dwarves.

Rass cowered against one of the walls. "So many."

"How far to the nearest exit?" Will asked.

"Not far. The next one to the right goes straight to the surface. But we'd still be on the grass and the Roven will see us."

"We could drop all our metal here and try for it," Patlon offered.

"Talen can fly faster than a goblin can run, right?" Will asked Sora.

"Easily."

"Then let's give them something else to chase," Will said. "What sort of metal do they like most?"

"Silver and gold," Sora answered.

"Anyone have any coins?"

Alaric offered him two, and Will, with a surge of calmness offered to Talen, pulled off the hood. The little hawk shifted and blinked into the darkness. A dislike grew in the bird, a discomfort with the closeness of the tunnel. "Tie the silver into the hood," he told Sora. "And then tie it to his leg. And let's hope it's not too heavy for him.

"A bit of coin's not going to fool them," Patlon pointed out.

"It just needs to distract them."

"What about the glimmer moss?" Evangeline asked. "Should we cover it?"

"The only thing that would make this situation worse," Douglon said, "is if it was happening in the dark."

"Agreed," Patlon said.

"Then let's at least get the light farther away from us," Alaric said. "Put the bowls out in the main warren along the edges. Then maybe we'll see them but they won't be as likely to see us. Unless that will make them suspicious."

"They're not that intelligent," Sora said. "They're driven by smell. Some odd lights won't matter to them."

"How long until the goblins reach us?" Will asked Rass as the moss was put out in the hall.

"Not long."

"Tell me when they're almost close enough to see."

She nodded and Will squeezed past the dwarves to stand hunched at the mouth of the main warren. The glimmer moss was spread along the tunnel, lighting it with the dim orange glow. Past it, the warren faded into blackness.

"There's a way out ahead," he told Talen, setting a restraining hand on the hawk's chest and putting the idea into the little bird's mind of the warren and the branch to the right, leading to wide open grass and endless sky. Talen shifted eagerly on his arm, but Will held him back.

A guttural cry cut through the darkness from behind him.

"They're here!" Rass hissed through the darkness.

Will thrust his arm forward and pushed the idea of freedom and open sky at Talen. The hawk spread his wings and flapped into the darkness of the warren.

Will ducked back in past the dwarves and sank to his knees next to Alaric. "And now we just need a wall that can block our smell."

"How can I help?" Alaric asked.

"I'm going to need a lot of energy." Will closed his eyes and cast out. Above the bright *vitalle* of the people around him, the energy of the grass dangled down in the roots. He set his hand on the ceiling and drew some in, turning to face the entrance.

Alaric wrapped one hand around Will's wrist and reached for the roots with the other. A stream of *vitalle* flowed into Will's arm.

More cries echoed down the tunnel, couched in grunts and rustles.

Concentrating on the air, he formed the idea of the wall. Not a clay wall this time, just a wall of dirt, like the rest of the tunnel. Anything to block their passage from the notice of the goblins. The energy seeped into his hand from above, singeing through the new skin on his palm and he fed it out his other hand, forming the air, shaping it, infusing it with the idea of earth. The air formed up immediately and the light of the glimmer moss shimmered as Will moved the air. The sound of the goblins faded until the warren was utterly silent.

Sora reached out and pushed her hand into it and there was a burst of pain across Will's hand as the magic was interrupted.

"Don't touch it," he gasped and she pulled her hand back.

"He's making a wall out of the air," Alaric explained to the others, his brow drawn in concentration. "It should trap any smell we have here in this tunnel."

"Should?" Douglon asked.

"Keep your axes handy." Will pushed more energy toward the wall.

"If any come through," Hal said, "kill them as quickly as you can. If they realize we're here, the rest will know too."

Sora and Douglon knelt facing the main warren with Hal and Patlon directly behind them.

Something pale flashed into view.

Will stopped and flipped through the book again, phrases of fear or hope or pain jumping out from each page.

CHAPTER FORTY-ONE

GREY, wiry limbs flew past the opening. Round eyes glinted like milky orbs. The group stood in silence, watching dozens and dozens of goblins rush past, scrambling past each other with sharp, jutting heads and claws that glinted in the mosslight.

The *vitalle* from the grass began to fade and Will grasped for more from above them, stretching out farther along the Sweep.

The skin around Will's wrist where Alaric touched him burned. Alaric shoved their sleeves up and pressed their forearms together, spreading out the energy until it flowed through with a bearable heat. Will funneled the new energy toward the wall.

Two goblins shoved into each other and the closest one flew into the wall of air, breaking through and slicing pain across Will's palm.

A grating screech ripped out of the creature's throat and a rotten stench filled the air. Sora grabbed the creature's neck and plunged her knife into its chest, tossing it down behind her. Douglon's axe swung down, severing the goblin's head. Blood pooled out onto the dirt in a steaming puddle of glistening black.

One of the creature's feet still stabbed into the wall and the pain across Will's hand was excruciating. Evangeline scrambled forward and grabbed the creature's arms, dragging it farther in.

The energy from Alaric faded and Will felt the wall begin to weaken.

"How many more?" he asked Rass.

She pressed back against the wall, her face terrified, her hand grabbing at the roots above her head. "So many."

Alaric grabbed the shoulder of the dead goblin and for a brief moment, Will felt a surge of *vitalle* before it faded.

"We need more energy," Alaric said.

Rass pointed to a spot on the wall of the tunnel. "There's a lot of roots behind there."

Evangeline crawled over and scraped away the dirt. Loose earth tumbled down until she was up to her elbow. With a grunt, she yanked and pulled a wide, knobby root out of the wall. Alaric stretched across the warren to grab it, and the energy poured into Will.

Another goblin tumbled through the wall with searing pain, scrambling and scratching. Patlon's axe fell almost faster than Will could see and the creature fell. Evangeline pulled it back, and the endless river of goblins flowed past.

"They're almost done," Rass said quietly. "Many of them followed Talen. The rest are heading toward the enclave."

Will's hand burned. His arm, where it touched Alaric, felt like it was pressed against hot metal. The root in Alaric's hand had withered to a thin, brittle stick and the flow of *vitalle* weakened.

The last of the goblins rushed past and the group stood still, waiting.

"Hold it as long as you can," Sora said. "Or they'll smell the metal and come back."

"They're turning down another warren," Rass said, her voice stronger. "And another past that...I think they're gone."

Alaric dropped his arm down and Will cut off the flow of *vitalle*. The air relaxed back into normal air and the glimmer moss glowed clearly through it again. The stench of rotten meat rushed in. Two of the moss bowls had been trampled.

"Let's get out of this wretched place." Douglon motioned for Rass to lead the way.

The main warren reeked of rotting meat and the sour stench of the goblins, and Will pressed the leather hawking glove to his nose while he hunched over and ran after the others. Rass turned them down a thinner warren that smelled more of earth and less of goblins. When the first hint of fresh air blew past, Will sucked it in like a drowning man.

They spilled out onto the edge of the grass near the base of the enclave mountain and streamed into the nearby trees. Rass waited at the top of the warren opening, glaring down into it.

"Are we being followed?" Will asked as he scrambled out.

She shook her head. "All the goblins near here are heading south."

Rass stood above the opening, her bare toes curling into the earth at her feet. She held out a hand, palm pointing down over the warren. Her lips pressed into a resolute line.

"I do not like these." Her fingers bent into a claw for a breath before she slowly closed them into a fist.

For twenty paces the surface of the Sweep sank down, filling the warren.

Rass kept her hand fisted, her tiny form quivering with displeasure, fixing a furious look at the sunken earth. "Let's not go in one of those again."

The group stood for a moment, looking between the tiny girl and the collapsed tunnel.

"Agreed," Will said.

"This way." Douglon led them through the trees, angling up the mountain.

Whenever there was a gap in the tree canopy, Will scanned the sky for any sign of Talen.

Sora pointed above them. "Top of that pine."

There sat Talen on a branch, gazing regally out over the Sweep. His feathers were unruffled, the hood still dangled from his leg. Will pushed his relief and happiness and gratefulness toward the little hawk and held his arm out. Talen shifted on the branch and didn't look down.

"Maybe he's mad at you," Sora said.

Will opened himself up toward the hawk.

Fierce freedom burst into him. Wind dragging its fingers over splayed feathers. Sharp heat from the sun soaking into the dark crest of his wings, seeping deep into muscles. Hunger and purpose and focus.

"There's only more tunnels ahead," Sora said to Will. "Let him stay outside. He'll find you again."

Will took another strip of dried meat out of his pack, broke it into small bits, and spread them on the top of a nearby stump. With a parting shot of gratitude toward the bird, Will followed the others up the slope.

It took only a few minutes to reach the base of the reddish colored cliffs that they were aiming for.

Douglon, Patlon and Sora spread out, looking for an entrance while the others sat with Hal. They had climbed steadily to get there and Will could see the long stretch of the Hoarfrost Range stretching to the east. The barren tops of the Scales were visible too, blocking the way off the Sweep to the east.

Will leaned a little closer to Rass. "There's a lot of new grass out there."

"I know!" Her face was so excited he thought she might burst. "Isn't it the most beautiful thing you've ever seen?"

The ground flowed over small rises and short bluffs covered with not-quite-green grass. Wind moved from one hill to the next, swirling and rippling and skittering off in different directions. The blue sky sat utterly still and vacant above it.

He cast out and instead of the tiny snips of energy he'd felt when they'd been walking north with the clan, he was met with a rising tide of life, swelling, growing, absorbing the decaying grass of last year and rising with a silent blaze of power.

"It's..." The echo of energy faded and he faced a Sweep

bursting with the verdant green of spring, pushing past last year's memories.

"Yes," Rass said smugly. "Now you see it."

"When I met you," Will said, "you snuck everywhere and hid in the grass. Now you're different. Braver. Or more daring."

"There was no grass yet then." She wriggled her toes into the dirt. "I always feel weak after a long winter, and everyone else seems so strong. But now…" She flexed her hands. "There's strength everywhere."

A strange little bird trill whistled across the mountain. Douglon stood half hidden by a large rock, motioning them to come. Hunching down behind boulders as much as they could, they made their way over and found him standing at the entrance to a thin, jagged hole.

"No more tunnels." Rass crossed her arms and stood back from the entrance.

"You don't need to come," Will assured her. "You can wait for us in the grass. Hopefully, we'll be back out this way with Ilsa in…" He glanced at the others. "Not too long. But be careful. There are a lot of Roven around."

"The Sweep is awake again." She gave a little smirk. "The Roven should be careful of me." She turned and scrambled down the slope, her arms and legs twice as thick as the first time he'd seen her.

Will slid through the gap in the stones. Ahead of him a cave twisted into gloom. This definitely wasn't a dwarven tunnel. The rocks around him were rough and irregular, the passage thinned and widened erratically, piles of stones jumbled on the floor. The passage was mostly naturally made, but in the narrowest parts, rough tool marks were visible. Up at the front, Patlon stopped in the dark, muttering and shoving against a rock blocking their path. He stood frozen against the rock for several heartbeats before it tilted and rolled forward with a crushing, grinding noise.

"If you don't shut up, cousin," Douglon's voice came from behind Will. "The entire Sweep is going to know we're coming."

Patlon shoved against the rock with a growl. "I'd be alright with an honest fight about now. I'm tired of sneaking."

"You beat the rock," Douglon pointed out, as he climbed over it.

A half hour and three more shoved rocks later, the tunnel narrowed again to a point blocked by a thick wooden door. In the orange glow of the moss, the door looked like slats of black, rough wood. Iron straps held it together and it sat snuggly against the rocks around it.

"This is the back end of the enclave tunnels," Hal said, "If we can get through this, there's nothing stopping us from reaching the enclave. But it's locked from the other side."

There was no handle or hinges visible, and Douglon and Patlon brought their bowls of glimmer moss up close to the edges of the door.

"It's barely locked." Patlon knelt down next to the door and peered through the crack.

"You should break the hinges." Douglon stuck something thin through the far side.

"Messing with rusty hinges, that's a quiet idea. Why don't we just scream until they come find us. Be helpful and oil the hinges."

"If you break the latch, the hinges are still going to squeak when you open the door," Douglon pointed out,

"Are you going to be helpful?"

"Already done." Douglon tucked a little tin back into his bag. "Have you gotten through the latch yet?"

A sizzling noise and a wisp of smoke trickled out of the crack in front of Patlon. "Almost. I need—"

Douglon set the handle of a thin saw into his cousin's outstretched hand. Patlon grunted in acknowledgment and slid the blade through the edge of the door. It took barely any time before he grunted again and handed it back.

"We'd have been through by now and back with the girl if you'd just have done the hinges."

Slowly, Patlon pushed at the door and it cracked open. A low, groaning came from the hinges along with a cool, damp breeze. Patlon worked the door back and forth in little nudges until the groaning stopped.

"You didn't oil them very well," he whispered to Douglon.

"You didn't open it right."

"Let's hope the big man remembers where he's going," Patlon muttered.

"Tunnels don't change," Hal whispered back, sounding annoyed. "Even over ten years."

Hal squeezed past the dwarves, taking the lead through the tunnel. Will brought up the rear, occasionally holding his bowl of glimmer moss behind them, searching the jagged, empty tunnel.

Through the forms of the others, Will caught the gleam of the dwarves' axes in their hands. They passed caverns spilling chilled, dank air into the tunnel. Long teeth of rock hung down from the ceiling dripping water as though the mountain was melting. Rounder, lumpy stone fingers reached up out of the floor toward them.

A little farther on, Hal turned into a thin tunnel winding off to the left, and came to an abrupt stop. The glimmer moss lit a pile of rocks completely filling the tunnel.

Hal swore. "This is—This *was* the tunnel that leads to the living quarters."

"Sometimes tunnels change," Patlon pointed out.

"Is there another way?" Will asked.

Hal scratched at his beard. "Through the main cavern. The Torches' enclave meets in a smaller cave off of it, hidden enough that it will be out of view, but if the meeting has started, there could be people in the main cavern as well."

Will's heart sank a little. "Maybe we got here before it started."

Hal's answering grunt sounded doubtful, but he continued down the tunnel. Only a hundred paces farther, another cavern opened up on the left. Will followed the others in and caught the smell of mossy water. On the far side of the cavern, a tunnel wound off and the mouth of it was not completely black. Hal ordered the glimmer moss covered, and motioned for silence, then stepped into the tunnel.

Without the orange moss, the tunnel rocks were bleached to a stale grey. The tunnel was thin to the point where Will's shoulders brushed the sides occasionally, and the only noise he heard was a curse from Hal as he squeezed through a particularly tight section. The wet, green smell of moss grew stronger as the tunnel grew brighter, and a shushing noise teased at his ears.

Ahead of him, Alaric turned sharply to the right, and Will blinked into brightness. Light and the sound of rushing water poured into the tunnel from a horizontal crack in the wall. The others leaned against the wall, squinting through it. Will stepped up between Alaric and Sora, and looked out into a long, thin cavern. Straight ahead, the far side opened in a gaping maw and sunlight streamed in, landing in a blinding patch on the stone floor. The cave looked out high over the rippled surface of the Sweep, stretching away to the hazy horizon. Straight below them, down a cliff face, sat a lake. It was flat and silty brown, reflecting smudged images of the drab cavern walls. A river flowed out from it, edged with pale green moss, sliding toward the mouth of the cave until it disappeared over the edge. Just before the mouth of the cave, a thin, arching bridge crossed the river. The constant wind of the Sweep blew the edges of trees and grass outside the cave, and the smell of the grasslands mingled with the moss.

An unintelligible tangle of voices echoed loudly through the cavern against the backdrop of the waterfall, and Will leaned forward until he could see through the crack. A little to the left, a smaller cave branched off, angling sharply away from the sunlit cavern. In the gloom, dozens of torches lit rows of long tables and benches. A couple dozen Roven congregated in small knots among them, grey-shirted slaves standing along the walls or carrying pitchers. Along the far wall the tables were laden with food. At the near end, just before the tables, a wide, flat stone like a platform filled the center of the floor.

"Killien's not here," Hal said in a voice so low it was almost hard to hear over the noise of the cave. "But I do see all the other Torches."

"And Lukas," Sora said.

Lukas limped among the groups of Roven, filling cups and keeping his eyes pointed down in a more servile stance than Will had ever seen.

"There's Sini and Rett." Will nodded toward a back table where the two were busy hunched over some food.

"I don't see Ilsa," Sora said.

"Each clan has its own permanent quarters," Hal said. "The Morrow's is, of course, the smallest. I'm sure it's been ignored over the years we haven't been here. Ilsa is probably there. And if Killien isn't here with the other Torches, he probably is too."

"It'd be easier to talk to Ilsa if Killien were doing something else," Will pointed out.

"Lukas doesn't stay away from Killien for long if he can help it." Hal nodded toward Lukas who was continuing to pour drinks. "I would guess Killien will show up soon. I don't think he'll bring Ilsa to the Torches' meeting, but it might be worth staying to find out."

Will pushed back a surge of irritation at the delay, but it wouldn't do them any good to sneak into the Morrow's quarters if Ilsa was on her way to this gathering.

An older Roven man in red dyed leathers climbed up on the boulder. His hair hung down his back in long, grey braids, and his equally long beard was decorated with glints of silver and red. A severity was carved into the creases of his face and his shoulders were set resolutely. He knocked a thick wooden staff against the rock and the cavern quieted.

"Torch Vatche of the Temur," Hal said. "One of the few Torches who allies with Killien. This mountain is on his land. The powerful clans demand gifts at the opening of the enclave, beginning with the least powerful, which would be the Morrow. But with Killien not here, Vatche will have to go first."

"We are pleased to offer these gifts to our brethren." Vatche's

Roven accent was harsh as he motioned for two slaves along the wall holding small chests. The first walked over to a tall, angular man wearing wine-dark leathers. His fingers glittered with rings and gems, runes were stitched or stamped into every surface of his clothes, and a large yellowish burning stone hung around his neck, swirling slowly with a viscous, murky light.

"Torch Noy, Sunn Clan," Will whispered to Alaric. "They have the most stonesteeps. And control the dragon."

"The Temur would like to thank the Sunn for their generosity in letting us hire their stonesteeps," Vatche said, his voice emotionless as the servant opened the chest, showing a pile of colored gems, the top of which shimmered with a greenish light.

"Doesn't sound very generous," Alaric whispered.

Torch Noy barely glanced at the chest before waving it away and turning back to his food.

"If the smaller clans don't offer bribes to the Sunn and the Boan," Sora said, leaning closer so Alaric and Will could hear, "the protective spells the Sunn stonesteeps place on the herds will be prone to inexplicable failures, and the Boan soldiers will *accidentally* raid their outlying settlements.

"The trick is to make both clans think they received the better bribe. One year the Boan chief thought that the Sunn clan's gift was more valuable than their own. They rode into Vatche's house, killed his servants and his two nephews."

Will scanned the main cavern, but there was still no sign of Killien. Or Ilsa. How long were they going to have to wait?

Vatche stood tall on the boulder and motioned to the other slave. The man shuffled forward and placed a slightly larger chest on the table before the enormously fat Torch of the Boan Clan. A chill dragged across Will's neck at the sight of the man. The stories of the Boan's Torch were uniformly cruel.

"Albech," Will whispered to Alaric. "Torch of the Boan. He has more warriors than the rest of the clans put together."

The slave opened up the chest and pulled out a corked glass bottle sloshing with grey liquid. Albech's eyebrow rose slightly and his hand flinched back away from the chest. With a quick nod, he flicked his hand at the servant to take it away.

"Poison." Sora let out a long breath. "The Temur dip their arrows in it. I've never seen them share it." Her eyes flicked from the Boan Torch to the Sunn. Neither man looked at the other. "Two decent gifts. At least neither wants what the other has."

With a slight bow toward the room, Vatche stepped down.

"This is taking too long," Will whispered to Hal. "Let's head to the Morrow's quarters and if Killien's there, we'll deal with it."

Hal nodded, then paused. Another Torch was approaching the boulder.

"Ohan of the Panos Clan," Hal said, his voice hard.

This Torch stalked forward like a wiry cat, his hands hung with an exaggerated ease, too still at his sides. His dark red beard was trimmed to a short point beneath his pinched face.

"The clan that betrayed Killien to the Sunn," Hal continued, "burned our grass, and tried to murder Killien in his home just days ago."

Before Ohan could reach the boulder a distant cry rang out. A shadow flickered across the sunlight on the edge of the cave and the grass along the mouth flattened to the side.

Torch Noy's head snapped toward the opening, his hand grabbing at the yellow stone at his chest. Ohan and the rest of the room turned.

A huge shape dropped into view and light scattered off garnet scales, darting through the cavern with skittering glints of blood red. The dragon flared massive wings, the membrane glowing crimson in the sunlight, dark veins and tendons stretching across them like twisted roots.

With scrambling claws, the creature sank down onto the cave floor next to the river and slithered toward the cave with the Torches, his wings curled back above him. The dragon slid forward until it reached the smaller cave and turned its emotionless face toward the Torches who had shoved back from their tables and scrambled away. Only Torch Noy stepped forward, the yellow burning stone held out before him, the other hand held up, commanding the creature to stop.

Red light rippled down the side of the dragon as he reached the boulder where Vatche had stood and stretched his head into the room. The Roven pressed against the back wall, utterly silent. Noy, his voice raising higher and higher, continued to command the dragon to leave.

With a long, ominous breath, the dragon relaxed its wings. A figure got to his feet on the wide scales between the roots of his wings, and slid down the dragon's shoulder, landing on the boulder.

"I'm glad we're still giving gifts." Killien rested a hand on the dragon's neck. "Because the Morrow have some to hand out."

CHAPTER FORTY-TWO

KILLIEN STOOD PERFECTLY CALM, his hand resting on the wide neck of the dragon. Even on the shadowed side, with every breath the creature took, glints of red skittered along his scales. The dragon pulled back his wings, folding them along his side. Thin, jagged spikes ran from the top of his head, down his spine to the tip of his tail.

The only sound in the cavern was the muffled rush of the waterfall. The Roven were pinned against the wall of the cavern. Lukas, Sini, and Rett stood along the side wall, watching Killien closely. Lukas's face was set in a pleased expression. Torch Noy stood rigid at the first table, his hand gripping his yellow stone.

"That's Killien?" Alaric demanded in a barely audible whisper. "Your description of him didn't do him justice."

"He's less impressive when he's not riding a dragon."

Douglon shook his head. "Why is it always dragons?"

"Does anybody happen to have a kobold?" Will asked.

"Oh, Tomkin and the Dragon! I love that story!" Evangeline whispered.

"I know that one!" Sora whispered back.

"Can we focus?" Alaric interrupted.

Evangeline leaned forward. "I definitely know that dragon."

"We all know that dragon," Douglon said from behind them. "It's tried to kill us. Some of us twice."

"Anguine," Evangeline said slowly, her head tilted slightly to the side as she considered the enormous creature.

"No, Evangeline," Alaric said. "Ayda knew that dragon. Even if you think you know it, *it* doesn't know *you*."

Hal hushed them all as Killien stepped forward to speak. "The first gift is for my friend Anguine." He ran his hand down the dragon's neck. He stepped down off the boulder and walked toward Noy, pulling a short sword out of the sheath slung across his back.

The seax. Will jabbed Alaric with his elbow. "He claims that sword was given to his father by Flibbet the Peddler."

Alaric's eyes widened and he peered at the sword.

"It turns out that even though Anguine is a dragon, he and I have something in common," Killien said. The seax glinted a dull silver as he set the tip against Noy's chest. "Neither of us is interested in being ruled."

Noy's face was white, but his eyes blazed with fury. "You raise your sword at the enclave?" Noy hissed through clenched teeth. "You declare war on every clan here."

An unhinged laugh burst out of Killien, and Noy flinched. "A sword?" He flung his arm back at Anguine. "I brought a dragon to the enclave. Yes. It's a declaration of war." Killien reached forward and ripped the yellow stone out of Noy's hand, dragging Noy a step closer by his neck. "Your days of crushing the other clans into submission are over. You no longer have your dragon." Killien drew his sword back and slashed forward, slicing through the chain.

He turned his back on Noy and walked back toward the dragon. Noy's hand dove into a pocket and pulled out a handful of gems. Anguine's head stretched forward and a deep, low growl rumbled in his chest. Noy's gaze flickered to the dragon and he froze.

Killien tossed the stone toward Anguine. The dragon's jaws

snapped shut on it, and the yellow stone sat pinned between jagged teeth for a heartbeat before Anguine bit down and the stone shattered.

A loud crack echoed through the cave and a shower of yellow sparks exploded from Anguine's mouth. The dragon spread his jaws wide and shards of yellow glittered from between his teeth. His head snaked closer to Noy. The scales on Anguine's back rose, bits of light scattering across them as he drew in a breath. Slowly he let it out and red flames flickered in his mouth with a sound like a distant wind. The fire licked along the dragon's teeth, reaching around his nostrils with clinging fingers of flame, setting the scales of his face glittering a bloody red.

When the flames stopped, the dragon's teeth shone jagged and clean.

Noy took a wooden step backwards while Anguine fixed him with a dead, reptilian gaze.

"How is Killien controlling that dragon?" Alaric whispered. "I thought you said he couldn't do magic."

"He can't."

"Could Lukas be doing it?" Sora asked.

The slave stood off to the side, gazing around the room with a satisfied smile.

"He doesn't look like he's doing much of anything," Will said.

"Look on the dragon's back," Sora said.

Nestled into the glittering red scales at the base of his neck, something flashed light blue. Like a bit of sky caught in his scales.

"That's the same stone he used to control the frost goblins," Sora whispered.

"A compulsion stone," Will whispered. "It can transfer thoughts into a creature."

"He's trying to implant thoughts into a dragon?" Hal asked. "He's completely lost his mind."

Sora studied the blue glimmer on Anguine's back. "That's what it looks like to me."

"That wouldn't work if Killien is next to it," Alaric pointed out. "He'd nullify the magic."

Will sank back away from the crack remembering Lukas's notes about compulsion stones. He spun his ring. "It could work. Killien keeps energy from being transferred near him. But Lukas discovered that if you put emotions instead of thoughts into a compulsion stone, that they'll *resonate*. Once he created a stone, the emotions would resonate into anyone the stone touched."

Alaric looked unconvinced.

"Trust me," Will said. "Emotions resonate. And he could use them to control a dragon."

"The Sunn still have stonesteeps." Noy's voice rang out shrilly. "Hundreds of them. Many of which are right outside this cave. You will never leave this enclave alive."

Killien let out a short laugh. "I also bring a gift to all the slaves in this room." There was a long moment of silence. "To you who have served these Torches, I offer you your freedom. Come to me and the Morrow will see you safely across the Scale Mountains, where you can return to the homes you were taken from."

A ripple of movement spread among the Roven and the slaves. Lukas's head snapped towards Killien, his eyes narrow.

"All you have to do is step forward. You have my word." Killien watched the huddled slaves at the back of the room patiently.

"Killien's freeing the slaves?" Will whispered to Hal.

The big man shook his head slowly, his face disapproving. "He's freeing *his enemies'* slaves, stripping the other Torches of any advantage they might have. You can tell from Lukas's expression that it's not a universal freeing."

Hal was right, Lukas's face was furious.

One elderly man stepped forward. The enormously fat Torch Albech grabbed at his arm, but the slave wrenched it away and walked toward Killien, his eyes flickering to the dragon.

"What land do you come from?" Killien asked.

"Baylon," the man answered.

Killien nodded. "We will see you returned." He faced the others again, waiting.

Slowly, other slaves stepped away from the crowd, walking over to join the old man until the only ones against the far wall were Roven.

"My final gift," Killien said, his voice as cold and sharp as the wall under Will's fingers, "is for Ohan of the Panos Clan."

Sora swore quietly next to him.

"A man I trusted," Killien continued, "a man who claimed he also wanted out from under the thumb of the Sunn and the Boan. A man who joined into an agreement with Torch Vatche and myself."

The Roven near to Ohan backed away. Vatche stepped up behind him and gave him a shove. Ohan stumbled forward. Lukas stalked over to the man and took a hold of his arm, while Vatche took the other.

Killien strode toward the man. Ohan tried to back away, but Lukas and Vatche held him in place.

"You convinced Vatche and I that you wanted an alliance. The Panos would join the Morrow and the Temur in our endeavors to break out from under the stranglehold of the larger clans."

Vatche shoved Ohan a little closer.

Killien stepped within reach of the man. "You burned my land. You sent men into my home under a sign of peace to kill me. You partnered with the Sunn, for what? To gain a little favor? To fawn at the feet of men more powerful than you?"

Ohan shrank back against Vatche, who didn't move.

"I have a question for you, Ohan." Killien stepped even closer. "And if you answer me truthfully, I will be merciful."

Ohan's entire body trembled. Killien pressed the edge of his sword against the man's neck.

"The night my father died, the night he traveled to broker peace between you and the Temur, was it a stray arrow that took his life? Or something more…cowardly?"

Ohan's jaw clenched and he stared into Killien's face, his eyes half-furious, half-terrified.

"A stray arrow." The words were rough and broken.

Killien stood very still, the blade still pressed against the man's throat.

"No, it was not." An older slave stepped forward from the knot of grey shirts who had come to Killien's side. "The arrow that killed Tevien, Torch of the Morrow, came from Ohan's own bow."

Ohan shot a blazing look at the slave and opened his mouth in rage.

"Do not speak." Killien's voice was thin. He glanced toward the slave. "Do you know this to be true?"

"I stood beside the Torch that night," the man said. "Like I have every night. He waited in ambush for your father and killed him from his hiding place. Like a coward. And the order to burn your grasses and kill you were from his very lips less than a fortnight ago."

Killien stood utterly still. A thin line of red dribbled down Ohan's throat under the sword. Killien drew in a long, trembling breath and took a step back, dropping the sword to his side.

"If you'd only told the truth, my gift to you would have been a quick death." Killien nodded to Lukas and shoved his sword back into his sheath. "You should have told the truth."

Will leaned forward, the rocky wall rough against his palms. In front of the dragon's enormous body, Killien looked small, but his posture was as vicious as the dragon's.

Lukas pulled an amber colored burning stone out of his shirt, dangling from a thick silver chain. He lifted it up over Ohan's head and Vatche yanked his hands off the man, stepping away. Lukas dropped the necklace over Ohan's head and stepped back, watching.

A strange glow formed in front of the man like wisps of fire. Tendrils of light slid out of his clothes and his neck, snaking out of his face.

"No." Alaric drew back from the rock, his breath jagged.

Evangeline drew in a sharp breath, then pressed her hands to her face, her fingers white.

"No, no, no, no," Alaric whispered, his eyes fixed on the man down in the cave.

"What is he doing?" Will asked.

Alaric pinched his mouth shut and shook his head. "That's an absorption stone—or a reservoir stone."

"It's pulling out his *vitalle*," Evangeline whispered, between her fingers, her voice pained.

Will stared at her. "Like Alaric did to you?"

Ohan screamed and Alaric flinched, turning toward Evangeline and crushing her to his chest. Ohan's screams rose, echoing through the chamber. He clawed at the necklace, trying to pull it off, but the gem stayed fixed to his chest. His screams changed to a shriek, feral and savage as he dropped to his knees.

Swirls of orange-bronze light tore out of his body and spun around the gem, sinking into it, mixing with the amber color of the stone, glowing like rusted honey.

Ohan's screams pierced into Will like daggers. Alaric clamped shaking hands over Evangeline's ears. Sora grabbed Will's arm, her face horrified.

With a final thin cry, Ohan tumbled sideways onto the ground.

His body was utterly still and the gem at his chest glowed with swirling light.

CHAPTER FORTY-THREE

THE ENCLAVE WAS SILENT.

Lukas knelt down next to the body and dragged the stone off Ohan's head. Standing, he offered it to Killien.

Killien held up the stone, watching the orange light for a long moment. "It is a shame that the Sweep has turned into this. Clan killing clan. Roven fighting amongst ourselves when we could be banding together."

Evangeline dropped her hands and looked into the cavern, flinching when she saw the body of Ohan sprawled out on the floor. Hal's eyes were fixed on Killien, horrified.

"We should be gathering our strength to fight the real enemies." Killien's words carried throughout the cavern. "Those who live across the Scales."

"That's unsettling," Alaric muttered.

Killien stepped away from Ohan's body with a disgusted look. The slave who had betrayed him stepped forward. Grabbing Ohan's arms he dragged the body out of the smaller cave and tossed it along the wall of the main cavern.

Killien nodded to the man and climbed up next to Anguine. He hooked the swirling orange stone over a thin spike on the dragon's neck. "Nothing is ever accomplished on the Sweep without bloodshed. And today is no exception. We have never come together in peace. Every change in our land, every bit of progress comes from pouring the blood of our people into the grass.

"But let today be the last." Killien toyed with the gem for a breath before turning away from it. "Let us purge the hatred out of our clans today so that tomorrow can dawn a new age for our people."

Lukas still stood where Ohan had fallen. All semblance of servitude was gone, and he stood with arms folded across his chest, eyes fixed coldly on Killien. The Torch met his gaze for a long moment, then nodded. A vicious smile lifted Lukas's mouth and he strode away, his steps echoing as he passed through the silent cavern and into a tunnel near the mouth of the cave.

"Only a little more unpleasantness." Killien stepped away from the dragon and walked toward the back of the room where the other Roven still stood pressed against the wall. He reached the farthest table and swung his legs over the bench.

"Come join me at the tables, and let us dream of what the Sweep can be." His words echoed more with a note of command than invitation.

The other Roven shifted.

"If any of you are concerned that troops or stonesteeps from the camp below will disturb our talks, let me assure you that they will not. The Roven below have their problems and we have ours. They will fight for today, but we must sit together and fight for the whole future of the Sweep.

"Come." Killien snapped across the room.

Torch Vatche stepped forward and sat at the table across from Killien. The two warriors with him sat as well. One by one the others sat until the only Torches that stood along the wall were Noy and Albrech.

"Do you not want a say in the future of the Sweep?" Killien spoke quietly enough Will could barely hear it. "Today you lose all the power you've had. Albrech, you will lose many of your warriors. Noy, you have already lost your dragon, and your stonesteeps will soon fall. A new era is dawning."

"What have you done?" Albrech demanded. "Do you dare attack my army with your pitiful handful of warriors?"

"My warriors are safe at home with their families. It is only yours who are in danger."

A horn rang out from the Sweep. Then another. Distant shouts and clashes echoed feebly through the cavern.

"The frost goblins," Sora whispered.

The Torches shoved themselves up from the table.

"Sit." Killien's voice cracked like a whip. A threatening growl rumbled in Anguine's chest. "The way to help your clans is to sit here, at this enclave, and discuss the future of the Sweep."

With a ripple of scarlet light, Anguine raised his head until it hung high in the air over the tables. The Roven sank back down in their seats.

"Now, if you would all hand your weapons to the good people who used to be your slaves," Killien continued, "we can get this discussion underway." The slaves stepped closer, taking swords and knives. "If you wouldn't mind staying close by," Killien asked them, "you might help the conversation to stay civil."

In moments a ring of grey shirts encircled the table, knives and swords held in their hands.

"Very good. Now, let us begin. Anguine will root out any who would disturb us."

The dragon's head curved around and the enormous creature's claws scratched against the floor as it crawled back toward the sunshine.

"If we're going to find Ilsa," Hal said, his face set in hard lines, "we need to do it now."

"Agreed," Will said, stepping back from the gash in the wall.

Hal led them back out into the original tunnel.

After only a few minutes they came to a hole in the floor. Following Hal, they descended a ladder, reaching another tunnel that wound forward with a hint of brightness. A handful of doors were set on either side.

"Storage rooms," Hal whispered. "This will lead us to the main cavern. Usually the Torches clear out this area when the enclave starts, sending everyone else down to the Sweep. So it should be empty. Let's hope Killien keeps them all back in that cave, because we're going to have to walk across the cave mouth to get to the living quarters."

Will nodded for him to continue, and they walked quietly down the dim corridor. Douglon and Patlon kept their axes out. Sora held a long knife in her hand. The tunnel brightened measurably around each turn until they could see an arched doorway where it spilled out into the bright main cavern. Hal motioned them forward, and they crept toward it.

A flash of red glittered in the sunlight and Sora drew in a sharp breath. A crushing weight of emotions flooded into Will. Anger, impatience, hunger. Sora grabbed Will's arm just as the dragon's head filled the arch. With a growl the dragon drew in a breath and the group scrambled backwards.

Anguine shot out a stream of flame that filled the tunnel with a stunning burst of energy. An answering burst of *vitalle* rushed past the other direction from Alaric, and they sprinted toward the turn. Will and Hal were the last to reach it, diving around just as a wall of flickering orange flame rushed by.

"Against the wall," Alaric hissed, holding his hand toward the fire. The flames flickered along an invisible boundary that angled out from the corner, pushing the fire back from where they huddled.

The heat reached them, though. A wave of scalding heat washed over Will, and he ducked away from it.

The flames stopped and the group stood frozen. The hallway was silent, but Will could still feel the crushing hunger of the dragon. The drive to kill.

Alaric shook out his hand, wincing. "There's nothing to draw *vitalle* from in here," he whispered. "I won't be able to make another shield."

"Is there any other way out?" Will asked Hal.

"Just back to where we came from. Or down into some storage cellars."

"The dragon isn't going to stop if Killien's commanded it to root out intruders," Douglon pointed out. "I think we need to consider retreating."

"We can't leave." Will shoved against Anguine's emotions, but he couldn't push them out. They pressed down, smothering him. "Ilsa's here. And the slaves. We can't leave."

Hal's expression clearly agreed with Douglon.

Will cast out. The huge head of the dragon was pressing into the end of the tunnel.

"We need a new plan, Will," Alaric said. "We're not getting past a dragon. And Douglon's right. As long as Killien controls him, I don't think he's going to stop."

Evangeline stepped up next to them. "Maybe we can get him out from Killien's control." She bit her lip and looked at Alaric. "It's going to be alright."

Then she stepped around the corner into view of the dragon.

Alaric made a strangled noise and grabbed for her but she moved out of his reach. She held her hands away from herself, palms spread to show she held no weapon.

"Hello, Anguine." Her voice was small and thin in the tunnel.

Will felt a spark of interest flare to life in Anguine and heard the dragon draw in a breath.

"My name is Evangeline," she said, "and even though you and I have never met, I…know you."

Curiosity from the dragon bloomed in Will's chest. The hunger receded slightly and the flames didn't come.

Alaric stepped into the tunnel behind her, but Douglon grabbed his arm to hold him back. "Give her a chance," the dwarf said quietly.

"It's alright," Will whispered to Alaric. "Anguine is just curious about her."

"It is *not* alright," Alaric hissed back.

Will leaned forward to see around the corner, but Hal grabbed him and pulled him back away from the door. "You stay back. He may still want to kill you."

Will nodded and moved until he could barely see around the corner. The dragon's head filled the end of the narrow tunnel, his yellow, reptilian eyes fixed on Evangeline.

Anguine slid his head forward into the corridor, his jaw inches above the ground until his snout was within reach of her arm. She stood woodenly, but didn't back away. Alaric strained against Douglon's grip, his face white. The dragon's nostrils flared and he breathed in. From deep in his chest came a low rumble.

The elf. The words rolled through Will's mind like a wave crashing over the surf. Everyone in the group flinched.

"Yes." Evangeline let out a relieved breath. "Ayda, the elf."

You smell of her.

"I...I do?"

Alaric still leaned toward his wife, but his eyes tightened in curiosity. Anguine drew in a breath again and Evangeline was pulled a half step forward down the tunnel, her hair whipping out in front of her face.

Your life, your...being. It smells like her.

"Well, that makes sense." Evangeline nodded shakily. "You see, Ayda was a friend of my husband. And she..." The tunnel fell silent for a moment. "She sacrificed her own life to save mine. Now I know things that she knew. And I recognize you."

The dragon considered Evangeline with emotionless eyes.

What would you and your companions lurking down the hall ask of me, Evangeline Elf Scent?

"We would like—um...Elf Scent?"

It is fitting.

"Yes, but..."

Anguine stared at her, unmoving. He let out a long, slow breath and Evangeline's hair fluttered backwards.

She stepped back. "We would like to get out of the tunnel and cross the cavern behind you."

That is not something I'm willing to allow.

"I think you might."

The dragon growled and Alaric flinched. Will felt a spark of irritation wriggle through Anguine's emotions.

"I mean," Evangeline said quickly, "I don't think it's *you* who doesn't want us to cross. I—*we* think that you're being controlled."

The growl from Anguine's throat was louder this time and Alaric took a step forward. Douglon's face was stony hard as he held the man back.

"Did you know there's a stone on your back? Right between your wings? It's blue."

Anguine's eyes slid shut and the dragon was perfectly still for a long breath.

I had…forgotten that was there. His voice held a low, roiling anger. *The Torch.*

"Yes, the Torch. We think he's using it to control you. Just like he sent you before to kill someone."

The Keeper. The words were hard as granite. Will felt a spike of hatred. *I want to kill the Keeper.*

"Well, the Torch wants you to kill the Keeper. I think if you took the stone off, you might not care either way about the man." She took a tentative step forward. "If you don't mind, um, with your permission, I mean, I could climb up on your back and take it off for you."

Anguine considered her for a long time. *You know the Keeper.*

Evangeline stiffened. "I do. And it would be good for him if we took the stone off of you. But it would be good for you, too. You'll know which thoughts are yours, and which are…not."

The dragon's anger and suspicion swirled in Will's chest.

I will not be controlled. Take it off.

Anguine stretched his clawed foot toward Evangeline and she flinched back. Alaric let out a pained gasp. When the dragon didn't move again, she put one hand out slowly to touch it. The claws pressed into the floor with knife-sharp points. The tops of his scaled foot sat at Evangeline's waist. She climbed up onto it, then scrambled on her hands and knees onto his back. She kept her head low so she didn't hit the ceiling.

"It's right here," she said, peering down at Anguine's back. "It's been tied in place with leather straps around three scales." She leaned forward and tugged at something Will couldn't see. "These knots are tight."

She yanked on something and Anguine hissed and snapped his huge jaw at her.

"Sorry," she said, holding her hands up. "I think that loosened it, though."

Anguine's head drew back slightly. With a little more fidgeting, she lifted something into the air with a glint of blue. Anguine closed his eyes and shook his head as though he were shaking off water.

That is...

A deep growl vibrated the floor under Will's feet.

That is better. His words flowed smoothly into Will's mind. *You are right, I care nothing for the Keeper.*

Evangeline slid down off Anguine's side and climbed down off his foot. She slung the gem over her shoulder by the long strips of leather and stood uncertainly in front of the huge creature.

My mind clears. Thank you, Evangeline Elf Scent. He breathed in and his scales rippled waves of red light along his side. *I owe you a debt. What would you ask of me?*

"Well, aside from a different title than Elf Scent, we would still like to pass. We have business across that big cavern."

Anguine turned his reptilian head toward the others. Will felt a mild curiosity form in his chest. *You may pass.*

Evangeline nodded, then motioned to the others to come.

Alaric let out a long breath. Slowly the group stepped into the tunnel and moved toward the dragon. Anguine's emotions were infinitely calmer now, a cross between boredom and vague curiosity. They were only a few steps away when he felt a flicker of recognition from the dragon.

I have met the black-robed one before.

"Yes, that is my husband," Evangeline said. "He was a friend of Ayda's. He was there the night you met her."

Will felt a low wave of anger. *I remember.*

There was a sudden spike of hatred and Will grabbed for Alaric's arm to pull him back. But Anguine continued to stare at them with an indecipherable gaze.

Will was still watching the dragon when Evangeline shifted, blocking his view. Her face twisted into a snarl and she lunged for Will, wrapping her hands around his neck and crushing his throat.

CHAPTER FORTY-FOUR

ALARIC GRABBED at Evangeline's arms, hissing words in her ear and pulling at her fingers as they dug into Will's neck.

Will's mouth stretched open, trying to draw in air. His chest burned. He shoved at Evangeline, but she leaned close to him, her face murderous, her breath hot on his face.

Black spots flashed at the edges of his vision and crept inward. Dimly, Sora's face appeared behind Evangeline with her knife raised behind Evangeline's shoulder. She sliced down and yanked the stone off Evangeline's shoulder, tossing it away.

Evangeline blinked and shoved herself back, her face filling with horror.

Will gulped in a breath of air, the coldness rushing into his lungs. He fell forward to his knees and Sora grabbed his shoulders, keeping him from toppling over. His vision cleared and he coughed, the air stinging in his throat.

Evangeline stared down at her trembling hands, backing away slowly. "What happened? Will…I'm so sorry. I don't know…"

"You were touching the stone." Sora motioned to the blue stone she'd tossed into the corner of the tunnel. "The one Killien used to convince a dragon to hunt Will."

"I hated you," Evangeline said, kneeling in front of Will, her face stricken. "I'm so sorry. I don't...I'm so sorry."

Alaric crossed the tunnel and pulled a cloth out of his pack. Carefully, keeping the fabric between his hand and the stone, he tucked the gem into the bag and tied it shut. "Doesn't seem like something that should be left lying around."

Will dropped his head forward, trying to slow his breathing.

"Are you alright?" Sora asked quietly.

He nodded, and she helped him stand.

Evangeline stepped back, her hand trembling and covering her mouth.

"It's not your fault." Will's words came out as a half-whisper. "Killien's really angry at me. That stone was strong enough to influence a dragon. Of course it would influence you, too."

"We should move," Hal whispered, pointing to the gap between Anguine's head and the tunnel wall.

Will nodded and Sora, after giving him a critical look, let go of his arm.

Alaric hesitated in front of the dragon. Anguine watched the Keeper, still calm.

"That stone." Alaric pointed to the one hanging on one of the spikes near Anguine's shoulder. "The one Killien used to pull the life out of that man, may I see it?"

I have no loyalty to that Torch, Anguine said, anger lacing the last word. *Do you intend to kill the Torch with it?*

"No." Alaric's hand went to his own necklace. "No. I'm strongly against killing people in such a manner. I want to see how much of the man has been captured, and whether there is a way to...heal the man it came from."

The dragon stared at Alaric for a long moment. *You are welcome to take the stone, but the Roven man smelled dead.* He tilted his head slightly and fixed a thin-slitted eye on Alaric. *Unless you can return people from the dead?*

"No." Alaric paused, considering the dragon. "Can you?"

No.

Alaric walked carefully between Anguine's neck and the wall of the hallway, sliding the amber stone off the long, crimson spike. He held it in his hand and closed his eyes. A flicker of darkness crossed over his face before he opened them again. "This was crudely done. There is too little *vitalle* here to do anything."

Anguine lifted his head and sniffed the air. Disgust rippled through him. *The caves fill with filth, and a battle bleeds below. Give me the sky.* The dragon's hunger returned, this time for the freedom of flight and the scent of blood.

He snaked his head around, twisting his long neck like a scarlet snake back out of the tunnel. With a dry slither, he disappeared into the main cavern.

Will cast out and felt the blazing *vitalle* of the dragon launch out of the cave and dive down toward the fighting with a swell of exultation that faded as the dragon fell away.

Sora suddenly tensed and spun looking back down the tunnel just as the scent of rotten meat slid into the tunnel. Footsteps slapped along the tunnel floor and a frost goblin scrambled around the corner.

Patlon stepped forward and crushed the creature's skull with a swing of his axe. Will cast out exactly when Alaric did and the echoes came back of three more goblins, rushing closer.

Douglon and Patlon took up positions next to each other, axes ready.

"About time we found something to fight smaller than a dragon," Patlon muttered.

"Did they follow us?" Douglon asked.

The wave of Alaric casting out ran down the tunnel again. "No. They're coming from somewhere down below."

"Storage cellars," Hal said. "They must have dug into them."

"This is our way out?" Alaric asked, pointing back the way they'd come. At Hal's nod, he turned to Will "We'll figure out where they're coming from and try to block it. You go find Ilsa."

Another goblin reached the corner and Douglon dispatched it

quickly. Will cast out again. A troubling tumult of *vitalle* echoed through the rocks below them.

"Alaric," he warned.

"I feel them. Hurry." Alaric's gaze searched around the tunnel. "It'd be nice if there was something to draw energy from."

Evangeline opened several of the doors near them. "How about fires? There are things in these storage rooms that would burn."

"Fires would be perfect."

"Let's go," Hal said. Will and Sora followed him, leaving Alaric and Evangeline to their fires, and the dwarves swinging at the next trickle of frost goblins.

They hurried down the tunnel the way the dragon had gone and peered out into the sunlight of the main cavern. Far in the back, muted voices could be heard echoing from the smaller cave the Torches were in, but no one was visible. Hal motioned for them to hurry, and they followed him across. In a few steps the main opening gaped next to them, overlooking the Sweep. Cries and clashes and screams came over the ledge. Below, along the edge of the lake, hordes of frost goblins poured out of warrens, streaming into the camps of Roven.

Will hesitated for a moment. Greyish-green bodies of the frost goblins piled up, but Roven bodies lay on the ground as well. The goblins seemed disoriented as they ran out into the bright sunlight, and the Roven took advantage of their confusion, shooting and hacking into the swarm. The stonesteeps from the Sunn Clan stood near two of the warrens, shooting arcs of energy into the midst of the goblins. Wisps of black smoke rose from dark smudges on the ground.

A new warren opened as Will watched, and a stream of frost goblins spilled out, plowing into a band of warriors. A quick fear for Rass's safety surfaced, but he pushed it away. She could take care of herself.

Sora nudged his back and he started walking again. Sunlight fell warm on his arm and face. Hal hurried them across the cavern toward the hallway Lukas had disappeared down. The passage was wide and smooth, roomy enough for the three of them to walk side by side. It dimmed as they walked farther from the main cavern. They came to a turn to the left and Hal raised his hands for them to wait. He stepped around the corner and Will strained to hear anything in the silence.

In a moment, Hal came back, his face troubled.

"This is as far as I'll be able to take you." Hal held up his hand to quiet Sora's objection. "Three of the clans have left guards at their rooms. I can lead them away so you can reach Killien's rooms. The Morrow's quarters are the last ones. Get Ilsa and get out of here." He turned to Will. "After everything we just saw, after everything Killien has done, I need to go to the enclave. I don't know if he'll listen to me right now, but at a time like this, my place is next to him."

Will nodded. "Thank you for everything. And I hope you can convince Killien to…"

Hal ran his hand through his hair. "Return to sanity? So do I."

"Will you tell him we're here?" Sora asked.

Hal shook his head. "But I won't lie to him either. He'll probably figure it out on his own. You won't have much time."

Will held out his hand, and Hal grasped it around the wrist in the Roven style.

"Around this corner there's an alcove you two can hide in. I'll have to bring the guards back past here, this is the only way out."

The alcove was a natural recess in the rock only a few steps deep, but it turned to the left, and Will backed himself into the darkest part until the rough stone wall dug into his back. Sora came in and pressed her back up against him, facing out of the alcove, a knife in her hand.

Hal disappeared. The tunnel was dim, so it was almost black in the alcove. Will could just see the outline of Sora's head. She shifted her shoulders and the light glinted off her knife. Her head was right in front of him and the earthy, woody scent of her leathers filled the space.

"You smell good," he whispered and she twisted around and he could just make out her incredulous look. "You always have. I thought it that very first night when you snuck into my room. You were terrifying, but you smelled good."

The edge of a smile crept into her face. "This isn't exactly the time, Will." The dim light caught on a strand of copper in her braid as she turned away from him.

He leaned close to her ear. "If this isn't the time, do you think there will be one? Maybe later?"

He felt more than heard her laugh.

"There's not going to be a later if you keep making noise," she breathed.

"You'll know when they're coming," he pointed out. "I'm just trying to determine if it's the sentiment or the timing you're objecting to."

"I'm objecting to the volume," she whispered. "And don't even think about using your creepy magical skills to read how I'm feeling."

"There's no need for that. I'm quite good at reading people even without my amazing magical skills."

"Then you know that Hal is about to betray us to Killien?"

"No, he's not."

"The moment Killien sees him, he'll know you're here."

Will let out a long breath. "Maybe, but that's hardly the same thing as betraying us. Hal can hardly help Killien while he's creeping around tunnels with us. You have to admit that today is a significant day for the Morrow. And Killien could use some help."

"Yes, with the murders and the threats and the slaughter."

"I'm not saying I approve of it," Will said. "But Hal has a level head, and adding him to the situation can only improve it. It's not like Killien's going to listen to *me* if I ask him to stop."

"It feels wrong to do nothing."

"I agree." Will leaned his head back against the hard stone. "I just have no idea what to do. He's taken his revenge on Ohan, and he's called the frost goblins. Anything we wanted to stop has already happened."

"They're coming," she whispered.

Will cast out and felt a jumble of *vitalle* coming closer down the hallway.

"Ohan's dead." Hal's voice echoed loudly. "The Torches are discussing the future of the Sweep."

Hal passed their alcove, facing away from them down the tunnel, followed by three other Roven. Will drew in a breath and pressed himself back against the rocks, but none of them looked into the alcove. In a moment they were out of view, and a dozen heartbeats later, not even Hal could be heard.

Sora motioned him to stay still and crept out into the tunnel. In a matter of breaths, she was back. "Empty."

He followed her out and around the next turn into the long tunnel with doors lining the right hand side along what must be the face of the mountain.

"If Lukas is in there with Ilsa," Sora said, "we'll have to keep him from leaving and telling Killien."

Will nodded. Lukas's scowling presence wasn't going to make this discussion any smoother. At the end of the hall, he pushed gently on the Morrow's door and it swung open enough to let him see a sliver of a stone room, well-lit with sunlight. The shushing sound of the endless wind filled it. He pushed the door farther to reveal a small common room with a wide, open window looking out over the Sweep. Several small tables sat near the back and a fireplace was carved into the outside wall. A few closed doors filled the wall to his left.

Alone in the room, standing in front of the fire with her back to him, stood Ilsa.

CHAPTER FORTY-FIVE

Will's breath caught in his throat.

There was something achingly familiar about the way she stood. He was young again, standing in his home, watching his mother cook. The longing that memory evoked in him took his breath away.

Ilsa pulled a shallow pan out of the fire and the Roven smell of roasting sorren seeds cut through his memory like a rusted knife.

He stopped in the doorway, unwilling to make a sound, suddenly terrified she would turn around and see him. He spun his ring. Ilsa stood at a wooden ledge in front of the fire, mixing the seeds into something in a clay bowl. The wind outside gusted past, filling the room with its irregular shushing sound.

Giving him a little push, Sora stepped into the room and positioned herself just inside the door, scanning the room, probably wondering where Lukas was, and keeping watch down the hall. The wind filled the room with a sound more like the ocean than the Sweep.

Sora looked expectantly at Will. When he didn't say anything, she said quietly, "Ilsa?"

Ilsa glanced over her shoulder. Her eyes widened at Sora, but when she saw Will she spun around, clutching a rag to her chest.

"You!" Her face grew pale.

Will opened his mouth to say...something, but her surprised look shifted to outrage and the words stuck in his throat.

Sora waited expectantly for a moment before sighing. "Ilsa, we're not here to hurt you."

Ilsa turned accusing eyes on Will. "Haven't you done enough to the Torch?"

The strangeness of the accusation freed his voice. "To Killien?"

"He's been furious since you left, stealing some valuable book."

Will stepped forward. "Left? You mean when I escaped from the prison he was keeping me in? While threatening to kill you if I didn't cooperate?"

She paused at his words, her eyes narrowing suspiciously. "The Torch has *never* threatened me."

"When he brought you with him to the rift," he said, his anger at Killien pushing its way to the surface, "he had a warrior behind you with a knife drawn, just so I wouldn't say anything he didn't want."

She shook her head. "Those warriors were there to control you."

"By threatening you!" he shouted and Sora hissed at him to be quiet. Will rubbed his hand over his mouth and pulled it down into his beard. This was not the way this conversation was supposed to go.

"Will you please just leave?" Her face was still hard, but there was a note of pleading in her voice. She wrung the rag. "He's so angry with you." Her eyes flickered to Sora. "And with you. If he finds you two here...I don't know what he'll do."

Will took a step forward and she flinched back, pressing herself against the ledge. The fear that flashed through her eyes stabbed into him like a knife, pinning down his next words—the words he needed to say. His heart pulsed in his ears with an almost feral thrumming as he shoved the words out.

"I can't leave without you."

She dropped her hands to her side and her eyes went flat. "Leave."

"I'm your brother, Ilsa."

She leaned away from him. "He said you'd say something crazy. That if you ever talked to me, you'd try to make me come with you. But you're a liar. You spent weeks with the Morrow lying to everyone."

"I'm a Keeper, from Queensland." Will wanted to step closer but Sora put a hand on his arm. "I did lie about that, for obvious reasons. But I'm here on the Sweep because I've been looking for you. For a very long time."

Ilsa's eyes flickered toward Sora. "The Torch trusted you," she accused. "And you're here, with *him.*"

Sora nodded slowly. "Will's not what Killien says he is. He's a good man, and he really has been looking for you."

"How could you know he's telling the truth?" Ilsa's tone was scathing.

Sora paused. "I believe Will thinks you're his sister." She gave a small shrug. "And you two do resemble each other."

Ilsa let out an exasperated huff. "That means nothing."

"You were two when they took you," Will said and Ilsa's gaze snapped over to him.

"Anyone could have told you that."

"I was eleven. Do you remember anything about home?"

Her jaw tightened and she shook her head slightly, and Will felt a jab of both heartache and relief. It must have made it easier for her not to remember, but it felt like a whole new theft, a violation to have also robbed her of those memories.

"We lived in a one-room cottage with our parents on a very small farm with a goat and a dozen chickens."

Ilsa shook her head quickly, raising one hand toward him. "Stop, you could say anything, and I have no way of knowing if you're telling the truth. What I do know is that you lied to people that I respect, so I have no reason to believe you. Please," she pleaded with him, "you two are in terrible danger. Leave before the Torch returns."

Will squeezed his eyes shut as the memory of her being pulled out the window came back with perfect clarity. Vahe's furious eyes, Ilsa's terrified face, her hand clutching her doll. Will's eyes snapped open. "You had a doll."

Ilsa stiffened.

"The night they took you, you were holding a rag doll. It was…really ugly. It had no hair and the face had rubbed off. The head was squished to the side because you slept with it every night."

Ilsa's hands clenched the rag against her chest, her face pale.

"It was so ugly, but I couldn't bear to tell you that because you loved it so much. So I told you it was hideous, because I knew you wouldn't understand the word. You thought I'd named her, so you called her Hiddy."

Ilsa flinched.

"A man named Vahe took you."

At his name, Ilsa drew in a sharp breath.

"He wasn't coming for you." The pressure of it grew in his chest until he could barely speak. "He was there for me."

Her eyes snapped open, but Will couldn't meet them.

"All these years, it should have been me here, not you." The words strangled out. "If I'd have just gone with him, he would have left you alone." He forced himself to meet her eyes. "I didn't know."

Ilsa stood with her hand over her mouth, her eyes wide, her other hand clenching the rag to her stomach.

"I'm so sorry." Will almost opened up toward her, but he couldn't tell if it was hatred or hope in her eyes, and if it was the former, the feel of it might kill him.

Footsteps rang out and Sora spun toward the door.

"Will can pluck memories out of your mind," Killien's voice came from the hall. "He knows exactly what you want to hear. Don't believe anything the man says."

CHAPTER FORTY-SIX

A WAVE of relief washed across Ilsa's face, fueling the rage growing in Will. He turned to see Killien standing in the doorway, his silver seax unsheathed, his face burning with the anger that always filled him. Behind him two servants stood, their swords drawn as well.

"No, I can't," Will said, fighting to stay calm. "I've never even heard of anyone who could pluck memories from your mind."

"So it's just emotions you can read?" Killien asked.

The words caught at him, leaving him feeling exposed, like fingers pulling open his cloak and letting the chill of the cave seep in against his skin. It hadn't taken Hal long to fill Killien in. "Yes I can read people's emotions. If I try."

Ilsa's eyes were on him, wide with disbelief. When he met her gaze she stumbled back against the ledge.

"Everyone's?" Killien asked, a tight curiosity in his voice.

Will nodded, ignoring Sora's small huff. Killien didn't ask the real question. "It's not like magic that can be countered. I can just feel people's emotions all the time. Unless I work to close myself off. It's like an extra sense. I can see you, hear you, smell you, and feel what you're feeling." He glanced at Ilsa's pale face. "But I'm not doing it now."

Killien studied him, his anger seething into coldness. "A useful skill."

"Sometimes," Will answered. "But in normal life, people express their emotions clearly enough for anyone to see."

Killien shook his head. "Everyone has secrets."

"Maybe." Will shrugged. "But you'd be surprised how hard it is to suss out a secret based purely on emotions."

Killien stepped into the room, and the two slaves blocked the door. "I'm sorry I left you alone, Ilsa." Killien walked past Will and Sora without a glance. Sora kept her gaze fixed on the two armed servants. Ilsa was still backed up against the ledge, gripping the rag so tightly tendons stood out on the back of her hands. "I had a suspicion the Keeper would reappear, but I didn't think he'd follow us here.

"There is no reason you need to be subjected to whatever lies he's spun," Killien continued calmly, motioning to the nearest door. "You don't have to stay. You're welcome to wait in the other room while Will and I finish something we should have finished long ago."

She hesitated a moment, the rag still clutched in her hand. She fixed her eyes on Will as though expecting him to lunge at her, or as though she finally saw a horrible monster she'd never believed was real. Her expression lit a mixture of gut-wrenching pain and rage in him.

"Ilsa—" Will stepped forward, desperate to get that look off her face.

Killien brought his sword up and leveled it at Will's chest, the Torch's face frigid and controlled. "No more talking to her."

At the coldness in Killien's words, a flicker of something crossed Ilsa's face, but she ducked her head, and hurried into one of the side rooms before Will could figure out what it was. The door shut behind her with a grim finality.

"The sword that you said was too serious for a mere fight." Will motioned to Killien's blade. "Should I feel honored that you're using it against me?" The blade was rougher than he'd expected, more primitive. The handle was sanded wood, the blade pockmarked near the hilt. The runes carved into the blade were roughly made. *Naj.* "What does Naj mean?"

Killien ignored the question. He motioned to one of the slaves. "Bind them."

When it was done, he ordered them to stand guard at the door. "You picked a very bad time to come back, Will. I only have a short time. Hal and the slaves are holding the Torches, but I need to return."

Will searched for a hint of the man he'd thought Killien was, but found barely any resemblance. "What happened to you, Killien?" The ropes dug into Will's wrists.

The Torch paced across the small room to where Ilsa had stood. "Where's my book?"

"Far away."

"Why aren't *you* far away? You'd escaped. And then…you came back."

"I couldn't leave my sister under the control of a man like you."

Killien spun to face Will. "I have been nothing but generous to that woman. As has Lilit."

"She's lived as a slave her entire life because of you," Will flung at him. "And you're using her to control me. What happens if you suddenly latch on to the mad idea that she's a threat to the Morrow? Then anything's acceptable, right? You can suck the life out of her as a demonstration of your power, without a second thought."

"That man"—Killien slammed his hand down and shoved off the ledge, coming face to face with Will—"killed my father."

Rage burst up from somewhere old and chained, a place that had smoldered for twenty years. He leaned forward until his face almost touched Killien's.

"*You* killed mine." Will's heartbeat pounded in his head, almost drowning out every other sound. "You sent Vahe to sneak into my home like a coward."

Killien pushed him back and looked away dismissively. "And if you'd ever had the chance to kill me, you would have. Grand ideas of peace evaporate very quickly in the face of a chance to make your enemy pay."

The memory of Lilit on the floor of the stifling tent, her life bleeding out into the ground rushed into Will's mind. Her *vitalle* weak, dying like old embers.

Will thought of Killien's face, his desperation that night. "You're blind."

The Torch's face twisted in anger and he raised his sword.

"Killien." Sora sounded tired. "Stop acting like Will is something you know he's not."

Killien's sword froze and he turned toward her. He studied her for a long moment before letting out a harsh laugh. "It's all true, isn't it? You decided to help Will, and from that moment, everything he tried succeeded. He escaped me. He convinced Hal to help him." Killien raked his fingers through his hair. "He escaped a *dragon*."

The Torch shook his head and paced the room. Sora watched him, her face stony.

"I hadn't thought it was true, Sora, but you are actually blessed." He stopped in front of her, staring her in the face. "Until the night Lilit almost died, I doubted. But the cursed part is coming true too, isn't it?"

Sora's eyes hardened.

"You've come to care about Will." Killien considered Will for a long moment. "And here he is, at my mercy."

Will held his gaze. Beside him, Sora's breath quickened.

"I met hunters from your clan. They told me how you held the power of life and death. How you passed on judgment from the Serpent Queen to your people."

Will didn't need to open up towards Sora to recognize the fury growing in her.

Killien continued, his tone low and inexorable, "How being

close to you was to court death...They told me about your little friend."

She flinched.

"They told me about your mother..."

Next to him, Sora's shoulders strained against her bonds as she stared at the floor.

"I didn't believe them. It took me a long time to see what you really are," Killien said, his voice dripping with disgust.

"Sora," Will said.

She kept her face down, her shoulders drawn in.

"Sora, please look at me."

She turned enough that she could just meet his eyes.

"He doesn't see you," Will said, leaning forward to hold her gaze. "There's no truth to what he's saying. He only sees what he wants."

"On the contrary, Will." Killien leaned back, satisfied. "I think I'm truly seeing her for the first time. I should thank you, Sora, for keeping yourself so distant from the people in my clan. And from me."

She closed her eyes and started to turn away.

"I see you, Sora," Will said, and she twitched to a stop.

She stood frozen. He could see her brow drawn and her lips pressed together. She stared at the ground, her face hollow.

"I see you," he repeated. "You are intelligent and strong and independent and kind." She didn't move. "And a little bossy."

She twitched at the word, a flicker of surprise crossing her face, clearing out the haunted look.

"There is no power that controls you and kills those you love. It's not the truth. It's just people grasping for power."

A spark of anger kindled in her eyes.

"You didn't go to Lilit because some distant goddess made you, you went for the same reason I did, because she was dying. You knew there was nothing you could do, but you went anyway, because of your own humanity."

Sora met his gaze. Her brow was drawn, but there was a resolve in her eyes.

"She's cursed!" Killien spat the words at them.

"Don't be stupid." Will was suddenly exhausted by everything. "And leave Sora alone. Your fight's with me."

Outrage flashed over Killien's features. "She betrayed me!" He lifted his blade to point at her. "After everything I did for you for three years, you helped Will escape. You helped him steal from me."

She stepped forward until the sword pressed against her neck. "*You* betrayed *me.* You took what I told you, the thing I hated most, and you used it against me." Her face was a mask of fury. "I told you the truth. I have no powers. I did nothing."

"Lilit was dying," Killien flung back at her. "If you have no powers, what saved my wife?"

Sora pressed against the blade, forming the next word slowly. "Will."

Killien's eyes flicked to Will, drawing the sword back slightly.

"I did nothing but pray that the Serpent Queen would take her quickly." Sora's eyes burned with hatred at him. "I told you there was *nothing* I could do. But Will stopped her bleeding. Your wife lives because of him."

Killien cast a harsh glance at Will. "Is this true?"

Will stared at him without answering.

"If it had depended on me," Sora said. "Lilit would have bled out onto the ground."

"Why?" Killien's voice was still harsh, his blade still at Sora's throat.

"Because she was dying." Will wanted to shake the man.

Killien kept his sword at Sora's neck, but his eyes shifted to Will.

"Because Sora wanted to, but couldn't. And I could." He paused, the chaos of the night coming back to him. Killien kneeling on the ground, desperate. "Also, because I believed we were friends."

Killien took a step backwards, his head shaking back and forth, his face a turmoil of anger and uncertainty.

"Lilit knows it's true," Sora said.

Killien dropped his sword to his side and he turned toward the window. A goblin screeched far below.

"You have to stop this, Killien," Will said. "Call off the goblins. Your father strove to bring peace to the Sweep. You're..."

Killien's face darkened.

Will searched again for the face he knew, but instead of finding intelligence and discernment, he saw only something raw and feral. Killien wore the same leathers. The same collection of gems glittered in rune-covered rings. But he found nothing familiar in his face.

Will felt unmoored. Like a leaf torn off the branch and tossed into the swirling winds. How could he talk to a man he didn't know at all?

"You can't convince me to be like you," Killien said.

"I'm not trying to. I'm trying to convince you to act on what you already believe."

The door to the room opened and Lukas stepped in, his customary scowl replaced by a look of satisfaction, wiping a needle-thin dagger with a cloth spattered with blackish-green stains. Sora stiffened and shifted slightly to face him.

Will's breath caught in his throat. For an instant, in Lukas's face he saw all the possibilities of what Lukas could have been. Raised by his family, brought to the Keepers, trained to use his powers. He'd have lived at the Stronghold for the last fifteen years.

A gaping void opened up inside Will. Lukas would have been another Alaric, another brother.

Lukas hesitated, taking in the room and his knuckles whitened on the handle of the knife. Will had always hated the grey slave's tunics, but the sight of it now was like a stab in the gut. Lukas should have been wearing a black Keeper's robe. Lukas stepped forward, his jarring limp a symbol of the life he must have lived.

Unlike Ilsa, Lukas must remember everything. They took him when he was eleven. He knew what he'd lost.

Guilt churned in Will's stomach.

The Keepers should have known. He'd known twenty years ago wayfarers were taking children, and yet he'd done nothing. It should have been Will in Lukas's town, not Vahe. It should have been the Keepers who found him and protected him. The wrongness, the failure was so foundational and so permanent, Will shrank back.

He couldn't help feeling that he had utterly failed this man. The Keepers had utterly failed him.

"Killien," Lukas said, all traces of servitude gone from him, "it seems you're being haunted by a Keeper."

He tossed the damp rag into a corner and shoved the knife into a sheath at his belt, limping toward Killien, grimacing tightly at each step. Will's eyes were fixed on him, each step tearing something out of him. "It is done."

"Good." Killien showed no surprise at the slave's demeanor. Lukas set one hand on Killien's shoulder and blew out a short breath, pressing his eyes shut, the grimace draining off his face.

Will opened his mouth to say something, but no words came. Lukas glanced at Will with an expression of hatred.

"The bulk of the goblins should be here by now," Lukas said, stretching to see out the window.

"Call them off," Will said. "Stop the massacre, Killien."

It was Lukas who answered, "This isn't Queensland where you mindlessly follow your queen. On the Sweep power goes to the strong. Those frost goblins are crippling the powerful clans. In a few hours the balance of the Sweep will shift to the Morrow."

"In a few hours," Killien corrected him, "every clan will have a voice."

Irritation flickered across Lukas's face, but he said nothing.

"And thousands of Roven, who want nothing more than to return home to their families," Will said, taking a half step forward, "will be dead."

"Let me guess, Keeper." Lukas's mouth twisted in contempt at the word. "You're against fighting."

"No. In fact, I'd gladly join any fight on the side of the oppressed."

"We are the oppressed, Will." Killien threw the words at him. "The Sunn and the Boan demand our barley, our herds, our warriors, and all under the threat of annihilation. *We* are the ones fighting the oppressors."

"You *were*," Will said, his frustration boiling up into anger. "And you wanted to fight back with ideas that could actually change the Sweep. But now that you have power, you've become one of them. And today if I want to fight the oppressor, I have to fight you."

"Oppressor? The night the Panos attacked we caught them trying to steal my son." The raw, feral look in his eye caught at Will like claws raking into his chest.

A man poised over a child—the image loosed a deluge of anguish and fury.

In that moment he recognized what he saw in Killien's face—the same hatred Will had carried for years. It hadn't started as hatred. It had begun with the terror that someone he loved was being hurt. But that terror gnawed down deep enough that it took root, and a savage hatred grew.

It wasn't the foreignness of the hatred in Killien that was so terrible. It was how profoundly Will recognized it.

The mirrored feelings in himself clawed their way to the surface, and he wanted desperately to push them away, to close himself off to Killien. But he couldn't ignore how much he understood them. Instead of pushing it all away, he faced it.

"I know what you want," Will whispered. "I know the terror and the guilt."

Killien's face grew hard and savage.

"And I know the hatred that grows from it."

"They *must* pay."

The words rang true and familiar. Killien's eyes glittered with a new sort of ferocity, and Will stopped keeping that at a distance, stopped looking for what he wanted to find in the man. "You want to rip away everything they love."

Something vulnerable joined the viciousness in Killien's expression, opened it up. Will grasped for that opening, letting his own rawness meet Killien's.

"You want to rip it all away and make him watch it bleed out on the ground." Killien's desire to control the frost goblins blazed up in Will, and he knew that hunger. He wanted the chance to release them on Vahe, tear the man apart.

Except, of course, it couldn't end with Vahe. Will followed the hatred in himself forward to Killien and the fire faded.

"At least you want to, until you ride over the Sweep with him, and learn who he is."

Killien's jaw clenched.

"He talks of things you love. He's married to a woman and every time she is near he's useless for anything else. He has friends who respect him, a clan that needs his leadership, and a son who needs a father."

Killien's eyes stayed fixed on Will.

"But there's more than that. Somewhere along the way you realize you understand him. You recognize the things about him that you respect as things you strive for yourself. And you recognize the darkness in him too, because the same anger has lived for decades inside of you, demanding to be recognized.

"One day you realize that a Keeper from Queensland and a Roven Torch aren't foreign to each other. Then the hatred starts to cool into something different. Something more complicated. And you're left with...more than you had. A tangle of things that feels like anger and failure, but also friendship."

The Torch shifted almost imperceptibly, but Lukas's face blackened further. Sora stood perfectly still.

"It has its own form of pain. A more internal, digging pain. And it's so tempting to go back to the hatred. But the new place is more...true. And the only reason you want to go back is that it's easier just to hate. But when you can look at it honestly, you know the hatred's killing you, and killing any hope that the future could be different."

Lukas's hand clenched on Killien's shoulder. "You know nothing of hatred."

Will took in Lukas's furious face and found he had no words to answer him with. "If you don't stop, Killien, the future will not be different. The clans will strike back. Sevien will never be safe. Lilit will never be safe. The others will regain their strength and they will destroy the Morrow."

"They deserve this." Lukas's tone held an unexpected authority.

Killien spoke in a hoarse whisper. "They have so much blood on their hands."

"They do," Will agreed. "But until today, you didn't."

"Until today we didn't have the chance," Lukas said.

"The Torches are here," Will continued. "Let this be the time when a Roven could have overwhelmed with force, but instead offered peace."

Killien turned away from the window. A shadow lay on his face, but also a clarity Will hadn't seen in ages.

He took another step forward, a bit of hope kindling. "Call off the goblins, Killien."

The frenzied screech of the goblins rose and fell, slipping between the rushing sound of the wind.

"I can't."

"Yes, you can," Will said. "You obviously have a frost goblin you've used to call the others. Just change what it believes. Convince it there's a vast mountain of metal far to the north. Let it spread that idea to the rest."

The Torch shook his head. "You don't understand. I *can't*. When we give a goblin the idea of all that metal, it goes mad."

Sora let out a long, defeated breath. "You had to kill it."

Killien nodded. "The only goblin I had is dead."

CHAPTER FORTY-SEVEN

Sora let out a long breath that was half growl, and stalked toward Killien.

The Torch raised his sword and Will's heart lurched in his chest. Killien held the blade only a handbreadth away from her neck, his eyes fixed warily on her.

"Untie me."

Killien stared at her for a moment, his face growing incredulous. "No."

She leveled him with a look that was all too familiar to Will. "You want to stop this," she stated, and Will knew she was using a great deal of restraint to not call Killien an idiot.

Killien's eyes narrowed at her words, but the tip of his blade wavered.

Sora blew out a short, irritated breath. "It's going to be harder for me to catch another goblin if I'm tied up."

"Back away from the Torch." Lukas pointed the thin knife at Sora.

Far more than Killien's blade, Lukas's face was so dark that a dart of terror stabbed into Will and he stepped up next to her.

"You can't go catch a goblin," Will said. "There are too many of them."

Sora ignored both Lukas and Will and kept her eyes fixed on Killien. "Untie me."

Killien still didn't move, his face unreadable. "Why should I trust you?"

"I have always told you the truth," Sora said. "I didn't leave you because of Will. You and I were done the night Lilit almost died. I told you that then."

"Back away from the Torch!" Lukas repeated, his voice harsher.

Sora turned a scathing look on him. "Are *you* going to catch another goblin?"

"We don't *want* to catch one." A thin smile pulled up one side of Lukas's mouth. "Everything is going exactly as we planned."

An idea whispered into Will's mind. Lukas stood next to Killien, shoulder to shoulder, and Killien didn't object. The slave's shirt was grey, but for the first time Will realized it was a disguise.

Lukas had lived with Killien for most of his life. Killien had taught him to read, taught him how to use the skills that the Keepers should have taught him. Lukas was always well dressed, rode one of Killien's horses, stood at the Torch's side, ate next to him, lived with him. Even if he hadn't wanted to be so close to the Torch, the pain in his hip would have kept them close. Lukas was part of every one of Killien's plans.

To Lukas, Killien wasn't his owner—he was his equal.

The understanding shifted everything. Lukas's face was bleak, and Will realized this discussion wasn't just with Killien.

"Every moment you wait," Will said, keeping his eyes fixed on Lukas, "more Roven are dying. More hatred is growing and the chance for the Morrow to live in peace is growing dimmer."

"You don't understand, do you?" Lukas said. "With every moment the Morrow grow more powerful and it is our enemies who grow dimmer. We finally have the power we need."

Lukas's face was determined, almost victorious, but out of the corner of his eye, Will caught the hesitation in Killien's. Lukas stood shoulder to shoulder with Killien, and hadn't even noticed that Killien had already surrendered.

The Torch nodded to Sora and she turned around.

"What are you doing?" Lukas demanded.

With a quick slice, her ropes were cut. Sora ran across the room and grabbed her knives off the floor. Will took a step after her, pulling at his own ropes, his mind scrambling for some way to help her, but she slipped out the door. Lukas's fingers dug into Will's shoulder, pulling him back.

Will pulled toward the door. "You can't let her go alone."

"Sora always does everything alone," Killien answered with a short laugh, walking back to the window and looking down at the fighting below. "Whatever it is you two have going on, you must know her enough to know that."

Will let Lukas pull him back a step. "Nothing had better happen to her."

"What could possibly happen? She's only running into an army of goblins," Lukas said. "We should send you with her. Solve both our problems at once."

Will ignored his words. "We should be ready when she gets back. Do you need to make a new stone? Or can you reuse the last one?"

Lukas gave him an incredulous look. "We're not actually going to do it."

"Let him go," Killien said tiredly.

Lukas's hand didn't loosen.

"Let him go." Killien sounded more firm. "And get a new compulsion stone ready."

Lukas stood perfectly still. "Why?"

"Will is right." The calm in Killien's voice barely hid the anger. "If the Sweep is going to change, it has to be done differently than this. We'll call off the goblins, give the clans time to realize that they aren't the only ones with power. And then, if I haven't already ruined it, we'll find ways to build peace."

When Lukas still didn't move, Killien leveled an unbending

expression. "Let him go."

Lukas shoved Will away. With a dangerous look at Lukas, Killien came over to Will and cut his ropes.

"Get the stone," the Torch commanded harshly.

Lukas wrenched the door open and turned down the hall.

Will rubbed at the skin on his wrists where the ropes had rubbed. Killien moved back to the window, his shoulders stiff.

"It's the right choice," Will said.

Killien stood unmoving, his jaw clenched. Every line in his body hummed with anger and Will felt a hint of loss that the man he'd talked to on the journey north seemed to be gone.

"What changed?" Will asked. "When did you stop looking for peaceful ways to change the Sweep?"

Killien didn't turn around. "I got tired of doing nothing and feeling helpless. My father's plans for peace got him killed, and mine almost did the same." He scrubbed his fingers through his hair and let out a growl of frustration. "I'm so angry at all of it. So tired of the Morrow being weak."

"They certainly weren't weak today."

Killien leaned on the windowsill, looking out. "And it just made us more enemies."

"Yes, but you got their attention. Killien, you flew on a *dragon*."

Killien glanced over his shoulder at Will and a small smile flashed across his face. "You saw that?"

In spite of everything, Will let out a small laugh. "It was impressive."

Killien grinned and for a moment looked like himself. "It was...like a dream. The power in his wings, the Sweep spread out below like a rug, covering hill after hill. We flew over this mountain." He flung his hand toward the ceiling. "Over it! It was icy cold and the wind almost ripped me off. But mostly it was...so removed from everything. Somehow from up there the Sweep felt small, the clans so close to each other, they seemed like one group. The idea of a unified Sweep felt...possible."

"Maybe it is possible."

Lukas pushed the door open and came back in, carrying a light blue stone on a long chain. It was small enough to fit in Lukas's palm and shaped like an irregular, broken column.

"Put in it the idea of metal far north in the mountains," Killien ordered him. "And make the desire for it so strong they'll have no choice but to go."

Lukas shook his head quickly. "We can't do this. If we give up the power now, they'll destroy us."

"The power isn't what's important." Killien's anger flared again. "Be ready when Sora comes."

"No." Lukas's jaw was set stubbornly. "Negotiate with the other Torches once you own the Sweep. This power is all that will keep us safe."

"Lukas." The note of command rang through the room.

"Killien, this is our chance. If we stop now the Morrow go back to being worthless and helpless."

"The Morrow," Killien said coldly, "have never been worthless or helpless. This path will see us all killed. Will is right. My father knew that. I knew it before…I forgot it."

Lukas's eyes tightened at the words. "One Keeper shows up and the Torch of the Morrow rolls over like a coward?"

Will opened up a sliver toward Lukas and a churning mass of anger rushed into his chest. Frustration shoved its way through and Will clenched his jaw in an effort to push the emotions back. There was nothing servile.

Killien took a step toward Lukas, his hand on his sword hilt. When he spoke, it was deadly quiet. "You forget your place."

The sharp slice of betrayal Lukas felt cut through Will's chest, and fury laced with fear bled out of it.

"My *place*?"

"Ready the stone," Killien commanded.

The fissure in Lukas split open, pouring out a cold isolation. Betrayal clawed up from deep in the bowels of Lukas's soul, looming over him, shadowing him with black, rending isolation.

Will shoved Lukas's emotions out, slamming himself shut. "Killien," he warned.

Lukas's face hardened into a mask. "You do it." He tossed the bluestone and Killien caught it by the chain.

"This is not the time," Killien snapped. "I need your support."

"No," Lukas flung back. "You need mindless obedience."

"You owe me that!" Killien roared.

Lukas froze.

"You were *nothing*. I gave you everything. I taught you to read, to use your powers, treated you like family."

"Until the time comes when I act like I am," Lukas said coldly. "And then you prove that all I am is a slave."

Killien's hand clenched the chain. "Fix the stone."

Lukas let out a harsh breath, somewhere between a growl and a laugh. "Get your Keeper to do it."

The Torch stared daggers into Lukas for a long moment. Then he held the stone out to Will.

"I don't know if I can," Will said. With a surge of frustration, he realized Alaric probably could.

His fingers closed around the stone and a buzz of energy rushed into his hand, like he'd grabbed a bees' nest. His hand clamped around the stone and the sensation flowed up his arm. It rushed into his chest like water bursting through a dam.

Yes, Alaric was the Keeper who needed to be here. Or any other Keeper for that matter. It was time Will accepted the idea that he was an utterly mediocre person. Which made him a pathetic Keeper. The words that had always felt painful, now felt…right. They were true. These sorts of heroic things were for other people. It was nice to acknowledge that. Liberating even.

The buzzing from the stone continued, and for a single, panicked moment Will recognized the rush of emotion from that compulsion stone Hal had put around his neck days ago to exhaust him, but this was so much stronger.

But then the world flattened to dullness. The walls of the room were lifeless. The anger on Killien's face was petty and worn.

Lukas's petulance was wearisome. The rush of the wind and the occasional noises from the window felt distant and unimportant. Nothing was important.

Will sank to his knees. The aquamarine was important. It was warm beneath his fingers. He wrapped his other hand around it, too, and the hum of energy surged into his fingers. His fingers glided over a facet of the stone as smooth as ice. He ran his thumb over a corner and the sharp edge scraped across his skin. A trace of light swirled inside the gem. Not filling it, just swirling in the bottom like molten stone. He tilted the stone and watched the light flow down to the other end slowly, like sluggish water.

There were voices somewhere, but he ignored them. He curled forward, trying to shadow the stone and see the light better.

A rough hand shook his shoulder and Killien's face was in front of him asking something. The Torch's face was so intense. All this intensity and scheming was so wearisome. Will ducked down, turning away from the Torch, holding the aquamarine closer to his face.

Killien tried to peel his fingers off of the stone, but when he touched it, he yanked his hand back. "What did you put in this compulsion stone?"

"Just a healthy dose of apathy," Lukas answered.

A slap on his cheek snapped Will's head to the side, and color rushed into the room along with the sound of the wind.

"Let go!" Killien's face was only inches away.

Sitting on the floor felt wrong.

Behind Killien, Lukas stood with his arms crossed, smiling. Will blinked to clear his head. Sora was coming back soon. They need to get ready for…something.

Killien shouted at him again, but what the Torch didn't understand, was that it didn't matter. The sludgy light had made it to the other end of the blue stone, and Will tipped it back the other way.

Lukas sounded terribly far away. "Let the Keeper rot."

CHAPTER FORTY-EIGHT

"We need to get back to the enclave." Lukas's voice was faint as he turned toward the door. "The other Torches are ripe for picking. If the fat fool Albech gives us any trouble, I have one more absorption stone. It'll be harder to fit it over Albech's fat head than it was over Ohan's." His voice took on a twang of regret. "I'd wanted to use it on Will, but I think it'd be put to better use in destroying the Boan Torch."

"Stop," Killien snapped. He clenched his fists, visibly trying to control his anger. "You're not the Torch."

Lukas froze, turning slowly to look at Killien with incredulous eyes.

Will wanted to tell them it would be easy if they just decided not to care. But it was too much work to talk. The world was dreary. Even the usually glittering gems in Killien's rings were dull.

Killien turned his back on Lukas. "Get the right stone for the goblin." He bit off the words sharply. "Now."

Lukas's body tightened and Will started to turn back to his aquamarine.

Lukas slid the thin knife out of his belt.

The movement caught at Will's mind, demanding attention.

He shoved at the feelings of apathy crowding into him. Killien was still talking, chastising Will to drop the stone. Lukas continued forward, his face twisted into a silent snarl. He raised the knife.

"If you're willing to give up the power we've gained and let all of us be killed," Lukas said, his voice chilled with contempt, "you shouldn't be Torch either."

Will dragged a word up his throat. "Killien—"

The Torch looked at Will just as the knife plunged down into his back. Killien arched away from it, but Lukas drove the knife in deeper. Killien's hands clamped onto Will's arm. His eyes unfocused, and he toppled to the floor.

Will stared, his hands clenching the stone. Shock shoved against the apathy and he leaned toward Killien.

"I'm not giving up everything we've earned." Lukas pulled out the blade and wiped it on Killien's sleeve before shoving it back in its sheath. Crossing to the shelves, he picked up a small, stoppered bottle. He dumped out some dried leaves and sank down on the floor behind Killien. His face was hard, but something in his eyes tore at Will.

"Did you know," Lukas said to Killien, his words muffled and dull, "that your ability to nullify magic is carried in your blood? The night of the goblin attack, when you were cut, some of your blood landed on me. It was as though I was touching you. I felt no pain at all. Even when the blood dried it still worked almost as well as you do."

Will shoved frantically at the apathy inside him, but there was simply too much of it.

Lukas pushed the bottle against Killien's back and a thin moan escaped the Torch, the noise cutting through Will's mind. Lukas's face was drawn, but when he spoke, it was clear. "So I don't need you anymore. All I need is your blood."

Will squeezed his eyes shut and listened to the frantic part of himself. There was something about Sora, something important.

Lukas shoved a stopper into the little jar and tucked it into his pocket. "Do you know how long I've dreamed of separating your powers from you? Of bottling them up and leaving this wretched land?"

Separate. Bottle up. That was it. Sora shoved her emotions away until they didn't affect her. She kept them so tightly controlled Will couldn't even find them half the time.

He pulled himself away from the emotions for a moment, searching out their edges, feeling for the shape of them.

He pressed the apathy out his arms, shoved it back down toward the stone. Color crept into the room again.

Logically he knew he should put down the stone, but he couldn't quite cut through the deadness inside him.

Beside him, Killien lay pale, his eyes closed and his breathing shallow. Lukas leaned out the window, looking not down at the Sweep, but up into the sky. He stayed there for a moment, before turning back to the room. His gaze fell on Killien, and he clenched his jaw.

"I used to think Keepers were some sort of magical beings that knew everything. They had everything under control. They protected us." Lukas opened his hand and a faded red scar filled his palm. "Vahe triggered it. He sent that fire out over the heads of the crowd and everything inside of me...woke up.

"That's when I knew I would be a Keeper. I just wanted to run home and tell my mother, begging her to take me to Queenstown. I tried to get my brothers to come with me, but they weren't ready to leave, so I went myself."

Lukas closed his fist. "Vahe found me before I'd gone far."

He walked slowly back towards Will. "My mother wouldn't find me, not tied up in Vahe's wagon. But a Keeper...I knew a Keeper would come. I believed it until we crossed the Scales and everything disappeared except the grass." His eyes dug into Will. "For years, I waited for you to come."

A deep guilt writhed through the apathy inside Will.

"Then Sini came...And still no Keepers." His face twisted in disgust. "Sini! If anyone deserves a life of happiness, it's that girl.

But they took her, too. At first, I thought you weren't coming because you were angry, because we'd begun to learn a sort of magic that the Keepers wouldn't like. But it was worse than that, wasn't it?"

Lukas's eyes searched Will's face. "You didn't even know we were gone."

Something sank into Will's gut, taking his breath away with it. He dropped his gaze to the floor.

"I believed all the lies about you," Lukas said quietly.

A complicated twist of emotions tore through the apathy and Will yanked one hand off the stone, reaching for Lukas. "If we had known—"

Lukas batted his hand away. "Now that I've met a Keeper, I know I was foolish to think they were anything but arrogant, useless men."

Will's hand dropped to the floor.

Lukas leaned over Killien and unfastened the sheath from around his chest. He slid the seax out a handbreadth and touched it with his fingertips. A grim smile crossed his face and he shoved it back into the sheath and slung it across his back. "I don't think I'll soil the seax with your blood." His gaze rested on Killien, and his jaw clenched. "This is not how I wanted things to go with Killien. I thought he could remember his anger at being controlled and make the decision to take what he needed. I had thought that together we might..." He blew out a breath and straightened. "His death is regrettable. But you, Will...I doubt I'll ever think of you again."

Will needed to move, but the part of him waking up was so small.

A voice rang in his ear. It reminded him of Sora.

Sora.

A wave of relief washed over him. She would come in and... do whatever needed to be done. Because something needed to be done, Will just couldn't pinpoint exactly what.

Lukas unsheathed his knife, his face filled with pure hatred, and Will knew it was coming. In a moment he'd be next to Killien, dying. The Torch lay still, his face grey. Will's mind recognized the wrongness of it, that he was going to be killed by a man who should have been like a brother. But there wasn't room for actually feeling it.

He dragged his gaze to the door, waiting for Sora to come and fix things.

"Why couldn't you be what you should have been?" Lukas asked in a ragged whisper.

Sora was too late. There was no one here to help. The truth flashed into his mind like a flare of light.

He was going about this all wrong. He wasn't Sora. She stuffed emotions away. He let others' emotions resonate within himself so that he could see them. Understand who they actually were. And recognize how much he was like them.

The apathy from the stone still filled him until he thought he might burst with the emptiness of it. He looked past it to his own emotions that had been shoved aside. The bright fear of the knife, the murky shame of what Lukas had been through, the hollow grief that Killien was lying so still on the floor next to him.

He latched onto the grief, and it was for so much more than Killien. It was still there for things long ago. His father. How his mother grieved for her husband and her daughter. The grief he'd carried so long for Ilsa. Even now, there was still a mourning for the years lost to knowing her.

It was his own grief and for the space of a heartbeat, focusing on it rolled the apathy back, making just enough room to open up to Lukas.

The little room left in him filled with bitterness and loss and guilt, a sharp ribbon of fear, and a fresh wound of loneliness.

And Will recognized every bit of it deep in himself.

"Lukas." He barely managed a whisper. "I see you, what you've been through. It shouldn't have happened. Any of it. But you can come back from all these things that are trying to consume you."

"You know nothing," Lukas hissed.

"I know about being alone." So much churned within Will, that he wanted nothing more than to shove it all out. But he sorted through it, gathering his own emotions bit by bit. Disappointment with himself over the sort of Keeper he was, the ever present loneliness he felt, the old, worn in anger at his father's death and Ilsa's abduction. "I know that something can happen that we don't deserve, and it can break *everything*." He gathered all the emotions and pushed them toward Lukas, letting him feel all of it.

Lukas's eyes widened, then he shrank back. "Get out of me!"

"You're not alone," Will whispered. He pulled everything back from Lukas. "It's not too late, Lukas."

"It *is* too late." Lukas's face was set in a dark look. "You don't know me."

Will felt a pang of sadness for how often he'd seen him that way. "What about Sini?"

Lukas flinched.

"She told me you're like an older brother who's always taken care of her."

For a fraction of a breath something gentle crossed Lukas's face. But then he shoved it away.

"The best thing that could happen to Sini," Lukas answered, "is that she grows up far away from me." He raised the knife and plunged the knife toward Will's chest.

Will twisted away and the knife bit deep into his shoulder.

Pain exploded in Will's arm, ripping through the apathy of the stone. Will's fingers spasmed open and the aquamarine clattered across the floor.

"Will!"

This time it really was Sora, standing in the doorway, her arms clamped around a thrashing frost goblin. Behind her Alaric and Evangeline ran into the room.

Douglon pushed past them, puffing. "Our way out is not an option any longer."

"The goblins are pouring into the cave—" Alaric stopped, taking in Killien, Lukas, and Will.

Lukas yanked the knife out. Pain shot down Will's arm and snaked across his chest. He grabbed his shoulder.

Lukas rose. The room stood still for a moment before the dwarves let out a yell and thundered across the room. Lukas fixed them with a look of pure fury, then turned and ran for the window.

"Stop him!" Sora yelled.

Douglon lunged after him and Will heaved himself up. But Lukas reached the wall, scrambled up into the window and threw himself out.

Will reached the window just as a flash of glittering red raced by. With the whip of his tail, Anguine rose into the sky, the grey form of Lukas clinging to his back.

CHAPTER FORTY-NINE

Douglon barreled up next to Will, scrambling toward the window and watching Lukas and Anguine fly southeast across the Sweep.

"Dragons," he grumbled.

Will sank against the wall, his shoulder throbbing. The room erupted in chaos. Ilsa yanked a door open and ran across the room, falling to her knees next to Killien crying out for someone to help. Patlon and Sora wrestled with the frost goblin, trying to get ropes around its limbs. Evangeline slammed the door to the hall closed, calling for something to barricade it with.

Alaric ran toward Will shouting question after question.

Will disregarded them all. "Help Killien, if you can."

He sank down next to the Torch and cast out towards him. Killien's body lay still. The little *vitalle* left in him sluggishly seeping out of the wound on his back. Will tried to gather some energy when Alaric knelt down next to him.

"You're in no condition. Move over."

Will nodded and sank back.

"Please help him," Ilsa whispered.

Alaric glanced up and his attention caught on her face, but he only nodded and then set his hands on Killien's shoulder and bowed his head. After a long moment he met Will's gaze and shook his head.

"He needs to live, Alaric," Will said. "He'd be an ally on the Sweep."

"The man who rode a dragon and sucked the life out of his enemy?"

Will paused. "You met him on a bad day."

Alaric's eyebrows rose. "What do his good days look like?"

"On those, he might be able to get the Roven to quit fighting. Maybe even reconcile the Sweep and Queensland."

Alaric looked skeptically down at Killien. The Torch's shoulder barely moved with shallow breaths, the ground behind him soaked with blood. Ilsa knelt behind him, tears on her face, pressing a rag to the wound.

"He's lost too much *vitalle*," Alaric said quietly.

"Give him some of mine," Will offered, holding out his hand.

Alaric waved his hand at Will's blood-soaked arm. "You don't have enough. None of us has enough—" He stopped.

"Whatever you're thinking," Will whispered, "do it."

Alaric shook his head, his face stricken.

"Alaric, please."

Alaric let out a long breath. He swung his bag off his shoulder and pulled out the swirling orange stone Killien had used to kill the Torch of the Panos.

"Is that still Ohan?"

Alaric shook his head. "Who we are isn't held in our *vitalle*. It's something more…intrinsic to us. What was Ohan is gone. This is just some of the energy that animated him. There isn't enough here to bring back Ohan, but there may be enough to save Killien."

Alaric rolled Killien onto his back and set the stone on his chest. Then, closing his eyes, he set his hands on Killien and tendrils of orange light snaked out of the stone. Ilsa gasped and pulled her hands back. Douglon stood behind her, watching Alaric with an unreadable face.

Evangeline called for help and the dwarf blinked. She stood with her back pressed to the door. "They're coming!"

Douglon ran to one of the tables along the back of the room and pushed it toward the door.

"Goblins are swarming into the caves," he said to Will. "The dragon flew off." He nodded towards the window. "Now we know why. And goblins poured into the tunnels from somewhere down below. We thought it might be time to gather you up and go. Which is when we found Sora fighting three of them, hollering about not killing one." He shoved the table against the wall and stomped back for another. "I assume this means you have some sort of plan."

Will glanced over to where Sora and Patlon had succeeded in tying up the goblin. The creature lay squirming on the floor, making a hoarse screeching sound. "We did."

Patlon went to help Douglon and Evangeline barricade the door. Will left Alaric to heal Killien and walked over to Sora. She grabbed a cloth from a nearby shelf, wrapped it around Will's shoulder.

"Do we have the stone we need to control the goblin?" she asked.

Will shook his head.

Sora pressed her eyes for a moment. With a tired sigh, she drew the knife out of her pocket and turned toward the goblin.

"Wait."

She glanced back at him. "They're pouring into the caves. This one will only draw more to us."

The goblin lay on the floor, pounding its bare, bony feet against the stone, eyes wide and feral. Its thin, wiry arms strained against the ropes, its leathery greyish-green skin scraped and raw from rubbing against it.

Will sank down next to the creature and the goblin twisted toward him. Sharp yellow teeth gnashing near his arm. Sora knelt down, pinning it with a knee to its chest.

Will opened up toward it. A howling mass of hunger and

anger rushed into him. Nothing defined, nothing nuanced. It was an animal, less complex than even Talen. It was consumed with a driving hunger and...something else.

Above it he felt Sora's tightly controlled fear.

Will reached out to touch the goblin's arm. The creature hissed and squealed, but Will wrapped his hand around the loose, leathery skin.

He needed to send them back into the mountains. He'd sent Talen places by imagining a picture. But it felt more complicated than that with the goblins. Talen's mind was calm and focused. The goblin before him was savage, and Will had no idea what the mountains looked like where the goblins were from.

Will closed his eyes against the goblin's thrashing. Almost everything was hunger. Gnawing, consuming hunger. He tasted the tang of metal on his tongue and it drove an insatiable need to possess it. Will tried to swallow the taste away and dove deeper into the hunger, searching for the anger he'd felt. Maybe he could redirect it.

He found the thread of the anger and focused on it. This wasn't one goblin's anger at being bound. This was a communal anger at...being controlled.

The goblins knew what Killien had done. They knew they were here not because they'd chosen to be, but because someone had forced them. And it was unraveling them.

Dimly he heard crashing and shouts from the door.

"Will." Sora pressed the goblin down. "Could you commune a little faster?"

"Shh."

Will focused on the anger. How could he change it? The goblin in front of him felt angry and desperate.

And hot.

Will caught the one emotion he'd missed.

The goblin didn't want to be here. The feeling was so familiar he'd passed over it as his own. The frost goblin was in a place it didn't want to be.

A loud crack came from the door and the mass of tables in front of it shifted. Long green fingers rooted through a gap in the door, scrabbling against the wood.

"Whatever you are doing," Sora hissed at him, "you are out of time."

Her words scattered the idea growing in his mind. "Stop talking!"

"Me stop talking?" Her voice was indignant. "I only talk when there's something important to—"

The door split with a long, tearing crack and a goblin wriggled through, clambering over tables. Patlon's axe swung down and the goblin collapsed on the table, but another took its place.

"I have to let go." Sora shifted her weight. "Don't let it bite you."

Will clamped his hand down on the goblin's arm just as Sora lunged off it and ran for the door. Pain ripped across the knife wound in his shoulder. The creature went mad, spinning and biting. Its teeth caught at the side of Will's pants and he shoved its head away. He grabbed the sides of the goblin's head, trying to still it enough that he could focus, but it was like trying to hold a thrashing fish—if the fish had thin pointed teeth and a great desire to eat him. Pain lanced through his shoulder and his hand loosened on the goblin's head. It twisted and bit into his arm.

A heavy weight fell onto the goblin's chest, pinning it down. It snapped its head toward the new foe, its teeth tearing across Will's arm. Hands pinned its chest down onto the floor and Will pulled back.

He looked up into Ilsa's face. She knelt on the creature, her face pale. Her terror echoed in his chest and he tried to shut her emotions out while still feeling the goblin's.

It took him a breath to find his voice. "Thank you."

Her eyes were wide with fear. "Whatever you're doing, hurry!"

Will dragged his attention back to the goblin. It wasn't the anger or the hunger he needed to work with.

He gripped the creature's arm and pulled out his own emotions. It was right there, the one he'd been living with for a year. The aching longing to go home. He thought of Queensland, trees, hills, farmland. The Stronghold, the library, the other Keepers. His mother's face that first moment when he showed up after being gone for too long.

He had found Ilsa. He could go home.

The yearning rolled through him like a wave, flattening everything else.

He let it grow until it filled him entirely, then he opened up toward the goblin and pushed the emotion toward him. Freedom to go home.

The goblin froze, its eyes wide and glazed. For a moment the longing warred with the hunger and the anger. Will pushed more of it in, letting it develop into its own sort of hunger for the familiar, the comfortable.

Will looked into Ilsa's terrified face. "Do you miss home?"

A flash of shock crossed her face and he let her longing pour into him, raw and frenzied. Will shoved her emotions toward the goblin, too.

The creature's anger dissolved, a wild freedom taking its place. In moments the craving for home was the only thing filling the creature.

It stopped straining to reach Will and stretched itself toward the window.

The door snapped and a wide gap opened. Greenish corpses were piling up inside the door, but more came every moment. Will cast out toward them feeling their hunger. But then one paused on its way through the door, a surge of homesickness filling it.

It snapped its attention to the window.

"Let it through!" Will yelled.

The dwarves and Sora paused, weapons raised. Sora stepped back and the goblin scuttled through the door, long, bony fingers grabbing the edge of a table as it scrambled over. It raced past, nails scraping on the stone floor, and clawed its way out the window.

Sora and the dwarves stepped back, leaving a clear path to the window. Goblin after goblin poured into the room, teeth and eyes glinting as they screeched and raced across the room.

Ilsa shrank back against the wall, and Will yanked at the knot holding the rope on the goblin in front of him, and threw himself over next to Ilsa. The creature thrashed itself loose and dove into the mass of goblins pouring out the window.

CHAPTER FIFTY

Two final goblins straggled through the room and outside. Will followed them to the window.

Down below the goblins that had been clawing their way through the Roven camp turned back on themselves like a school of fish and drained back into the gaping warrens. Hoping Rass was smart enough to stay out of the goblins' way, Will turned back to the room.

Killien groaned. Alaric had dragged him over against one of the walls, leaving a streak of blood across the floor. The last of a thin orange haze sank into the Torch's body. Killien's face had regained most of its color and he blinked slowly up at Alaric, scowling. Will came over and knelt next to him.

Killien reached a shaking hand toward Will. The moment Will touched the Torch's hand, a burning anger smoldered up in Will. He slammed himself shut, but the anger continued. He dropped Killien's hand and it faded.

A glint of blue caught his eye. The ring with the blue stones, the one Killien had taken from the traitor early in the trip north. The blue of the stone perfectly matched the aquamarine Will had just spent so long enthralled with. He reached out tentatively to touch it and the anger seeped back in.

Will twisted the ring off Killien's fingers and threw it into the corner. Killien stretched his hand, and started to take a deep breath, but cut it short with a grimace.

"What was that?" Killien looked up at Will, confused. His gaze traveled through the room and horror spread across his face. "What have I done?"

"How'd you get that ring?" Will asked.

"Lukas gave it to me," Killien said weakly. "Said it could hold magic and we should find a use for it." He shook his head, as though trying to clear cobwebs, and winced.

"It certainly held magic," Will said. "He turned the gems into compulsion stones to keep you angry. It looks like Lukas was against your plans to spread peace."

"That doesn't make sense." Killien's shook his head gingerly. "The stones wouldn't work on me—no magic works on me."

"If Lukas just used it to store emotions it would," Will answered. "He learned that emotions have their own resonance so once he created the anger in the ring, it wouldn't take any magic to transfer it to a person. The natural resonance of the emotions would do it for him. You just had to be touching it."

The Torch pressed his eyes shut. "The goblins...What have I done?" Killien breathed a long, defeated breath. He looked up at Will, stricken. "Ohan. I didn't mean to kill him...I was just going to threaten him. I..." He ran his hand over his face. "I couldn't hear anything inside of me but the anger."

The aquamarine Will had held for so long swirled with a light blue light from the floor. "I believe you."

Killien's eyes sank closed. "What have I done? I've ruined everything. I can't build peace on a murder and a goblin attack."

Will set his hand on the Torch's shoulder. "You have created a few more obstacles."

Killien opened his eyes and noticed Alaric. "Who are you?"

"This is Alaric," Will said. "Another bloodthirsty, evil Keeper."

Killien grunted. "The one I *should* have captured."

Alaric raised an eyebrow.

"Yes." Will picked up the now dark stone that had held Ohan's energy. "And the one who just saved your life. With this. Which feels…ironic."

Killien drew away from the stone. "You healed me with…Ohan?"

"It wasn't him anymore." Alaric's eyes glittered with an anger that surprised Will. "It was just the leftover energy that you didn't waste during the murder."

Killien stared at Alaric for a long moment. "So it's safe to say the healing wasn't a sign of friendship?"

"It was a sign of his friendship towards me," Will said, "not you. Alaric just saw you fly on a dragon, command an army of goblins, and kill a man in a way he's unusually sensitive to. You didn't make a great first impression."

Killien let his eyes slip closed again. "If you didn't want to save me, why did you?"

"Will seemed to think it was important. And I trust his judgment of people." Alaric pushed himself up to his feet, taking the empty stone and tucking it into his bag. "Even when I don't understand what he sees.

"And I didn't heal you, not completely. Your body won't let me. While you were weak I could pour energy into you, but the stronger you grew, the less you would let me. You're strong enough now that no magic is going to work on you. You're not going to die, but you still have a lot of healing to do."

Killien squinted up at Alaric. "Thank you."

Alaric walked across the room toward Evangeline without responding.

"You Keepers are complicated." He tilted his head and strained to look around the room. "Lukas?"

Will opened his mouth to answer, but couldn't decide what to say.

"Your man, Lukas, stabbed everyone he could, stole your sword, then flew away on your dragon," Douglon said, tossing some broken table pieces out of the way.

Killien grabbed for the strap that had held his scabbard on his back, but found nothing.

"How did he get the dragon?" Will asked. "I thought we took the compulsion stone off."

Alaric shrugged. "Maybe he had a second one?"

"So Lukas was prepared to escape on the dragon all this time?" Killien asked.

Douglon let out a snort. "People don't control dragons because they might need a quick escape. Dragons are for destruction. Who does Lukas hate?"

"Me," Killien said, his voice heavy. He pushed himself up to sit. "Obviously."

Douglon shook his head. "He already killed you. Who else?"

"Keepers," Will answered.

Douglon leveled an annoyed look at him. "So if I stay with you Keepers, I'm going to see that dragon again?" He shook his head and stumped back over towards where Sora and Patlon were clearing debris from the doorway. "I need different friends."

Killien shifted his shoulders, stretching his back. "I almost died, didn't I?"

"I thought you were dead." Will paused. "I couldn't put that compulsion stone down. I'm sorry. I wanted to, but…"

"You don't have to explain to me." Killien turned to the window. "I didn't think Lukas would…" He fell silent for a moment. "I trusted him."

"Do you…" Will paused, wondering if it were even possible now that Lukas was gone. "Do you want to know why he did it?"

Killien's attention snapped to Will. Interest warred with trepidation on his face, but he nodded hesitantly.

Will brought back the memory of Lukas's emotions and let the echo of the feelings fill him again. They came back surprisingly easy, and he opened himself up toward Killien, pushing the feelings toward him.

The sharp slice of betrayal. Fury and terror bleeding out.

The fissure split open and the cold isolation flooded him. Betrayal clawed up from the deep, shadowing him with black isolation.

Killien's breath tore out of him and he threw his hands over his face. Will closed himself off, letting the emotions fade until they were just a heart-breaking echo.

The others had cleared the broken tables away from the door. Alaric had found a stack of books and sat against the wall poring over them. Ilsa stood with her back to the wall, watching Killien and Will with a troubled expression.

"Ilsa."

Will jumped at Killien's voice, and Ilsa, after a short hesitation, came over to them.

"As far as I can tell," the Torch said to her, "Will really is your brother. What he told me matches what Vahe said."

"I know," she said quietly.

Will's heart clenched.

Her eyes flickered up to his face. "You were right about the doll. I had her until she fell apart."

He opened his mouth to say something, but there was too much.

"Enjoy this," Sora said from behind him. "It's almost impossible to get Will to stop talking."

Ilsa laughed a short, nervous laugh. Her face, smiling like that, was so much like it had been when she was tiny, he couldn't breathe.

"What he'd like to say," Sora continued, "is that he's really happy to have found you. He's been looking for you for a very long time."

"Would you—" The words caught in Will's throat and he swallowed before trying again. "Would you like to come home?" At the flicker of uncertainty in her face, he added, "To Queensland."

"I believe your mother is still alive," Killien added.

Ilsa's gaze snapped to Will's face, and he nodded.

"She's always believed you'd come back."

"I think," said Ilsa, her voice wavering slightly, "I would like that."

Will wanted to smile, but something too big pushed up from his chest.

After a moment's silence, Sora stepped in front of him. "He's not always this awkward." She motioned toward the fireplace. "Let's gather some supplies while Will gathers his wits. And if you have the ability to make him speechless this often, you and I are going to spend a lot of time together."

"Speaking of going home," Douglon said, peering through the broken door, "it's probably time for us to do that. This is all very touching, but despite getting rid of goblins and a dragon, we're still not—" He stiffened and raised his axe, before muttering and pulling the door open.

Hal stepped in, stopping to take in the room and eyeing everyone warily. "The goblins are gone," he said to Killien, "but the Torches are getting restless. If you're going to talk to them it had better be soon. I don't know how long the freed slaves can keep them there, even if they are armed." He glanced around. "And you're going to lose any influence you had if you're caught with…" He gestured at the room.

Killien nodded and gingerly stood up, rolling his back muscles and grimacing slightly. Hal's face paled at the blood covering Killien's shirt, but the Torch waved it off.

"There's one more thing before we go," Will said to Killien. "Lukas should have been raised as a Keeper. Sini and Rett should have been too."

The Torch's eyes narrowed. "No."

The too-familiar frustration with Killien rose to the surface, and Will tried to keep his voice even. "What would have happened if the Panos had taken your son?"

Killien's face hardened, but there was an edge of panic in his eyes.

"Would he have been raised as a slave in their clan? Never

going back to his own family? Never learning who he was or what his life should have been?"

Killien shook his head stubbornly. "You're not taking Sini and Rett. I have lost my book, my goblins, my *dragon*."

"The dragon was not my fault," Will protested.

"Really? Because it was firmly under my control."

"Oh, the stone. That part was us." Will glanced around at his companions. "You know, a few hours ago, I didn't think we had a chance at any of this."

Killien gave him a flat stare. "Yes, you've done very well."

"Sini and Rett should have the chance to go home."

"Rett won't remember what that means," Killien said, his face unreadable.

Will bit back the angry retort that came to mind and opened himself up the smallest bit to Killien. Grief blossomed in through the crack, faded and worn around the edges before he closed himself back off.

"Raina should have had the chance to go home, too," Will said.

Killien flinched at her name. "I know you think it's terrible that they're slaves, but they've been treated like family."

"Lukas thought he was family, that he was your equal. The truth that he wasn't is what finally turned him against you."

"I feel like they're family. Or something close to it." He looked up at Will. "What if they don't want to go with you?"

Will's chest tightened at the very real possibility. "Then they don't. The whole point is that they get to choose."

Killien studied him for a moment. "Hal, bring Sini and Rett here."

"You don't have time for this," Hal objected.

"Hal."

The huge man's nostrils flared in annoyance, and he walked out of the room.

"If Sini and Rett leave," Killien said, quietly enough that only Will heard, "the Morrow have lost everything."

"You still have everything that was rightfully yours," Will

pointed out. "Now that Lukas isn't making you angry, maybe you can salvage the old ideas you had for peace."

"And what do I tell the Torches who just lost Roven to my goblin attack? Or the Panos Clan about Ohan. That my slave was controlling me?"

"I have no idea," Will said, "but you wanted the balance of power shaken, and you've definitely achieved that. The Morrow aren't the most powerful clan, but, in a rather belated fashion, you did choose peace over domination. And that's an idea the Sweep needs to keep hearing. You've gotten the attention of the Sweep. Now use it to say all the things you've always wanted to say."

"And if they don't listen?"

"Some of them won't. But some of them will, and it will be the start that you wanted."

Hal returned quickly with the others. Sini's eyes widened when she saw Will and Sora, and the sight of the dwarves made her step back against the towering form of Rett who set a protective hand on her shoulder. Alaric let the book sink into his lap, watching the two of them closely.

"Sini," Killien said, strained, "we've become infested with Keepers."

Sini's eyes flashed to Alaric.

"You know," the Torch started again, "if you'd stayed in Queensland…"

When he didn't continue, Will finished it for him. "You would have come to the Keepers, and we would have tested you to see what talents you have. And then, if you wanted to, you could have joined us. And Rett too." Will glanced at Killien. "Rett and Raina both would have come to us. And Lukas."

Sini's gaze darted around the room at Lukas's name. "He's gone," she said in a small voice. "Isn't he?"

At Killien's nod, she closed her eyes and let out a pained sigh. "How did he go?"

"On the dragon," Will answered.

Sini's shoulder drooped and she sagged back against Rett. "I'd hoped he wouldn't."

"You knew?" Killien asked.

"The moment you had the chance to control the dragon, he began talking about it."

Killien's jaw clenched. "Is he coming back?"

She shook her head. "He wanted to go somewhere safe, where he could learn and prepare." Her eyes flicked toward Will and Alaric. "To attack Queensland."

Will exchanged worried looks with Alaric.

"He took my sword." Killien sounded bitter.

Sini shrank back even further against Rett again. "Your seax has some kind of power. You wouldn't be able to tell, obviously, but we could feel…something in the blade. It has a…something."

"That's not very specific," Killien said.

She shrugged. "I don't know what it does. I only touched the blade once, but it made my finger tingle. Lukas doesn't know what it does either. But he thinks it's powerful."

"If it was given to you by Flibbet the Peddler," Will said, "that isn't too surprising."

He paused and spun his ring. "Sini, would you like to come back to Queensland with us?"

Sini stiffened.

"You haven't been with the Morrow long. You can come with us, back home. To your family."

Sini's eyes locked onto his, a desperation rising in her making her look even younger. "Home?"

Will nodded, but a flicker of distrust crossed her face.

"I know you don't trust Will yet," Sora said, stepping forward. "But I'll go with you too. I'll make sure you get back to your family."

She glanced toward Alaric, taking in the black cloak. "Will I have to join the Keepers?"

Will laughed. "No. Although you have no idea how happy we'd be if you decided to. We've been searching for you and Rett and Lukas for years, although we didn't know who you were. And if *you* joined, we'd be especially thrilled. It's been sixty years since the last female Keeper died."

"In the past," Alaric said from the floor, his fingers thrumming excitedly on a book, "female Keepers have manipulated energy in different ways than the men. I would love to know what you're capable of."

"I..." She looked around uncertainly. "I can't do the kinds of things Lukas can."

Killien looked at Will with a pointed expression. "Lukas stabbed Will in the shoulder."

Sini's gaze snapped to Will, interested.

"What does that have to do with anything?" Will demanded. "If we're comparing, he stabbed you in the back."

Sini's attention flipped toward Killien with a worried look, but he waved her away. "The Keeper healed me." A little smirk lifted the corner of his mouth. "Even if it took him a while."

"A while?" Alaric said indignantly. "You were almost dead."

Killien just laughed and motioned toward Will. Sini stepped closer, her eyes watching Will warily for a moment before she lifted her hands up near his shoulder. She set her palm on the bandage and Will tried not to wince at the jolt of pain that sliced into his arm.

"That's deep." She pulled her hand back. Her brow wrinkled as she focused on his shoulder, and traced lines in the air with her fingers. Thin trails of pinkish light hung in the air behind them, forming a rune.

Alaric scrambled to his feet and stepped closer. A strange rune that reminded Will of *sunlight* faded and she drew another one. The fingers on both hands danced through the air, leaving trail after trail of light.

A warmth started deep in his shoulder, growing hotter until Will had to try not to squirm away from it. The heat radiated down his arm as though his bone was smoldering. It burned over to his neck and he clenched his jaw. The heat moved toward the surface of his shoulder, leaving a tingling warmth behind.

With a final stretching sensation across his skin, the heat faded. Sini dropped her hands and Will pushed the bandage down off his shoulder and saw nothing but a ragged red pucker of skin. He lifted his arm and felt only stiffness and a dull ache.

Killien looked at her proudly. "You're getting better all the time."

Will raised his eyes to Sini, stunned. "How did you do that?"

Alaric stood behind the girl, staring at Will's shoulder. "There's nothing in here to pull energy from besides us. You couldn't possibly have done all that from yourself."

Sini looked up at him uncertainly. "I used the sunlight."

The room was completely shadowed.

"What sunlight?" Alaric asked.

"From out the window." She pointed outside hesitantly. "Where else would I get so much warmth?"

For a long moment, the two Keepers just stared at her. Alaric opened his mouth then closed it several times before settling on, "How did you make the runes?"

"Oh." She brushed her hair back out of her face with a nervous motion. "That energy does come from me. But it's easy." She moved her finger through the air in a long arc and left a thin pink trail behind that faded slowly away. She looked at the two Keepers curiously. "You can't make the air glow?"

Alaric blinked and reached toward the waning line.

"It looks like what the stone did," Will said, "when it sucked the life out of Ohan—and when it put that energy back into Killien."

Alaric's eyes widened. "The air glows! The energy moves through the air...and it glows. How did I not see that?" He turned toward Sini, his face so intense that she took a step back. "How does the air *glow?*"

"Alaric," Will said mildly, "you're scaring her. And the rest of us."

Alaric pressed his lips closed and backed up.

"I don't know how it glows," Sini said. "That's the first magic I ever did. Of course it wasn't a smooth line." She turned her hands over. The tips of each finger were shiny and smooth with old scars. "It was more of a...cloud."

"It came out your fingertips?" Will turned his own hands face up, showing the healing burns and the old white scars on his palm.

Alaric held out his as well, a patchwork of old faded scars filled his palms. In a tightly controlled voice he said, "*Please* come to the Stronghold. Even if you don't stay. Please come and show us what you can do. I promise you we will do everything we can to help you learn more."

"If you stay on the Sweep," Killien said, sounding desperate, "you can have your freedom. You can keep living with us as a real part of the family."

For a moment, Sini looked interested. But then she shook her head slowly. "I'd never really be free among the Roven." She considered Alaric and Will, tapping her fingers on her lips. "Lukas will come for you. I don't think yet, though. There were things he wanted to learn first, but it's always been his goal to destroy the Keepers."

"Do you know where he's gone?" Will asked.

"Probably Napon. He wants to learn from the blood doctors there."

Alaric made a disapproving noise.

Sini straightened her shoulders and a determined look settled on her face. "I'll come with you. Lukas is...I might be able to help you prepare for him. He's not as terrible as he probably seems to you right now. If I could talk to him, maybe..." She shrugged and her words trailed off.

Her gaze fell to the book in Alaric's hand. "Do you have any books at the Stronghold?"

"Eighty-two thousand three hundred and twenty. Or there about."

Killien's mouth fell open and Sini's eyes widened.

"Yes, I'll come," she said quickly. She turned to Rett and looked up into his face. "I'm going to go back home, to Queensland. Do you want to come with me? Or stay with Killien?"

Rett shook his head. "Come with Sini."

"We need to wrap this up," Patlon said. "I hear people in the hall."

"If you go out the window," Killien said, "you should be able to get around to the back of the mountain quickly. Don't linger."

"Sounds good," Douglon said, scrambling up to the window and peering out. "Everything's chaotic enough down on the Sweep that no one should pay much attention to us."

Evangeline followed him. Sini, paused before giving Killien a quick hug. Then she clambered out the window followed by Rett, Alaric, and Patlon. Sora started toward the window.

"I'm sorry," Killien said to Sora. "About the night Lilit almost died."

Sora hesitated. "I understand the desperation you must have felt. And if you hadn't called for me, you wouldn't have gotten Will, and Lilit would have died." She gave him a reluctant shrug. "So I suppose I'm glad you did."

Killien gave Will a sidelong glance. "What do you think she'd do to me if I pointed out that she'd just claimed to be the reason Lilit was saved."

Sora fixed him with a dangerous look. "I'd finish the job Lukas started on you."

Killien let out a short laugh, then grimaced and shifted his back. "If you're ever near the Morrow again, Sora, you'll always have a place."

Sora nodded in acknowledgment and went to the window. Ilsa gave the Torch a hesitant smile and followed her.

Hal gave Will a crushing pat on the back. "The fact that you introduced me to dwarves has tipped the scales. I've decided I'm glad to have met you."

"And I you."

"I have a feeling you might see Lukas before I do," Killien said to Will. "If you do, tell him…"

Will waited, but Killien shook his head.

"Maybe there's nothing to tell him." Killien held out his hand to Will, and he took it, clasping Killien around the wrist. "Thank the black queen you were here. I feel as though I should offer you some sort of reward for saving me, both from the knife and from the ring. But you might ask for more slaves, and you've already taken enough of those."

"Is that bag over there full of avak?" Will pointed to a shelf. "Because you know we don't have those in Queensland."

Killien let out a short laugh and winced. "You drive a hard bargain, but I suppose two dozen fruit will help you feed the many people leaving with you."

Will grabbed the bag and slung it over his shoulder.

"Next time you're sneaking across the Sweep," Killien said, "you should stop by the Morrow."

"I'm done with the Sweep," Will said. "It's your turn. Come to the Stronghold. We have a lot of books."

Killien opened his mouth to refuse, but Douglon interrupted from the window. "Hurry up, Keeper. Or we're leaving you behind."

Killien extended his hand, and Will grasped his wrist.

"Good luck, Will."

CHAPTER FIFTY-ONE

WILL CLIMBED through the window and into the warm sunlight on a slope scattered with trees. The last goblins from the battle below drained back into their warrens. Ahead of him, the others scrambled among rocks and bushes. It took endless, exposed clambering across the steep slope before they'd moved around the mountain enough that the Roven camp was out of sight. But the Roven were busy dispatching any wounded goblins and beginning a victory celebration. On the north side of the mountain, trees grew more densely, hiding the Sweep, and they hurried downhill through them. But climbing along the side of the mountain took much longer than walking through tunnels, and the sun hung low in the sky before they reached the place they'd come out of the goblin warren.

Any rangers that had been patrolling must have gone back to the camp during the fight, because the swath of grass between them and the mountain range sat perfectly empty. Douglon led, angling for the entrance to the dwarven caves. Will scanned the grass for any sign of Rass and the sky for any sign of Talen.

They were almost across the grass before Talen's little form winged out of the sky to land on Will's arm. And when they reached the last stand of thick grass before the ground rose into the mountains, Rass's face popped up out of it in time to hear Sora explain to Ilsa, Sini, and Rett that the way back to Queensland involved several days in dwarven tunnels.

Rass crossed her arms. "No more tunnels."

Will crouched in front of her. "The rest of us can't slip through the grass unseen like you can. There are too many Roven for a group as strange as ours to get home safely." He tried to keep the disappointment out of his voice and added. "If you don't want to come, I'll understand."

She frowned. "I do want to come. It's just too long away from the grass."

"It's easy enough to take some with us." Douglon studied the grass she stood on. "But that's too tall."

He climbed uphill to a little patch of short mountain grass. Taking a small shovel, he began to dig. In a few minutes he'd dug up a square of earth and grass an arm's length on each side. He rolled it up and tied it to his pack. "That should stay alive long enough to get us through the tunnels."

Rass reached her hand up and ran her fingers along the bundle, knocking loose a shower of tiny bits of dirt. "You're very smart, Douglon."

Douglon winked at her. "There are caves that get sunlight, you know. And water. Deep in Duncave there's a garden with a floor of grass. Every bit of it got in there rolled on a dwarf's back."

Unlike Rass, Sini was unabashedly excited about the idea of dwarven tunnels, and so Rett followed along perfectly happy as well. Ilsa balked only a few moments before Sora assured her she would walk with her.

Will followed behind them with Talen. A thousand questions swirled in his head to ask Ilsa, but he felt oddly nervous at the idea of asking them. Sora and Ilsa talked for a bit before Ilsa turned to him. "What's our mother like?"

In the dim glimmer moss, her face mirrored his own nervousness.

"She looks exactly like you." At her surprise, he continued, "I've been afraid for years that I might walk past you and never know it. But anyone who's met our mother would know you instantly."

She hesitated. "And our father? I heard you tell the Torch…"

Will answered before the emotions had time to make him hesitate. "He was killed the night you were taken."

Ilsa turned away for a few steps. "I think I knew that. I don't remember it, exactly, but I've never thought my father was alive." She glanced back at Will again. "Do you remember much of me?"

Will launched into every memory he could remember of her as a baby. Learning to walk, chasing the goat, dragging her ugly doll behind her wherever she went. Then he continued on with stories about their village, their mother, their father.

Ilsa turned out to have a subtle, dry wit and he found a hint of comfortableness growing. Not an ease, exactly, but the awkwardness began to smooth away. She didn't talk about herself, and he bit back the countless questions he had for her.

Ahead of them, Alaric and Sini walked together, peppering each other with questions, Douglon and Patlon hummed rhythmic, deep dwarfish tunes that echoed along the tunnel, blending back into themselves, creating their complex thrumming song. It took a couple of hours to reach the same dull cavern they'd slept in the night before. With no chimney to allow a fire, they gathered the glimmer moss together and sat around it eating a cold meal.

Douglon spread out the little square of grass, and Rass settled into it with a contented sigh.

"You're growing soft in your old age, cousin," Patlon said.

"Are you really cousins?" Rass asked.

"Patlon's father is my uncle," Douglon answered, sitting down next to her grass. "But most Dwarves call each other cousin, to remember we're all related."

"I like it," Rass said. "I've never had a cousin."

"You're too little to be a cousin," Patlon said. "You're a nibling."

Rass giggled. "Sounds like nibble."

"It's like a niece," Douglon explained. "Or a nephew."

Rass considered the idea. "Well then, thank you Uncle Douglon, for the grass." She stood and wrapped her little arms around his neck.

Douglon's eyebrows shot up, but he patted her back awkwardly. "You're welcome, wee snip."

With a contented sigh, Rass settled back down on her grass.

Ilsa, Sini, and Rett sat along one side. A thin divide of air and uncertainty formed between the three of them and the others.

Will wanted to feel celebratory, but mostly he felt exhausted. He felt a responsibility to fix the awkwardness in the group, but it was hard enough just to keep his eyes open and eat the dried meat and cheese the dwarves passed out. Will added avak to the meager meal, and everyone who hadn't tasted it before was suitably impressed with it. The fruit perked his mind up for a few minutes, but even that couldn't dull his exhaustion.

With all the humans and the small elf worn out, the dwarves carried the evening, telling tale after tale of the pranks they'd played on High Dwarf Horgoth. Douglon, it turned out, was such a close relative to Horgoth that until the High Dwarf had some children, the case could be made that Douglon was next in line for the throne—an honor he was decidedly unhappy about.

The dwarves entertained them, until one by one they fell asleep to long, slow echoes of dwarven songs.

The next day Will walked with Alaric through the darkness. Ahead of them, Sora, Ilsa, and Evangeline chatted animatedly. There was something subtle, but almost masterful, about the way Evangeline drew the other two out. Sora's laugh was as light and easy as it had been when she'd found him after the fire. And Ilsa joined in the conversation more and more as the hours passed.

Will and Alaric continued to fill in gaps for each other from the past year.

"When we reach the Stronghold," Alaric said, "I'll put Ayda's memory of the elves into the Wellstone. But I think you should be the one to write those down. The elves deserve to have the story told right."

"I can't believe they're all gone. I can't believe Ayda's gone."

They walked in silence.

"Where's her body?"

"Douglon took it to the Elder Grove in the Greenwood."

"She really *is* gone, right?" Will asked. "I mean, it sounds like Evangeline was essentially dead, and you brought her back. Could Ayda…?"

Alaric shook his head. "I've asked myself that every day. But she isn't like Evangeline. Ayda gave up everything. There's no life left in her at all. Although"—he paused, as though reluctant to continue—"she did put a lot of herself into Evangeline, and into Douglon once when he was dying. And into the Elder Grove itself. I can't find anything particularly unique about the *vitalle*, but maybe you could feel something else?"

They reached the Cavern of Sea and Sky at the end of a long day of walking. The air in the cavern glowed blue with the sunlight that trickled its way in. Glints of orange flashed across every surface from their glimmer moss. A reverent silence muted the group, both from those who'd seen it before, and those who hadn't.

Patlon and Rass made a fire, roasting some yams and onions, scattering countless glints of light across the cave. Ilsa, Sini, and Rett explored the cavern. Will took off Talen's hood, and the hawk flew in circles around the cavern.

Alaric drew Douglon and Evangeline aside and explained Will's talent. "There's a chance that he can sense what Ayda put in you better than I can."

Evangeline looked at Will sharply. "Do you think there's a

chance that it's part of her? That we could somehow get her back?"

"I don't know," Will said. "That's what I'd try to find out."

He opened up to Evangeline. A rush of gratitude and unworthiness filled him, laced with guilt and something that felt like a desperate, clinging sort of...greed. Alaric squeezed her hand and what had felt like greed settled into what it really was—a tight bundle of joy and desire and friendship and fear, all wrapped so tightly together there was no name for it except love.

Will took a breath and opened up toward Douglon. A gnawing ache flowed into him. Grief. Still new enough to be eroding everything else. Every experience of grief Will had had surged to the surface in his own emotions, resonating with Douglon's pain. The sheer weight of it threatened to overwhelm him.

There was something similar in them, but there was too much chaos to figure out what.

Sora shifted, watching them with interest. That's what he needed, Sora's calm.

"Could you help me?"

She stepped closer. "Anything."

"I need to feel what you feel." He reached out and took her hand.

A flood of emotions crashed into him. Admiration, curiosity, excitement, sympathy, and over it all, a warm, glowing blanket of eagerness, pulling him toward her, wrapping around him. His stomach twisted into a knot of nerves and he couldn't breathe.

He closed his eyes and drew in a breath. "That's very distracting."

A snag of hurt pulled her emotions back and she loosened her hand.

His eyes flew open. "No!" He tightened his grip. "It's nice—very, very nice. I like it a lot. But what I need from you is that eerie calm you have." He gave her an apologetic smile. "Just for now. There's so much here, I can't concentrate."

She laughed a self-conscious little laugh. "Oh...I'll try." She closed her eyes and he felt her emotions recede a little. She cracked one eye open. "It's harder around you than it used to be." She closed her eyes and her brow drew down in concentration. Slowly her feelings drained away until he felt a deep calmness, giving him room to sort through everything.

"Thank you."

Will started with Evangeline, pushing past the tangle of emotions. Below everything something tranquil caught his attention.

He squeezed his eyes shut. Serenity. The peace that infused forests and mountains and storm clouds. The kind that endured for eons and stretched across the heavens at night.

It did remind him of Ayda. But it wasn't the elf exactly. It was more like an echo.

He felt a twang of his own disappointment and realized he'd been hoping that he'd find something recognizably her. That somehow the elf was still alive.

What Evangeline carried wasn't just emotions, though. There was something like *vitalle* about it. He could feel it sitting like a bubble of energy inside the intangible swirl of feelings.

Will focused on Douglon, reaching past the grief. There it was, the same serenity that Evangeline had, part emotion, part *vitalle*. Instead of sitting below everything, Douglon's was completely surrounded by grief and a desperate sort of possessiveness.

Will pulled at it the way he would pull at *vitalle*, and felt it draw closer to him.

If he wanted, he realized, he could pull it out. Which was interesting, but not necessarily useful. He lingered for a moment, trying to claim a hint of the peace. But there was nothing in himself that was like it enough. The serenity of it was foreign. He could recognize it, but it didn't resonate with anything inside of him.

"It's not Ayda," he said quietly. "It's just...elfishness. I don't think there's anything of her left."

A flash of disappointment flashed through Douglon's emotions, but his face stayed impassive. "That's what I thought."

Will closed himself off from both of them, the ache of loss from Douglon still ringing in his own chest. The dwarf walked over to the fire, and Evangeline and Alaric moved away together, talking somberly.

CHAPTER FIFTY-TWO

Sora, still holding Will's hand, pulled him toward a side tunnel. They turned down it, and the ethereal blue of the cavern began to darken. The tunnels felt different than they had the first time she'd brought him here. The fear of them had disappeared, replaced with the feeling of being cocooned in something safe. The disappointment of not finding Ayda couldn't quite follow him in here. It fell off somewhere in the darkening tunnel leaving just himself and Sora and the mountain.

"I'm glad you snuck into my room that first night," he said.

Sora laughed and led the way around another turn. The tunnel darkened to a deep grey. "You didn't always feel that way."

"True. You were too frightening for me to be glad." He thought back to that night. "When you said, 'I see you,' it was the most terrifying thing I'd ever heard. Because I knew you saw more than I wanted you to." The fear of her felt foreign now. "I'm not sure when it turned from terrifying to freeing."

"Somewhere on the Sweep for me." She slowed. "At first it was just frustrating that you seemed to understand me. But it kept drawing me back."

"Flibbet the Peddler has a rule that says, *It is a terrifying thing to be truly seen—but it is infinitely worse not to be.* I don't think I really understood what he meant before I met you." He laughed. "You managed to teach me both parts."

She turned toward him and he could just make out her face in the dark. She smiled, but there was a hesitation in her face. "How much past Kollman Pass is your home and Queenstown?"

"Are you in a hurry?"

She paused. "I told Sini and Ilsa that I'd see them to their homes, so I will, but then I need to leave."

"What?" He clenched her hand. "Why?"

"I need to go back home." There was an ache in her voice. "You were right. The holy woman from my clan took what was *my* story, and I've let her control it for too long. She controls who I am, who the clan is. I have to go back and stand up to her, tell them all the truth. Or they'll never be free of her...*I'll* never be free."

"I'll come with you." Her fingers felt cold. "I love telling people the truth."

She let out a little laugh and leaned against him, laying her head on his shoulder. He ran his free hand down her braid, his fingers finally tracing the plaits of copper like they'd wanted to for...how long *had* he wanted to do this?

"This isn't something an outsider can be a part of, Will. Especially one that would be chasing after me wanting to record my every word."

"Oh, this should definitely be written down." He cleared his throat. *"The Huntress and the Holy Woman: A tale of corruption and truth."*

She breathed out another laugh and leaned into him.

He ran the end of her braid through his fingers. "When do you have to go?"

"Not yet. There's a ceremony on midsummer that I always played a main role in. She won't be able to stop me from taking that position. If I want to talk to my people, that will be the moment. But I have a couple weeks to help get Sini, Rett, and Ilsa to their homes."

"Let me come with you," he pleaded.

She shook her head against his shoulder. "You have things you need to do. Like prepare for a dragon attack."

Will wrapped his arm around her. She melted against him and he stood there absorbing the feel of her. He caught a scent of leather just like the first night she'd appeared in his room and terrified him. "Would it help if I begged? Or cried like a baby?"

"It might."

When she started to pull back, he tightened his arms, an ache in his chest. "What if I *can't* let go?"

She looked up into his face for a breath, her brow drawing down in concentration, until a rush of longing and resolve and warmth burst into him, all wrapped in a sort of grasping need and desperate hope that caught his breath.

She leaned up and pressed her lips against his, and he opened up to her, letting everything else she felt swirl in. He pushed as much of his own emotions back into her as he could, until it was impossible to tell the yearning and eagerness and hope and heartache apart. It churned around them, a tangle of things beginning and ending in the same moment.

She pulled away and it felt like she tore something out of him. "I'm not leaving until everyone gets home. And it won't be forever. If we've learned anything, it's that you're incredibly easy to track."

"You'll come find me?" He sounded desperate. "When you're done?"

She nodded and he pulled her back against him.

"You won't even have to track me. I'm very famous and important in Queensland. Just ask anyone and they'll point you in the right direction."

He could almost feel her eye roll.

Calls that food was ready echoed down the tunnel and Sora pulled away. "Food is still one of the only reasons to leave a tunnel."

They walked slowly back to the cavern. The sun must have set because the cave had dimmed to a blackness sparkling with the orange glints of firelight.

"I've talked to Douglon," Alaric said, as they drew near, "and he has an exit from the tunnels that will put us less than half a day from the Greenwood. We can get to the Elder Grove and bury Ayda." He glanced at the group. "Unless everyone's in a big hurry to get to their homes."

"We could see the Greenwood?" Sini asked excitedly.

"I haven't seen many forests," Ilsa agreed.

"I'm definitely not in a hurry." Will gave Sora a small smile. "Let's take the scenic route."

The group settled down around the fire and the split happened again. Sini, Rett, and Ilsa sat a bit apart. It wasn't as pronounced as the night before, but it was still there.

Will waited for a lull in the conversation before clearing his throat. "The night I was rescued from the rift"—he gave Rass a little bow and she beamed at him —"Killien had demanded a story from me, and I was planning to tell the story of Sable."

Alaric made an approving noise. "I haven't heard that one in years."

"If we're to have a story, we need wine." Patlon pulled a wineskin from his bag, and Douglon pulled out another. "The Roven just left these lying around. Everyone seemed too tired last night to enjoy them."

The dwarves passed the wineskins and Will pulled out the bag of avak. He took a bite of the fruit, letting the freshness wake up a little hope that the gap between them all could be closed. Passing it to Alaric, he began.

"Sable was still small enough to crawl through the broken plaster wall that led under the floor of the abandoned warehouse. And she was still small enough that finding such a place to spend the night was a necessity. Dirt, pebbles, and broken shells jabbed into her hands and bare knees as she scooted in. It was dusty and lonesome, but it was quiet and safe."

He opened up to the group and felt the normal chaotic swirl of emotions.

"Early the next morning, though, heavy footsteps broke the silence. Terrified that it was one of the dockside gangs, Sable crawled silently backwards until a glitter of fairy light caught her eye through the wood slats. Glints of red and gold and blue. She moved her head slowly, letting the colors shimmer down into the gloom where she lay."

One by one, the feelings of the people in the cave focused on the story and the first sparks of curiosity formed.

"There was laughter, but it wasn't the harsh laughter of the street packs. And there were snippets of songs, but not loud, bawdy tavern songs. She'd never heard voices like these. For it was sheer luck that a street mouse from Dockside had slept under the practice room of the Duke's Figment of Wits traveling troupe."

Sable's story continued, and the emotions of the group began to seep out from themselves and mix with those around them, creating a cloud of anticipation and amusement. It filled the cavern, each listener resonating with the emotions of the others until any divisions between them dwindled away.

The rock walls wrapped around them all, glittering with firelight. In here were no slaves, no goblins, no dragons looming on the horizon.

There was nothing but infinitesimally small glints of hope scattering across everything he could see.

THE END

FROM THE AUTHOR

Thank you for reading *Pursuit of Shadows.* I hope you enjoyed Will's story.

A review is worth more to an author than a solid rescue plan would have been to Will around chapter 14.

If you enjoyed *Pursuit of Shadows* and have the time to leave a review, you can do so on Amazon.

The third and final book of The Keeper Chronicles is *Siege of Shadows*, and is available on Amazon.

You can see a list of all my books on my website at jaandrews.com.

Thank you,

Janice

Tomkin and the Dragon

A bookish, unheroic hero, a maiden who's not remotely interested in being rescued, and a dragon who'd just like to eat them both.

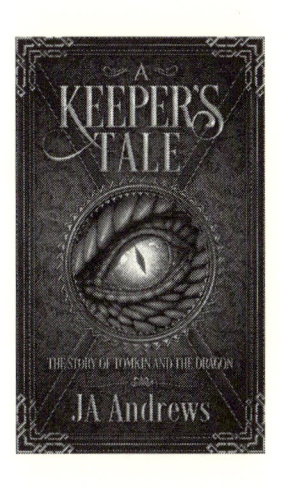

"When they request a story from you,
tell *Tomkin and the Dragon*. I love that one."
~ Evangeline

If you'd like to read the story of Tomkin and the Dragon that was mentioned in both books of the Keeper Chronicles, it is published under the title ***A Keeper's Tale: The Story of Tomkin and the Dragon*** and you can find it for sale on Amazon.

ACKNOWLEDGMENTS

Thank you Karyne Norton and Cheryl Schuetze for endless conversation about plots and helping to corral the bloated early drafts of Will's story. You two helped more than I can express. Cecilia Sells, thank you for your unending patience and enthusiasm through my year and a half of complaint and whines about writing. You're a constant encouragement to me. Katie Cross, thanks for the emergency story structure Facetime meeting. It's what put this story right.

To Fantasy Faction, thank you for the excellent critiques and unfailing enthusiasm for talking about writing things.

To the unnamed order of authors who have taught me so much and given me hope that this writing thing might work, you know who you are, and I adore you all.

Thank you Dane at ebooklaunch.com for the beautiful cover and Wojtek Depczynski for the amazing artwork. And Ren, thank you for the beautiful map.

Thanks to my three kids for your patience while mom wrestled with the book, and for giving me quiet time to work when you had so many interesting things to talk about.

But as always, most of all, thank you to my husband. You are the only reason I've kept going through the times when I felt like I couldn't do it, but you believed I could. You make me a better person. Thank you for letting me ramble about writing and story structure and marketing, and for coming up with the best ideas. I love you so much. Can't wait for the next 20 years of our story.

ABOUT THE AUTHOR

JA Andrews is a writer, wife, mother, and unemployed rocket scientist. She doesn't regret the rocket science degree, but finds it generally inapplicable in daily life. Except for the rare occurrence of her being able to definitively state, "That's not rocket science." She does, however, love the stars.

She spends an inordinate amount of time at home, with her family, who she adores, and lives deep in the Rocky Mountains of Montana, where she can see more stars than she ever imagined.

For more information:
www.jaandrews.com
jaandrews@jaandrews.com

Made in the USA
Middletown, DE
26 May 2023